MONSTERLAND
BELOW

(BOOK III)

MICHAEL OKON

"…and that which is below…"

– The Emerald Tablet of Hermes Trismegistus

For Dad.

"True guidance is like a small torch in a dark forest. It doesn't show everything at once. But gives enough light for the next step to be safe."

– Swami Vivekananda

Thanks for being my torch, Pop.

BELOW

AS BELOW

50 Miles off the Tober Trench deep in the Pacific Ocean.

QUIET SURROUNDED HER, not the quiet of serenity or peace. It was calm, not even a ripple. The silence filled the entire length of her body until she felt she would explode from it. It was the absolute absence of sound that made her realize all was not right in her world.

She moved upward, the temperature changing rapidly, indicating something strange had happened. She meandered at first, not quite sure what was different. She refused to allow emotions to take over and calmly poked around, her impatience giving way to unease.

Don't get nervous, she told herself, but the tingle of tension traveled up her body like an electrical current, zapping the region just above her arms. Her stomach felt weightless, and the meal she had recently finished caused her to gasp, expelling fluid and a bit of food leaving a bad taste in her mouth.

She wriggled, her arms expanding widely propelling her to heights she'd never dared travel. She knew her expression had changed, she didn't need to see her reflection. She was sure that anyone who was familiar with her would say she looked worried.

Glancing up, she knew she wouldn't stop. She had to go *there*. An invisible force tugged her upward.

There were rules about it, and consequences, too. She understood that heading in that direction led to trouble if she were discovered. She paused, twisting backward to stare at the gloomy abyss, waiting for something, or someone to make her return.

Minutes, or maybe hours passed. Sighing, she made her decision.

Slowing her movements, she studied the murky expanse around her. Hanging suspended, she allowed the currents to caress her, wrap her in their loving embrace.

It was beautiful here where the light penetrated the water, highlighting the glories of the sea. *Orange, blue, green!* She had never seen such colors, so bright they hurt her eyes.

It was forbidden, yet curiosity niggled at her like a worm. *How could something this exquisite be hidden? Did the ocean not belong to them all?* With a shiver that ran through her body, she shook off any doubt.

She moved toward the light, the weight of her three hearts slowing her ascent. Traveling at a snail›s pace, she rose little by little, listening, tasting, feeling for a disturbance. She clicked her beak, the sound muffled by the water surrounding her.

She smelled and tasted nothing. Higher, she had to go higher. There had to be more.

It was quiet, she could hear the water rush around her. She drifted, keeping as still as possible so she would never be detected. She floated, her arms spread out as if a puppeteer were holding her motionless. Her large eyes scanned for danger. Her skin rippled with excitement, her suckers crimped as if they were spasming, but she barely noticed, so fast were her hearts pounding. Once or twice she paused, a slight eddy or whirlpool causing her to slide back into the shadows.

She waited, barely breathing, pretending she was a fossil encased in rock, spellbound. She was further above than anyone in her consortium had ever ventured.

Scanning the area carefully, she detected nothing. Satisfied she was alone, she surged onward. Her circles widened as bravado made her fearless.

How did this happen? Who opened the way?

Anticipation—or maybe it was uneasiness—made her frantic, uncoordinated. Her arms flailed in a spastic dance causing her to lose control. It made the water churn as if caught in a powerful undertow. She felt something slide down one of her arms and she jerked, causing a shimmering curtain of fish to surround her. For a minute, she couldn't breathe.

Blinking, she opened her mouth to inhale, and the school of pilot fish scattered. She was exposed, the water cleared and the vastness of the ocean opened up. Disoriented, she rolled, unsure of which way to go. Up or down, right or left. She didn't know. *There was too much space! Too many creatures.* She pulled her arms wrapping them around her shaking body.

She shouldn't have done this! She was out of her element, a stranger. Her frame of reference was off-kilter. She had never traveled this far up, not ever, not for millions of years. No one had. It made her pulse beat faster and her hearts vibrated with powerful intensity. *Didn't they always warn me not to be attracted to the light?*

Some of the elders said the light warmed. She convulsed instead. Others swore the light was a myth. Once you got there, it was nothingness. You'd be swallowed into the great vortex, never to be seen again.

By nature, she was not brave and didn't like making waves. She was biddable, reliable, and followed the rules. She never wanted to test the theories. She realized she liked the secrecy of depth, the velvet void enabling her to exist in quiet anonymity.

Light warmed. *No, that is a lie.* It didn't. Light meant exposure; light meant disruption; light meant… danger. Light charmed, though. Like a magnet, it pulled her upward.

She circled as she ascended, her mouth closed tight with expectation, mixed with dread. The light was close. She reached out, tentatively wanting to touch it.

CHAPTER 1

SEA SHANDY

**Four Weeks After Vincent Konrad's
Escape from Monsterland**

ON A HOT night, when the fog obscured the moon, a grizzled sailor limped into a bar on the *Isla de la Condensa,* the Island of Doom. It was a forbidding place, where brigands met to swap stories between raids.

The old man told a captive audience of a hair-raising tale of disaster, an impossible attack. A captain and his two crewmates about to leave, paused as the frightened man spun his tale. It had all the ingredients of a good sea yarn, all the right characters, mixed together with secrets and danger, and it was just the information they had been searching for. They returned to reclaim their table in the middle of the room. The four sailors who had taken their seats scattered as they approached, spilling their drinks on the greasy floor.

The stranger was a typical seafarer, his skin burnished from years in the strong sun, one eye patched, a scar bisecting the skin above, attesting to a savage fight. A golden earring glinted in the gloomy interior, becoming a beacon to the listeners. The old tar scuffled across the room, his knobby hands balled into fists as he retold a horrifying encounter with a fantastical beast.

Drinks were flowing in the tavern, a pall of smoke hung like a thick cloud. It was late, and the captain was tired. Jötnar, the bosun, straddled the other chair at the table. They watched as the mariner warmed to his tale, his burly arms flying as he related the epic battle of man versus perils of the sea.

Jötnar waved a ham-sized hand in dismissal. He rose to interrupt, scowling, his voice booming loudly. "Enough with the fish tales, you dirty bilge rat! Tell us what really happened to the ship!"

"Six months ago, that guy was piloting a cruise ship from New York to Miami," another man called out. He wore a sword belted to his waist and stood at the bar. He held a drink up as if to toast the room. Snorting, he bowed mockingly to the boatman standing indignantly in the center of the room. "He's full of crap. The most exciting thing that ever happened to him was when a tiki torch set fire to someone's hula dress."

"It's true!" the old sailor spat back. "I was there! I saw the monster with my own eyes!"

"You only got one o' those, and who knows how good that one is?" Jötnar snickered.

The older man raced across the room, his chest puffed out like a pouter pigeon, his fist curled and ready to deliver.

Jötnar stood to reveal an astonishing height. He towered over everybody else in the saloon at just about eight feet. There were a few gasps as the worried patrons exchanged looks.

The captain placed a restraining hand on the big man's arm,

pulled him back, and said with a lazy drawl, "Let him finish. I want to hear his yarn."

"You don't believe that hogwash about a bloody octopus. We need to know what really happened to the *Windward*," Shandy, their third companion, said. He was the oldest of the three and the first mate of the ship. He had a shock of white hair and a face so wrinkled it looked like a prune. "We've crawled through every dive and gin joint, and they all have the same story...."

"I said, let him finish," the captain repeated firmly, and the room grew quiet again. At last, the captain nodded. "Go on, old man." The command was final.

Jötnar grumbled, his face grimacing as he lowered himself to his seat. Shandy sat down as well, folding his arms across his chest. The captain eased back into a chair, then leaned forward.

The audience turned to face the sailor, listening raptly.

There were stories of a great beast circulating seaports from Shanghai to Tortoga, a monster so big it was able to crush a ship with its many tentacles. Here was finally something more substantial, the man claimed to be an eyewitness. It was said the creature was elusive and as insubstantial as fog, gone before anyone could capture it.

"It squeezed the ship and all on board until there was nothing but pulp."

Someone hooted, setting off the rest of the room with a low rumble of laughter. The sailor spun, his face fierce. "You think that's funny? This thing, this beast will kill all trade. It's insatiable. It will not stop at one vessel. It made a meal of hands all on board my ship!" the old man said, his voice an angry hiss.

The crowd murmured, a few shifted uncomfortably in their seats. A waitress cried out, fainted, going down with a tray holding several glasses of rum. "Not the entire crew," the captain said, with a wry smile. "Apparently *one* survived."

The two stared at each other as if they were measuring an opponent.

"I have proof and I won't take no worthless paper money." The sailor held up a shaking hand. Clutched in the grubby fingers were photos, grainy images with blurred lines, the beast's movements so fast all the camera could catch was a ghostly shadow.

Every head craned forward, the silence interrupted by the plunk of a bag of coins on the wooden table.

"What's your name, swabbie?"

The sailor's head swiveled toward the captain, his cloudy eye on the money. "And why should I tell you?" he shot back.

The giant stood menacingly, his massive hands reaching out to grab the sailor by his scrawny neck.

The old tar backed away, intimidated by Jötnar's enormous size. He volunteered his name in a quavering voice. "They call me Harry… Harry Who."

"Alright, Harry Who, how do we know you are telling the truth?" the captain asked quietly.

"I am the sole survivor. Held onto a piece of the deck for four days until they found me."

Shandy exploded with chuckles, spitting out his drink. His shoulders shook with mirth. "Everybody's saying the same baloney. They all want the reward money."

The old salt straightened his back and replied, "It's the truth. Ask my rescuers if you don't believe me." He pointed to a group sitting behind him.

"Yeah, we picked him up," one of them yelled, then went back to his card game.

"I'll buy those pictures from you," the captain's voice rang out.

The old man plastered the photos to his chest as if they were his most valued treasures. The captain took in his grimy appearance, his tattered clothes, and trembling hands.

"What do you want from *El Fantasma Gris*?" Harry Who demanded. The patrons all began talking, repeating the name of the monster.

Jötnar half rose in a threatening manner, a growl erupting from his throat.

"Easy, Jötnar. Stand down," said the captain.

"Wot's he mean by that?" Jötnar's hands were balled into fists that resembled cannonballs.

"I said, stand down." The captain's voice cut through the din in the room like a dagger. The big man sat abruptly, his large size dwarfing the chair. Steely eyes narrowed, the captain said softly, "*El Fantasma Gris?*"

The old sailor gulped, his Adam's apple bobbing nervously. His single eye appraised the burly giant, then held out the photos to the captain, who nodded to the bag of coins. He snatched the leather pouch, dropping the pictures onto the tabletop, his gaze never leaving Jötnar.

"*The Gray Ghost,*" he explained. "She's been sighted, alright. Her attacks are bold, and she's moved into the shipping lanes."

"Go on," the captain encouraged.

"Shipping is the only way left to move products now that everything's been grounded."

The captain nodded in agreement. "That's true. Since the battle for Monsterland, governments everywhere have collapsed."

"Aye. Trade's frozen like the tundra. Nothing's getting in or out," a woman next to the captain lamented.

"Not to mention air traffic controllers all over the world have abandoned their posts." Another man grimaced.

"Yes, I know." The captain concurred, then added, "But there's work to be had for those willing to shake hands with the devil."

"And you willingly did that," Shandy muttered, earning a dirty look from the captain.

This comment brought a few sneers, coupled with sniggering.

A man spoke up. "It's chaos out there."

Everyone grumbled in agreement.

"Aye, leaving what's left to those of us willing to risk our lives to get it," the captain responded. "The seas were riddled with ex-cruise and shipping employees living their pirate dreams, and don't tell me you all don't love it."

Laughter broke out, the mood changing in the bar. Glasses clinked as they toasted the absence of law and order.

"You spoke of a ship called the *Windward*," Harry Who said.

The captain took a long swallow of rum, then replied, "Aye. A sailboat, a sleek yacht taken from a Miami shipyard and captained by a guy named Cranston, one of the best skippers in the world."

"Cranston." The walnut face cracked a smile, the remaining eye glittering feverishly. "Cranston. A fine captain. He ran small yachts down from Vancouver to Cabo, but no match for *el Fantasma Gris*."

The captain leaned forward. "Will you take us there? Will you take us where she went down?"

"I… I don't…" The sailor backed away, stumbling into a chair.

A handful of gold coins rained down on the scarred table. "There's more where that came. A lot more."

Harry Who licked his lips, his eye straying to the pile of coins strewn on the wooden tabletop. "Yes, I'll show you where she went down." He held up a crooked finger in the air. "But first I want to know why."

The words died in the sailor's throat as he watched the captain and shipmates stand up to leave. The captain never looked back, but Shandy motioned to the money and jerked his head impatiently. "If I know my captain, we set sail… now!"

The old tar swept up the money and followed them out of the seedy pub.

Finally, news of the *Gray Ghost, el Fantasma Gris!* The captain walked briskly toward the harbor.

The streets abounded with hushed conversations about heavenly retribution. People stopped where they walked to watch the foursome make their way down the dimly lit street. They gossiped on corners, whispering about the strange new threat to commerce. Living on the lawless islands, they all understood that if the stories were true, trade goods everywhere would be imperiled. Who would be able to sail when ships were being snapped in half by monstrous creatures?

The captain's thoughts whirled. The *Windward* had been destroyed with the entire crew, battered and beaten by a creature so big it tossed the ship in the air like a toy.

"I don't like it," Shandy groused.

"You don't like anything," the captain said with a laugh. "You kicked up a ruckus when I hired Jötnar."

"What do we know about him—?"

"Enough! I trust him, gentle giant that he is. He has the strength of ten men." The captain paused to let the words sink in. "What do we know about anybody, Shandy? I have a pocketful of gold, and that's going to land us the discovery of the century. We need this. We promised we'd find the thing and bring it back to Prendick Rock to trade that old whaler they unloaded on us."

"It's a good ship." Shandy gave a twisted smile. "Better than nothing." He shook his head and spat into the corner. "You made a deal with the devil. You know it. I know it." He pointed to his large nose. "I also know, that's not the only reason you want to catch this thing." Shandy looked angry. "*Bah*! It's easy to throw around money that isn't yours. We should have taken the old ship they gave us and cut out of here."

"We can't disappear with that tanker following us like a lost puppy."

"Aye. That's what I'm saying, Capt'n. Them that organized this crazy mission don't trust us and sent that tanker to watch our every move." He leaned in close to whisper, "You know you could have shaken them off at any time. I taught you enough to be capable of it!"

"What? And miss all the fun?" The captain left Shandy to leap up the gangplank, giving orders to set sail.

The captain and crew soon followed the supposed wake of the doomed ship. Harry Who directed them west and then south into the warmer waters of the Pacific off the coast of South America.

The two ships, the antique whaler and a cumbersome tanker, set sail to the isolated patch of sea where the crew of the ill-fated yacht had supposedly met their deaths. After a week of fruitless searching, the captain ordered the tanker to stay behind lest its massive engines scare off their prey.

A heated argument erupted between the two commanders. The larger ship was forced to veer off to the east, keeping a minimum of a two-day distance between the two vessels.

The sea was smooth as glass. The dark water glistened like polished obsidian. The captain watched the flat surface, waiting for a sign. This was the spot where the *Windward* had gone down just over a month ago.

The silent sea revealed nothing. Playful dolphins broke the surface of the ocean, but of the massive creature, there was no sign. They traveled for days, tireless in their pursuit, the crew restless with the inactivity. The captain watched the endless horizon, impatient and feeling foolish.

With little sleep and barely any food, the crew was nearing exhaustion. They complained about returning empty-handed, their mission scuttled with nothing to show for it. It was a dangerous game, but the captain was not ready to give up yet.

There will be hell to pay, the captain thought ruefully, anticipating the introductory meeting with the new employer on the mysterious Prendick Rock.

They had never met face-to-face, and the captain knew it would go much better with the presentation of a priceless trophy.

After all, the captain thought ruefully, first impressions were the most important and lasting impressions of them all.

CHAPTER 2

RITA MAE'S

HOWARD DRUCKER AND Wyatt trudged through the desolate landscape. They had started their journey from Copper Valley a couple days ago, avoiding the renegade gangs marauding the highways.

The entire trek had been grueling from the start. Everywhere Wyatt and Howard traveled, they saw communities coated with the gray residue of the Glob. The alien fuel left every town in a two-hundred-mile radius around Copper Valley devoid of life. The only remnants of humanity were in the form of lifeless husks.

The roads to LA were deserted as well. Wyatt and Howard prudently kept a low profile, walking miles off the major freeways, avoiding the bands of crazies who terrorized the roads. Carter had mapped a crude route, estimating their trip to LA to be no more than one hundred hours, a few days at the most. It turned out to be a total miscalculation. By skirting areas where the gangs operated, they went miles off-course and it wasn't long before they realized they were lost. Wyatt's chest constricted with worry. *What if he disappointed Carter?*

The landscape was totally barren. It felt like he was on Mars. He should have made contact with some sort of authorities already. *Where the heck had the army gone?*

The third day dawned with a merciless sun. Wyatt's throat was parched as they traveled the packed sand of the desert.

Wyatt held up the map, the hot breeze ruffled the paper.

"Wyatt, man, you're holding the map upside down. Did you look at it that way before?" Howard's eyes were worried.

Wyatt stared at the squiggly lines. He missed his GPS. Turning the paper sideways, he wondered if he *had* read it wrong. Glancing up at Howard's blanched face, he said, "No, no. I'm sure."

Howard turned in a small circle and muttered, "I think we might have gone… " Howard didn't finish the sentence, shading his eyes, he said, "None of this looks familiar."

"It can't be familiar! We never strayed off the freeway. We don't know any of these small towns," Wyatt responded, out of patience; a well of panic lodged in his gut making itself known. "We'll be fine," he assured him.

Howard did not look convinced.

By the fourth day, they started conserving their water. The detour off the beaten track took them miles south.

Wyatt stared at the endless desert with the grim knowledge they made a mistake. They were exhausted. The beef jerky they'd been eating left them both hungry and unsatisfied.

"I could use one of Manny's burgers right now," Wyatt said. They were taking a break sitting in the shade of a joshua tree.

"Me too," Howard agreed. "Lots of fries, but hold the salt, I'd tell Manny. Man, I'm thirsty."

"What if nobody's left?" Wyatt's hands dropped on either side of him. They were heavy.

Howard looked at him. "What do you mean?"

"What if we're like the last people on earth?" Wyatt looked straight at Howard. "This is worse than a zombie apocalypse."

"The odds are the further we get from Monsterland, we'll start running into people."

"Yeah, but what kind of people?" Wyatt said more to himself.

Howard didn't answer. He was leaning forward, squinting his eyes. "Is that a mirage, or am I seeing a structure?"

Wyatt peered in the direction Howard indicated. The horizon seemed to shimmer, the umber colored sand taking on an iridescent shade of silver and blue. A long low building took shape. Wyatt rubbed his tired eyes. "I think… I think it's a … diner."

Wyatt got on one knee and shaded his face with the paper map. "It *is* a diner!"

It was as if they'd hit the jackpot. "What town do you think this is?"

"Who cares? Bet they have Whisp in there!" Howard yelled rising to his feet.

"I would lick a salt stick before I'd ever drink that stuff again." Wyatt laughed, relieved at finding a hint of civilization.

Howard grabbed the map from Wyatt's hands and consulted it again. "It might be Pyrite Junction."

"There's a sign. It's called…." Wyatt bit his lip as he tried to read the sign. "Rita Mae's. Never heard of it."

"Look around. Why would you have? We're in the middle of nowhere. Let's go!"

They ran to the abandoned building, slowing when they reached the outskirts of the town.

"Calling this a town is a real stretch," Howard observed..

There were two gas pumps outside the diner under a flimsy awning. A small general store stood like a squat toad on the sunbaked pavement, the windows blown out. A few trailers were spread around, one listing on its side, not a person in sight. The wind blew making a rusty hinge creak as it swayed.

Wyatt eyed the vacant street suspiciously. He moved his gun to point forward.

Swallowing was hard, his throat felt like sandpaper. Wyatt held out his other hand to slow Howard. They approached the diner cautiously, their guns ready. Opening the door slowly, Wyatt eased in. No lights were on. A breeze stole through a broken pane of glass, ruffling the paper napkins on the counter. It smelled of old grease and spoiled meat. Flies buzzed around dried plates of food left midmeal.

"Where do you think they went?" Howard asked.

Wyatt shrugged.

They examined the half-eaten food, the congealed grease on the grill. Howard spied a glass case holding a doughnut. He slid open the door, the loud squeak filling the restaurant. There was one doughnut left. Howard snatched it, then tapped the stale pastry on the Formica surface. He broke it in two, tossing half to Wyatt. Wyatt caught it, and his eyes spied an ant crawling on the pitted surface.

"*Yuck.*" Wyatt held it up.

Howard licked off an ant making its way across his treat. "Protein, bro. No time to be finicky."

Wyatt nodded. "We may need this doughnut."

"How so?"

"Well," Wyatt continued, "if Whisp killed the mummies, you never know what doughnuts can kill. Maybe Gremlins?"

"Only kale kills Gremlins," Howard said as a matter of fact.

"Kale?" Wyatt replied. "I thought sunlight…"

"Don't reference 80s movies if you want to learn how to kill a monster. They're never right. Basically any cruciferous vegetable will do the trick."

"How are you gonna get a Gremlin to eat—" Wyatt imagined Gremlins munching on a salad.

"Who said they have to eat it?" Howard said.

Wyatt looked back at the doughnut and nodded in amusement.

"Besides," Howard Drucker said. "Gremlins would probably love a doughnut. However, I could possibly see how doughnuts may kill the New Jersey Devil, even dragons."

Wyatt tapped the stale treat on the counter. "Only if you throw them. Besides, the Jersey Devil is thousands of miles from here. Who the hell knows what's happening on the east coast." He shook his head. "I'm thinking this fried morsel of artery-clogging goodness is more of a formidable weapon against giant insects. *Kingdom of the Spiders*, maybe. *Them!...* " They were falling into the old routine of comparing the strength of monsters.

Howard's eyes widened as he nodded in agreement. "*Starship Troopers*. I can see that!" He looked at Wyatt. "*Gee*, I miss Melvin."

Wyatt agreed. "It isn't the same without him." He considered the insect on the doughnut. "Sorry, man. Survival of the fittest." His stomach rumbled noisily. His mouth watered. Closing his eyes, he took a big bite, chewed quickly, then swallowed. His eyes opened with a bit of a shock. He hadn't tasted the insect at all. He finished the doughnut, sucking the remnants of sugar from his fingers. "Definitely giant insects." He looked around the funky-smelling restaurant. The refrigeration was out. That was no surprise. "Looks like they cut out of here before the mummies or Glob got them."

"Yeah, no purple dust." Howard slammed the door of the appliance with a loud crash. "What a waste. All that spoiled bacon."

"Doesn't look like they have a generator like Manny."

"That's probably why they left." Howard rummaged through the cabinets.

Manny owned their favorite hamburger joint, Instaburger. Not only did they love the food, Howard, Wyatt, and Melvin all worked... *well*, Wyatt thought ruefully, *used* to work there.

"Someone's cleaned the place out already," Howard said, his head deep in a cabinet. "Not much here. Lucky for us, they missed the doughnut." He rubbed his stomach, belching from the stale grease. He felt his guts do a little dance. "Maybe they missed it on purpose."

Wyatt walked to the end of the café. He wasn't sure what he was looking for. He saw a crumpled piece of material pushed into a corner of a red leather booth. Using the muzzle of his gun, he pulled it out. It was a flimsy scarf. He touched the gauzy material and brought it to his nose. A fragrance wafted from its folds. Wyatt held it thoughtfully, wondering how long it had lain there, still retaining the perfume of its owner.

Howard continued poking around the closets. Wyatt heard him yell, "Eureka!" His friend pulled out a can of beans and looked for a can opener, leaving drawers open.

The roar of multiple car engines filled the restaurant. Wyatt shouted, "Duck!" They threw themselves on the floor.

Wyatt crawled behind the counter, where they met, keeping his backpack and gun close to his body. He looked at his hand, realizing he still held the scarf wrapped around his wrist. He stuffed it under his shirt.

"Did you see them?" Howard whispered.

Wyatt shook his head. "I don't need to. Who else is driving around here? We need to hide. Let's move into the back of this place."

Using their forearms, they dragged themselves into the storeroom behind the counter, their bodies soon coated with the grease that stained the floors.

Howard got to his knees, directing Wyatt with his head to squeeze into a dark corner. A row of empty boxes surrounded it. Several pieces of cardboard were on the floor, as though someone was breaking up the piles of boxes that surrounded them. It was as good a hiding place as any. They edged themselves into the tight confines of the space and pulled the boxes in front of them.

Wyatt felt an unyielding lump beneath him, as if he had stepped onto an old carpet. He carefully placed the boxes making a wall enclosing them, but there was something interfering. It blocked the space, leaving them exposed. He crouched down to investigate, pushing blindly in the dark. He pounded the bump with the butt of his gun.

Wyatt heard a swift intake of breath, realizing he was not alone.

Dropping his backpack, he stood, pointing his weapon at the man lurking in the shadows behind one of the stacks of cardboard cartons. Wyatt had hit the hard surface of the man's booted foot. The stranger's face was half-covered by a scarf, like the ones the military wore in the desert. His eyes were shaded by dark glasses. Wyatt wondered why he was wearing sunglasses in the dimly lit interior. "Easy," Wyatt warned him.

The stranger held his hands up as if surrendering, but Wyatt sensed the coiled strength of his rangy form. Watching the other man size him up, Wyatt saw him turn his head to the doorway as if he were gauging it for escape.

"I wouldn't if I were you," Wyatt said, his voice low. "There are others outside."

The man glanced through a crack in the cardboard wall and nodded with understanding. Wyatt could see his white teeth gleaming in the dark. The door to the café squealed when it opened.

"Get down!" Wyatt pushed him to the floor, covering him with his own body. "If you make a sound, I'll shoot."

The man relaxed.

Howard, Wyatt, and the stranger lay flat on the floor, squeezed into the tight space, screened by the empty cartons and boxes.

There was the tinkle of broken glass from the front of the cafe followed by the crash of something big being thrown down. A few voices called out to each other.

"See anything?" someone asked.

"Rita Mae! You there?" a male voice shouted.

There was laughter. "She probably left after the last time we was here."

"It stinks. I wouldn't eat anything from this dive even if we found something."

The heavy tread of boots crushing debris into the floor drew closer.

Wyatt, Howard, and the stranger's heads snapped up; the noise of the interloper on the other side of their hiding place froze

Wyatt's blood. The enemy shoved aside something bulky, knocking it over to crash on the floor. Wyatt was so tense, he thought he might be vibrating.

Fighting the urge to gag from the stale taste of the doughnut, Wyatt's mouth watered. Bile fizzled in the back of his mouth; he knew it was suicide to clear his throat. The man below him was so silent Wyatt wondered if he was dead. He exchanged a look with Howard, who gestured with his eyes to the man's sleeve. Wyatt squinted in the dimness making out khaki army fatigues. Wyatt jerked his head with understanding. Howard patted the man's shoulder as if to comfort him.

The unmistakable sound of a gun being cocked caused them all to freeze where they were sprawled. Nobody breathed. Wyatt grasped his own gun, leveling it so it pressed against an opening between the cardboard boxes.

Wyatt's prisoner placed his hand around the muzzle of Wyatt's gun. He had pulled down his glasses, his eyes making contact with Wyatt, pleading for him not to open fire. Wyatt blinked back letting him know he understood.

Still, Wyatt simmered resentfully at the man's high-handedness, as if he had taken on the role of commander. Sucking in a silent breath, Wyatt knew the more pressing problem was on the other side of their hiding place.

The space filled with the scrabble of tiny nails. Looking down, Wyatt saw a fat rat run in front of them, squeezing out of the bottom of the box. The intruder on the outside yelped. Wyatt watched him take a bead on the rat as it raced from the room. A shot rang out followed by a triumphant yell, "I got dinner!"

Peeking through the opening, Wyatt observed the hulking outline of the man. He walked quietly around the small confines of the area then stalked off. Wyatt heard his captive exhale with relief. There was the sound of a door slam, and after a few minutes, the roar of the engines filled the air. They lay there quietly until the noise of the cars receded.

Howard rose and sprinted to the doorway. He stood sideways, searching the main dining room. "It's all clear. I'm going outside to make sure. Look!" Four uniformed people walked out from behind several structures. Three men and one woman were carrying heavy guns.

"It's okay," the stranger said. "They're friendlies."

"How do we know *you're* a friendly?" Wyatt demanded. They had stood up. The man was lean and somehow intimidating, despite his size.

He shrugged, but Wyatt couldn't tell much about him, what he was thinking, or where he was looking. His gaze was once again obscured by the glasses, and it infuriated Wyatt. He wanted nothing more than to reach up and snatch the spectacles off. Wyatt's gut tightened with the knowledge that he didn't trust this man.

Wyatt shoved the man backwards. Howard looked at him, his face shocked at the display of force. "He didn't betray us, Wyatt," he said.

Wyatt snapped at Howard, "He didn't betray himself either. You have to stop being naive, Howard."

The man ignored them, then gestured at the door. He said, "My crew. They've been out looking for a car."

"Howard, go out and see if they have a car," Wyatt ordered.

Howard grabbed his gun and opened the door. Wyatt backed out of his spot, the gun trained on the stranger. "Who are you?" he asked.

The man didn't respond. He seemed to be looking at something behind Wyatt. Too late, Wyatt twisted. A baseball bat glanced off the side of his head. The room faded, and Wyatt dropped to the dusty floor.

CHAPTER 3

IT'S A WEREWOLF'S LIFE

MELVIN SAUNDERS STRETCHED out on the banks of the artificial lagoon. The sun beat down, drying his wet body. He propped his head on the palms of his hands, satisfied with his life for the first time he could remember. He licked his lips, tasting salt from the marshy water.

Melvin watched the movement of the clouds as they scudded across the crystal sky. Nothing made any sense in his world. He knew the water inside the now-defunct Werewolf River Run was fresh water, as if it were supplied by a lake. The lagoon, complete with the little bump of an isolated island he now called home, was surrounded by salty water. Why Vincent Konrad had made the two different types of ecosystems was beyond him. Melvin shrugged. Not that it mattered. At least there was shrimp and saltwater fish rather than bass and trout, and that was fine with him. Who knew what was in the mind of that nutcase?

He and Jade had put down roots in what was left of the Werewolf River Run attraction. He had dismantled the bridge; no one could get across except by swimming or using the one boat that remained. He had sunk every other floatable in the park when they'd decided to live there. He wanted to keep everyone out. Melvin had dragged the last boat from the flume ride into the moat, giving them access to the rest of the park.

In the past few weeks, people ventured into the ruins of the park. Melvin created a credible show of snarling and growling to scare them off. Worked every time. Humans were so easy, he snickered.

He and Jade lived on the island. He refused to use the former pens where Vincent Konrad had housed his old pack. Melvin made adjustments to a straw awning that had been erected to keep people in line shaded from the sun. He had added four walls made from planks of wood scavenged from Main Street. The little hut was created from a hodgepodge of materials, it didn't look like much, but he was proud of it.

It was dim inside, but they had enough of a supply of scented Monsterland candles to last them twenty years. He had to admit he was getting tired of the Wafting Werewolf candle and preferred Vampire Vantasies better. He'd have his canines removed before he shared that tidbit of information with Howard Drucker. He missed Wyatt and Howard fiercely, but he knew things would never be the way it was before Monsterland. It didn't matter. He had Jade, and, well, he had to admit, he liked that part of his life, a lot.

Melvin couldn't believe that a girl like Jade had chosen life with him. She seemed to have no regrets. It was something he worried about all the time. She had adapted to their new surroundings with the enthusiasm of the cheerleader she used to be. Jade had made their place homey, filling it with shells, rocks, and other things she found lying around the park. The place had an organic feel to it. It was the nicest place he had ever lived, and he didn't want anything to change. It sure beat the trailer he shared with his grandfather.

The evening birdsong stopped when Jade called Melvin for dinner, her voice soft in the misty air. They had a good thing going, a sweet life. He caught and cleaned the small game and fish that shared their home. Jade had gotten proficient at cooking it over the fire she'd learned to create using twigs and leaves.

If the kids at school could see us now, Melvin mused. Jade, the most popular girl in school in Copper Valley, was his wife. They lived together in paradise. They had decided to marry as soon as the Battle for Monsterland was over. He still winced thinking about how her father had taken the news. After Melvin turned Jade into a werewolf, no amount of discussion or apologies could put that genie back into the bottle. He snorted loudly. *That ship had sailed.*

Melvin knew by the position of the moon and constellations at night that it was nearing July 4th. If their world hadn't imploded, he would have been roasting marshmallows and practicing beer pong with Wyatt and Howard while shooting off kick-ass smoke bombs at Lake Almanor. They were certainly going to lose the vacation house rental deposit, but that was all water under the bridge. So much for celebrating graduation and the impending entrance to assorted universities across the United States.

Melvin had won a free ride to Caltech and Jade would have been admitted to a local nursing school. Instead, the unlikely couple had found a peaceful way of life away from society and its craziness. Not in a million years had he thought he'd end up with someone as perfect as Jade.

All that time in school, he'd never let on how he felt about her. Wyatt, his best friend, had been wild about Jade for all of the twelfth grade, but Wyatt seemed to be more interested in Lily now, the girl from the reservation. While guys didn't do that to other guys, Melvin had decided that after Monsterland, things were different. The world was no longer the same place. He realized life was too short not to go after what mattered most, and he knew that Jade mattered most to him. He had loved her silently and from afar for years. He would have been okay—well, sort of okay—if she and Wyatt had made a go of it. They didn't. Once things became dicey, Wyatt realized he and Jade were not a good fit. Part of Melvin was angry at Wyatt; the other side rejoiced that the field opened up for him.

Melvin pulled at a tuft of grass, placed one blade in his mouth, and sucked on it thoughtfully. The truth was that once Vincent Konrad's Monsterland had destroyed society, it felt like every man for himself. Not that it mattered to him. Melvin always had lived on the fringes of his small community. He never knew his father. According to the stories, he was a guy passing through Copper Valley on his way to Alaska, where he worked the crab boats. His mom was a hopeless groupie with some of the popular vampire groups. Gramps, her father, threatened all kinds of things, but she couldn't stay away. What did they say? *Once bitten…?*

She served as a drone for a band of vampires for a while until she disappeared from his life. Melvin remembered her sprawled on the couch, never making his lunch or dinner, too dazed to function. Only Howard Drucker's mom took pity on him and fed him regularly. Took care of his clothes too. She replaced the ripped shirts and ill-fitting shorts he'd outgrown with stuff from her kids. Never made him feel bad about it, either.

The Druckers were special people. They even formed a search party when Melvin's mother went missing, vanished without a trace after the band *The Bleeding Ticks* gave a concert in the local park.

Melvin looked at the calm water of the lagoon. *Do I miss my mother?* He shook his head. Not much. It was actually easier without his mom around. Less embarrassing.

Still, he knew that his whole life, all he desired was to belong somewhere. He had the unlikely trio of Howard Drucker and Wyatt. Even Sean, Wyatt's kid brother, joined them sometimes, but while they made him welcome, Melvin always hung back. He never quite felt a part of anything.

There was no doubt he was different, even before he was bitten by a werewolf. He couldn't put his finger on it, but he longed for his own home and family. On the occasions when his friends included him, he was the puzzle piece that somehow didn't fit.

Guess the apple didn't fall far from the tree. His mom craved the bite of a vampire, and for him it was a werewolf's peck that finally brought happiness. Melvin found peace among the werewolves, altering his life forever when they made him one of their own.

Billy, the lead wolf, had nipped him, mingling their blood. Just thinking about the transformation made Melvin shiver, not with fear but with primal delight. It felt *so right*. He remembered looking down and seeing auburn fur-covered paws with their wicked claws at the end. He folded his hands over his face, sniffing them, the canine odor filling him with jubilation.

Melvin loped around the domed enclave on the opening day of Monsterland, seeing Billy watch him with pride, as if he were his son. Melvin had never seen anything like that before in anyone's expression when they looked at him. He was used to tolerance and perhaps pity from his friends, scorn from the cool kids. Billy and his pack of werewolves positively beamed at him. They surrounded him. He could feel their panting chests close to his own. Nobody had ever stood that close to him.

The kids at school always treated him as if he were a leper, or a zombie even, as if being a nerd was something they could catch. Not Wyatt or Howard Drucker, he had to admit. But they were not enough. He shook his head. He wanted more, and for a few hours, he'd had it all, a clan that accepted him as if they were a family.

He was happy until Vincent Konrad blew all the wolves' heads off. Every werewolf, every last one, was destroyed by Vincent Konrad.

Melvin had gotten his revenge, or so he thought. An eye for an eye, he ripped off Vincent's head that very day in front of Howard Drucker and Wyatt. He thought he had avenged the werewolves, but Vincent had somehow survived.

Melvin looked around his peaceful home. He still had a score to settle with that monster, and he was planning to finish the job once he rebuilt his pack. For now, he wanted to enjoy the fact that he had a place and a family. He had Jade, and she was his home.

Melvin had rescued Jade from the Glob when it invaded Copper Valley, saving her from certain death. He discovered all Jade wanted was to be taken care of, and he was prepared to do that. That left only Wyatt as a loose end, and Melvin loved Wyatt just about as much as Jade. He worried about a confrontation, but to his surprise, Wyatt adjusted to the whole idea easily. It seemed his friend wasn't in love with Jade after all.

Melvin was happy and, in the destruction of his old world, had found a spot of serenity where he could live the way he wanted.

They say that opposites attract. Melvin thought the expression was speaking directly about him and Jade. Melvin, the boy who never fit in, and Jade, the most popular girl in school—they did make an odd couple. He laughed. He was awkward; she was sublime. He was ugly, *he never lied to himself,* and Jade was the most beautiful girl in the world. It almost hurt to look at her. She was perfect.

Maybe he wouldn't go looking for Vincent. He woke every day at peace. For once in his existence, Melvin thought, life was perfect.

He stretched. At least his body had changed in his transformation. It was sleek and muscular, and despite being covered with freckles, he had to admit he looked pretty good. While he never worked out, somehow after the initiation, as he called it, his body morphed into a veritable clone of a movie-star werewolf. He put it down to one of the best side effects of his mutation.

This morning, he and Jade awakened cuddled together, marveling at their good fortune.

"Are you happy?" He kissed her as he pulled her close.

"Never better."

She had the biggest blue eyes he'd ever seen on a person.

"This is not where I thought you'd be after graduation," he growled, nipping her cheek.

Jade fussed with her hair. She looked down at the ragged shorts she wore, the dirty shirt. Melvin licked a smudge from her cheek. Jade's face reddened. She moved to get up to check her appearance in the sliver of a mirror Melvin had hung up for her on a pole.

"Leave it." He smiled. "You're a hot mess, but I like it. You're perfect the way you are."

She giggled. "No." She shook her head. "I used to be perfect. It's a hard job staying that way. This is easier." Jade stood, brushed herself off, and went to work on her wild hair. "I always had to have everything in place, watch my weight. Being flawless was demanding."

"*Oh, so much pressure.*" Melvin rose, working the kinks from his body.

"Really." Jade moved around the hut. "You have no idea. I was anxious all the time that if in some way I failed, I would lose everything. I'd be a nobody."

A nobody? His gut tightened at her tone. *Is this enough for her?* he wondered. A feeling of icy dread settled in his stomach. He looked at the deserted hut, the abandoned park surrounding them.

"You… you don't feel like a nobody here?" he asked, his voice nervous.

"Oh no, Melly." She ran close to hug him. "I feel like the most important person in the world here with you."

Melvin rubbed his chin on the top of her head. "You're not sorry, you know… that you didn't go with Wyatt?"

"Wyatt?" She looked up at him, her face filled with tenderness. "I like Wyatt. I love you."

"You don't regret what I did to you?"

Jade held his cheeks with both palms. "You saved me from the purple foam. It killed everyone, and I couldn't have moved fast on two feet. When you bit me and made me your own, you saved my life."

"I made you into a werewolf, Jade. You can never go home."

"You took me from there and gave me security. This is where we belong."

Melvin kissed her then. He pretty much kissed her as much as possible. He loved everything about Jade and couldn't believe she loved him back.

They separated for the morning, both having things to do. Jade traveled to the wreckage of the stores in the center of the park while he fished and caught a turtle for dinner.

Close to sunset, Jade walked back into the clearing, holding her blonde hair off the back of her neck. She moaned, "It is so hot."

Melvin watched her under heavy-lidded eyes. She wore cutoff jeans, so frayed they had more holes than material. He was going to have to go clothesline shopping again. This time he'd have to travel further away from here. Most of the local towns were uninhabitable. She had on a faded Monsterland tee shirt that was too big on her slim body. Jade knotted it, a lump of material resting on her tanned hip. Melvin chuckled when he read the shirt. "Where'd you get that?"

"I was poking around what's left of stores today. You like it?" She tightened the shirt across her body so he could see it.

My Other Pet is a Werewolf, Melvin read silently, then held out his arms. "Am I your pet?"

Jade jumped on his lap. She brushed the frizzy red hair back from the sides of his face. "You are now." She kissed him.

Jade rose abruptly, pulling Melvin by the hand. "Come on. It's hot. Let's go swimming."

Melvin shucked off his clothes and ran after Jade, who splashed noisily in the lagoon. Just when he grabbed her arm, she dove down. He lost her in the murky depths. Melvin went in after her. They played in the water, Melvin catching her and tossing her casually into the middle of the pond.

"You beast," Jade said, spitting out a mouthful of water. "*Ugh*. Why is it salty water?" she asked. "And it's full of trash."

"Yeah, I know. The park goers were pigs. We gotta clean it up little by little. That stuff won't go away by itself. I was poking around

Vincent's old office buildings the other day and found some reports about them using the salty water for harvesting alternat food sources."

"Another one of that megalomaniac's horrid experiments. Melvin, stay away from there! You don't know what that fiend was up to."

Melvin smiled at her indulgently, "Megalomaniac."

"Whatever." She shrugged.

Melvin went on, "There were rows of tanks, like they were studying fish, but everything was destroyed. It's a mess. Nothing survived. Well, the good news is at least we can get better seafood from here other than the funky catfish from under the dome."

"Ugh, they're so oily. But you gotta be careful of the gators." She splashed him. "I'm not afraid of them as long as you're around." Her blonde hair was sleek against her head. Her blue eyes sparkled.

Melvin swam lazily around her, evading her grasp when she tried to catch him.

They floated idly, talking about dinner and maybe a little exploring after they ate, when Jade gasped. She dipped, swallowing water, then sank, disappearing from sight.

She resurfaced abruptly, her eyes wide with fright. "Something… I can't…" She choked, going under again. Melvin heard her gurgle as she swallowed water.

Melvin screamed, "Jade!" His heart pumped like a piston. He dove deep, swimming frantically in a circle, searching for her under the water.

Something brushed him from behind. Jade's panicked face filled his vision. Dark arms held her by the neck. Clear air bubbles escaped from her mouth.

Melvin kicked to get closer, grabbed Jade by the waist, and tried to pull her from the intruder.

An elbow lashed out, hard and sharp, jabbing him in the face. It abraded Melvin's skin as if he were being dragged on a rocky surface. Long fronds were tangled in the stonelike fingers that grabbed him.

Melvin took hold of an arm; it was like touching armor. He pulled closer, coming face-to-face with the floating figure.

They grappled. Melvin recoiled with shock. It had two slits for a nose and huge round eyes on either side of its fishlike face. Whatever held onto Jade was not human. It was a creature, right here in his lagoon, Melvin thought wildly. He swam around the back of it. It was tall, with a rusty-colored exterior. Melvin pounded its broad expanse of shoulders, the water buffering the blows so that they did little to the enormous creature.

Jade's eyes fluttered, her hands flailing. Melvin grabbed the slippery arms holding her. He pulled Jade, but she was trapped, bubbles of air escaping her mouth. Her eyes went wide with fright.

Melvin kicked, holding onto the creature's iron grip until his fingers bled. Fury roiled through him when he saw Jade go limp, her eyes drifting shut.

Melvin concentrated on morphing, feeling power rip through his body. He howled in the water, his back going rigid. Muscles undulated. His torso elongated, reshaping into a canine's form. Fur rippled in the water.

His jaws clamped on the arm of the being, crushing the shell-like exterior. His teeth clacked, but he refused to let go. Tasting the tangy metallic flavor of blood, Melvin clamped the enemy with his savage jaws. Relief filled his chest as he felt the arm rip from the torso, releasing Jade. She bobbled upward, free from the monster's hold.

The creature punched Melvin's snout with its other fist. Then, holding the stump near its shoulder, he kicked Melvin in the face and swam into the deep recesses of the lagoon.

Melvin raced to Jade's side, whimpering. He still had the creature's detached arm in his jaws.

Jade hadn't moved or tried to swim away. She floated above him, alarmingly still, her arms outstretched on either side of her limp body. Her face was pale with a deathlike quality, her eyes closed.

Gently, Melvin nudged Jade with his nose. She rolled over, her face breaking the surface of the water. He raised his head above the lagoon surface, paddling furiously. Jade sputtered, then coughed. Melvin gave a triumphant howl.

Tears pricked Melvin's eyes. He dove underneath her, using his body to bring her back to shore, his only thought for Jade.

By the time he reached the sand, he dropped the creature's arm and transformed back to his human body. Breathing hard, he lifted Jade from the water and carried her to their hut.

She opened her dazed eyes. "What was that thing?"

"I'm not sure, but I am going to find out," Melvin answered grimly.

He heard Jade protest, her arms reaching out to keep him from leaving once he settled her on their nest of blankets. Fury made him stomp to the water's edge, ignoring her pleas. He stood ankle deep in the lagoon, staring at the cloudy depths.

"This is my home!" Melvin shouted. "Mine!" He watched the still surface of the water, ready to defend his territory. A shiver raced through him. In another time, he would have been thrilled. Next to movies about werewolves, *The Creature from the Black Lagoon* was his favorite film of all time. Now all he felt was revulsion. Everything had shifted. Melvin no longer cared for those things. He cared only for Jade.

There was no movement. The silence wrapped around him like wool smothering him.

"This is my home," he repeated. "Nobody is going to take it from me." HIs voice cracked.

He spied the abandoned arm lying in the shallows. He bent down to peer at it. The fingers twitched and then stilled. Melvin picked it up and brought it into the hut.

CHAPTER 4

EL FANTASMA GRIS

THE MOON HUNG low overhead, sparkling on the impenetrable water. There was no movement that night, nothing. A fog rolled in, muting the sound so that it seemed like the ship was wrapped in cotton wool.

They were deep in the Pacific Ocean, in the middle of nowhere. It felt like they had been adrift for weeks. Food and water were running low. *Perhaps the old tar played them false, sent them on a wild goose chase so other ships could scoop up all the prizes,* the captain thought glumly.

Placing a capable hand on the wheel, the captain moved the ship ever so slightly east, where the sun peeked above the horizon. It formed a thin line of gold, painting the sea amber.

"It's here, Shandy. I know it's nearby, maybe underneath us as we search for it." The captain turned to the ship's first mate who stood in a silent vigil against a wooden mast.

Shandy slipped off a knitted cap from his thick white hair. He had a two-day-old beard that covered the bottom half of his wind-beaten face. Bright blue eyes peered intently at the captain.

"I don't know, Cap'n. We can't stay much longer. We're running out of provisions." The older man moved in as if to confide in the captain and kept his voice low. He spoke with the confidence of a long-standing friendship. They had known each other forever. "The crew is unhappy," he continued. "They are here for the prizes, and if we don't deliver the goods-" The older man shook his head. They were both thinking about the dismal battle yesterday where the ship sunk before they could claim any prizes.

The captain whipped him an angry stare. "What, and would you have me abandon our true mission? Surely this is the closest we've gotten to finding it." Doubt hung between them like a thick curtain.

"The beast is a myth, a fish tale, and you've fallen for the bait. Jötnar was right about him. That swabbie sold you an empty bill of goods. We shouldn't be doing this kind of work. It's not worth the gold they're paying us. And on top of it, I don't trust—"

"The *Windward* is still missing. Cranston was a good skipper." The captain cut him off swiftly. "Besides, it's not about the money, and you know it."

"Pirates off the coast of Peru could have gotten them. It's a cold world out there now, Cap'n." Shandy touched a bent finger to his face. "I have a nose for sniffing these things out, and I'm telling you, I don't like it...."

"Enough, Shandy." The captain motioned behind them for Jötnar to take over steering the ship. The huge man separated silently from the shadows, his sausage fingers gripping the wheel.

Shandy shook his head, staring at Jötnar›s hulking form. "I'm not sure if I trust that one. I don't know what you see in him," Shandy said under his breath.

The captain glanced at the large man, not sure what to make of him either. He had joined the crew recently and certainly pulled his weight, but he remained as enigmatic as a puzzle. "He carries his load and then some," the captain said grudgingly. "It doesn›t matter how you feel about him. All that matters is what *I* think."

Shandy laughed softly.

The captain looked at him sideways. "You find that amusing?"

"You learn your lessons well. I tol' you to trust your gut."

The captain nodded graciously, their good humor restored. "You see. I was always listening to you."

They both turned to study the giant at the wheel, each deep in thought.

Shandy cleared his throat. "*Jeez*, he's just so… so…"

"Big?" the captain's teeth gleamed in the early morning light.

"I was going to say, mysterious."

The captain laughed. "Sure."

Jötnar's bald head sat on his squat body as if his neck couldn't support it. He wore earrings the size of bangle bracelets. Shandy shook his head, wondering how he carried the weight of the heavy gold. He fingered his own gold loop, bought over fifty years ago when he first went to sea. A big but necessary expense, insurance that if his body was found having died at sea, the gold would go to the cost of a coffin. "Ship's become a regular menagerie. You and your strays," he added with an indulgent chuckle.

"Easy, Shandy. Don't make me lose my temper." The captain stalked to the lee side of the ship. "He serves a purpose." They both leaned against the railing to continue to observe the mountain-shaped outline of the first mate. "He's loyal and a good sailor," the captain added as if an afterthought.

Shandy reluctantly shrugged. "You don't know anything about Jötnar. Came out of nowhere…"

"Most of us came out of nowhere," the captain responded.

Shandy nodded. That was true, but still, the man was so… unnatural. Shandy turned to see the captain bending over the side of the ship. "We're not sure about anything he says—"

"I said that's enough." The captain searched the impenetrable darkness of the water. "I know you're here," the captain crooned, ending the conversation. "There've been sightings of you, pretty beastie. Come out, come out." The captain turned to Shandy. "It's been all over the maritime radio today… sightings of it."

"It's the ramblings of the weak, a yarn, nothing more. We've been sailing together for twenty years. I've been at it longer, close to fifty. I've never seen the likes of something they're describing."

The captain seemed to stew over the remarks, then answered, "Just because you haven't seen something doesn't mean it can't exist."

Shandy opened his mouth to reply, snapping it shut when he saw the stubborn tilt of the Captain's chin.

The floor vibrated as a collision shook the ship taking them all by surprise. Both the captain and Shandy jerked at the impact. "What was that?" Shandy's voice sounded nervous. He grabbed a barrel to keep himself upright.

They peered over the railing to see a broken bit of flotsam, a piece of wood or metal floating in the dark water. Weak rays of morning sunlight bounced off the debris, illuminating it. The captain motioned for a sailor to use the winch and reel in the broken bits rocking on the waves. The wreckage landed on the deck with a heavy thump. Shandy leaned over, eyeing the splintered material. It was at least seven feet wide and four feet tall.

"It's part of a ship." The captain went down on one knee. "Fiberglass… a light craft."

Shandy squinted as the captain pointed to an uneven border. He crouched to get a better look at it. He traced the jagged edge with his finger. "Looks like something took a bite out of this." Shandy measured the arc of the crescent shape and shook his head. "If that was a bite, the mouth would have to be… eight to ten feet wide. It's impossible."

"A shark?" Jötnar asked.

"No," the captain answered. "What do you make of this?"

Shandy pulled at his lower lip. "Beats me. I've never seen anything like it."

"*El Fantasma Gris.*" Harry Who staggered onto the deck. Clearly he was enjoying too much of whatever he was drinking. He walked unevenly toward them. "We're doomed…. It's here."

"Shut up, you old sot!" Shandy shouted.

They turned to stare at the vast ocean, ignoring Harry, who slid onto the deck next to the debris.

"It's *her,*" Harry Who wailed.

"That bit of wreckage doesn't prove anything. You can't trust the chatter you hear on the radio either." Shandy spat toward the water.

The captain turned with a grim smile as if it were evidence. "I tell you, it's nearby. I made a promise to bring it back."

"A promise to a maniac doesn't count. Let's cut our losses and get out of this," Shandy responded, his face shadowed. "We don't have to do this. We could go back to cruising the coast up north, working for ourselves."

The captain flashed furious eyes lit with a dangerous gleam. "Would you have us relegated to the backside of hell when there is money to be made? If we lose this ship, we're returned to square one. Where will we get the money to buy a new one? You forget, I made a deal!"

Shandy snorted. "Since when did that stop us? This is nothing but blood money!"

The captain turned to face the other direction. "'Money is the operational word here. It's what we need, and this is the only way we can get it. That old rust bucket you called a ship sank in the Cook Inlet nearly killing us all. It left us literally high and dry. If not for this opportunity, we'd still be working in that canning factory."

"Only for a short time," Shandy hissed, earning him a dirty glare from the captain.

The sails creaked; the wind pushed the ship over a swell. Shandy rolled with the deck, moving with the rhythm of the boat. He liked this old craft. It made him feel he was connected to the ocean below him, not like the modern jobs that used technology to tame nature. That was the one good thing to come out of this venture—the ship. He still felt they should seize it and make their way to more isolated waters away from the likes of their new employer. They were too exposed.

Shandy complained to anyone who would listen that one lost something with modernity. It placed barriers so that common sense was replaced by machines. Working on this job with a shifty crew appeared to have affected the captain. They couldn't seem to agree on anything anymore.

He watched Harry Who babbling, a long line of drool dripping from his mouth to the deck. Jötnar glowered at Harry with contempt.

"Take him below," Shandy ordered to two seaman.

The two sailors hauled Harry and dragged him below deck. Shandy heard his cries become fainter until they stopped abruptly. Shandy exchanged a satisfied smile with Jötnar, knowing Harry would be nursing a sore jaw tomorrow thanks to the crew. At least they found something they had in common.

Shandy was an old-fashioned man who liked to see things with his eyes, touch them with his hands, and judge their value based on his own understanding. He had never trusted the newfangled ideas that made people feel invisible, as if they were better than nature itself. He felt he never belonged in this time, but in another era.

Shandy respected the endless ocean and its denizens, knowing that if Mother Nature decided to sneeze, this ship and all aboard would be nothing but a bunch of splinters.

He slapped the wooden railing with a bit of affection, then caressed the smooth wood. They were on an antique whaler, built over two hundred years ago, swiped from a museum in Boston. He knew his captain was the only person who could sail something as old as the *Hampton*.

It was almost eighty-eight feet long and still had the stink of the boiled blubber ingrained in the wood. They had bolted on two cannons, taken from some decrepit fort in Puerto Rico when they'd stopped for provisions this summer. She was considered small for a whaler, with capabilities of moving when they needed to evade the criminals terrorizing the seas. The white canvas above Shandy snapped as it caught a puff of air, the jib and mainsail billowing. The ship lurched forward. He inhaled deeply. No matter what the captain said, he liked this old boat.

Shandy and the captain anchored themselves to the rocking deck. The horizon had lightened to a dull pewter. His experienced eyes scanned the dark waters.

"It's dangerous out here alone," Shandy muttered. "We should have never separated from the tanker."

The captain nodded to the east. "The *Mirage* isn't far. All I have to do is call and they'll catch up. Her engines are scaring off my monster. We have a job to do, Shandy, and I am determined to finish it."

"Ain't no monster, Cap'n. Probably just a big fish, if it exists. For the record, I still don't like this job."

"Not quite a fish, Shandy, but it exists." the captain ignored the last comment.

"More 'n' likely we'll be blown to bits by one of the varmints that pirated the Colombian navy."

The captain grunted a response.

Shandy wouldn't let the argument go. "This is crazy business, if you ask me."

"I didn't." The captain's eyes were glued to the horizon.

"Even if it does exist, what do you expect to do, put a leash on it and drag it home?"

"Are we doing this again? You know they gave us a special sedative to bring it back."

"Still, it's nasty business." Shandy paced the deck. "And all for the wrong reasons, I may add."

The captain waved a hand. "You'll like the money enough when we get paid."

Shandy grumbled about taking unnecessary chances, but the captain ignored him. "We're not even sure about the DNA thing—."

"Leave it, Shandy," the captain ordered quietly.

"Let me finish."

"If you're going to rehash the argument about coincidences. I don't want to hear it." The captain stalked away.

Shandy sighed with a pang of sadness. He'd fought his share of battles in his lifetime, working for the side that paid him enough. More often than not, he was not proud of his friendships. He bit his lip. He'd have to cut the captain some slack, even if he didn't have a good feeling about this. He watched the waves finding comfort in their ebb and flow.

In the captain's defense, Shandy was having a hard time telling the good guys from the bad right now. The entire world had gone crazy—no law, no rules, everything faded to shades of gray. Most didn't even know what they were fighting for anymore, the lines between right and wrong blurring into on indistinguishable border.

They had been warned by the locals on the island that both the Chilean and Colombian navies had mutinied and were now taking any ship they could find. The seas were full of enemies. They couldn't sail more than a day without exchanging gunfire. Some used speed-boats; others were on old ships like this one.

They had chosen to evade the American navy. Shandy wasn't sure who they sided with. They had come across a strange looking aircraft carrier last week.

It had been painted black, and the crew didn't look like any he'd ever seen before. With some deft maneuvering, they evaded them. They radioed the *Mirage* about that one. Shandy knew it needed some investigating to find out who was piloting the big warship.

The breeze died; the air grew heavy. It was as though they had entered a vacuum. Shandy cocked his head, listening intently.

They had been attacked by a torpedo earlier that year. It had been in the waters of Africa, when they were hugging the coastline, looking for a place to get supplies. He remembered the sound of something barreling through the water, parting the waves like silk. He recalled describing it as a quiet but steady pulse.

Shandy heard that same sound now. He paused, tilting his head to listen with his good ear. He ran to the captain as fast as his bandy legs would carry him.

"Watch out!" he called, gripping the captain's arm.

Something hit the ship hard, rocking them on their feet. Shandy would have fallen, but the captain's steady hands held him firmly.

"What in the hell…?" Shandy peered over the rail, looking for damage. Whitecaps surrounded them, the waves lapping against the hull. He looked toward the horizon and spotted the choppy wake of something large. *No, something huge.*

Shandy's eyes opened wide with shock. "It could have sunk us. Must be a whale!"

"Perhaps she only wants to play." The captain's face was alight with excitement. "There she is!" The captain pointed as the enormous tentacle rose from the water as if it was waving. They observed the creature in silent fascination.

"What the—?" Shandy's jaw dropped to his chest. "I don't see no fin."

"Change course," the captain ordered, interrupting him, and shouted to Jötnar, "Follow her!" The giant bosun pushed his shoulders, his jaw tight as he spun the wheel.

Everyone stopped moving. The ship heeled sharply, changing direction to pursue the creature. They watched as the beast slowed in the sea, soon becoming a dark shadow mirroring their course from a safe distance. Shandy peered at the fathomless ocean. "What the hell is that thing?"

"*El Fantasma Gris,*" the captain said with awe.

The creature, or whatever it was, moved to glide lazily aside them, matching their speed. It had to have been over eighty feet long, according to Shandy's reckoning of the body and the long tentacles trailing behind it. "Look at the size of that head." He shivered, imagining the creature›s beak. He squinted. "That's one big calamari. You think it's an octopus?"

"No." The captain shrugged. "Not sure. Something like, perhaps."

"Never seen nothin' that size." Shandy shouted. "Maybe it's something that got caught in a nuclear test blast."

"Kraken!" Jötnar called from his spot behind the wheel. "There are stories about them in Norway."

Shandy observed the gray skin glistening where the early morning rays gilded it. It had faint melon-colored markings, like tiger stripes. He had not seen anything with that type of coloring in his life.

The breeze was picking up along with the crew›s response as they realized the scale of the beast. The tentacles trailed for what looked like a mile.

"It's more than ten feet wide," Shandy whispered to the captain, his eyes bulging from his head. One flick of its massive body would crush the aged wood of the ship and send them into the abyss. He touched his earring reassuringly.

The captain ran across the deck, ordering the crew to get the sedative ready. Massive barrels lining the side of the ship were punched open, and giant harpoons were coated with the liquid. A longboat was lowered. It hung over the sea as crew members leaped over the rail to man it.

Shandy watched the animal swim in the other direction, creating a gulf between them. A great sigh of relief died in Shandy's throat when the creature paused and turned. It maneuvered lazily as if it had all the time in the world. It started traveling, racing toward them, slicing the water like a buzz saw.

"It's coming right at us! Hit that thing with a harpoon!" Shandy cried. He tugged the gold hoop in his ear. *Not even a burial at sea, just oblivion*, he thought. *If that thing hits them...*

There was the crash of wood against flesh, the smack of their collision. The ship rocked, water sloshing over the railings. The longboat shattered as if it were made of twigs. Shandy heard the cries of crew members as they fell into the ocean. He grabbed one of the ropes attached to the longboat, his knuckles white from the effort. Four tentacles with giant suckers slapped the deck, flicking barrels and supplies away like bothersome insects. The tentacles wrapped themselves in the rigging, shaking the ship like a child's rattle.

Shandy prayed he'd stay put. His fingers had long since grown numb with the effort of holding tight. For a minute he was weightless. Closing his eyes, he heard the screams of sailors as they were washed into the roiling sea. "Crew overboard! Crew overboard!" he yelled as the salty water poured over him, drowning the sound of his voice.

The ship righted itself. Shandy got onto shaking legs and rushed to the railing. His old eyes searched the water but could find no sign of the sailors or the longboat crew on the choppy surface, just splintered wood floating. Tentacles as thick as logs slapped the water. He scanned the deck searching for the captain, his breath coming out in a rush when he saw the familiar face on the top deck. He turned back to the sea.

Shandy's fingernails left crescent dents in the rail. The ocean calmed once again. He peered over the edge, expecting to see a hole with rushing seawater on the side of the ship. He blinked. The wood was undamaged.

He looked up to see Jötnar hugging the wheel, his feet planted firmly on the deck. *At least the giant was good for something,* he thought.

Crew members watched the water, looking for survivors.

The captain ran across the deck. Their eyes met. "We're bruised, Shandy, but not sunk."

"The crew!"

The captain pointed to the lookouts. "We'll find them, I've no doubt. Let's get this beast!" The captain called to the crew. "Get into the other longboats!"

The well-rehearsed sailors sprang into action, jumping into longboats, the harpoons dipped in sedative and ready to do their job.

"Go, go, go!" the captain shouted with a voice sounding oddly muffled. "I knew I'd find it."

Shandy leaned over the edge, feeling frozen. "It's a monster!" He yelled into the buffeting breeze. "You can't capture a beast this big! You'll sink us all!"

"I've waited too long." The captain's mouth twisted. "If you don't have the guts for this, Shandy, then go below."

Shandy straightened his five-and-a-half-foot frame. Drawing a deep breath, he challenged the captain. "Aye, I have the stomach for the capture, but do you have the power to drag that thing back? There's a reason one has never been caught!"

The captain shrugged. "Nobody believed they existed. Call the *Mirage* for help. They can't be more than a few hours behind us."

"What?"

"Didn't you know? They've been tailing us all day, keeping enough distance to keep me from firing on them."

"They don't trust you?" Shandy asked, but they both knew the question was rhetorical. *Who could trust a pirate?*

"Would you?"

Shandy raised an eyebrow, knowing the captain had a point.

The captain's fierce eyes glowed with passion. "You've never understood why I have to do this. I know these waters like the back of my hand. I studied the stories. Once we met Harry, I knew we'd find one here. We need to bring this to Prendick Rock to prove—"

"You and your blasted promise," Shandy grumbled, then turned to face the crew jumping into their positions. "You're obsessed with that man."

Four sailors leaped into the longboat. Shandy heard the grind of the pulleys. The boat was lowered, followed by the sound of a splash when it landed on the ocean.

The creature had moved away, picking up speed as it dipped from sight. It looked like it had gone deep.

"Faster, faster!" the captain called. The crew moved with practiced ease, the longboat taking off in pursuit.

Shandy watched a harpoon being loaded into a gun by the experienced hands. A crewmember stood on the rocking boat, his bare feet bracing against either side of its narrow space. The air was spliced with the *whoosh* of the weapon when it fired, only to fall harmlessly into the sea.

"Captain!" Shandy shouted, pointing to the crew.

The giant octopus had turned and was speeding toward the longboat like a heat-seeking missile. It collided with the sound of shattering wood and screams of the sailors.

Shandy watched in horror as the beast emerged from the water, its parrot-shaped beak of a mouth snapping a man in half. Several tentacles gripping sailors swayed above the white-capped water, their screams pathetic as the life was squeezed out of them.

The giant maw had to have been twelve feet wide. Shandy had never seen anything that big. "It's… the devil," he whispered, his face drained of color.

"The devil is in New Jersey, Shandy, and you know it."

"It's going to kill us all!"

The great beast came up to grab flailing crew in the water with one of its many arms, dragging them into the murky depths.

"Not if I get it first!" The captain shouted to the second crew to get into their longboat. "Pick up the survivors!" The more subdued group took off in the direction of the downed crew, the oily water now slick with blood. Another boat was dispatched to deal with the monstrous being. The air was filled with the screams of the sailors in the water.

"*Oh* no," Shandy muttered, his eyes widened in shock as the octopus twisted, hitting the rescue boat with a *thwack*. Crew spilled into the water. The captain cursed loudly as they were stuffed and devoured one by one by the massive beak. "What the hell is that thing?" Shandy asked.

"It's an octopus, a big one, and we're going to bring her in! That thing took out half my crew!" The captain's eyes were narrowed with hatred.

"You have to stop! Let's get out of here and save the ship! You can't beat something this massive!" Shandy shouted. He blocked the captain.

"I can, and I will," the captain told him through gritted teeth. "Don't make me choose between you and *El Fantasma Gris*. This is my destiny." The captain shoved Shandy out of the way.

"Aye, and your destiny will be the death of us all."

The captain ignored him and ran to a giant harpoon gun. "Hold her steady!" the captain shouted to Jötnar.

Sweat poured down Jötnar's reddened face. Veins bulged on his temple. Shandy reluctantly admired the strength of those massive arms holding the wheel, keeping it from spinning out of control.

The captain pivoted, turning the gun turret, the rocking waves making aim difficult. Shandy observed as the captain carefully aimed, not moving, waiting for the opportunity to strike. The beast made mincemeat out of the crew. The captain followed its movements with steely resolve.

Shandy watched the captain, angry and at the same time proud of the display of skill as the weapon was trained on the monster's broad face. The sun was full out now, and the old man shaded his eyes from the glare. "Pisses ice water, that one does," Shandy mumbled, looking at the silhouette of the captain taking aim.

He heard the *twang* of the harpoon being fired, followed by the *thunk* as it embedded itself in the rubbery flesh. The sailors cheered loudly.

The giant beast jolted high out of the water, its massive beak snapping impotently at the rope, its platter-shaped eyes rolling backward until only white showed.

"We got her! Hold it steady!" the captain shouted. "She's going to drag us for a bit! Get another boat in the water to pick up the survivors before she eats the rest of them!"

Shandy ordered another craft dropped. It skimmed the water even as the whaler moved. He released the new rescue team to row to the flailing survivors moaning in the water.

The octopus dove deep. The rope on the reel spun so fast it smoked from the friction. It went taut with tension. The creature took off, pulling the ship like a towboat. They traveled faster than the whaler could have ever sailed. The sails snapped overhead, billowing out as they filled with wind. The beast zigzagged across the waves, dragging them behind her.

Shandy looked back. The remaining longboats in the water soon looked like toys in a bathtub.

They crested the waves like a Nantucket sleigh ride and could see the octopus ahead of them, racing forward. It slowed for a bit, then turned, its head rising above the water. It was silent, the remaining crew frozen watching to see if the octopus was well and truly drugged.

The powerful sedative did its job. The animal slowed. It jerked several times, turning as if to attack the ship again, instead rolling up for a minute or two as it fought the drug coursing through its bloodstream. It dove feebly, bobbed twice, finally landing on its back, floating, its pale flesh exposed to the bright sky.

The exhausted crew roared in triumph, moving to one side of the ship to observe the dazed animal.

"Yes!" the captain crowed.

"You done a bad thing today." Shandy shook his head. He removed his cap and looked at the captain. "I changed your nappies when you was a child, I did. Took care of you like you was me own when your mother died. Taught you everything I know."

The captain turned to look at the sailor. "And you will have my eternal gratitude for that, old man. Cut the Popeye crap and talk normally. You've been weird ever since we boarded this old ship. Maybe now I'll be able to trade up and get us a decent boat. I've had my eye on a destroyer for a long time."

"But this is wrong, Rosemary. It's all about greed, and you know where greed gets you?"

The captain had lost her hat in the melee, her dark hair blew wildly around her narrow face. She moved forward and grabbed Shandy by the shirt, her eyes blazing. "Don't call me Rosemary. It's not about greed. This is about something else."

"What, then?" Shandy demanded, his face inches from hers.

Rosemary bit her bottom lip, looking twelve years old again, erasing any anger from Shandy. He couldn't be mad at her. His eyes widened when he realized her expression reflected indecision and confusion. *She wasn't sure.*

Rosemary turned her gaze to the sea, changing the subject. "Did you call the *Mirage*? Tell them we need help hauling in our prize?" Her lips were set in a firm line.

"We lost twelve men!" The veins on Shandy's neck stood out.

"Collateral damage."

Shandy's face turned so red it looked like steam would come out of his ears. "You did *not* just say that!" His shoulders slumped. "You've changed. Ever since that man found you, you're…you're different."

"I am not!" The captain's head lowered. "Any loss is devastating. You know it's killing me inside. Besides, I didn't ask to be found." The voice was all defiance.

"You sound more and more like your *alleged* father every day." Shandy said with disappointment. He stalked off to make the call. "I know why you are doing this, and I can't figure out where I went wrong. It's all for attention and, make no mistake about it, my girl, no mistake at all." He pointed to the large creature being tethered to the ship as he left. "That thing is the devil's spawn, and it will be the death of us." The old tar stomped off, mumbling about tampering with nature being a very dangerous thing. It was clear Shandy was disappointed with the young woman and angry with the world.

The captain watched them attach the animal to the side of the ship with a net. "Give it room to keep moving," she advised.

The sailors stayed glued to their spots. Rosemary's face grew thunderous. "It's sedated, you fools! Nothing will happen, but if you don't get water circulating around its body, it will die! Now!"

The sailors rushed to do her bidding. She motioned to one of them. "You! Make sure you keep it heavily sedated until we hook it up to the *Mirage*!" She turned to Jötnar. "Contact the base. Tell them we're coming home and bringing a present. A very special present."

I told him I would do it, and I did, she thought to herself. *He might have pulled me out of a two-bit job in a backwater town, but I'll show him what I'm made of.*

Rosemary Konrad smirked, and he'll know he'll have to meet me on my terms.

CHAPTER 5

THOSE AMAZINGLY TALL GIRLS

WYATT CAME TO, his head resting on his backpack, the quiet murmuring of Howard Drucker's voice filling the aching cavity of his skull.

The stranger filled his blurry vision. Wyatt blinked and tried to rise.

"Don't. You took a nasty blow to the head," *GI Joe* said with an air of authority that Wyatt found condescending.

His head felt like it had been rolled over by a monster truck, and when Wyatt groaned, the sickly sweet, half-digested doughnut rose to the back of his throat. He must have turned a different color, as steady hands twisted him sideways, enabling him to throw up into an aluminum bowl. Wyatt pushed away the help as soon as he was able.

"Concussion." He heard Howard Drucker's voice say from a distance.

Light pierced his irises as each eyelid was raised. He batted away the hands from his face, grumbling, "Don't touch me." A soft, cool palm persisted, combing the hair from his sweaty forehead, and an auburn-haired girl with a triangular face swam into view. She leaned over him, her tresses brushing his cheek. He inhaled, knowing instantly she was the owner of the scarf he'd found earlier.

He looked up to see a tiny snub nose covered with a sprinkling of freckles. Wyatt's mind wandered for a minute, then came back to rest on her face. He thought the freckles were endearing.

"I'm sorry," she said with a sympathetic smile.

"You look like an elf," he murmured.

The girl laughed prettily and blinked large, colorless eyes. "*Ha!* An elf. This isn't Vermont. I'm sorry I whacked you, but you were going to shoot Etan."

"This is Etan, and he's with the army," Howard said in a rush. Howard looked dazed himself. He was rubbing his head as if he were the one who had been clobbered.

"Marines," Etan corrected Howard.

"Yeah, marines, I thought that other guy said army." Howard sounded vague. "We're going to travel with them to Rancho Cucamonga," Howard continued.

"Etan who?" Wyatt demanded, still woozy. Nobody answered. "No, we're not going to travel with them." Wyatt struggled into a sitting position. The room tilted. He forced his eyes to focus. "We're going to LA."

"It makes more sense to check out places where an army could mobilize. Rancho Cucamonga has a large mall."

Wyatt tried to rise, shaking his head. "Thanks, but no thanks. We don't need to stop there."

Howard grabbed his arm. "Yes, we do. My parents might be there."

"They hit me on the head!" Wyatt shouted.

"Yeah, sorry about all that, kid, but..." Etan shrugged. He

sounded like a cop from a television show. "You know how it is. Besides, I had to protect the girls."

Wyatt glanced up, groaning until the room righted itself. He was surrounded by six girls, all giggling and strangely alike. They had wavy auburn hair and pert noses with scattered freckles. Wyatt blinked, then rubbed his eyes. *Am I seeing double? What do you call it when you're seeing six?*

Howard must have read his thoughts. "You're not seeing multiples. They're sextuplets."

"What?" He shook his head.

"Sextuplets. Sisters."

"Yes. We're heading to the base with Etan," the ever-helpful one who had smashed him with a bat offered. Wyatt twisted his head, and it pulsed from the effort. He looked at the girl. Even crouching, she appeared smaller than the other five by a few inches.

"We want to join the army," the one leaning over him added.

"You mean the marines," a different one giggled.

"I heard the navy is fun," another suggested.

"We travel in groups but could use another set of hands," a fourth said from across the room. Their long legs seemed to stretch from one end of the floor to the other.

They were identical, all six, and amazingly tall, dressed in layers of clothing as if they didn't want to be exposed to the sun. Wyatt's thoughts were muddled, and he opened his mouth to say that they must be sweltering in the heat. He looked dazedly at the one who had stroked his head.

"My name is Danai. We're all named from the first six letters of the alphabet. It's easier to remember us that way."

"Astounding." Howard Drucker took a large bite of beef jerky. "That's Adriane, Becca, Candice, Danai, Erin, Frannie." He pointed to each one accurately.

Wyatt looked back at Danai, studying her. She seemed to tower over him even while they sat.

"You'd better get some sleep. We leave at first light." Etan stood and stretched.

"Who are those other guys?" Wyatt demanded.

"Soldiers. We're all soldiers on our way back," Etan responded, his voice calm. "We're searching for our units." Wyatt cast a glance at the rest of the people in the cafe. They certainly looked like soldiers. Even though they appeared relaxed leaning against the walls, Wyatt could tell they were not as casual as they seemed. He touched his head and winced. None of them wore a uniform. Wyatt narrowed his eyes.

Two of the sisters produced a couple of cans of tuna. Etan ordered them to see if they could find more. He stood and followed the soldiers outside of the cafe. They disappeared through the opening. Wyatt bristled at the way Etan had assumed command.

Wyatt watched Howard create a few beds out of towels they'd all dug up in the back room. "Howard!" he whispered fiercely. He grabbed his aching temples, the noise bouncing in his bruised brain. "I don›t want to travel with them! We don't know who they are!"

Howard glanced over to see if anyone was listening. He grabbed Wyatt's arm and gave a gentle squeeze. "We need all the help we can get."

Wyatt opened his mouth to argue, but the tall girl interrupted him. "He's right," Danai said, patting his shoulder reassuringly. She tugged him, and he fell over.

Wyatt felt compelled to pull away, but another part of him stayed still. He wanted to yell at Howard that they had battled vampires, zombies, and werewolves. They had defeated mummies, the Glob, and a reanimated monster named Vincent Konrad, but exhaustion pulled at him. Besides, Howard stood and walked away as if they'd finished their discussion.

Wyatt looked at the oversized hand of the girl resting on his arm. She started stroking his forehead again. His headache vanished.

"Etan said he's going to push straight through the desert tomorrow without stopping. You should try to rest."

She smiled sweetly, and Wyatt felt his eyelids grow heavy. He wanted to tell her he didn't care when Etan was leaving, that he wasn't going with them, but his eyes closed. He tucked his hand under his cheek, drifting off into dreamless sleep.

Wyatt heard them getting ready to leave before he was truly awake. He opened one eye to see the group loading up knapsacks with whatever they could salvage. He rose, his head no longer aching. He touched the spot where the bat had connected with his skull, and there was not even a bruise.

"We decided to let you sleep as long as possible," Etan informed him.

Wyatt stood and looked for his gun. He realized Etan was holding it. He held out his hand, his face set.

"I thought I'd carry it for you," the older man told him.

"I can handle it."

Etan's lips tightened as if he wanted to refuse. Wyatt hardened his gaze, and Etan tossed him the gun. Wyatt watched as Etan rested his hand on a sidearm tucked into his pants declaring his authority.

Wyatt cradled his firearm. He looked at Howard, who was helping Erin, or maybe it was Becca tie a towel filled with supplies on her back like a rucksack. Howard had to stand on a stool to help her. These were the tallest females Wyatt had ever seen.

"What are you, a traveling basketball team?" Wyatt asked.

They all looked at each other blankly; then Danai stepped forward with a forced laugh. "Right, basketball." She nodded, and they all agreed.

Wyatt watched them suspiciously. They were basketball players like he and Howard were ballerinas.

Danai went from booth to booth. One of her sisters called out, "Did you lose something?"

"My scarf," she answered, her head ducked under one of the tables. Wyatt's hand went to his chest and then stilled. He could still smell the fragrance of the scarf under his shirt and was reluctant to let go of it. It was not his nature to be cruel and withhold something, but for a reason he couldn't explain, he didn't want to give it back. It was silly, he knew, but he felt it gave him some sort of advantage, as if he knew something they didn't.

Etan had an amused smile on his face, almost a smirk, that irritated Wyatt. Wyatt jutted out his chin and looked for Howard.

Howard was nowhere to be seen. Resentment filled him. Gritting his teeth, he set out to find him.

"Howard!" He opened the door to see his friend loading a truck. "Stop! Let's get out of here!"

Howard looked up, his face filled with surprise. "We decided yesterday. We're teaming up with Etan and his group."

"We didn't decide anything."

Howard's face paled to almost translucent. Sweat dotted his temples.

Wyatt's brows grew thunderous. He grabbed his backpack and stormed from the diner awning toward the main road. Howard ran after him.

"Wyatt!" he called. He caught up and pulled Wyatt by the shoulder. They stopped to talk, Howard in his reasonable manner. Wyatt was seething. They stood staring at each other for a long minute.

The pickup truck Howard had been loading earlier was parked at the entrance.

One of the commando types was filling the gas tank with a row of cans. Wyatt watched him work. Two other soldiers were walking down the road carrying heavy gas cans. Wyatt admitted he was jealous of the truck.

"How could you make a decision like that on your own?" Wyatt said through gritted teeth. He spun to face Howard angrily.

It was so early, but it was still dark outside. The desert was cold at night when no sun warmed the earth. Wyatt shivered convulsively as he saw the clouds of condensation escape his mouth.

Howard watched him attentively. "You okay?"

"I'm fine. Let's go."

"*Um*, Wy, I really think it's safer if we…"

"We don't need them!"

"He's going to find my father, Wyatt. He promised. I'm not even sure where they could be. We could use his help."

Wyatt fumed for a few minutes. He didn't want to travel with them. There was something about Etan that ticked Wyatt off. "You don't know that guy from Adam."

Howard paced the area as if he was thinking. He turned to face Wyatt. "You think you shot a few bad guys and mummies and you're all badass now. Well, I don't think so, Wyatt. It was only a few months ago when the only thing we had to worry about was how much salt to put on the fries at Instaburger. You don't know anything about survival." He paused and said half to himself, "I sure as hell know I don't. I still feel like I'm a teenager." He rubbed the back of his head as if he were the one who had been hit in the head with a bat.

Wyatt's gaze held Howard's, and he thought his friend looked twelve years old. He wasn't feeling so sure either but crushed the monster of insecurity with a shrug of false bravado. "No matter what you just said, I still don't like it," Wyatt replied.

Howard's face went red. "Well, I don't like *anything* anymore. The town where I've lived my whole life has been destroyed, the entire population wiped out, my parents are missing, the world is in a meltdown, Vincent Konrad—a psychotic of the first order—is maybe on the loose… there is *nothing* to like anymore!"

They stood staring each other, breathing heavily. Wyatt fought the urge to throw his backpack down and storm off. Howard was all he had left. He looked at the dim shadows of the desert. He didn't want to go alone. He heard a coyote or one of Melvin's hybrids howl a long, mournful cry.

Tears stung Wyatt's eyes. He missed his old life too. Melvin was not with them. Nothing was the same; nothing would be the same. He wavered on his feelings, watching Howard's taut face.

"We have to stick together, Wy."

"We don't need anybody else," Wyatt declared, feeling independent and brave.

"Wyatt! We've come across werewolves, vampires, zombies, the Glob, mummies, a prospecting ghost, shapeshifters, a hunchback, and a reanimated corpse! And that was just in our hometown! Even the lawyers, dentists, and accountants have gone crazy! You don't know what to expect out there!" Howard implored, "We need all the help we can get."

Wyatt's chest heaved with indignation. He bit his bottom lip, a bad habit that told everyone he was nervous or indecisive. *Did he need their help?* They had managed quite well on their own, he thought resentfully.

Etan walked out of the restaurant, the girls clustered around him like adoring fans. He spoke quietly with the man filling the truck. They both stopped to observe Wyatt. He had to admit that Etan more confident that Wyatt felt, and he was just standing there, watching everybody. Wyatt gritted his teeth.

"They have a truck," Howard pleased. "We'll get there quicker."

Wyatt thought for a minute, kicked the dirt with the toe of his sneaker and gave in ungraciously. Howard Drucker had a point. "Just for the ride," Wyatt muttered.

"You won't be sorry," Howard shouted, his face relieved.

Wyatt looked at them, wanted to ask Howard how he knew he wouldn't be sorry, but his mouth snapped shut.

The girls surrounded Etan like a barrier. They weren't heavy, *just big*. Wyatt studied them. They seemed to tower over the males like a tribe of Amazons. They chattered amongst themselves as if they were going on a grand adventure.

"Are you done yet?" Etan yelled at Howard.

"I am," Howard replied. Wyatt saw him run over to fall into place next to Etan. "Let's go, Wyatt."

Etan quietly directed everyone where to sit. Howard turned his basset hound eyes on Wyatt. Wyatt grudgingly caught up to them.

He could see Etan's rank now on his jacket. Captain—no surprise there. He acted like a leader.

"We could have done this alone," Wyatt repeated to Howard in a low voice.

Howard glanced at the girls walking to the truck. He had to trot to keep up with their long-legged strides. One by one, they hopped into the bed of the pickup.

Howard looked at the carrot-topped beauty next to him and then at Wyatt. He shook his head with a dopey smile and asked, "Why would you want to?"

"I thought you had eyes only for Keisha," Wyatt snapped.

"I do. I do. This is for observation."

CHAPTER 6

THE TROUBLE WITH MINKINS

A TALL GROUP OF six stood hunkered-down in the shade under a high rock ledge that jutted from a crack in a barrier of stone. It rested on an enormous boulder leaving a tight space behind it. It was just enough room to hide them from the people fleeing in a vehicle. One of the six ordered them to crouch so their size wouldn't give their hiding spot away.

They squeezed tighter, the smallest of the group shoved toward the back of the space. Wind-milling his arms, he tried to push the others away, but a harsh word from the one next to him left him subdued and simmering. But for his angry face and shorter stature, they were completely identical, down to their homespun clothes and handmade shoes.

They bent low, their bare knees being scraped raw against the boulder, where they waited for the humans to leave. The giggles of the six girls drifted in the morning air. Stiffening shoulders and jutted chins revealed the laughter irritated each one of the men.

Grillos crushed a small rock in his hand angrily. He felt the stone give way sliding through his fingers like sand. *Foolish, foolish, foolish,* he thought, adding a silent curse. The commandments dictated sunlight was forbidden. Looking at the harsh morning rays hurt his light eyes. He blinked, his eyes burning from the early morning sunshine.

He glanced back at Brontes, his baby brother, whose face was wet with tears of frustration and worry. Grillos put a reassuring hand on his brother's shoulder. "We'll get them, brother."

Brontes sniffled noisily.

Grillos scanned the wide open space beyond the border of rocks. Exposed and vulnerable up here on the surface, fury made him crush another stone in his powerful fingers. Selfish girls to put all of us at risk. Soon it would be full daylight and the buttery sun would crest the horizon to beat down on them. It would burn through the fair hair on their heads, making their skin tight as dried parchment. He flinched with the notion of his skin sizzling. He should have worn the hat he left on the hook by the door, but they were in too much of a rush.

Foolish. He shook his head again. He looked at his younger brother who was suffering the most. Brontes head was bowed as if he was praying. He barely reached any of their shoulders. He was the runt, and as the smallest, the girls were under his authority. He was their biological father, after all.

Grillos was the eldest of the clan, so the responsibility of bringing them back fell to him. He could see that Brontes was getting agitated again by the expression on his face, and had to quiet his brother before he gave away their location.

He nodded to Fangi and Zaf. They rested their powerful hands on Brontes's arms, ensuring he didn't bolt after the truck as it took off down the road. Grillos could feel his brother quivering with rage, knowing an explosion was coming.

Brontes stamped, howling with frustration. His muscles bunched under the cloth of his homespun shirt.

Grillos looked at the speeding truck, his face grim. "*Hush*, Brontes!" he whispered fiercely..

Brontes ripped free and pounded his chest, a loud roar erupting from his throat. His eyes were wild, devoid of reason. Grillos slapped Brontes then, the sound ricocheting off the rocks hiding them. It shocked his brother into silence.

Brontes gasped. A sob escaped as he slipped down onto the dirty canyon floor. He sniffled. Tears streamed down his broad face. His orange hair stood in wild tufts where he pulled at it. Grillos winced, then reached down and ruffled his younger brother's hair.

"I know," he said in as soft a voice as he could manage.

He squinted at the desert spread out before them, the stark landscape as bleak as his mood. Not a tree or a building to hide them as they trekked across the hills. He was the leader of the tribe, granted that authority from his uncle before him. He had to get everyone back to safety. The runaway girls, his loyal brothers. It was too much.

Silly little children. Risking everything out of curiosity. Exposing themselves and all of their kin to discovery. Shameless, he thought. Selfish and brash. He studied the calluses on his hands counting months. On top of everything, they were close to sprouting time.

Brontes wailed. At least the truck was too far to hear him. He begged them to follow the vehicle in broad daylight.

"Should we galloping behind the truck like a herd of cattle?" Grillos shot back. Sometimes he was as impulsive as his daughters, Brontes was. Grillos grunted with indignation. He opened his mouth to say what he was thinking, that if the girls were his, he would have made sure they didn't pull a stunt like this. One look at his brother's anguished face made him snap his mouth shut. He shook his craggy head. *That's what happens when you let them have too much freedom.*

"We could follow," Fangi said, in support of Brontes.

Zaf nodded. "We could bend really low."

Grillos sighed from the deepest part of his stomach. He was shepherding a pack of idiots. "Are you all sun blind as well as stupid?" he demanded.

Even if they hunched over and draped themselves with layers of clothes to hide their size, they stood out like beanstalks in a garden of grass. Grillos scratched his head. His nieces would have a lot to answer for when he got his hands on them.

He shuddered with resignation. He hated coming up here. Pure risk and no reward. One sighting and the minkins would know about them. They wouldn't stop until they figured where they were coming from. Then they'd ask probing questions, demand answers, explore and finally invade their domain. It made his insides shake with fear. The minkins would wreck their homes, destroy their world, make them slaves, like they've done throughout history with anyone who was different on this planet. He shivered at the thought. Look what they did to their own kind. They were animals, monsters.

"Let's go… now!" Brontes bellowed, interrupting Grillos's dismal ponderings.

Grillos shook his head. "No. We must wait. We wait until dark, brother."

"I want to go now!" Brontes stood.

"It's too hot." Grillos gestured to the sun. "Too much light. You'll fry out there."

"I don't care." Brontes was petulant.

"No." Grillos looked away, ending the conversation. He knew Brontes would not defy him. It was their way. Still, he admitted, he felt Brontes' pain.

He glanced up at the scorching sun bathing the sand with its relentless heat. The wind raked their tender skin, already burned from the harsh early-morning rays. *What would the elders do?* he wondered.

He was the elder now. The weight of responsibility sat heavily on his shoulders. "We need a plan," he said, scratching his head.

"A plan? Let me go." Brontes rose to his full height, muscling his way through the tight corridor. "I'll rip those little grubs to shreds."

Grillos laid a heavy hand on his brother's shoulder. "You will not. They have guns."

"A mere nuisance," Fangi muttered.

"We have strength," Zaf added.

"That might have worked many years ago, but you know it doesn>t work anymore. The girls are too exposed to steal them back. We need a plan. Let me think." He sat down and stroked his chin. *What worked with minkins? What do those little creatures care about?*

Grillos contemplated a few thoughts in his head. Minkins didn't care about the planet. Most were selfish and greedy. In the rare instances he'd negotiated with them, he knew you had to get what you wanted first. Minkins like to cheat. He looked at his large hands. He clenched them into tight fists. *What did he have that a minkin could possibly want?*

They needed something to negotiate, something that a minkin would want more than the girls. Grillos grinned. He needed a trade. They had to have something the minkins valued. Now, with most of the human population dead or gone, there wasn't much to barter.

He had seen humans hanging on in this barren wasteland. Like the carnivorous grubs his clan battled underneath the earth, the minkins had dug themselves in, surviving on what they could find. They were a stubborn lot.

While Brontes banged his head against the rock wall with impatience, Grillos snapped, "Be still. Let me think. I may have something." A plan was shaping inside his thick skull. If only he could make his brother>s sobs cease. "First things first." He stood and slapped the dirt from his hands. "We wait until dark," Grillos said, trying to give his brother hope. "We'll make better time then."

"That will be hours!" Brontes brows lowered..

"After sunset?" Arog, another brother, interrupted.

"Later." Grillos pointed to the bright disk in the sky. "When the moon is high, it will be safe." He gestured for Zaf and Fangi to come closer. "I have an idea, but you will have to move fast."

Brontes whined in protest. "Let me help."

"I could go too," Arog said. Mantos, the last brother nodded.

Grillos shook his head. "Arog's too loud. Zaf and Fangi are the fastest of us all. Mantos you need to keep an eye on Brontes." Mantos was the most reliable of the brothers.

"What about me? They're *my* daughters!" Brontes insisted.

"You're useless right now. The girls belong to us all. They are the future of the clan. Without them our line will die out," Grillos told Brontes, then turned to Zaf and Fangi. "You must be quick, or we will lose the opportunity."

"What do we have to do?" Zaf asked.

Grillos proceeded to give them his commands. Brontes settled down into a helpless, whimpering hulk while his brother shared his plan.

"It will never work." Brontes shook his head.

"Of course it will, Brontes. They'll travel fast. You'll see." Grillos felt sorry for his brother. This was hard for him. Hard for them all. "We'll catch up with them in the land to the west." He pulled his brother up. "There." He pointed to a rock outcropping, a gaping hole that would allow them respite from the heat. "We'll stay in the caves yonder until it's safe and our brothers do their job. Come, Brontes. Let's go." Grillos walked toward the cave, Brontes, Agog, and Mantos following furtively behind him. Their large feet dragged on the ground, leaving a trail.

The last two, Zaf and Fangi melted into the landscape as if they had never been there.

CHAPTER 7

THIS CESSPIT HE NOW CALLED HOME

THE CREATURE SURGED around frantically, moving quickly in the water, his body clumsy with only one arm. Even lopsided, he was powerful. He was in his element, after all.

Where were they? He floated, searching the floor of the lagoon littered with rusty cans of soda and plastic trash that wouldn't degrade. He hovered over the bottom, waiting for his beating heart to slow, the water to settle.

He made a face. They were slobs, those humans, all of them. Even the canine ones. *Negligent of their own home*, he thought with distaste. *Am I truly any better than them?* he wondered for a panicked second.

How could I have misplaced them? Had he been so lazy that he'd forgotten where he put them? *Oh, this is trouble, very bad trouble.* He swam in a tight circle, his fingers gliding along the slimy rocks. He moved closer to the bottom, his large eyes finding nothing. He bit his lip with apprehension and growing dismay. *What could have happened…?*

He could feel the tingle of regrowth on his shoulder where his arm had been ripped from his body. He glanced down to see tiny flame-colored spikes protruding from the wound. They dotted the area, sprouting as if by magic. He'd have the beginnings of a new arm by nightfall.

He came upon a turtle and lifted it gently with his remaining arm. He felt the turtle jerk as it retreated into his shell, pulling back its four feet, its head disappearing into the largest opening. *No, no, don't be afraid.* He stroked the shell, tickling the pale underside of the animal, a worried smile forming on his mouth when the turtle poked his head from his hiding place.

Do you know where they've gone, sir? he communicated, silvery bubbles escaping from his mouth.

The turtle observed him, his face solemn. *The girl. She collects them.* The reptile sighed.

The creature's mouth opened with a silent scream.

That's not so bad, the turtle assured him. *The boy eats the likes of me. They got Jeffrey this morning*.

No! He released the turtle with anger and shock. *Why?* he demanded. *Damn these beasts!* His hand cradled his cheeks as tears mixed with the lagoon water. *I was here first! I was willing to let them share my home if they behaved!*

The turtle floated toward the bottom of the lagoon. *That doesn't matter. It's survival of the most dominant in their world,* the turtle told him sadly. *They care only for themselves and their own pleasure. Look what they've done to our home.* The turtle gestured to the filth littering the seabed. Cans and bottles, plastic bags, and dangerous straws rested among the plants and rocks.

Why would she do that? he asked as the turtle landed on the seabed in a pile of netting.

After disentangling himself, the turtle pushed upwards. *Who knows the ways of them?* The turtle's feet fluttered, and he swam around him in a slow circle. *I don't think they understand what they do.* He paddled off, leaving the creature to sink onto a boulder, his head bowed.

What does she want with them? he wondered. He kicked a loose pebble. He had just gotten used to this cesspit he now called home. It had taken an age for him to adjust to the temperature and salt content of the water. He didn't want to go back to the tanks or that crazy caretaker who keeps looking for him. He had seen him lurking in the shadows of the laboratory. It was only a matter of time before he discovered that the lagoon was salty water now. The only thing holding his caretaker back was his fear of the dog-boy.

He hated this place and all the people associated with it..

He had awakened in the interior of the park in a huge tank after being abducted from his home, deep in the sea. He had to admit the lagoon was better than the lab and the putty-skinned professor who poked and prodded him. He had especially hated the one they called Vincent, his caretaker's superior. Cold-blooded and emotionless, the ringleader had directed the white-coated one to study him, breaking off pieces until there was little left for more of their harebrained experimentation.

When all hell broke loose in the theme park, he'd managed to push through a crack in his tank. Using up all the potato chips and hot dogs in the park, he managed to salinize this sewer and grow back his legs. He had scoped out the surrounding area. There was no escape; he'd dry up like a sponge in the desert.

When he realized there was no way back to the ocean, he accepted his situation. He adjusted, grew roots.

They're mine! he bellowed, looking up toward the surface angrily.

They are mine! How would you feel if I took something from you? His fury created a bubbling whirlpool.

The creature sank lower, glowering until he rested on the gritty floor. Fish swam above him. He simmered, the water fairly heating around him. This was war.

CHAPTER 8

THE ELEPHANT IN THE ROOM

WYATT KNEW GETTING to Los Angeles was the first step to reach Washington, the capital.—that is, if it even existed anymore.

Wyatt rolled over on the dirty mattress to look at the people in the crowded room. They were in a deserted suburb hours northeast from the city limits of Los Angeles. He remembered Howard Drucker's mumbled response when they arrived in the town of Rancho Cucamonga last night.

Etan took command, much to Wyatt's dismay and insisted they head to the small community rather than the city. Wyatt had wanted to press on but was overruled by Commander Etan.

Wyatt wasn't even sure if Etan was his first name, last name, or even an invented name. Their new fearless leader asked a lot of questions but revealed very little information about himself, Wyatt thought resentfully. Still, he had to admit that if they were searching for a large group of armed forces, it made sense to stop in an area that housed a sizable mall that could serve as a meeting point.

Wyatt was sick of the trip, sick of Commander Etan, and sick of Howard Drucker's slavish devotion to the man. He missed home. He thought about Copper Valley; Carter; Sean; and, Lily, his heart aching dully in his chest. He stifled the maudlin thoughts.

Home, he thought, reminding himself wasn't Copper Valley. He hated every minute he lived there. He wanted to leave from the moment they relocated to the isolated desert town. Los Angeles was his real home, and that's where he needed to be, not in some backwater hick town waiting for life to happen. He wanted to be in the center of the action.

Wyatt frowned, thinking about how his life had changed over the last few years. First his parents divorced, and his mom took them to Copper Valley where she got a teaching job. Then his father abandoned them. Not really—Wyatt had to be honest. His father had been none too interested in his family for a long time before his parents broke up.

He always considered Los Angeles his real home. That's what he had told Carter all the time he lived in Copper Valley. He missed LA and his former life there. In the city, he wasn't considered an outsider or a loner. He didn't stick out like he was different. Wyatt felt a connection to the diverse metropolis. Los Angeles was vibrant, full of life. There was something for everyone and he was able to blend in with his surroundings.

Aside from his comfort level, Los Angeles had the resources to overcome the difficulties of living so far off the grid. One, he could prove to Carter they'd be safer in LA, he'd convince him to relocate. Yet, he bit his lip deep in thought, Lily might not want to leave. He patted the kestrel feathers in his shirt pocket. He wasn't sure how he felt about that. The idea of finally arriving in LA made him jittery with a new feeling. He was nervous.

Something strange was happening. The closer they traveled to

Los Angeles, the more foreign everything looked and felt. It was increasingly desolate. He was expecting to see crowds of people helping each other get their lives back. *Where was the community?* Where were all the cars, the people pulling together to survive?

"Of course things are different," Howard told him when they talked about it. The Glob had killed off half the population, the mummies the other half. Survivors had fled, leaving towns from the desert to the coast abandoned.

Even if that were true, Wyatt thought, *where did they go?* There were no moving vehicles on the roads except for the roving bands of highway robbers grabbing anything with an engine. So far, Howard Drucker and Wyatt hadn't made contact with anyone except *GI Joe*, his band of commandos, and the weird group of girls who followed them. The whole journey was beginning to feel like an epic mistake.

He wished he could share his turbulent thoughts with Carter. Wyatt missed his stepfather's common sense. He was able to lean on Carter and unload his perceptions without judgment. No matter what Wyatt said, Carter gave his comments consideration, even if he vehemently disagreed. Carter had proved to be a much better parent than the man who actually was his biological dad.

Either way, Wyatt was uncomfortable. All he had wanted was to escape Copper Valley and get to LA. The closer they approached the city limits, the more uneasy he was feeling about his decision. On top of that, he and Howard had been absorbed into some guy's renegade army, taking orders from this shady commander.

Wyatt wasn't as thrilled as Howard with their new group of friends. In theory, he understood the notion that safety in numbers was a better way to travel. It was just that everything about Etan bothered him.

Wyatt couldn't shake the feeling that he knew him. Etan kept his distance and was usually surrounded by one of the four oversized goons who never seemed far from him. There was something about that guy that didn't sit well with Wyatt.

Wyatt wished he could get a closer look, but Etan never took off the dark sunglasses or removed the wrap from his head. Wyatt remembered seeing desert soldiers on the news reports wearing the checkered scarves around their neck. Why was he wearing it here and now? *What was he hiding?* .

He couldn›t fathom Etan's age either, which bothered him no small bit. Etan was built well. His stubble showed mostly dark but for a few streaks of gray on his chin. The lines radiating from his eyes under the glasses were weathered from action, Wyatt supposed, or maybe he just enjoyed a good tan.

Wyatt shifted uncomfortably on the bed, trying to remember if that Etan guy was with the army or the marines. He couldn't recall exactly what he'd said when they'd encountered each other in Rita Mays.

There were other small things that bothered Wyatt, too. Carter was a vet and had served a couple of tours of duty. He always looked like a soldier, even when he was just plain standing. The three dudes and single woman who traveled with Etan stood that way, but oddly, Etan slouched. He didn't look military at all, yet they acted as if he was their leader. Nothing about him made sense.

"The Glob really traveled far." Wyatt gave up his attempt to sleep and sat up.

Howard nodded absently. Wyatt watched his friend swipe a finger along the windowsill, leaving a long trail in the gray dust. They peeked through the broken glass and watched the tattered remains of a mummy decomposing on the lawn. Once they destroyed the source of Vincent's power, the mummies collapsed on the spot, but not before they did serious damage to the surrounding population.

"Shame," Howard whispered. "I hope they didn't make it to LA."

"We shut Vincent Konrad down in the Battle for Monsterland. How do you think he's keeping his reanimated body functioning now that he doesn't have the fuel supply?"

Howard rested his gun in his lap as he sat back against the

doorjamb. "Once Dr. Frasier reanimated that body and attached the head, I think Vincent didn't need the alien fuel anymore."

"You don't know that," Wyatt said.

Howard took a while to answer. "Yes, it's just a theory. He might even be dead by now. We really have no way of knowing if he survived."

"*Oh,* he's alive," Wyatt said through gritted teeth. "I'd know if he were dead."

Wyatt had once worshipped the billionaire, thought he would be the savior of the world with his theme park. Dr. Vincent Konrad had planned to eradicate the virus that created zombies. He'd promised stability, economic security to return and world peace. Using his strategies, he guaranteed a bright future. Instead, he'd unleashed the apocalypse.

Howard went on, oblivious to the turmoil in Wyatt's brain. "With all the life he sucked out of every town in Southern California, my guess is he had enough to revitalize himself for years."

"Yeah, but we destroyed the machines they were using. If I know Vincent Konrad, he's reorganized."

"Yes," Howard agreed. "I think he would have planned something. We have to make sure the people in charge know he's still alive and dangerous." Howard stared off into space. "Maybe he needs only small amounts of the alien fuel to keep himself juiced up." He looked at Wyatt and said, "I really need to talk to Keisha about this."

Wyatt sighed as if he hadn't heard him. "Nothing kills that guy. I mean… Melvin ripped off his head. We destroyed the source of his energy. I'm stumped. You'd think without the fuel he'd be a dead man." Wyatt was thinking of the lumbering giant in a reanimated body flying a helicopter to escape. "Even if he did die, his plans may still be in motion. I wonder if he had a succession plan." He hit the palm of his hand with his fist.

"What do you mean?" Howard asked, intrigued.

"A guy like Vincent Konrad always has another strategy. He's playing a dangerous game; he's got to have a successor in the works."

"It was Nate Owens, and he's dead too," Howard said.

"I spent only a little time with Vincent Konrad, but the man was a genius. Nope, he's got something else up his sleeve."

"*Hmmm...*" Howard shrugged and cleared his throat. "The world is getting stranger and stranger."

"Howard." Wyatt swallowed, his Adam's apple moving convulsively. "You think we're ever going back to the way it was?"

"We have to; otherwise, our existence will start to look like the Stone Age."

Wyatt raised himself enough to peer out the window again. The town where they were squatting looked abandoned. There wasn't a human in sight. Doors hung open; cars were left with the keys in the ignition. He searched the deserted community, the empty streets filled with tumbleweeds. He recalled the destruction in Copper Valley, the corpses strewn all around. The waxy remains of people dotted the lawns like frozen garden ornaments. It looked as if they had been caught as they tried to escape the insidious Glob.

"Too late." Wyatt shook his head. "I think the world as we know it doesn't exist anymore." Wyatt shivered, imagining what they were going to find when they reached the city. *What if nobody was left?*

Etan, their *de facto* commander, pushed in the door of the small ranch house and stopped when he saw Wyatt and Howard. Their erstwhile leader looked as furtive as ever. Wyatt wanted to knock the aviators off his smug face. What he could see of his sun-darkened skin was covered with dust and sweat. The ever-present scarf was wrapped around the top of his head. Even half-covered, Wyatt had to admit he looked way cooler than any of his friends ever would. It was no wonder all the girls following them clustered around Etan like he was a rock star. *Was it his commanding ways or his rugged good looks?* Wyatt couldn't tell. It was like the groupies and the vampires all over again, he thought resentfully.

The four oversized baboons that completed their group worked like a well-oiled unit. They called him *sir* all the time and hung on his every word. Maybe that's what Howard Drucker liked about him, Wyatt reasoned. Etan had the charisma of a vamp.

Well, he sighed, they were stuck with them now, recruited into the *A-team* whether they liked it or not, and Wyatt didn't like it. He was itching to get up and leave.

Wyatt told Howard they didn't need to travel with this circus. His lips turned down as he glanced around the room. He had never wanted to join the group anyway. He had been coerced, plain and simple.

Wyatt looked at the dusky-colored sky, knowing another day was dawning, and all he wanted to do was reach Los Angeles. That was his turf, he'd feel safe there.

He glanced longingly at a brown Toyota in the driveway of the house, wishing he and Howard were miles away from Commander Etan and his crew.

"It's out of gas," Etan said as he slid wearily onto the floor. "I know what you're thinking, Baldwin, but it's smarter to wait and travel in a pack."

"Yeah, a pack," Howard repeated, exchanging a glance with Wyatt, who gave a brief nod, knowing his friend was thinking of Melvin.

Etan looked at his watch. "It's six a.m. I want to get moving by five this afternoon." The timepiece was a delicate thing, something you might get at graduation for some great achievement, like being valedictorian.

Wyatt frowned. Carter had a massive metal watch that could do all types of cool stuff such as let the authorities find you if you were lost at sea. Wyatt could tell that all Etan's watch was capable of was telling time. Also, Carter always used military time. His stepfather would have said he wanted to leave at seventeen hundred, not five in the afternoon.

Wyatt turned to Etan and asked, "What unit did you say you were with?"

Etan rose as if he hadn't heard him and went to talk to one of his ever-present goons.

"Don't you think he looks familiar?" Wyatt whispered to Howard.

Howard scrutinized Etan and shook his head. "*Nah.*"

The vehicle they had appropriated back in the desert was out of gas as well, and the abandoned gas stations they passed along the route had no power to pump out their reserves. Forget about stealing an electric car, power had been out for almost a month. That was a bad bet, those stupid electric cars.

"You'd better get some sleep," Etan ordered in that quiet way that brooked no argument. Wyatt had been up for more than thirty-six hours straight. "That's not a suggestion," Etan told him.

Wyatt opened his mouth to protest. He wasn't obligated to do or listen to anything Etan ordered. Wyatt answered to nobody but Wyatt Baldwin.

Wyatt wanted to push on, find another vehicle, but his tired muscles rebelled, and he folded back onto the mussed mattress they had dragged under the window. His eyes slid shut, but he fought sleeping out of spite.

His skin prickled. Etan irritated him. He stretched, wondering if he should give up trying to rest and walk out. He smiled, thinking it would piss Etan off if he disobeyed an order. He would then tell him he hadn't violated anything; Etan was not his superior.

Wyatt sighed, cataloging what irked him about the other man. Etan never answered any of Wyatt's inquiries. Even when they talked about age, Etan was vague. Wyatt was sure he was much older than he implied.

During their journey west, Etan informed them he'd been on leave when all hell broke loose. He immediately began traveling toward the coast when the expected orders from his commander failed to arrive. Wyatt narrowed his eyes with distrust. How could his orders have arrived if Etan wasn't at his last known address? Wyatt wanted to ask if his orders had arrived by magic, able to find him like a magnet. And why were the others willingly following him?

Etan's story was like a puzzle that didn't fit together. Why had

Etan assumed command of the group? When Wyatt questioned his leadership, Etan laughed and said he collected people wherever he went, like the *Pied Piper.*

It rankled Wyatt to be thought of as a follower, but the way Etan worked with the pack of people in the group didn't ring true. Wyatt watched how they treated Etan. There was a respect that seemed to imply that theirs wasn't a brand-new acquaintance. When Wyatt questioned the others, they clammed up as if he were the enemy or something.

Even their guns seemed out of the ordinary. Each one of the four soldiers carried submachine guns. Etan used mainly a sidearm.

Etan certainly wasn›t the strongest. He often deferred to one guy, a muscle-bound meathead who went by the name, Yerbol. Yerbol spoke in a gravelly whisper and treated everybody with contempt.

Wyatt wanted to yell that he had experience, that he had battled mummies and could boast of more than a few kills. He wasn't a kid anymore.

Then there was the matter of the girls. Wyatt's brain was close to overload with unanswered questions. The girls were attached to Etan's group as if they were part of his troops, only they didn't act their age. Their conversations were silly and bizarre, and that barely touched the real elephant in the room, their identical faces and unusual size. Nobody addressed any of those things, yet Etan seemed happy to include them.

Wyatt laid his forearm over his eyes. He shifted slightly so he could observe the group of females traveling with them. They followed Etan's every movement as if he were a god. All six girls fussed and cooed around him like a flock of doves.

Wyatt shifted his gaze to Etan. The older man had coiled strength in his lean body. Wyatt could see that even with the ever-present sunglasses, Etan's watchful, foxlike face was alert, as if he were ready to pounce. He was always searching, like he was looking for somebody. Wyatt couldn't shake the feeling that he knew him.

Every time they came upon a corpse, Etan appeared to hold his breath and expel it with relief once the face was revealed. Wyatt's eyes narrowed with distrust. Yes, he was looking for someone, Wyatt knew it in his gut.

Etan was sitting in the corner, tracing the floor with a stick. One of the girls—Wyatt still couldn›t tell them apart—was seated so close, their forms melted together, her softer shadow swallowing Etan's slighter one.

Those girls were… *big*. Not heavy, just amazingly tall, and so alike, they looked like clones. It gave Wyatt a healthy dose of the creeps. Another girl sat at Etan's other side, but their fearless leader seemed lost in thought and ignored the female presence.

It wasn't that Wyatt didn't like Etan. Well, he thought, if he were being completely honest, he didn't. He supposed Etan was okay. Howard certainly thought so.

Howard's hero worship irritated Wyatt. His friend appeared to be in ecstasy when he described Etan's abilities as if he were extraordinary or something, Wyatt thought glumly. Etan didn't seem so special to him. It wasn't as if he had fought any werewolves, vampires, or zombies either. Etan said he'd spent his time in the army stationed in Hawaii. He probably surfed really well too. Seriously, like all he ever had to worry about was finding a good wave.

A coyote howled, followed by the call of another, then a third. Wyatt smiled. He made eye contact with Howard, but his friend was eagerly talking to Etan, too absorbed to notice Wyatt. Wyatt exhaled in disgust.

Maybe one of the cries was Melvin's. Melvin. Wyatt missed him. He'd made up the third part of their trio. Wyatt glanced resentfully at Etan, the interloper.

Nothing was the same anymore. Even if he hadn't liked his life in Copper Valley, the comfort of the consistency had had a certain appeal. Everything had changed. Wyatt worried his bottom lip with his teeth. Melvin had changed. A welcome bite from a werewolf had altered the course of their friendship, propelling Melvin to a new destiny.

Well, thought Wyatt, *at least he wasn't alone.* Jade, Wyatt's old girlfriend, had joined Melvin, and they seemed happy enough together.

It was full daylight now. Wyatt rose to search the skies through a broken window, wondering where Vincent had flown. Carter and his friends had estimated the range of the chopper, calculating the fuel from the direction he took off and coming up with the probability he was headed for California's coastline.

There were islands off the coast where a man could hide. Rumors circulated of a zombie colony on one of the many islands. *A person could get lost there… or rebuild his empire*, Wyatt finished the thought grimly. Wyatt had convinced Carter to let him leave. Carter was reluctant but admitted someone had to communicate what was going on. Besides, Howard was desperate to find his parents.

Wyatt's thoughts circled back to Lily again. He hated leaving his new girlfriend. She and Keisha, Howard Drucker's girl, had stayed back on the reservation, helping Carter and John Raven to rebuild Copper Valley with the remaining people.

Howard was busy describing the Battle for Monsterland to Etan. The commando seemed most interested when Howard spoke about Vincent and his henchmen. Wyatt caught a look that passed between Etan and Yerbol. Something Howard related sparked their interests. He wished he sat closer and heard the entire conversation.

Wyatt grumbled, thinking back to a few days before they had been commandeered into Etan's unit. He looked at the other man resentfully. If only he and Howard hadn't entered that town, walked into that diner, they'd have never met. The mere thought of that made Wyatt grit his teeth.

CHAPTER 9

SPECIAL DELIVERY

ROSEMARY KONRAD, AS she styled herself presently, held the fragile stem of her wine glass with her blunt fingers. She had the hands of a man, large and callused from years of working at sea. Growing up with Shandy was not easy. The old tar pulled no punches, treating and demanding the same from her as any other of the crew.

Shandy had been her mother's companion. He stayed with them whenever he was in the Cornish port they called home. Fifteen years ago, around her eight birthday, her mother died in a car crash. The memories of those days were a hazy blur and Rosemary barely remembered the circumstances around her mother's tragic passing. Shandy took her to sea rather than allow her to be placed in a foster home or juvenile facility. It was shortly after the plague outbreak and the world was in a maelstrom of disorganization.

Rosemary's hometown had been hit hard. The illness had been

brought into the seaport by travelers from foreign countries, infecting a huge portion of the population. Schools closed; public resources were overextended. Nobody seemed to care about a homeless, orphan child.

She remembered hating her new life, wanted to go back, but understood things had changed. Shandy grudgingly adopted her. Gratitude for his act didn't come until she had traveled enough to see the devastation wreaked by the zombie plague. People were unemployed, children were reduced to begging, and homelessness abounded. The more places she visited, the more she realized she was one of the lucky ones.

Eventually Rosemary grew used to the grueling pace, forgetting about a softer way to live. She felt more comfortable with the misfits and refugees whom Shandy preferred.

There came a time when she yearned for the sea and the denizens of her world, land becoming more like a prison. She shuddered now, looking at the rock walls surrounding her, enclosing them in the island's deep embrace. She missed the freedom of the open sea, the honesty of the pirates rather than the harried and artificial lifestyle she associated with landlubbers.

Jötnar sat like a great hulking mass to her left. He dwarfed the chair. His shoulders took up an entire side of the table. Most people found him strange, not her. She was comfortable with his company. He spoke only when he needed to, and she liked that fine. Jötnar was a no frills kind of crewmember; he followed orders without fail and had remarkable strength. He may not have been the brightest guy on the boat, but he was dependable as the sun rising in the east.

Rosemary studied him. She couldn't tell what drove him. He said so little. Even after all these months, she knew virtually nothing about him. It didn't matter. Everyone had things they wanted to hide, including her. Shandy didn't trust him, but then, she laughed, Shandy trusted no one, especially, her alleged father. The way he discovered her identity still rankled, although she was loathed to admit it.

Rosemary watched under lowered lids as Vincent Konrad

considered her crewmember. "Where did you say you were born?" he asked Jötnar.

Rosemary shifted in her seat, uncomfortable with the avid gaze examining the crewman. She didn't know where Jötnar's past, never asked. It wasn't important.

She bristled, Jötnar's was his own. As a member of her crew, he answered only to her. "It doesn't matter," she interrupted. "It's immaterial where a person comes from." She waved her hand dismissively. "It's what we do with our lives that counts."

Vincent's eyes turned to her. "And you've all accomplished so much."

Rosemary's tone was frosty. "Given our circumstances, I can't complain."

Vincent laughed, his awkward hand slapping the tabletop.

She didn't feel obligated to share hers or any of her crews story with anybody. Pirates had an unspoken code—*don't ask me where I came from because you may not like the answer*

Rosemary continued to stare distastefully at her father, the hybrid human. Searching his face, she looked for something, anything to link them together.

She heard a hefty sigh and saw Jötnar place the utensil on the side of his plate carefully. Those big fingers moved with surprising delicacy. *Aye, Jötnar,* she thought, *not much to my taste either.* She hated Tex-Mex. *What the heck is it anyway? Is it Texan or Mexican?* She disliked all things hybrid.

Rosemary felt her father's gaze resting on her. He smiled crookedly, copied Jötnar's careful movements, then gestured to the big man as if he were sharing a private joke. Rosemary's sighed, *I can't believe this, the man is a bully.*

Vincent called her name, not once, but twice. Taking a deep breath, Rosemary cleared her throat and said, "Jötnar is important to me."

"Is that your way of telling me that he's off-limits?" Vincent's shoulders shook with silent mirth as if he found her amusing.

Rosemary stiffened at his condescension. Placing her cutlery down, she assessed the creature before her. He was not what she'd expected. Truthfully, she wasn't sure what she'd find.

Drilling her fingers on the table, Rosemary squirmed. It's not as thought she was looking for her biological father. She accepted the fact that he lived in the murky past, a secret her mother took to the grave. A chance injury at a canning factory where she and Shandy were working in Juno. DNA samples from a bloody wound sent to a world data base. She never consented to it, never would, yet, here she was, identified and found.

Vincent's people swooped in and rescued them from the drudgery of a dead end job with the promise of a ship and a hefty reward if she joined the search for the elusive octopus.

It couldn't have been at a better time. She was broke. Between the plague and economic meltdown, she was scrambling to find a new berth anywhere. It didn't matter how Vincent found her, she argued with Shand, this could turn into a pot of gold for them. She couldn't believe her luck, Vincent Konrad, of all people!

She studied her father. On paper, Vincent was everything she wasn't: successful, brilliant, educated, rich beyond her wildest dreams. Sight unseen, she felt her stomach flip with excitement at the thought of being connected to such an important person. He was a super star. A genius. A financial titan! She wondered if their shared DNA would reveal she had a touch of his brilliance as well, an undiscovered well of something extraordinary that would make her rise head and shoulders above the mediocrity of the rest of the world. She was filled with excitement at the thought of meeting him. It was delayed only by her mission, as though she had to prove her worth before he graced her with his time.

When they finally met face-to-face, she had to admit her thrill evaporated to be replaced with disappointment and disenchantment.

Shandy had warned her to lower her expectations, as if he had some insight she didn't. That man could read her like a book, she sneered with no small amount of rancor.

When she and Vincent first made contact and he offered the old whaling vessel, she couldn't explain the pride she felt or quell the excitement building in her chest. No one had ever given her anything. Even if he had missed out on her entire life whether by circumstances that were out of his control or her mother's secrecy, she discovered to her chagrin, a strange burning desire to please him.

Devouring everything she could find about Vincent on the internet, she learned he was one in a billion, a philanthropist who wanted to improve the challenges facing a fractured planet. Vincent Konrad offered to lift those burdens plaguing the world at his own expense and alleviate suffering. He proposed a way out for everyone.

His connections and wealth could elevate her to heights previously untouchable. Rosemary could carve a place where she would be respected, crew a real ship and not some smelly scavenger boat looking for the leftovers nobody wanted. Vincent contacted her often, his words of encouragement inspiring. In time, he boasted through one of their many communications, she'd be an admiral of the fleet. Vincent's attention made her feel special; as if she were touched by starlight. For the first time in her life, Rosemary knew what it was to feel hope.

She could not wait to finally meet him, and then she did.

All that time Rosemary swaggered with importance as she walked the deck of the whaler, made her face reddened with shame. Shandy warned her about the effects of having power. *How did Shandy and the crew tolerate her?* Looking sideways at her mentor and first mate, she sank a bit lower in her seat, humiliation keeping her eyes downcast.

Shandy rewarded her with a wry smile. He knew she was embarrassed. She blushed to the roots of her auburn head, partly with chagrin, partly with anger.

Rosemary's jaw tightened. Vincent had ended up being nothing more than a criminal hiding behind phony philanthropism. Despite her disappointment, her mind waged a war. Things didn't add up. His intentions sounded as noble, there was the promise of great things and yet… yet, she looked at her father, wondering who he really was. She recognized a monster when she saw one, didn't she?.

Her conscience flip-flopped, keeping her off-balance. *Who was she to call the kettle black?* With her checkered past, she was not in a position to judge others.

There had to be more. Vincent certainly spouted politically correct propaganda and claimed he wanted to fix the world's issues. He had dedicated his fortune and resources to protect the poor souls affected by the zombie virus. He charged in when the governments failed. The press had dubbed him an angel.

More like a devil.

Whatever he was, Rosemary found herself drawn to him like a moth to a flame. He attracted and repelled her simultaneously.

A memory surfaced filling her with a mixture of fear, dread, and something more… something she couldn't quite identify.

She had always been afraid of the dark. An all-consuming terror plagued her from the time she was a child. She slept with a light on, never walked into a dark room, but there was one dark place that attracted her.

She had a closet in her bedroom, a black void of a place. Most would think it was benign, an empty space with a dress or two, nothing more.

Rosemary knew it was so much more. Shandy would shine a light inside and assure her there was nothing there. Rosemary sensed something in that place that no one else could see. It repulsed and attracted her with its darkness. When the door opened, she could hear it suck the oxygen from her room like a giant vacuum.

It would start as soon as they tucked her into bed, a gentle creak of its rusty hinge. The yawning gash widened so the obsidian interior beckoned her. She heard soft cries that turned into moans, calling her into the smothering gloom.

Stuffing her fist against her mouth and squeezing her eyes shut, she would stifle the screams bubbling from her chest. She'd cover her head with her quilt, her breathing fast and labored, but the darkness beckoned. The siren's call of the abyss lured her into the deep folds of emptiness. She wasn't sure what drew her to its malevolence. Maybe it was the intoxication of cheating evil.

Creeping toward the closet, her small feet barely touched the floor. No matter how fast her heart beat or the current of chills that ran up her spine, she remembered only anticipation building. Her breath came in short bursts as she made her way toward that door. The thrill of the unknown grabbed her and tugged with an invisible cord that pulled her unresisting body. Whispering voices filled her head.

Monsters were in there and she needed to hear their secrets.

Exhilaration. Fascination. Horror. She couldn't stay away from it, just as she found she couldn't resist the creature sitting at the table. Her father, Dreg; his revolting companion, even Jötnar, they all repulsed her in some way.

Rosemary made a disgusted sound, admitting they attracted her too. She shivered with dread, or perhaps with anticipation. Shandy always yanked her kicking and screaming from the confines of the closet. She gave him a sideways glance at the table, wondering if he was going to haul her out of this hellhole as well.

Vincent coughed pulling Rosemary from her memories. He smiled a toothy grin as insincere as it was titillating. His mouth opened revealing a rotted cavern, a dank hideaway filled with skeletons that teased her. His darkness had a familiarity. Her eyes widened with the realization that Vincent Konrad was another version of the closet. His sibilant whispers and sinister explanations were more compelling than any cave-like interior. Vincent Konrad drew her with the same intensity.

She firmed her jaw, she would not allow Shandy to pull her away.

What kind of monster would she find? She rested her gaze on Vincent, her father and considered his warped features, wondering what her mother had seen in him. *Had her mother been drawn to evil as well?*

She understood this parody of a human was not the same man her mother must have known. A different body was attached to this strangely hued head. A faintly purple hue to his skin. Electrodes adorned the sides of his neck, where some wacky scientist had brought him back to life. Vincent had explained as if it was commonplace to be resurrected from the grave. She glanced at the misshapen lump of a human next to him. if Dreg hadn't found and saved her father's head, she never would have met him.

It seemed too fantastic to be true. She shrugged. Every day she was learning there was a new line between fantasy and reality. She had seen many unbelievable things in her travels with Shandy, but this—and the strange octopus she'd caught—rose to the top of her list.

Rosemary stared at Vincent's long, thin nose, then touched her own.

"*Hmm…* it's the same." Vincent's voice grated. His clumsy hands were attempting to spear a piece of seafood. "We are similar in many ways."

The fork clacked against the fine bone china, missing its target. Vincent didn't seem to care. The twin black holes that served as his eyes watched her with quiet intensity.

She thought about the accident of nature that had created her. Was it a grand passion, long-lasting love, or was she the result of a careless fling between a lab assistant and her employer? She sifted those thoughts while the men chewed their food noisily.

"Why did you search for me?"

Vincent shrugged. "I wasn't specifically looking for you. I've been around, you know. Known many people. It was bound to happen."

Rosemary's eyes widened. "Do I have siblings?"

Vincent smiled wistfully. "Still looking."

"You haven't answered my question."

"Perhaps, I am thinking about my legacy."

They sat at a long stone table, surrounded by four walls of thick plexiglass windows displaying the glorious seafloor. Huge fish—marlin, sharks, the bright neon of a yellowfin tuna—contrasted with the silver-gray of the dorado fish. Rosemary watched them swim in lazy circles, their unblinking eyes surveying the inhabitants of the room. Strange spiky, rusty-colored globes littered the seabed. Every so often she turned to look at them. She wasn't familiar with the spheres and wanted to ask what they were, but the hypnotic effect of the swaying seaweed pushed the question from her mind.

"You like my aquarium?"

"Pardon?" Rosemary asked.

"This undersea delight was originally known as my Great White Shark Park, an underwater aquarium I own."

"I never heard about it," Shandy said. "Or your involvement."

Vincent leered at him. "It was common knowledge. It prepared me for my theme park Monsterland."

Shandy grumbled, his lips turned down. "The island's nothing more than a zombie dumping ground."

"They're safe here, and so are we with them patrolling the grounds."

"*Humf,*" Shandy scoffed. "Not happy to be surrounded by them."

"A useful diversion to keep the riff-raff away." Vincent laughed. "They make excellent guard dogs."

Jötnar growled, or maybe it was Shandy, Rosemary wasn't sure. The food was tasteless in her mouth. She had to get them out of here before Shandy provoked her father. "Look." She pointed the glass wall enclosing them hoping to distract them.

Two dozen divers in black wetsuits appeared to be gathering samples of something. They were absorbed in their work, and spread out across the vast windows.

Water dripped around them in the cavernous room, there were

small puddles on the stone floor. It was dank and damp. Rosemary swore the cold humidity went through her skin to her bones. She felt uneasy being this far below the surface of the water. It was unnatural.

The carved rock walls of the room weighed heavily on her. It was like they were buried deep in the bowels of Prendick Rock, hidden by this ghastly aquarium.

Vincent observed her closely. There appeared to be no warmth in his gaze, no welcome in his words. She felt like a specimen in a test tube. She stuck out her jaw in stubborn defiance causing Vincent to chuckle. He pointed his fork at her and said to Dreg, "A chip off the old block."

Rosemary cleared her throat. "I'd like to know more about you and my mother." She paused. "I'd like to know about your parents as well."

"I never talk about my parents," Vincent snapped.

Vincent's head lurched as if his neck were too weak to support it. HIs fingers lacked coordination. Vincent growled, frustrated when he failed to spear a piece of fish on his fork. He was a giant patchwork quilt of a man, his mind clearly out of sync with the host body. She heard he had been able to pilot a helicopter out of Monsterland in a wild escape. This person could barely walk across the floor without help.

Vincent turned his burning gaze to her. "You must excuse my manners," he said smoothly. "I am having a problem with this host."

"Your host?"

"Yes, this body. It cannot stand up to the rigors of my schedule."

Shandy put down his wine glass and sputtered, "And how are you going to fix that?"

Vincent shrugged. "I have a team of scientists working on a solution. I'm confident they'll come up with something."

Vincent turned to stare at Jötnar, sending a chill up Rosemary's spine. "What if they don't?" she asked.

"*Oh,* I expect they have something in the works already."

Rosemary stiffened. She could feel Shandy's tension. Jötnar's face was devoid of expression, but she saw the coiled strength of his muscles flexing. She wished the meal were at an end, but curiosity kept her in her seat. She wanted to know more. She wanted to know everything. She could feel the pull enticing her to stay in her seat.

She barely remembered her mother. There was no way for her to ask what drew her to this hideous man. What was it about him that had made her drop her guard? His oily charm? His saturnine face? Was it love? She looked at him. He must have been handsome once. *Maybe he was funny*, she thought. *Women love a guy with a sense of humor.*

"It was for a few paltry dollars, money, m'dear," Vincent said without looking at her. He was attacking a piece of meat now, his uncoordinated hands sawing it into dust. He snarled, then threw the utensils, which clattered to the floor. "She worked at my plant. An assistant in one of the labs. Our union bought her some extra creature comforts."

Rosemary shuttered with revulsion, violated. Vincent was tramping through her most secret thoughts. It must have shown on her face because Jötnar jumped to his feet, making the heavy table tremble as if they were caught in an earthquake.

Vincent picked up a clump of the seafood and stuffed it into his mouth. His fingers crawled from his chin, chewed specks of meat flying from his lips. He looked at her blanched face with an evil grin. "You're a rather poor specimen for a woman. Aside from the Konrad nose, I can't quite figure out who you resemble. My memories of your mother are at best vague. Mary was..."

"Her name was Marie." Rosemary said the name with a French inflection, digesting the fact that she was apparently the product of a business transaction.

"Mary, Marie, whatever." Vincent spat when he spoke, fluids leaking from an unhealed seam around his neck. He could barely sit, this monster of a man. He touched his neck, cursing, "This damnable body! It's failing, Dreg. Failing fast."

"Don't worry, Vincent. We are solution-oriented," Dreg reassured him.

Dreg, the servant who never seemed to be far from his master's side, explained again the story of the mad doctor who had stitched her father's reanimated head onto this hulking body to act as a host for his brain to survive.

"Yes, yes. You told us this already." Rosemary turned her face to the ceiling with impatience. Rosemary glanced at the door, longing to escape for the first time since sitting down to this macabre meal.

Vincent looked sickly, pale.

Juices from the masticated food leaked down his violet-colored chin. The hunchback, Dreg, leaped up and wiped her father's face with a napkin.

Rosemary shuddered. "Where is that doctor who did this?"

Dreg laughed, the sound echoing in the cave-like structure. "He stayed behind. He was a cold man, stone cold." Dreg tittered. "Get it, Vincent? Stone cold."

"I don't understand," Rosemary said, her voice lacking warmth.

"I heard he got turned into a statue… by Medusa." Shandy pushed his plate away, his appetite apparently gone.

"None other." Vincent nodded.

"These are strange times we are living in," Rosemary said slowly. "Enormous octopus, Medusa, reanimated mons…" Rosemary's voice died.

"Monsters? Are you referring to me?" Vincent finished. His eyes narrowed. He looked pointedly at Jötnar.

Rosemary froze. Who was he to call Jötnar a monster? Jötnar was the gentlest person she knew.

Vincent continued. "I assure you, I am no monster. They are the monsters." He lurched up.

"Who are the creatures you are speaking about?" Shandy demanded.

Vincent looked at Shandy with contempt. For a minute, Rosemary was nervous for the older man. She felt her side for her pistol, cursing softly knowing Vincent had insisted she sit at his table unarmed. Her body tensed. She glanced at Jötnar, relieved to see that the big man's muscled back went completely rigid as if he was ready to spring on Vincent if he attacked Shandy.

Vincent went on, oblivious to the undercurrent of tension in the room. "Those vile children, Wyatt Baldwin and his beastly friends—they did this to me!" he shouted, flecks of spit flying from his purple lips. Vincent moved jerkily as if his brain couldn't control the muscles. He swayed and would have fallen if not for Dreg. The little man propped him against the window.

Rosemary made a face. She caught his dark eyes studying her again. "Children?" she asked.

"Yes, children. 'Parents are the bones on which children cut their teeth.' Well, they dined on my bones, those cannibals, and have gnawed me near to death." Vincent tapped on the window moodily. The fish swam by, and he placed his cheek on the glass.

"Are you telling me, sir, that I do indeed have siblings?"

"No, you stupid girl. That's not what I am talking about. You understand nothing." He waved his hand as if he'd had enough of her. He watched her, his face filled with loathing. "I wanted to change the world for them. I wanted to save it for their future." He began walking again, his large body halting with each step. He looked at the seafloor. He rambled talking more to himself than anyone in the room. "The children of the world—don't they see the monsters were going to destroy them all? I was going to give them a peaceful future." He spun then. "No, Rosemary, you are my only child so far," he sneered at her. "They turned me into this, and for what?" he demanded. "For what? To punish me for wanting to fix the mess they've made of this planet? No child can appreciate what I was doing for them."

Rosemary watched her father gnash his teeth.

"I would have made it better." He pounded his chest. "Those

little monsters, they ruined my dreams. I could have killed them, but I showed mercy and let them go."

Dreg fawned and preened around Vincent, turning her stomach. She met his gaze without fear.

Vincent›s keen eyes stared at her. "You think *I am* the monster? You are not afraid, my dear? I told you, I am not a monster," he repeated. "Do you even know what a monster is? Dreg, define *monster* for our guests," he said with exaggerated patience.

"There is no need—" Rosemary stammered.

"Silence," Vincent ordered.

"A monster is a creature or beast that is usually huge, ugly, and scary," Dreg recited.

Both Vincent and Dreg looked at Jötnar. Rosemary heard the big man whimper. She placed her hand on his forearm soothing him.

Vincent did an ungainly pivot. "While I am large, so are you, dear Rosemary. We are almost the same size."

Rosemary inclined her head. "I am tall."

"Indeed. And while I am tall, no one can call me ugly or scary, can they?" He leered at her, the seam on his neck a mocking smile.

Rosemary didn't answer.

"People overuse that word," Vincent went on. "Clearly, I am not deformed, merely stitched together." He laughed, and Rosemary tilted her head, wondering if he was mad. "You have brought me a monstrous creature." He pointed to the ocean. "My octopus. Is it a monster or merely a large example of its species? Does its size make it a monster, or does its intent make it the stuff of nightmares?"

"It's an animal. It has no intent but to survive," Rosemary responded. Vincent wasn't listening.

He strolled along the glass walls of the cave and watched the octopus. "All I wanted to do was make the world a better, safer place." Vincent looked sad. His shoulders sagged. "No." He shook his head. "I was attacked by monsters. I was savaged by the worst monsters on the planet. They attempted to thwart my plans and sacrifice peace for Earth. They tried to crush my intention to bring unity and harmony to the world with wanton disregard for my carefully thought-out programs."

He turned to them, his eyes burning coals of anger. Rosemary recoiled in her chair from the heat of them.

Vincent continued, "They are the monsters, the ones who are filled with their own self-righteousness. They will kill first without question to maintain their status quo. Someone had to make the hard choices, and do what needed to be done."

"That's right." Dreg put a consoling arm around Vincent's back. "They didn't give any of Vincent's ideas a chance. Destructive and selfish. Right, Vincent? They killed my son too."

Rosemary watched the two standing by the panoramic windows, their deformities stark against the perfection of the schools of beautiful fish. The room narrowed, the air thinned and she was having a hard time drawing in breath. Eying the exit, Rosemary longed to leave. She exchanged a look with Shandy, his mouth pursed, disgust evident on his face. The unholy duo shuffled back to the table.

Rosemary pushed the unfinished food around her plate, her appetite gone. The massive body positioned itself before the throne-like chair, and Vincent eased into the richly cushioned seat. The room darkened as if the light had been extinguished from it.

Shandy cleared his throat, then jerked his head to one of the glass walls. "Look at those dorado."

She turned to see the group of fish do a jittery dance taking up the expanse of the glass.. Rosemary sat up abruptly. The dorado turned vibrantly gold, the scales flecked with blue. The school of fish twitched their tails in unison, darting into the depths of the ocean, leaving the area deserted. It lightened for a second.

A shadow fell over the room again, a gloomy portent of negativity. Fish scattered, even the sharks. Both the tiger and the great white made a hasty retreat as a massive form intruded into the space.

The hulking body of her octopus slid along the glass, its curious black eyes finding her. Its body with the strange pale melon-colored striping spanned the entire wall. The octopus's body billowed as it opened its arms shooting across the panorama of the sea. Rosemary watched it glide through the water. It had a beauty about it, the movements poetic. For a moment she forgot the deadly encounter with her crew. It bounced around the confines of the space, scattering fish everywhere. Feeling a vague sense of pride, Rosemary decided it was a female. She was like a queen, and this was her domain.

Squinting, she noticed a small transmitter bobbing on the translucent skin of the octopus. The enormousness of her catch struck her, and she held up her glass to Vincent.

Vincent sat back, his face a cold sneer. "You mock me?"

Jötnar shifted nervously in his seat. She gave a nearly imperceptible shake of her head, a clear command to both her crew members. Rosemary worried about Jötnar, not completely confident of his reactions. "Forgive me, Vincent. Not at all. I have only respect for your noble mission." She knew people like her father, men drunk on power who felt they had the right to do or say whatever they wanted, people who lived without consequences. She decided it was best to humor him. "Do you like my… acquisition?"

Vincent got to his feet in another spastic movement. Dreg grabbed his elbow to help him. They made an odd couple—Dreg, hunched and with a clubfoot, and her father, Vincent, almost seven feet tall with his head sewn onto the body of a decaying athlete.

He walked along the window, his finger grazing the glass, ignoring her question.

"Is that a leash?" Rosemary laughed.

"Why, yes. Dreg, fetch me my mobile," Vincent ordered.

"Cell service is not working," Shandy said.

"It is with my satellite," Vincent responded, pointing to the heavens. "Here, let me show you. Where is that app? *Ah.* Tell me what you want, right or left?"

"What? Left," Rosemary said, not understanding what he was talking about.

Vincent pressed an icon on his phone and shouted, "And here we go, to the left!" The octopus shivered as if shocked, then made a sharp left, it's great eyes bulging from their sockets.

"You can make it follow your directions!"

"Precisely. Watch this. Up seven feet and bring me a seal!" Vincent typed, his fingers moving erratically. The octopus surged upwards, returning a moment later, a man in a wetsuit trapped in its massive arms. Threads of blood oozed along the currents of water. The man flopped in the current, his eyes glazed over, his mouthpiece floating next to him. Vincent peered closely at the window. "Darn. That's not a seal."

He pressed a command on the phone and shouted with ecstasy when the octopus ripped the man in two and stuffed the body in its huge beak.

Rosemary gasped. Shandy shot to his feet. Jötnar hid his eyes in the crook of his elbow.

"That's horrible, reckless and irresponsible," Rosemary shouted. "How could you do that to your employees?"

Vincent inclined his head and replied, "I didn't mean for that to happen. Someone call Bill in HR. *Oh* well. Damn fingers aren't working right!" Vincent dropped the phone into his hip pocket.

Rosemary looked away. "I think I'll be going." She began to rise, her crewmates following her.

"Sit down!" Vincent ordered in ringing tones. They all resumed their seats. "I'm not done with you yet."

Rosemary shimmered with rage, her hands fisted at her sides. She had seen enough. Vincent had no allure.

They sat in thick silence. Shandy cleared his throat noisily. He stammered, "What are those round things?" He gestured to the rust-colored spiky globes on the seafloor.

Vincent leaned against the glass as if it were holding him up. "You don't know? Should we tell them, Dreg?"

Dreg raced to his side, his excited face wet with drool.

"It's part of my collection." Vincent eyed them all up and down contemptuously and said, "Haven't you figured out that I collect oddities, things the world conveniently labels as creatures or monsters?"

Rosemary felt the heat rise to her cheeks. The insinuation was clear. She looked away.

"I didn't mean you." Vincent glanced at Jötnar with a slick smile. "We discovered them in the Tober Trench."

Shandy's eyes opened wide. "Nobody's been that deep in the ocean!"

"So you think, old man. I have submarines that are able to go to such depths. They have gathered these specimens and more. Most of these"—he waved at the seafloor covered with round spheres—"have come from the Tober Trench. We took them to study. I had an entire lab dedicated to them at Monsterland. It was destroyed by those bothersome marines. No matter. We saved enough to continue our experiments." He pointed to the large octopus. "Do you know what this is?"

Rosemary shrugged, her lips twisted with resentment. Hurt and confused, she didn't like the way Vincent spoke to her. He undermined her confidence with his contempt. At least with Shandy, she knew where she stood in his affections. Rosemary felt as if she were standing on the highest mast in a raging storm, her feet slippery and uncertain. Vincent raised an eyebrow, and she stammered, "An octopus?"

"An octopus!" Vincent sputtered, lurching along the wall as if she had told a hilarious joke. Dreg followed him, tittering behind his hand in agreement. "With these strange-colored stripes?" he mocked her.

Jötnar called out, "Tiger octopus?"

Both Vincent and Dreg dissolved into a fit of giggles. "Tiger octopus, he says. As if there were such a thing!"

Rosemary opened her mouth to retort. Shandy met her eyes with a look of warning.

When he calmed down, Vincent said, "This is an Octopus *Giganteus*."

"That's impossible. It's a mutant!" Shandy blurted.

Vincent went on smoothly, "They were alleged to be a myth. You have broken the *Guinness Book of World Records*." He laughed. "Your friend is correct. They were said not to exist, and not only have you located this one, but you've also brought it back to me." Vincent duck-walked toward Rosemary, grabbing her cheek with his fingers. He gave the flesh a hard squeeze. "Your proud papa." His voice dripped with malice.

Tears sprang into Rosemary's eyes from the pain. Fisting her hands, she fought the discomfort, smiling in spite of his punishing grip. She refused to let him see his effect on her. She looked away, but something made her face turn to him.

A memory trigged. Rosemary was back in the closet, the monster so close she could see, hear, and smell him. *I know this place,* she thought, *and I am not afraid.*

Their gazes were frozen in a silent duel, and she pushed her fear into a tiny knot into the center of her chest. His cold stare locked with her equally icy regard. From the corner of her field of vision, she saw Shandy begin to rise, his face set.

Jötnar's chair scraped the concrete floor as he pushed himself away from the table.

Rosemary tore her cheek from Vincent's cruel grasp, her face red and stinging. She held up a hand, halting them. Vincent seemed oblivious to danger. Perhaps he didn't feel threatened by them. She knew Shandy would be squashed like a bothersome insect, but Jötnar could annihilate Vincent.

Vincent studied her while she glared at him.

"What are you planning on doing with it?" she demanded.

"Should we tell her, Dreg?" he asked, his tone playful once more.

He made his way around the table, cursing his uncooperative legs. "I will crush the world into submission. He who commands all the monsters rules the world. I already control the land, and now I will control the seas."

"That's ridiculous." Rosemary stood up. "It's a fish."

Vincent laughed at her.

"Alright," she added, "it's nothing more than a gigantic cephalopod. It's not a monster. Besides, you said this was about fixing the problems facing the world."

Vincent's cheeks purpled. It was the first emotion she'd seen from him all day. It animated his face, and he stopped resembling a corpse for a minute.

"You have no idea what you are talking about. I will bring order!"

"How?"

"With monsters. I will unleash their terror on the land and sea, and force humankind into submission."

"You can't make a mindless beast do your bidding," Rosemary said, knowing she had felt his power and had indeed become submissive. She tucked her feelings away for later reflection.

Vincent smiled cryptically. "We shall see about that." He looked out at the tank affectionately. "Won't we, Magnus?"

"You've named the octopus?" Rosemary laughed.

"I name all my pets, my dear." He moved toward her.

Rosemary hated intimacy and allowed only one person, Shandy, to call her anything close to an endearment. She opened her mouth to tell Vincent her name was Rosemary, she didn't like his false sense of closeness. Her father grabbed her wrist and squeezed it until her hand was forced to open palm up. It felt like some sort of surrender. He dropped her hand, and she rubbed her bruised wrist.

"We're the same, you and I. The difference is that my goals are for the betterment of this planet, and you care only for your next meal. There is a bigger picture here, and you could be in the center of it rather than a minor player on the fringe. I have plans for you, my dear."

"I am not *your dear*," Rosemary spat back.

Vincent ignored her outburst. He walked away from her. Shandy stood as Vincent passed his chair. They did an odd shuffle, and Shandy knocked into her father.

"You clumsy fool!" Vincent roared, shoving Shandy away. "Let's go, Dreg!"

Vincent and Dreg staggered out of the room. The automatic door *whooshed* behind them.

Rosemary and her crew sat in silence for a moment. She studied Shandy. "What was that all about?"

Shandy smirked. He pulled the cell phone from inside his sleeve.

"That's stupid. He's going to know it's missing," she said with a shake of her head. "Go give it back to him."

"He's too full of himself to know it's missing. I told you he was mad. I say we pull anchor and leave him to his crazy plans."

Jötnar grunted in agreement.

Rosemary eyed the two men, her lips thinning. "I don't know. I'm not ready to leave yet."

"Why? What is his strange hold on you?" Shady demanded.

Rosemary walked away, her arms folded over her chest. "I'm not sure. I wanted to know about them. I wanted to understand—" She stopped, her face troubled.

"Rosemary." Shandy approached her. "Stop looking at the past, child. If you keep your eyes backwards, you'll never see what's coming at you in the future until it hits you full in the face."

Tears stung her eyes. She willed them not to leak lest she humiliate herself. She opened her mouth to respond, then snapped it shut, stalking from the room, frustrated by the fact that she couldn't explain what she needed to know. She never realized that Vincent had hadn't told her what the strange rust-colored globes on the floor of the ocean were or that Shandy never returned the phone.

CHAPTER 10

HELLO MISTER

"WHERE DO YOU come from?" Wyatt asked Danai. They were sitting on the floor sharing a can of *Spam* they found in a cabinet, alone in the house. Howard has eagerly joined Etan and his crew for a recon mission.

He considered the girl next to him. Danai was at least a whole head taller than he, and he was one of the tallest kids at school.

"*Oh*, over there." She waved airily out the door.

"No, really, where?"

Danai looked up and around the room. Her five sisters were spread throughout the house. Three were sleeping, and two had taken guard duty at the windows. She lowered her head and answered in a hushed voice, "The mountains. We live in the mountains."

"Which mountains?" Wyatt asked, his voice equally quiet.

"The ones that run underneath Copper Valley," she said in a rush, compressing her lips when others entered the room.

Etan arrived with Howard Drucker, looking as if they had just finished filming a buddy cop movie. Howard was walking with a swagger, but the gun was too big for his skinny arms, and when he swung it like he was a cool guy, it went off, shooting a hole in the ceiling. There was a whole lot of screaming and flying plaster. Etan snatched the gun from Howard's hands and put on the safety.

Wyatt suppressed a smile, torn between wanting to laugh at Howard, the dork and not wanting to hurt Howard, his friend. Once Howard started staring at Etan with slavish devotion, Wyatt shook his head with disappointment. His friend looked so silly, he wanted to puke.

Danai guiltily stood, brushing white dust off her cutoff shorts. They were busting at the seams. Wyatt wondered if she and her sisters were having some sort of growth spurt. Wyatt caught Etan looking from him to Danai, his face grim.

Howard leaned against the wall, his expression haggard. "Well, we found something."

Wyatt smiled and sat down next to him. "That's good news! Where?"

Howard mumbled, "In the mall."

"That's as good a place as any. Let's get going," Wyatt said eagerly.

Etan responded, "The mall was deserted, completely empty."

"Your parents?" Wyatt directed this to Howard, who was now looking up at Etan as if he were the Messiah or something.

"We found their car." Again, Etan answered. Wyatt was wondering if he was now their spokesperson. "There were signs that a large group had been there."

"What?" Wyatt poked Howard's shoulder to get his attention. "That means they must be okay."

Howard shrugged. His face looked bleak until he gazed at Etan. Wyatt wanted to slap him like in the movies when someone was acting weird.

"Who knows? The mall is deserted now. If they were there, they left in a hurry. A lot of stuff was abandoned." He sounded forlorn.

"If the car was there, they can't be far," Wyatt persisted.

Howard looked at their fearless leader with something akin to awe. "That's what Etan thinks. He says we'll head out to the Valley tomorrow."

Danai asked Etan, "The Valley?"

"Yes, the Valley. It's the next logical place," Etan responded as if he were an authority on everything.

Wyatt snapped, "The mall, the Valley, makes no difference. We can't stay here. That's what I've been saying for days. Howard,"—he turned to his friend—"let's head out today." He stood and brushed off his pants. Leaning over he grabbed his backpack.

"Not so fast." Etan looked as if he were going to add "little buddy" or something, and that would have required a punch in the mouth. He rested his hand on Wyatt's shoulder. Wyatt shook it off, ignoring him.

"This is crazy! We don't need this menagerie. We can head out and find your parents." Wyatt directed his comments to Howard alone.

"'Menagerie' is a little harsh." Howard looked as if he was about to cry. "Etan says—"

"I'm sick of hearing about what Etan says!" Wyatt exploded.

Howard jumped forward, his face filled with rage. "Well, I'm sick of hearing about what you want to do. This isn't about you, Wyatt. Sometimes it's about other people. Just because you took out a few pathetic monsters doesn't mean you're a soldier. Etan has seen action."

Wyatt drew back, horrified. "You want to tell me that Monsterland wasn't enough action for you?"

Howard shook his head, his eyes softening. He pulled Wyatt to the corner of the room away from the others. "Wy, you were amazing. For that matter, so was I, but, but, but..." he stuttered. "I'm afraid now. This isn't a theme park anymore. This is real. Monsterland is real, and I want to go out there as prepared as I can be." Howard struggled with his next comment, his bottom lip quivering. "This isn't a video game. It's for real."

Etan was standing off to the side, watching their exchange. He looked at Wyatt with pity and said, "Wyatt's right. Pack up, everybody. We're pulling out."

Wyatt wasn't sure why Etan did that, to make him save face or to show who was in charge. It didn't matter, he thought bitterly; it was a hollow victory.

They gathered their belongings. The room emptied except for the two friends. Wyatt saw Howard stuffing whatever he could find in the kitchen into his backpack. He heard him sniff loudly.

Wyatt patted his shoulder. Part of him wanted to storm out; the other half felt the familiar tug in the center of his chest he remembered from when he'd lost his mother. He was pissed at Howard's abandonment but understood the pain of loss. Warring with his pride, he forced his resentment back where it came from and said, "I'm sure they're okay."

Howard choked on a sob. "We don't know that."

"You'd know if something happened to them."

"Did you know when your parents died?" Howard asked, wiping his face with his sleeve. "If I knew I wasn't going to find them, I would have never left Keisha."

"Why? You seem pretty happy to be in Etan's company."

"You have to be kidding me! Aside from your stepfather, he's the only other person I've met who seems experienced with more than just video games. Did it ever occur to you that I was trying to protect you too?"

"I don't need—" Wyatt's face was flushed with anger.

"Yes you do, Wyatt. We don't have the faintest idea of what to do."

"Carter trusted me." Wyatt pointed to his chest.

"What choice did he have? Do you think he would have if things were normal? You know, Wyatt, the people who get themselves killed are the overconfident ones. Maybe you should look at what Etan is doing and learn a thing or two."

Wyatt shook his head. "We could argue about this all day. We don't need Etan and the tribe of Amazons traveling with him. I bet that's the real reason you want to be with them."

Howard looked at the six large girls lining up outside the window. "They're entertaining, I'll give you that, but they're not Keisha." He grinned. "I should have never left her back at Copper Valley."

"You have to find your family, and I have to tell the authorities about Nate Owens."

"She may be all the family I have left." Howard slung his heavy bag over his shoulder and walked out of the room.

Wyatt followed him, his lips tight with unsaid words.

Etan grabbed Wyatt's arm as he left the building, halting him. "What about Nate Owens?"

Wyatt pulled away, angry that Etan had eavesdropped. "Nothing."

"You know something...."

"I don't have to tell you anything." Wyatt straightened his shoulders.

"I don't understand you, Baldwin."

Wyatt watched Etan's eyes size him up. He stood taller, his fists balled. "I don't owe you anything."

"You don't trust me. We're all on the same side."

"I don't know the sides anymore. I'm not sure of anything."

Wyatt didn't know why he didn't answer. He thought about all that had happened to him in the last few weeks. He didn't trust anyone anymore.

Wyatt watched Etan leave, the girls filing after him. Danai turned around, waving for him to follow. It was only then that he realized what she had said about the mountains, that they were *under* Copper Valley. Wyatt forgot about Etan and his argument with Howard Drucker as he tried to catch up with her, but her long-legged strides put a large distance between them.

It felt as if they had walked for hours—eleven hours, to be precise. They stayed off the freeway, skirting towns. Here and there, red paint was sprayed on the large freeway signs saying, "Stay out" or "Enter and die."

There were no signs of life. The windows of the apartment buildings stared back blankly. No movement stirred but for an occasional breeze.

It was so quiet, Wyatt felt as if he were walking on the moon. Their feet scraped the pavement, the sound echoing down the empty streets. Here and there, an empty husk of a body lay on the side of the road, a victim of the Glob. Old, shredded blankets covering deserted homeless encampments flapped like streamers. Occasionally, the screech of a bird or a dog barking sent them scrambling for cover, but they could never find the source of the sound.

"I wonder where everyone went," Howard murmured to no one in particular.

"If the Glob didn›t get them, my guess is they've been evacuated," Etan said.

"By whom?" Wyatt demanded.

Etan shrugged. "That's what we're going to find out."

Wyatt rolled his eyes at Etan but got no response from Howard.

No matter what formation they walked in, Etan was surrounded by his four commandos. For a bunch of people who claimed they'd started out as strangers, they seemed a pretty tight-knit group, Wyatt thought suspiciously.

The freeway at the first Pasadena exit was barricaded. A group of people sat on different levels of the junk they had piled, separating their street from the outside world. There was no way around it. A lone gunman sat on the top level of trash. He pointed his gun at them but said nothing. His face was blank.

Etan motioned for them to hide behind an abandoned tractor trailer. Wyatt watched him scope the area out.

"You three." He motioned for Howard and two of the tall girls.

Wyatt couldn't tell any of them apart. "Go that way." Etan pointed to a deserted street right in the line of fire.

"That's crazy," Wyatt challenged. "They'll be sitting ducks."

"How else do you want to get around?" Etan pointed to another barrier behind them. "We have to get past the freeway entrance in order to get to the heart of LA."

"We should have headed straight for the coastline," Wyatt grumbled.

"For what? There's nothing there. There's no place for an army to camp. We have to find the base. The only thing large enough for the troops would be something like the Hollywood Bowl or the Crypto Arena."

Every time Etan gave an order, Wyatt questioned it. Etan managed to countermand whatever came out of Wyatt's mouth. It had gotten so tiresome, after an order was given, they all sat down to wait for the confrontation and heated argument that followed.

"I disagree. You have no guarantee that's where they are located," Wyatt told him.

"Okay, Baldwin," Etan drawled, "you got a better idea?"

"Griffith Park," Howard blurted, trying to defuse the charged conversation.

Etan shrugged. "Maybe."

"Dodger Stadium is where I'd go. We'd be enclosed, but I have to admit, Griffith Park is so big—" Wyatt added, his voice emboldened.

Wyatt watched Etan wrestle with the idea. For the first time, he looked as if he was considering something they suggested.

"It makes sense, Etan," Howard added. "Hollywood Bowl wouldn't be my choice either, and while Dodger Stadium is on a hill and easily defensible, I think the park makes perfect sense. It's big and hilly, and you could spread out there."

"No commander worth his salt would put his army in a valley." Wyatt shook his head.

Chests puffed out as if they were spoiling for a fight. Wyatt and

Etan stared angrily at each other. Etan's lips thinned. He gave a curt nod. Wyatt detected he was being reassessed.

"We have to get around this barricade, first and foremost. Any ideas?" Etan asked.

"I'll just go talk to them," Danai interrupted, pushing her large body into their trio. Her clothing looked as if it had shrunk overnight. "Look, they won't see me as a threat."

"You don't know that," Wyatt rounded on her.

"They're people, plain old people protecting their homes." She smiled sweetly. "I can handle them."

Howard shook his head. "You have no idea what stuff like this does to folks. We saw ordinary citizens—accountants and dentists—turned into gangs of roving killers."

Etan nodded. "It isn't safe."

Danai waved her hand. "They are scared. Look at their faces."

"Scared people do terrible things," Wyatt said.

Danai stood and held out her hand. "I don't see another solution. I have a feeling we'll be fine. Besides, this always works on… never mind. Just watch." Without giving them a chance to react, Danai and Erin walked out into the street, their movements mirror images. Holding hands, they threaded together.

Wyatt made a move to follow them, but Etan grabbed his arm and said, "Look."

The street was quiet. There was no noise except for the sounds of the twins' boots hitting the blacktop.

The man sitting atop the barricade stilled, he ducked behind a large armoire that made up part of the wall. He appeared to have traded his gun for an axe. His brows lowered, his eyes widening in fear as the girls approached.

Wyatt heard their voices ring out on the empty street, the monotone sound sending a chill down his spine.

"Hello, mister." Danai's and Erin's colorless voices filled the silence simultaneously, their timbre flat. "Come play with us."

Their tall shadows reached the man, although they weren't that close. He peeked out, his head half-hidden, his face paling.

"Hello, mister," they repeated. "Come play with us."

Two more of the sextuplets left the safety of their spot, walking in that same hop-skipping stride. "Hello, mister. Come play with us."

Their strange singsong voice unnerved Wyatt, and he knew them to be totally harmless. He wondered what their actions were doing to the guard.

The guard's face grew panicked. Now both sets of twins were repeating the sentence over and over. The man looked at each set of girls and scrubbed his face, as if he could wipe the image of them from his eyes. When the last set walked from their spot, he yelped. His erratic movements sent a computer table crashing to the floor, the sound deafening. He scrambled down the side of the barricade, screaming about murder and a guy named Johnny. Wyatt rushed into the street to see the stranger flee from them, the axe held tightly in his hands, his eyes bugging from his skull.

Wyatt exchanged a look with Howard. "What's wrong with him? He was petrified."

"Hey, you gotta admit that they were creepy," Howard replied.

"I don't see it." Wyatt shook his head.

"Who knows what makes people scared?" Etan strolled over to them. Wyatt was in no mood to include him in the discussion, but Howard appeared to be delighted to have the attention.

"I think it's the duality. Their perfection as twins, sweet and innocent yet without any emotion."

"Stop overthinking it, Howard. Their freakin' size unnerved them." Wyatt hefted his gun to his shoulder and stalked away.

Danai caught up with him, her face alight with humor. "Come on. It's safe now," she giggled. "Works every time on minkins, except I have no idea who Johnny is and what's he's going to do with that axe." Her sisters skipped happily down the road, Howard, Etan, and the rest of the men bringing up the rear. Danai hung back walking a few feet before them.

"What do you mean 'works every time'?" Wyatt whispered..

"Who are minkins?" Howard asked, but no one responded.

Danai looked back at them with a sly sideways glance. "Nothing."

"No, you said it. What did you mean?" Wyatt called.

"Come on. You have eyes. Howard's right. We're all the same. It invites comments. Doing stuff like that stops them." She laughed. "Did you see his face?"

"I wish Melvin could have seen it," Howard said, deep in thought.

"Who's Melvin?" Danai asked, then without waiting for an answer took off after her sisters.

CHAPTER 11

SOMETHING FISHY IS GOING ON

LONG AFTER JADE had gone to sleep, Melvin stared at the amputated arm of the creature he had battled. He tossed and turned, finally rising to examine it. Its spiky hard exterior closely resembled the rusty colored surface of a starfish. The bluish underside had a tough, leathery surface. He ran his forefinger along the prickly appendage. It had dried, becoming as fragile as glass. He broke off a piece, crushing it into coarse sand.

He swept it into a small pile, absently playing with it. He looked at the stack of rocks Jade had laid along their hearth. They were similar in color. He crouched, picking one up and hefting it in his hand. It had the same jagged points. Melvin tapped it against another rock. It crumbled from the contact, surprisingly delicate. He watched it intently as a mound of sand grew. Using his palm, he moved all the debris into a pyramid.

Melvin thought for a bit, then took a broom they'd stolen from one of the maintenance rooms, sweeping the mess from his hut.

He heard Jade murmur. "What?" he asked. He watched her on the bed, her face flushed from sleep. She had fallen instantly into a deep slumber when they'd returned from their encounter with the creature.

"What do you think it is?" she asked, rubbing one of her eyes.

Melvin shrugged. "Who knows? It's got a shell-like exterior."

"Where do you think it came from?"

"Vincent might have mutated something. He was working on all sorts of crazy things. It might be some experiment gone bad."

Jade raised an eyebrow. "How do you know it's gone bad? Maybe it wanted to communicate with us."

Melvin touched a bruise on his shoulder. "I think there are better ways to get a message across." He crouched down and sifted the strange sand between his fingers. "They are remarkably alike, this substance and those rocks you've brought into the house."

"Maybe it wants them back," Jade said.

Melvin picked one up in his hand and tossed it from palm to palm. "Finders keepers. I dunno; maybe you're right. We'll try to speak to it tomorrow."

"You'll be careful?"

"*Duh*, of course."

"What if it wants us to leave? What if this is its home?" Jade asked, her face uncertain.

"No way. This is our home, and we aren't leaving. We'll tell that thing tomorrow. Go back to sleep."

Jade patted the nest of blankets. Melvin lay down, making himself comfortable. Jade rested her head on his chest. He must have dozed for a bit. He wasn't sure what awakened him. Carefully, he slipped out of their bed and walked to the door. The moon hung low in the sky, its glow dazzling the surface of the pond, turning it silver. It was hot, the air sultry, yet he shivered as if someone had danced on his grave.

He walked out and looked at the pile of sand he deposited outside his hut last night. He tripped on one of the round objects Jade had collected. He bent down to pick it up and studied it for a bit. He let it drop from his hands as the agony of transformation rippled his skin.

Daybreak was about an hour away. Melvin stared at the moon, feeling the primal pulse sound through his veins. His chest expanded. The familiar pain ripped through him. He didn't fight the transformation; it was easier on his body.

Dropping on all fours, his face elongated, his skin turning into a reddish-gray pelt. He stifled the howl that rose in his throat.

Trotting to the water's edge, he peered down. It was quiet in the marsh, an occasional burst of chatter from night birds in the trees interrupting the silence. A bullfrog croaked. The sound cut off instantly as if it had been smothered. Melvin's pointed ears shifted; the tufts of hair on the edges quivered.

He scanned the darkness, then went back to the water and dunked his face in, letting the liquid cool his body. Shaking his head, he watched the flying droplets making circular pockmarks on the still surface of the water. He looked down, a howl erupting from his throat when he noticed two glassy black eyes peering up at him.

Melvin touched the water with his paw. He tried to talk, but it came out as a harsh growl. He yelped to soften the sound, but it had the opposite effect.

The crustacean man rose from the water. It was huge, its entire body covered with that spiny, shell-like exterior. One arm was missing, yet the stump was powerful. The creature reached out and grabbed Melvin by the neck.

Melvin wriggled free, whimpering, resisting the urge to defend himself. Backing away, he dodged the beast, willing himself to transform back to a human so he could communicate. His body refused to cooperate.

Melvin's breath came in short pants as he ran from one side of the beach to the other. He was terrified Jade might hear and come outside, so he lured the monster away from his hut. Snapping, he tried to nip the creature's leg, but his teeth glanced off the brittle material.

Melvin locked eyes with the starfish man, but the orbs he saw were dead and lifeless. No help there.

Fingers like rocks gripped him by the neck, choking him. Legs as strong as stone lashed out. The monster's fisted hand came down on Melvin's head with the force of a jackhammer.

Stars burst into Melvin's vision. He tasted blood in his mouth. The strong canine body saved him. Melvin saw the sun peeking over the mountaintops, his muscles beginning to feel the lassitude of change. He willed his body to stay lupine, now knowing that to change into a human and fight the creature meant death. His fragile human form was no match for it.

Melvin twisted groggily, dragging the creature in a circle. Jade! He had to protect Jade! He was going to die, and then the creature would go after Jade. Just the thought of it gave Melvin renewed strength. He tried to speak, but again it came out as a strangled snarl.

Melvin wove drunkenly toward the pilings, smashing his attacker against the wooden posts. He held him pinned against the rotting wood, hoping he might reason with the creature. The shell-like hand reached for Melvin's eye with the intent of poking it from its socket. Melvin ducked, and the creature grabbed the skin at the werewolf's neck, ripping the fur from his body. Melvin yowled when he felt his pelt tear.

His thoughts racing, he wiggled against the hands holding him captive. Werewolves were the master of all monsters! What was going on here? His brethren had bested both vampires and zombies. What new creature was this, challenging his superiority in the monster universe?

Using all his body weight, he shoved hard and heard the crunch of the shells as they impacted with the round logs.

The beast was winded. The hold on Melvin's neck slightly weakened, and the werewolf used this respite to push his massive paws into his opponent with crushing strength. The crunch of the shell shattering rent the morning air. It seemed to go on for hours. Gritting his teeth, Melvin pressed harder. Using all his body weight, he gave a hard shove.

The creature›s eyes closed as its body separated into two halves.

Melvin rolled off onto the sand, breathing heavily. He lay flat, his torso melting, his face constricting, the hair disappearing. He was human once again. He couldn't move even if he needed to. His body had no strength.

He watched the bisected creature, afraid to look away. It lay in two parts on the beach, its feet half in the water. He looked for blood but saw nothing but a puddle of greenish seawater staining the beach. Melvin watched the still chest, alert for any movement. There was nothing. The thing was indeed dead.

Melvin threw his arm over his eyes, waiting for his strength to return. Slowly, he sat up. The upper half of the body of his attacker lay drying in the sand. He crawled over to it to touch it. It was made from the same surface as a starfish. It had a small head with a red comb similar to a rooster, which was now hardening in the warm sunlight to a brittle consistency. The lower half was a slight distance closer to the water. A long fin ran down the wide back, terminating at the base of its spine. The legs lay splayed, ending in webbed feet that were being washed by the water.

Melvin rose unsteadily. It hurt to swallow. Blood ran from a gaping wound on his neck. He touched it, his vision swimming from the pain. Cursing, he moved around the dilapidated dock to further examine the upper half of the monster.

Lifting a foot, he stamped it on the monster's head and watched it crumble into dust.

Melvin was dizzy. He had to hold onto the wood to steady himself. For a second, his whole world darkened.

A loud splash brought him back. Melvin shielded his eyes to see the bottom half of the creature roll itself into the water. It scrabbled, not unlike a crab. Melvin took off after it, but his legs wobbled, forcing him to his knees.

He returned to the remains of the dead monster, watching the water lap up the pile of dust. It was dead. It had to be. Nothing could live without a brain. It must have been reflexes returning the bottom half to the water, he reasoned.

Melvin walked back to the hut. Grabbing one of the rounded rocks Jade loved, he threw it into the water. He crushed another one as he watched the growing concentric circles fade from sight.

CHAPTER 12

DID US A SOLID

ROSEMARY KONRAD WALKED along a ridge on a mountain that looked down on the coastline of the island. Shielding her eyes from the dazzling sun with her hand, she scanned their surroundings. "We're not far from the mainland. He's not as isolated as he thinks," she observed. "It was close enough for people to come to this aquarium."

They studied the circle of empty aquarium tanks that surrounded the massive structure of Vincent's hideaway. It was a vault-like building made from coral buried in the soft sand, and must have served as an educational center at one time. It had a row of narrow windows that made it look suspiciously like a World War II bunker. A blue and yellow sign lay on its side by the broken dock, the bold letters spelling out; *The Great White Shark Park, Meet the Great Monsters of the Deep.*

"Strange," she murmured. "No cameras, minimal security as far as I can see." She studied the camp below her.

"He don't need none of that." Shandy stood on the promontory next to her. "Not only is he completely isolated, he's stocked the entire lower portion of the island with zombies. He's safer than a Colombian drug lord." Shandy pointed to the beach three hundred feet below them where plague victims wandered aimlessly, bumping into each other and ripping off body parts to feed. Rosemary grimaced with distaste.

"No more fish," Jötnar complained, pointing to the empty tanks. He pouted.

Rosemary smiled. "The aquarium is closed. The fish are where they belong, in the ocean."

"Unlike us," Shandy grumbled. "There's something wrong with exploiting—"

"Some would say he's keeping them safe from predators," Rosemary interrupted. Closing her eyes tightly, she felt slightly nauseous. She had seen no glimmer of compassion in her father's dead eyes last night, not that she was known for sensitivity or understanding. *What did she expect? They were nothing more than strangers, really.* She was a pirate captain. Rosemary sighed. There was some small part of her that wanted more. *A shared connection of sorts.* Common sense told her to run, but her feet stayed strangely rooted to the soil as if they were planted in the earth.

Rosemary weighed everything she'd read about her father. Vincent Konrad wasn't wrong about zombies being persecuted. He understood that werewolves had to be protected, and vampires were nothing more than parasites on society. The monsters were draining civilization, sucking the life from it.

It was true, Vincent was harsh, but tough times took strength and daring. Afterall, being in leadership meant being the one to take action, and not always embracing the popular choice. In the cold light of day, was he any different than she was on her pirate ship?

"Perhaps we're being too hard on him," she said.

"Take off your rose-colored glasses. I never took you for an idiot, Rosemary."

"Maybe we're not giving him a chance," Rosemary said halfheartedly, not sure why she was defending Vincent.

"Liked what you saw yesterday, did you?" Shandy demanded. "I'm not a fan of your *Jötnar* there." Shandy pointed to the hulking giant to their side. "But I sure as hell didn't like the way Vincent was eyeballing him neither."

Jötnar rolled his eyes and mumbled, "Minkins, *ugh.*"

Rosemary and Shandy ignored his remark.

"Jötnar's part of our crew. I won't let him touch him," Rosemary said, her hands fisted.

"A crew he conveniently disbursed to different ships when we arrived. We're all the crew you got left, girl."

Jötnar grunted in agreement.

Rosemary shrugged. "They were scum, the lot of them. They could have fought to stay with us."

Shandy gave her a look that would have melted ice. "Only a fool thinks he can't be bested. I'd be careful of him. I don't trust him." Shandy shook his head, and his face colored up like a boiled shrimp.

Rosemary laughed. "*Ha!* like who did you ever trust?"

"Your mom. I trusted her. And for the most part"—he paused—"I trust you."

They stopped walking to look at each other. "Thanks, old man." She paused and considered him. "Only for the *most* part?"

Shandy turned to face the sea, his eyes tearing from the wind. Rosemary watched him. Shandy swiped a hand across his face, wiping wetness from twin trails down his creased cheeks. They stayed quiet for a few minutes.

"What are you not saying?" She came up behind him. Shandy buffered her from the warm winds pounding the top of the cliff. The rancid odor from the decaying flesh below floated upward. Rosemary gagged from the smell. "I can hear you grumbling from here, Shandy. Just say it."

"I never wanted to tell you, lass. I never did."

"What? Shandy, what?"

He looked from her to Jötnar.

"Whatever you have to say, you can say it in front of him," she said, gesturing to Jötnar. "I trust him with my life."

Shandy wiped his eyes. "Your mom didn't die in no crash, Rose. She died like those poor souls down there, infected with the plague."

"What?" Rosemary turned. "You said it was a—"

"I know what I told you. Would it have made you feel better to know she died not even knowing her own name?"

"How did she contract the plague? I don't remember anybody having it near us."

"She was one of the first victims. She got it at work. At Vincent Konrad's plant."

"Are you insinuating that somehow Vincent was involved in her death?"

Shandy was quiet for a long time. "I'm not saying nothing, Rosemary. I don't know. I can only put one and one together, and I can't figure out why he wants this *ginormous* octopus and why he wants you." He looked right at her and said, "Surely his behavior at dinner last night proves the man is crazy… if you even want to call him a man."

Jötnar nodded in agreement. Rosemary sighed.

"Don't tell me you don't agree with me, Rosemary. He's a maniac."

Rosemary didn't answer.

Her new ship lay anchored in a secluded harbor. It was not the destroyer she had demanded. She considered her conversation.

"Damn fine ship." Shandy rolled back and forth on the balls of his feet as if he were on the deck of a vessel.

Jötnar stood to examine the greenery around them, or maybe he left to relieve himself. Rosemary wasn't sure.

"I would feel a whole lot better on the deck of that ship and miles from this godforsaken place."

She could hear Jötnar's large form thrashing through the dense underbrush. He sounded like he was excavating. A bird screeched, taking off like a rocket and setting off a racket from the surrounding bushes.

Rosemary shrugged, her face sad as she stared at her ship. "It's small," she said, dismissing the neat Coast Guard cutter bobbing in the water. A long, dark shadow twice the size of her boat swam next to it, creating a wide wake. "I was thinking of holding out for a bigger one. He owes me. I brought him that creature."

She sat down on a rock surrounded by thick shrubbery. A breeze blew over them, bringing the tangy smell of the ocean. Her dark eyes watched the waves restlessly.

All the way to the east, a school of dolphins broke the surface of the water, their gray skin sleek and shiny in the late afternoon rays. They swam closer to shore and made an abrupt change of direction, taking off like torpedoes. Jötnar pointed to them. "Sharks nearby" he said. The others stayed pensive each in their own thoughts. "Compact." Shandy nodded toward her ship. "Sturdy. A regular workhorse. She'll outrun anything else on the water."

Jötnar sat down on the ground, resting his head in his palm, his thick brows lowered. His face looked so much like the craggy hillside that Rosemary found herself staring at his features instead of the choppy waves. He pursed his lips, the rubbery skin twisting to look like an overripe peach.

Rosemary reached over to pat his stubbled bald head and smiled. Even with him sitting, she had to reach up. Hard to believe that he was probably taller than her father. Had he grown overnight? He looked bigger than she remembered. She opened her mouth to say something, but Shandy interrupted her.

"I'm tellin' ya, lass, she'll skim the waves and outrun anything following us. I don't like the man, your father," he spat. "I have to admit, he did us a solid favor with this ship."

Rosemary inclined her head, conceding Shandy's point, her lips thinning as if she didn't want to admit it to him. They sparred like this often, but usually she allowed Shandy to guide her.

She heard Shandy mumbling. Rosemary knew he was losing patience. She wasn't sure she agreed with him, and it was making her mentor angry. Truth be told, she was equally conflicted. It wasn't as though she should be casting any stones or pointing fingers. She hadn't had such a squeaky-clean existence her entire life either.

While they'd spent a lifetime breaking laws, they technically didn't hurt anybody. They had a strict code of ethics. Pirate ethics. Not the old crap Blackbeard or Morgan lived by. It was a new creed, developed by poor victims of greed and avarice who merely evened the playing field. It worked. She shrugged, her thoughts whirling in her head.

Now here was her father with a new ideology, a grander one. He didn't steal. He was strictly out to improve the world, or so he claimed.

She shifted on her behind, feeling uncomfortable in her own skin. Sticking her blunt fingers between the crevice in the boulder, she dug deep as if to anchor herself. She was as unsteady as a ship on a stormy sea. Common sense warred with the hazy notions Vincent spouted.

Rosemary scratched her head. Nothing added up, but she was confident and unafraid. She wobbled on the rock, then steadied herself. Vincent claimed his goal was benevolent. He wanted to restore order and world peace. He was bigger than stealing.

She wondered where she fit in his schemes. An image of her mother intruded, her beautiful face filled with sores, her eyes dull and lifeless. Rosemary's heart broke, and she swallowed convulsively. The damn plague. *Why did it have to be the plague?* She glanced at Shandy, who was watching her intently. He raised a gray eyebrow and nodded solemnly.

She knew Shandy recognized her unease when he softened his voice and continued talking. She realized for the first time that he didn't know what she was thinking. He assumed she was upset about the ship. "If overturned, those ships right themselves within thirty seconds. Don't know of another vessel that can do that." He cleared his throat and spit into the bushes.

Rosemary shook her head. "Can't argue with you there, old man. Still…"

"Still nothing, Rosemary. You don't owe that fiend anything," he said with disgust. "I just want to know what we are *still* doing here!" He paused and went on. "I can tell you're uncomfortable with the whole deal. He's a strange one." He parted the green leaves of a palm and pointed to the ship. "We can take that boat and make our way back to the Alaskan coast. Don't need much crew anyway, just your big guy here and me."

"*Ha!* So now you like him?" She laughed.

Shandy shrugged. "He'll do."

Rosemary pursed her lips but didn't respond.

"Ain't nobody policing up there. We could do what we want," Shandy said.

Jötnar nodded his head in agreement.

"You'd like that… *hmmm*, Jötnar?" she asked, looking at him sideways. "Fewer people to stare at you. Did they make fun of you growing up?"

Jötnar looked at her quizzically. "Wot?"

"At home… when you were growing up… did they make fun of your size? Is that why you ran away?"

Jötnar's pale skin reddened. He shook his head. "Didn't run away."

Rosemary studied him and laughed. "Yeah, sure. And you, Shandy?" She turned to the older man. "Is that what you want to do? Go back to slumming the waterfronts, looking for some crumbs so we can exist for another few months until the next bit of gossip? I brought him that… that…"

"Creature," Shady said in a gravelly voice. "It's a monster, and that man is evil. Nothing good is going to come out of this." He looked her full in the face. "He's powerful. Brought the world to its knees. *For what*, Rosemary? He cares for nothing."

"He had intentions of making the world a safer, better place."

Shandy laughed, his round belly jiggling. "You don't believe that balderdash about werewolves, vampires, and zombies, do you? I thought you were smarter than that."

Rosemary bristled. "He was keeping them contained. They were wrecking the world," she said stubbornly.

"He used them to convince the population he was all heart, concerned for both us and them. Those phony politicians were happy to fob off the problems dogging the cities on him. He captured and wiped out the werewolves by annihilating them all. Took out the vampires, but I bet he's got a supply of their blood stashed somewhere. It's perfect to subdue a population. The zombies, poor souls, were just a tool for him. He exploited them all." Shandy's face was mottled, his voice raised. He gestured angrily with his hands.

"What do you care about them? They were all monsters," Rosemary stated.

"They were *people*," he said angrily, shouting the last word. He looked pointedly at Jötnar. "Innocent victims of whatever made them that way. Vincent Konrad's the fiend capitalizing on whatever he can get his greedy hands on to manipulate the world to its collective knees."

"He meant well," Rosemary replied stubbornly, hitting her fist in her palm. "I know he did."

"What, you can feel it in your bones?" He laughed. Shandy took a long look at her. Rosemary lowered her eyes, fighting the sinking feeling of shame. She turned away, guilt making her angry. "Are you worried the apple doesn't fall far from the tree? You're nothing like him, Rose, nothing. You don't have to worry about that. I'd be more worried about what you picked up from me than that creep. Aye, go ahead. Say it, girl."

"'*To thy own self be true*,'" she said softly, almost to herself.

Shandy sat down wearily next to her on the rock. She made room for them both, and their shoulders touched with a sweet intimacy. "It was the first lesson my ma taught me and the first one I taught you. '*To thy own self be true.*' Don't lie to yourself!'"

"Okay," she responded. "But what if we're wrong? What if we're judging him from our perspective? I'd like to give him the benefit of the doubt."

Shandy chuckled, his voice low. "If that's what you want to tell yourself, Capt'n, alright, then." He stood and walked behind the boulder.

Jötnar raised his head, brushing the leafy canopy.

"*Hey,* look there, Jötnar. If we had one of those zip lines, we could zip right down to that ship." Shandy pointed to the boat bobbing in the water.

Jötnar shook his head and made a motion with his hands. "Very fast."

Shandy nodded. "Like one of them rides in his damn Monsterland park."

Rosemary ignored them and started down a narrow path toward the inlet, Shandy and Jötnar close behind, talking of zip lines and escape routes.

Rosemary called back, "We'll leave through the front door whenever we choose."

"Okay, sure. And I got a nice bridge I want to sell you. Listen to me; he'll dump you as fast as he dumped your ma once he was done with her."

"You don't know that," she spat.

"*Oh,* don't I, now? I had a front row seat to it all. Left your ma high and dry. Never took no interest in her. She wrote him, begged her to help."

Shandy was huffing and puffing from the rough terrain. Rosemary sat down on a tree stump and made room for him. "Did she tell him about me?"

"I never had a chance to ask her. She disappeared into a

containment camp." Shandy hung his head. "I had to get you out of there before Children's Service put you into their system."

Rosemary nodded. "I know. I know. But maybe he would have…"

"A lot you know," Shandy sniffed. "He gave her a job at his plant. Strung her along for some time."

Rosemary shrugged. "Obviously she didn't allow herself to be 'strung along' for too long. She was with you… " Rosemary stared at him, her eyes narrowing.

"Don't go there, girl. We was friends, 'doncha you remember. We was good friends." He shook his head, his face sad. "I loved your ma from the minute I met her, but it wasn't like for her. Don't know what she saw in him, but she did."

Rosemary watched him carefully. She was never sure of their relationship. She stuck out her lip stubbornly. "Still, he claims never knew about me."

" So what! What has he done for you aside from giving you a few paltry boats? We don't need him."

Anger forced Rosemary to rise, her face twisted. "I'm not leaving yet." She took off down the rocky hill, her shoulders rigid. "I want to know what he's planning with *my* octopus."

"Not his octopus and not yours neither, girl." Shandy's voice followed her.

She stomped to a clearing, stamped her foot, and turned to respond. She stared up at the empty incline. Shandy was gone. For that matter, so was Jötnar. She hadn't heard them leave.

She opened her mouth to call him, then snapped it shut. She was the captain. She wasn't ready to shove off yet. She just wasn't ready.

CHAPTER 13

LA LA LAND

THEY WALKED FOR an hour, skirting small communities, all barricaded with cars and household junk. The streets were mostly deserted. They heard whistles and other signals but were left alone.

Wyatt stayed in the lead, despite Etan insisting they keep a tighter formation. The four other soldiers always seemed to surround Etan as if they were his bodyguard detail. Wyatt observed that they walked like the muscle-bound people who hung out at the gym on Main Street at home. They must have weighed a thousand pounds collectively, except for Etan. Etan was tall and rangy, and while physically fit, he was more like the joggers or bicyclists Wyatt was used to seeing exercising on the weekends. Carter called them weekend warriors. For a minute, Wyatt wished Carter were here to evaluate them.

The rest of the soldiers were jarheads, even the female, which to his mind meant marines, but where Etan fit in, he couldn't quite figure it out. Etan wore that damnable scarf around his head, and Wyatt yearned to rip it off to see if he had a military-type haircut too.

Howard Drucker followed orders enough for both of them, he thought angrily. He could hear Howard asking questions that Etan answered patiently. Every time the soft-spoken, confident response came, Wyatt gritted his teeth. Etan certainly knew how to sound like the commander. He was a real commander-in-chief, Wyatt smirked.

It felt as if they had been walking for days. Vultures flew overhead, filling Wyatt with dread. That meant only one thing: there were dead people behind all these barricades.

Nobody talked about the rest of the country, politics, or the failure of the entire infrastructure. If there was any conversation at all, it was in short spurts, direct and to the point.

They crossed a road to walk under an overpass. The shadows cooled their overheated skin. Wyatt glanced back at Etan. The guy was an animal. No matter how hot he was, he never took off the scarf from his head or removed his sunglasses. The girls chatted noisily amongst themselves.

There was a noise from across the street. It sounded like metal hitting the pavement. Four of the imperial guards, as Wyatt called them, crouched, ready to protect Etan as well as the rest of their group. Wyatt stayed out front. The largest of the group shoved him behind and pushed them into a protected triangle, herding them like sheep.

A stranger separated from the shadows and watched them warily. He was barefoot, dressed in rags, his hair wild. His eyes settled on Etan, and Wyatt watched the man's expression change from distrust to anger. He dropped what he was holding and ran toward them, his fingers pointed to Etan. "What have you done! What have you done to us!" he shouted.

With a scream, he leaped toward them. The soldiers formed a barrier in front of Etan. Etan automatically shoved Howard to the ground.

"Drop," Yerbol shouted.

Everyone except the soldiers fell to the ground. The man crashed into the wall of commandos, one of them neatly smashing him in the head with the butt of his gun. The attacker collapsed like a rag doll.

"Is it safe?" Etan asked.

Yerbol walked to the man and nudged him with his boot. He gave a quick nod. The group rose shakily to their feet and moved on, the girls much more subdued than before.

Wyatt grabbed Howard under the armpits and helped him get up. "What do you think he meant by that?"

"What?" Howard asked.

Wyatt waited until there was some distance between them and the group. "That was directed at Etan. It was like he knew Etan."

"He was crazy, Wyatt. The whole world's gone batshit crazy. Etan's just a regular guy."

Wyatt wanted to argue, but really, he had no proof except what he observed, and it seemed that nobody wanted to hear it anyway.

They crossed wide streets, empty and covered in discarded paper. Broken electronics, stolen in haste, lay smashed on sidewalks. Wyatt and the group came across a school bus abandoned beside a median in the middle of the road.

"Check it out," Etan ordered.

Yerbol, jumped inside, then stuck his head out. "There's gas in the tank. I'll see if I can start it."

"Do you want to go in *that*? It's a bit obvious," Wyatt asked Howard.

Howard raised an eyebrow. "It's better than walking out in the open. Etan says we are targets—"

"And riding up like we're going to school is not making yourself a target? You know, Howard, he's not the smartest guy in the world."

"He might not be, but right now he's the smartest guy in our group." Howard leaned against a metal stanchion and wiped the sweat from his face.

Wyatt felt his face flush from his neck to his forehead.

"Wy, you've been acting like an asshole for the last few days. There's nothing wrong with accepting help from people with more experience."

"You didn't used to be so gullible. How do you know if this Etan guy is really in the army?" Wyatt whispered harshly.

"How do you know he's not?" Howard rose off the metal barrier he was leaning on. "Right now I trust him a lot more than I trust you."

Words choked in Wyatt's throat. He looked away from his friend and thought about leaving, walking away. Etan and his crew had the hood of the bus up and were trying to get the engine to turn over.

Howard cleared his voice. "I didn't mean that, Wyatt."

Wyatt swallowed hard but didn't say anything. He felt the same burn in his chest when he realized he'd lost his mother. It hurt, deeply.

"Wyatt?"

"Forget it." Wyatt moved past him. Howard grabbed his forearm.

"No. Listen. I didn't mean that."

Wyatt made a rude noise.

"Please," Howard implored. "It's just that he does make sense. He says things my dad would say."

Wyatt refused to make eye contact with Howard.

Howard paused, as if to choose his word carefully.. "I think what happened with the mummies was a miracle, and we dodged a massacre. Experience tells me we can't rely on luck. I'm scared it may run out."

Wyatt turned to face him.

"You know I have been lucky with only one thing in my life, Wyatt," Howard said.

"With what?" Wyatt asked, his voice stung.

"My friends, you idiot. I think we've pretty much lost Melvin. You know he's never coming back to us. Can't you see that I'm doing this as much for *you* as for myself? I can't lose another friend."

Wyatt felt the ice melt between them. The stood silently for a minute.

"Still mad?"

Wyatt looked at the bleak landscape, the empty buildings, and deserted streets. Howard was Howard. Sometimes he didn't think when he spoke, but there was always an element of truth to what he said. Wyatt sighed, the fight knocked out of him. "Howard, does Etan remind you of anybody?"

Howard considered Etan and said, "*Rambo*?"

"Forget it." Wyatt laughed.

"I don't know why you don't like him."

A minute later, Wyatt heard the engine turn over. There was a loud cheer from the girls, whom Etan silenced with a look of warning. Etan paused to acknowledge Wyatt and Howard. His eyes locked with Wyatt's. Wyatt scrutinized the other man, trying to decide why he didn't like him.

Howard asked, "What do you want to do?"

Wyatt turned to him. "You said you wanted to stay with them."

"Logically it makes more sense, but ultimately, I'll do what you want."

"You'd leave them and go with me?" Wyatt asked softly.

Howard nodded quickly. "I think my dad would tell me staying with a group is the best strategy." Howard dipped his head shyly and continued, "If you are so against it? I didn't mean to say I didn't trust you. I do."

Wyatt shook his head. "I trust you too. And I trust your judgment. Except when it comes to vamps."

He started walking toward the school bus. He and Howard were the last of the group to climb on board. Etan halted Wyatt before he could enter the vehicle. "I'm not your enemy," he said.

Wyatt shrugged. "You're hiding something."

Etan raised his eyebrows so that they were visible above his sunglasses and said, "I don't know what you're talking about. Haven't I proven we're on the same side?"

Wyatt moved to the back of the bus, not sure which side Etan was talking about.

The bus gave a loud groan, followed by a grinding noise, then a shaky leap forward. They were on their way to Los Angeles.

"Barton, use the side streets." Etan ordered one of his four men to take the wheel.

"Sorry, GPS ain't working," Barton replied with a laugh.

"Never mind. I'll tell you where to go." Etan sat behind the driver, leaning over the partition, and directed him through the deserted streets.

"Have you lived here?" Wyatt asked.

Etan didn't answer right away but glanced at Wyatt through the rearview mirror. "I've spent some time in LA with my dad."

"Where exactly?" Wyatt asked, but Etan was leaning over the seat, giving directions to the driver.

"He's using back roads," Wyatt murmured.

"Wise choice." Howard nodded. "Less going on here than on the main arteries."

Wyatt sat next to Howard and fought the response that he would have done the same thing. It didn't take an Einstein to know they'd be easy targets on the freeway.

Howard had gone quiet since they entered the city limits, passing the neat pastel-colored stucco homes.

"Looks like Zombieville," Wyatt commented. He glanced at his friend. "You'll find your parents," he said, watching Howard's face for a reaction.

Howard shrugged. "I'm not so confident. What do you make of them?" He gestured to one of the sextuplets.

Wyatt moved closer. "They're so… so…"

"Identical. Like clones," Howard finished.

"You think they're clones?" Wyatt whispered, watching Danai move to a seat a few rows ahead of them.

Howard shrugged. "Not sure. They're taller than anyone I've ever met. Can you imagine the size of their parents?"

Wyatt looked at the six identical auburn-haired girls. "They might be giants." Wyatt smirked.

Howard laughed out loud. "I don't think so." They were quiet for a moment. Howard was pensive.. "Everything about them is super-sized," he said. "I've been studying them, talking to Becca."

"And here I thought all you cared about was Etan," Wyatt answered.

Howard snorted. "You should know me by now, Baldwin. I know you don't have faith in him. I have my reservations too. The whole world is upside down. I wish Keisha were here to compare notes."

Wyatt nodded at the girl sitting in front of Danai. "Is that the one you've been talking to?"

"No, that one." Howard pointed to one of the sisters sitting alone in the third row. Her legs twisted so that her long thighs stuck out in the aisle. It was clear from the six sets of legs that none of the girls could fit in the row seating. "They're strange. Never saw a television set in their entire lives."

"So?" Wyatt shrugged. "They could be part of a sect. Danai told me she came from the mountains."

Howard shook his head. "Melvin was weird like that sometimes too. But he knew about everything, like milkshakes and stuff."

"It's as if they've lived under a rock their entire lives. Danai said the mountains were underneath—" Wyatt blurted but never got to finish.

Etan yelled for them to take cover. Shots exploded all around them. They slammed onto the floor. The bus came to a slow halt. The driver listed over the wheel, a red circle in the middle of his forehead.

They continued to roll, the girls screaming. The vehicle moved over a median; the underbody lodged on the concrete. Two tires lifted off the surface of the road.

"Did you see them!" Danai yelled.

"What were those things!" Becca cried, her face a mask of terror.

Wyatt tried to move upward to see what had attacked them. He caught a glimpse of storefronts and a street sign. They were in Glendale. A large billboard towered over them.

"Crap. We're in the Valley already. This isn't good," he told Howard.

"Who's attacking us now? What could be worse than vampires, zombies, or werewolves?"

Wyatt poked his head up, his eyes going wide. He shivered with a mixture of fear and a healthy dose of revulsion. He fell back into the seat, his legs giving way. His head felt light as if it were detached from his body. Bile rose from his stomach, and he fought the urge to hurl. After the Battle of Monsterland, not much scared Wyatt, but there was one thing that frightened him more than anything else.

"Wyatt!" Howard shook him. "Are you hit? What did you see?"

Wyatt wouldn't answer. He couldn't. He was hyperventilating, his eyes squeezed shut. He'd fought all kinds of creepy things that frightened most people. He'd tangled with a ghost in the Copper Valley Inn and battled zombies in Zombieville, but this was the stuff of his nightmares. He was frozen onto the seat, bent in half, his arms wrapped around his midsection. His breath sounded like a chainsaw. Lights danced before his eyes. Wyatt knew he was close to passing out.

He opened his mouth twice. No sound emerged. When he spoke, his voice finally came out in a squeak. He couldn't spit, his mouth was so dry. "Clowns. We're being attacked by clowns." He felt his rib cage constrict. Nothing in the world scared him more than clowns.

"*Ugh.*" Howard shook his head. "I hate clowns."

Wyatt didn't just hate clowns; he had a pathological fear of them.

The bus was sprayed by machine gun fire, shattering all the windows. "Take cover!" one of Etan's men shouted.

Everyone dove onto the floor except for Wyatt. Howard was screaming at him to get down, but Wyatt couldn't hear him. Everything moved as if they were underwater. He heard Etan shout at Howard to stay put. Wyatt stared blankly ahead.

Etan raced over in two steps, grabbed Wyatt by the midsection, and threw him down onto the seat. He held his head down against the vinyl. "What's wrong?" he demanded.

"I... I..."

"It's okay." Etan patted his shoulder. "I hate carnivals. The smell of fried *Twinkies* can send me into a catatonic state. Bearded women paralyze me. When I was in the air force—"

Wyatt closed his eyes with shame, then opened them. "I thought you said—," he gasped.

Etan shook his shoulder, interrupting him. "It's okay, buddy. Everybody is afraid of something."

Wyatt wanted to hate this man, and yet he was helpless here. A bullet could have taken him down like the dead soldier in the front of the bus, and Etan had risked his own life to save him. On top of that, he was consoling him in the middle of a gun battle. *Was there anything this guy couldn't do?* Wyatt wheezed, his breath still coming out in a thready gasp. He couldn't draw oxygen into his lungs.

The rear window burst open. A small canister landed on the floor with a thump. The canister made a loud pop, then squealed like escaping gas from a balloon.

Wyatt leaned over his seat, still choking, his heart ricocheting in his chest. He saw Howard move to pick the canister up.

Etan stopped him. "Don't touch it. It could be a grenade that didn't explode."

"Well, it smells like crap." Howard made a face. "It's just a stink bomb," he explained, a strange giggle escaping him.

"We can't get off the bus. They're all over the place." Etan was looking out the window.

Wyatt peered over the edge of the seat. They were surrounded.

Hundreds of clowns were watching them. He squeezed his eyes shut, panting like a racehorse. Smoke was making it hard to see inside the bus. It stung Wyatt's eyes.

Clowns were hiding in the doorways, their faces covered with white makeup, their eyes and mouths garishly highlighted, each with the ubiquitous red ball of a nose.

"They all look like *Bozo*," Howard said with a giggle.

Wyatt caught a glimpse of a clown dressed like a hobo in a threadbare business suit, carrying a rifle with a green scrap of cloth tied to the end like a banner. He was scrambling across the pavement. He whistled loudly to the other side of the street and ducked inside an empty storefront.

"Watch out!" Etan shouted. Everyone dropped to the floor of the bus. Etan coughed then started to laugh.

Three men and one woman dressed in shabby clothes with exaggerated shoes scuffled out, blasting the bus with shotguns. They then raced across the street, disappearing into a darkened building.

"Got any ideas?" Howard asked. His face was filled with a silly grin. "We're trapped."

"I don't like them, Erin," one of the girls whimpered. "Are they minkins?"

"*Hush*," Erin said then guffawed.

"But they scare me," the other girl replied. She was rolling back and forth in her seat, chuckling, tears streaming down her cheeks.

If Wyatt had a breath in his body he would have shouted, *Me too!* Struggling to regulate his labored breathing, he eyed the door on the bus. He wanted to run. Holding his hands over his mouth, he smothered the screams in his chest. For a minute, he wanted to die, so ashamed he was of his panicking.

A cloud of foul-smelling smoke hung over the occupants of the bus, but Wyatt barely noticed it. A window shattered above him, sending a waterfall of glass tinkling down.

A giggle escaped from the girl in the seat in front of Wyatt. "Oh no," Candace said with a chuckle. "They're funny. Look, Erin."

The girls poked their heads up to peek out the window. Wyatt crawled to the edge of the seat to see what was going on.

A small man dressed like a tramp gazed adoringly at the two girls on the bus. He wore a painted frown that covered the bottom part of his face. Tears created with makeup trailed from his eyes. A huge daisy drooped in his lapel. He brought the paper flower to his bulbous nose, inhaling deeply.

Etan raised his gun. Howard touched the muzzle, halting him. "He's unarmed," he said quietly, then choked. Howard waved his hands, fanning away the smoke.

"Yerbol, get rid of those cans." Etan's voice was funny, as if he was holding in his laughter.

They observed the clown duck-walk across the street.

"Hold your fire," Etan ordered, lowering his weapon.

The bum fell to one knee outside the bus, and though no words escaped his mouth, he appeared to be singing gustily to the girls. He grabbed the flower and held it up to Candace, waving it in front of her as if he were proposing.

"What do you make of this?" one of Etan's men said through a mass of giggles.

"I always said LA was filled with a bunch of clowns," Etan called back, then exploded with laughter. He doubled over trying to control it..

A door swung open in the apartment building across the street. Another can popped into the bus, letting loose more noxious gas. They all ignored it, caught up in the drama in the street.

A tall female emerged. She was as big if not bigger than the girls on the bus, with an exaggerated red Lucille Ball wig. She was dressed as a washerwoman, an apron stretched around her ample hips.

"She looks like Aunt Henny!" Erin pointed to her.

The female clown spied the tramp on his knees by the bus,

planted her hands on her waist, and began a silent diatribe. Stomping toward him, she moaned and groaned, holding her head, and *boo-hooed* fake tears. She dwarfed the smaller man; he looked like a toy next to her.

Wyatt heard Etan chuckling. Soon the soldiers were doubled over chortling.

"You're laughing at them?" Wyatt glanced up. He was incredulous. "Stop! They are not funny!"

"I… I can't help it." Etan tried unsuccessfully to look serious. His lips twitched, and Wyatt could see he was having a hard time stifling his hysterics.

Just then Howard collapsed with a loud howl. It was as if the laughter was being forced from it and painful to watch as it was to hear. Wyatt rose, still breathing heavily, his knees shaking. He moved to the center aisle of the bus, watching Etan and Howard break into giggles. Tears streamed down their face, and their eyes had an odd look of terror.

Clowns surrounded the bus, their filthy gloved hands touching the windows. He could hear tinny music in the background. One of the guards sobbed and tittered at the same time, his head in his hands.

"What's wrong with all of you?"

"Look! That one is so tall! She does look like—" Becca said after a spate of silliness.

"Be quiet!" Danai cut her off, holding her belly which shook with mirth.

The large red headed female reached into her oversized purse. All of the clowns in the street stopped to watch her. One left the group. He was holding a can that hissed with gas. He handed it to Candace through the window, who took it and held it to her chest.

"*Awww,* he's so cute," she said and dissolved into tears mixed with chuckles. "They don't want to hurt us. They're our friends," she said with a dreamy smile.

"*Oh* my God, it hurts!" Howard cried, holding his stomach as he laughed.

The female clown pulled out a brass bugle and blew taps. The group on the bus convulsed with laughter. Panting, Wyatt watched as each person sat breathlessly attempting unsuccessfully to stop. Dots were dancing in front of his eyes. He couldn't understand what they thought was funny until he glanced out the window again. The little clown looked sadly at the redhead, who was tapping her oversized shoe with impatience.

Wyatt felt hysteria bubble up from his stomach. It warred with the horror filling him until he felt he'd be split in two.

The red-haired female took out a pistol and shot the little clown point-blank in the cheek. Wyatt reared in fright but couldn't stop his shout of laughter. He was not alone. The bus was rocking with it.

The female turned to goose-step back to the building from where she first emerged.

Wyatt held his hands over his ears. Taking a deep breath, he realized he wanted to laugh again. He pulled his tee shirt over his mouth and yelled, "It's the gas!" His words were muffled by the material and had little impact on the others.

A man dressed in a colorful harlequin suit fiddled with the door of the bus. His fingers were squeezing in, prying the folding door open.

Wyatt did a double take at the canisters rolling around on the floor. He raced down the aisle, grabbing them and throwing each one out a broken window.

Etan's eyes opened wide with the realization that there was something in the stink bomb. He pulled off his scarf, revealing the stubble of salt-and-pepper hair, wrapping it around his mouth and nose. "Shoot them!" he ordered. "They want the bus!"

The three remaining guards followed Etan's lead, covering the lower part of their faces with their shirts.

The gas must have started to dissipate because the girls began screaming. There was the sound of more breaking glass, and each of the soldiers pointed their muzzles outside and sprayed the crowd with bullets. The clowns dispersed quickly, running for cover.

"Let's get out of here, Wyatt!" Etan shouted.

Wyatt pushed the dead driver from the seat and tried to shift the bus. It didn't move.

"We're stuck on the median."

Outside, the little man clown jumped up, blood leaking from a round hole in the side of his cheek, and ran after the oversized redhead holding his flower. Uproarious laughter bounced from the buildings on the street blasted from loudspeakers.

"They're trying to distract us," Howard said, his shirt collar covering his mouth and nose. He was shivering as if he was trying to stop giggling. "That's why they're dressed like clowns."

"I can think of another reason they're dressed like clowns!" Wyatt said sarcastically.

Howard Drucker nodded. "Clowns are frightening. It's the unknown. You can't guess what they are really thinking."

"I'm not in the mood for this right now." Wyatt grimaced. He was struggling with the stick shift, trying to get the bus to move.

"You're not alone, Wyatt. It's not uncommon to be afraid of clowns. It's called coulrophobia, from the Greek word—"

"Not now, Howard!" Wyatt shouted, feeling more in control of himself.

"Why wasn't he laughing?" Candace asked, pointing to Wyatt.

"Hyperventilating," Howard responded. "I might hate clowns, but apparently Wyatt's terrified of them."

"Can't you get this thing to move!" Etan yelled to Wyatt. He was leaning over Wyatt's shoulder. Their faces met in the mirror, and once again the fleeting feeling that he knew this man shivered through Wyatt even though Etan was still wearing sunglasses.

Music filled the air. Two cars pulled alongside them. All the girls moved to one side of the bus, absorbed in the scene taking place.

Wyatt looked sideways to see a group of people in macabre face paint perform a fire drill where they poured out of each car and switched vehicles. He shuddered but refused to move, his knuckles turning white on the steering wheel. Trying to concentrate on getting the bus off the median, he fought with the stick shaft, but dread made him glance up every so often to observe the clowns. Four gaudily dressed clowns kept exiting identical Volkswagens, rushing in a frantic but coordinated manner to the other cars.

Wyatt paused for a second, his eyes opening wide as a clown fired a pistol toward the driver's seat on the bus. He was frozen, his hand locked on the handle of the gear. Etan leaped toward him and grabbed Wyatt's shoulders, pulling him down to land on his side. Groaning, Wyatt rolled on the floor and stared at the bullet hole punched in the window where he'd been sitting. A red line scored Etan's sleeve. He had lost his sunglasses.

"You're hit," Wyatt whispered as though he couldn't find his voice.

Etan glanced at his shoulder. "It's just grazed."

"Sir!" Yerbol yelled. He raced to help Etan up.

"I'm fine, Lieutenant. At ease."

Yerbol handed Etan his own scarf to wrap the bloody wound.

Wyatt saw Etan's glasses on the floor. He picked them up and handed them to Etan so he could put them back on. Wyatt nodded with understanding. He knew that face; he just couldn't place it.

"Thanks," said Etan.

Outside the bus, there was a ripple of laughter followed by the beep of the horns as the two cars sped away. Shots peppered the bus again. Then it went silent.

Wyatt ventured a look. "I don't see anyone."

They sat in stupefied silence on the bus. "They're gone," Danai said.

"No, they're not," Howard observed, pointing to several doorways. "They want the bus. They don't want to destroy it trying to get to us. They don't want to hit the fuel line. They're finding another way to attack."

"Why are they dressed like that?" Adriane whined. "I don't like them now."

"It's a method to distract us while they incapacitate us with the laughing gas."

"Yeah, I was so distracted I almost peed," Frannie agreed.

"You know, it's laughing gas, like dentists use? Thanks to Wyatt's realization, it didn't work," said Howard.

"Dentists?" Becca asked. "What's that?"

"What do you think that was all about?" Danai redirected the question.

"The circus is coming to town?" Yerbol said dryly.

"We have to get out of here." Wyatt shook his head. He had questions for these girls, but now was not the time.

The bus lurched as the girls rose one by one, making it teeter precariously.

"No!" Howard shouted. "Stay where you are. I'll tell you when to move." He pointed for Etan to get into the driver's seat. "Make this sucker go when I tell you." Howard hopped over the seats to the front and stood in a wide-legged stance to combat the rocking. "Candace, Erin, move over there."

"What are you doing, Howard?" Wyatt shouted.

"Counterbalancing their weight." He pointed to the rear of the bus. "Walk slowly!"

The bus heaved as the large girls shifted. The metal groaned as the vehicle fell back onto the road off the pavement. It landed with a jolt. Etan instantly shifted gears, and they took off. A crowd of clowns followed them, gunshots and rocks hitting the side of the bus.

Wyatt felt them swerve onto a narrow winding road. The streets were quiet. They each took positions at the windows, watching for any signs of more attackers. Wyatt stared out the glassless window as they got onto the freeway. The dry wind cooled his overheated face. He realized where they were headed with shock.

Wyatt moved up to Etan and said, "You're going to Griffith Park? I thought you said you wanted to head to the Bowl or Arena."

Etan looked at Wyatt through the rearview mirror. "A good leader listens twice as much as he speaks."

Wyatt opened his mouth to reply, then snapped it shut. Sitting back, he thought about the man in front of him. Etan had saved his life. Wyatt resisted the growing feeling of respect for Etan. He tried to hold onto both his distrust and resentment, but he was bone tired. Hate was hard work and had to be stoked like a fire, and he found he couldn't summon those feelings. Though Etan still wore dark glasses, he knew the older man was observing him. Wyatt shuddered and turned his gaze to the passing scenery counting the exits to Griffith Park.

"You okay?" Etan asked him.

Before Wyatt could respond, he felt the bus slowing. Two jeeps were pulled horizontally in the street, blocking their route. Etan slowed the bus.

"There's the exit." Yerbol moved to the front of the bus. "Get off here." He pointed. "Anybody know how far it is from the exit?"

"It's just a few hundred—," Wyatt responded, the words trailing off.

Before anyone could finish, Etan's next comment ended the possibility of a discussion. "Company!" Etan called out.

The group pushed to gather at the front of the bus.

Wyatt saw the entrance to Griffith Park looming before them. Memories flashed of going to the LA Zoo with his father. It was always filled with bikers, joggers, and parents with their kids. There were no long lines, no crowds now, no radios blasting or excited pedestrians waiting to watch the animals. They turned onto the road that took them into the park.

A truck moved behind them, boxing them in. Wyatt exchanged an uneasy glance with Howard, who raised his eyebrows so high, they appeared to connect with his hairline. A skinny guard with a concave chest walked out, a helmet shading his eyes. He trained his gun directly on Etan.

Howard Drucker gasped, surging through the mass of girls blocking his way. He fumbled with the door mechanism. Wyatt watched with dawning horror. Howard was trying to get off the bus.

"Howard! No!" He reached for his shirt, his fingers coming up empty.

Howard burst through the folding doors of the bus and screamed, "Sheldon!"

He leaped off the steps, and Wyatt saw the muzzles turn to focus on Howard. "No!" he screamed.

The skinny guard lowered his gun and yelled, "At ease!" He raised the visor on his helmet and said, "Howard?"

CHAPTER 14

SCRAMBLED EGG

"WHATEVER YOU DO, don't go near the water," Melvin advised Jade.

"But you killed it, Mel. Smashed its brain to smithereens. It's not like it's going to grow a new brain or something." She moved closer, leaning into him. "I feel perfectly safe. I'm not afraid of anything as long as I'm with you."

Melvin felt his chest puff up with pride. "Yes, I did kill it. Still, I wish you would go with me."

Melvin had double-checked by swimming every inch of the lagoon. There was no sign of anything other than the resident fish and turtles.

Jade shook her head. "I'm not up to seeing my father just yet." She frowned. Her father was living on the reservation, and he hadn't adjusted well to the idea of Jade and Melvin's relationship. "After he told you to *fetch* last time… I don't know. It bothered me. He's…"

She searched for a word to explain her feelings. "He's disrespectful." She pouted. "It's rude."

"Well, he didn't take our wedding very well." Melvin smiled at the thought of their hasty marriage a few weeks ago. "I still would feel better—"

"Hush." She covered his mouth with her fingertips. Holding up an arm she flex her muscles. "I'll be fine."

Melvin smiled at her. She made him happy.

Jade walked away to tidy up the hut. She continued, "John Raven did such a nice ceremony. Keisha was so pretty with the flowers in her hair instead of snakes."

"It certainly made her more approachable. I wouldn't want to piss her off. Especially when she has this new ability to turn a person into stone."

Jade giggled. "She only tried to do that to Vincent Konrad and his followers. Besides, she swore she wasn't going to do that anymore. John Raven is teaching her to be a different spirit animal, but she won't tell me what it is yet. If it were me, I'd pick a bird."

Melvin looked up, his eyes questioning. "You... *you don't like wolves?*"

"No, silly." Jade placed a comforting hand on his arm. "I meant for Keisha. I'd pick a bird for Keisha. Someday," she said dreamily, "We'll start a family. Can you imagine me sitting on an egg?" She sighed loudly. "I wish Daddy could find some happiness with my choice."

"It doesn't bother me, Jade," Melvin told her as he loaded a Monsterland backpack with supplies.

She leaned over to observe his bundle. "What are you doing?"

"Offering up some trade with Carter Wright. I took a bunch of supplies from the dispensary."

"Yes, they do appear much more fragile than we are. I definitely enjoy the side effect of increased strength," Jade agreed. "What are you hoping to trade for?"

Melvin looked out the quiet pond, the mirror-like surface sparkling in the sunlight.

"A gun." He wrapped her in a tight embrace. "Remember what I said: don't go near the water."

"Mel, you said it was safe. I'm not worried."

Melvin shrugged. "Still, stick to our camp. I should be back sometime before nightfall."

"Got it." Jade squeezed him back. "I'll be waiting for you right here."

"I really wish you'd come with me," Melvin said hopefully.

Jade shook her head. "It's dead, pulverized. If I see anything strange, I'll morph and outrun it. Don't be such a worrywart." Melvin rested his chin on the top of her hair. He hated leaving her. "Trust me to take care of myself. You've taught me so much. I'm not as stupid as everybody thinks," she said indignantly.

"I never thought you weren't smart!"

"Well, when you carry on like this, you make me think you don't believe in me."

He kissed her and hefted the bag onto his shoulder. "I believe in everything you do and say. I'll be back as soon as I can."

Melvin stripped off his clothes and transformed as soon as he left Monsterland, his four paws and increased speed making better time than human walking. He kept a grueling pace, knowing he wanted to get to the reservation, exchange goods, and get back.

He was not happy about leaving Jade, but he felt a responsibility to protect their home. He knew, too, that Jade's father had upset her. He was planning on having a talk with him. He knew Jade missed her dad, and if he spoke to him man to man, without Jade there, maybe he'd thaw out and come visit her.

The ground scorched the pads of his feet. Twice he made contact with a pack of coyotes. He stopped for a quick chat. They shared whatever information they had.

Glad I caught up with you! Melvin greeted them. *I need a favor.*

Sure, Buster, the largest coyote's bobbed his head. *What, can we do for you, brother?*

He asked about Wyatt and Howard, first. His request would keep for a minute. The four-legged grapevine indicated they'd made it to the outskirts of LA. They'd had to fight their way into the city.

Who saw them?

Some cat I know. Lives in the hills. Terrorizes the rich idiots, Buster snickered.

They told him the towns were deserted, the human world upended. Whatever people had survived the Glob had run to the inner cities to find there were no supplies to live.

The cities are a wasteland. Food ran out. I heard they were acting like animals, Buster finished his tale.

His buddy Jacomo added, *Lawlessness. People are being corralled in giant stadiums to stay protected. Safety in numbers, that type of thing.*

What about the gangs?

Most of them died with the mummies. Just got to worry about ourselves now, Buster murmured.

Melvin grunted. Many of these guys had relatives in town, family dogs that could no longer be provided with food. *Shame.* Buster shook his head. *Domesticated animals don't know how to survive. They're used to taking Prozac when it's thundering. How in the hell are they going to make it in this hostile world? I got a cousin who can't eat meat! You believe that? She's allergic.* They all chuckled at the thought of being allergic to meat. *She eats quinoa and berries. Ha! They aren't going to waste food on a pet no matter how much they say they love you.*

Did you offer to take her with you? Melvin asked.

Dude, they're from LA. They don't do camping. They're into glamping.

Glamping? Is that even a word? Melvin asked.

Beats me. Humans. Some can't live without pets. Made the brethren soft. I feel for them, but they ain't gonna last.

I hear you, Melvin growled. *See anything else you want to share?*

Jocomo gave Buster a furtive look.

What? Melvin asked.

You're gonna think we're crazy, Buster answered.

All coyotes are crazy. They all laughed.

What's up?

Buster moved closer as if to whisper into Melvin's fur-tufted ear. *I saw monsters.*

Melvin howled with laughter. *Yeah, and who hasn't?*

No, dude. Buster moved in a tight circle with nervousness. *Really, six identical monsters.*

Yeah! Jocomo interrupted. *They were tall.*

How tall? Melvin asked, his head tilted. His eyes were all seriousness.

Jocomo nudged Buster with his nose. *Show him, bro.*

Buster turned. *See that crease in the hills?*

Melvin studied the craggy facade of the sandstone mountains. *It's a cave. It doesn't look so big to me.*

Well, six big dudes the size of... you know that big rock at Haskin's Pass, down by—

I know where it is. Wow, that tall? Melvin nodded.

Dude, Buster added in a lowered voice, *I saw them come out all at once. One of them was kicking up a big fuss. Lost something and was screaming fiercely about it. They parked themselves outside Victorville and waited for the sun to go down. Then they headed straight for the reservation.*

What do they want with the reservation?

Buster shrugged. *Who knows? Who cares? They were some big mother...*

Okay, I get it. Tall?

Taller than a two-story building.

Melvin grinned. *You chewing on the peyote bush, bro?*

I swear on the great star of Sirius. They were big.

Hmmm. Melvin was thoughtful. *I have to head past there.*

Be careful, Jocomo advised. *Did you hear what they're saying about Konrad?*

All three of them spat on the ground in unison.

What? Melvin asked.

They say he escaped.

I saw him on the helicopter.

Rumor is he's holed up on Prendick Rock.

Reliable source.

Buster smirked. *Gonna trust a human over a cat?*

Well, it's impossible to check out unless you have a boat. Besides, they say there's a zombie colony there.

What are you talking about? There's a network of caves by the Sign that will take you right there. You can walk underground, straight across the channel.

Under the water! Network of caves? Melvin's brows rose to the top of his canine head. *Who built that?*

Maybe the big dudes made them. Who knows? This cat told me Konrad's got some kind of underwater aquarium there. Humans are too stupid to figure it out.

Humpf. The Great White Shark Park. Melvin added, then clarified. *That's been closed for years.*

I think there's a connection between those caves and the monsters we saw, Jocomo added.

Melvin didn't care about caves. All he thought about was Jade. It wasn't that he wasn't concerned about his friends; he had other worries now. That brought him to his favor.

They nodded and wished each other a safe journey. Melvin asked them to keep an eye out for the road leading to Monsterland. *Jade's back there.* He nodded toward the broken-down theme park. *Can you keep an eye on the place for me? Oh, and don't let her know, okay.*

The coyotes looked back at the wreckage of Monsterland.

Yeah, sure. We'll watch the place for you.

Enjoy catching the Road Runner. Melvin laughed.

What roadrunner, bro? You saw a roadrunner?

Nah, forget it. human joke. Melvin took off toward the reservation, feeling lighter about Jade but troubled about the cities.

Yes, he thought, that's what he liked about his new world. They all helped each other. The animals didn't compete. There were no petty jealousies or competition… well, he had to admit, except for when a female was involved. Then it was a simple fight, winner take all.

He thought about the changes in the big world. The roving bands of outlaws from the nearby towns had quieted down. The mummies had claimed too many of them to be an effective fighting source. People were migrating to the big cities. Melvin understood the need. There was little in the desert, and unless they had the skills to hunt for food or find water, most people wouldn›t survive

The last coyote he'd met on the trail had directed him to a small stream where he would find water. Melvin ran, his feet kicking up clots of dirt, the heat barely affecting him. He panted a bit more, and just when he felt genuine thirst, he found the twisted trickle of water that served as hydration to the animals living in the area. The stream seemed to start in the same place where the other coyotes had shown him the caves. Melvin walked on the uneven ground carefully. He was hot and thirsty.

He lapped up the water. It was cold, bitingly refreshing. He scanned the direction from where it came. It poured from a fissure in a rock wall that allowed water to spill from underground. Melvin's nose twitched. It looked a lot bigger here than from downhill.

It was too quiet, he determined. No birds flew around. A hot breeze *whooshed* past him, but that was the only sound.

He tasted the air, knowing the odor was unfamiliar. It was musty and damp, like mushrooms or when laundry is left wet where it won't dry. He moved closer, sniffing. His ears wiggled, the small tufts of fur swaying from a soft wind coming from the fissure in the rocks.

Melvin climbed an incline, loose rocks making the hill slippery. He looked down to see pebbles fall onto the surface of the desert.

Must be an earthquake, he thought. *I'd better get out of here.*

A boulder groaned, rocks made a sound grinding against each other, and the earth shook . The terrain shifted under Melvin's feet, and he lost his balance, his four feet splaying, the backpack swinging wildly, sending him crashing down the hill. Melvin gripped the dirt with his paws, his nails scoring a trail as he slipped down.

He gritted his teeth, angry at himself for taking a chance. *Curiosity killed the cat*, he cursed silently.

He turned in a tight circle and leaped across a gully in time to see the ground heave as if an earthquake were shattering it. The rocks parted, releasing a torrent of water that rushed down the cliff.

Melvin shook his head. He heard a steady pounding. Turning toward his destination, he took off as fast as he could. Heading back to where he came from, he decided he would use a different route. He already started planning his return. He needed to get in, see Carter Wright, and get the hell out of Dodge.

Melvin had adjusted to human form and dressed by the time he reached the outskirts of the reservation.

The caw of a raven made him look upward and smile. The bird flew past him, followed by two kestrels, who brushed the top of his head with their feathery wings. *Keisha must have chosen a bird*, he thought. *I have to tell Jade she was right.*

Gray and small, they whizzed over his head, whispers dancing around his ears. *Keisha and Lily*, he mused. They landed on a large rock. He heard the raven screech loudly.

Melvin turned, shading his eyes against the glare of the sun. By the time he faced forward, Keisha and Lily were sitting on the rocks in human form, smiling expectantly at him. He trotted forward, and they embraced in a three-way hug.

"You didn't bring Jade?" Keisha pouted. Her braids were gone, and her hair was now puffed out in an oversized Afro. She was almost as tall as Melvin. Dressed in doeskin breeches and a tunic courtesy of Lily's people, she looked leaner and more toned than he'd ever seen her.

Lily was softer looking, shorter, with a black waterfall of hair, gray feathers dangling from the side. She waved to the raven, who circled around them, then headed west toward their encampment.

"How are things with the newlyweds?" Keisha asked.

Melvin blushed, and both girls burst out laughing. "Don't go all shy on me now." Keisha punched his shoulder.

"What happened to Medusa, Keisha? Jade said you were giving it up. I thought you *rocked* it."

The teens all chuckled at that.

They started walking toward the fence surrounding reservation land. "Too hard to practice. I almost turned Jade's father into a statue, so I gave it up. John Raven's been teaching me more useful shapeshifting. You should try it."

"*Aw*, shapeshifting is for the birds." He laughed. The girls giggled with him. "Looks like you got a good teacher." Melvin nodded with appreciation.

Keisha exchanged a look with Lily.

Melvin watched the two girls. "What? What's that all about?"

"Nothing," Lily said hastily, changing the subject. "Tell me how Jade is doing. Does she miss her dad too much?"

Melvin snorted. "I don›t think so." He paused and shrugged. "Maybe a little bit."

"Well, she shouldn't, especially not after the way he behaved at the wedding," Keisha said grimly.

"Any word from Wyatt… and Howard Drucker?" Keisha asked, then looked away.

"Raven and Tocho caught sight of them outside Victorville." They walked over the rocky trail.

"Tocho?" Melvin looked up at both girls. "Who's Tocho?"

"Just one of the guys," Lilly said hastily. "My great-uncle and Tocho hooked up with some soldiers returning to their bases. Raven said it was strange. They were commando types. He couldn't go further, so we don't know if they are in LA yet." She turned to Melvin. "What about you? You hear anything from your furry friends about them?"

"They made it to Los Angeles. A mountain lion saw them and told some of my local pack about it. How are things here?" Melvin asked quietly.

They passed through an opening in the fence and headed toward a trailer down an unpaved dirt road. The door opened and Melvin smiled. Carter Wright bounded down the two wooden steps, his hand outstretched. "Nice to see you, Mel. Come on out of the sun."

They moved out of the heat into the dim interior of the trailer.

"We've set up a provisional police force. I have a spot for you if you want to move here, Melvin." Carter Wright poured Melvin a cup of black coffee.

Melvin looked around, squinting. Jade's father sat at a desk, drumming his thick fingers. The tattoos inked on his fingers were bright on his freckled skin; *D-E-A-D M-E-A-T*, it read, more appropriate for his old profession of a butcher, less politically correct now that Jade's father was an acting police officer.

"Hi, Mr. Zadowski."

Jade's father ignored him. His eyes had a glassy quality to them. Melvin shivered from the hate emanating from them.

The former butcher was watching Melvin through slitted lids. "How's my daughter?" he ground out.

"Doing well." Melvin dipped his head, annoyed that his voice squeaked. He peered at the other people in the room. "I'd like to have a word with—" the words died on his lips.

Mr. Zadowski shook his head. An uncomfortable silence hung over the small room. Melvin changed the subject. "It's dark in here," he said, changing the subject.

"Yeah, no electricity yet, but Raven's been working on getting something up with gasoline," a voice said from one of the corners of the room.

Squinting into the dark recesses of the railer, Melvin tried to locate who was there. He heard papers rustling and when a drawer slammed shut, he saw a tall, rangy man rise from the desk. He glided from the shadows and brushed past Melvin, without saying anything. He seemed annoyed at the intrusion. Keisha laughed nervously.

"Tocho, this is our friend, Melvin." Her voice was strangely high, as if she were anxious.

"I know who it is." Tocho continued walking away ignoring Melvin's presence.

Melvin smirked and looked at Carter who explained, "He's new. Came from the north."

"He's my cousin," Lily offered. "I don't know what's come over him. He's usually much friendlier." She jumped when Tocho exited the trailer loudly, the door slamming shut behind him.

Melvin blew on the hot liquid, took a sip, and closed his eyes as if Tocho rudeness was unimportant to him. Truth was, it wasn't. "No matter how many times I show Jade, she doesn't know how to make coffee." Melvin glanced at her father, who still ignored him.

"Can we talk?" he asked Carter.

Carter nodded.

Melvin lowered his voice. "Couple of things. I met a few friends on the way here. They said Vincent Konrad hiding on Prendick Rock."

"Prendick Rock? Isn't that the…"

"It used to be his aquarium. The Great White Shark Park."

"Who else knows?"

"Not sure. Truth is I have something else on my mind." Melvin swallowed. "A funny thing happened back at my home, *um…* you know, where Monsterland used to be." He began telling them of the conflict with the sea creature.

"You sure all you're drinking is coffee?" Keisha asked from where she sat cross-legged on a desk. She was peeking out of the window, her face concerned.

"I know; it's hard to believe," Melvin retorted.

"As hard as believing people can turn into werewolves?" Carter poured more coffee.

"Maybe it was a bear?" Lily offered.

"No. I saw it fully. I pulled off one of its arms." Melvin put down his cup, looking down. "I fought and broke the creature in half. Then I crushed its skull."

"And you left my kid there?" Archie Zadowski, exploded.

"She'll be fine. I told her to stay out of the water," Melvin assured him.

"Why didn't you bring her?" he demanded.

Melvin took a rapid breath, his face coloring. He avoided making eye contact with his father-in-law, who giggled. "*Umm…* she didn't want to-"

Archie stood up, his fists raised. "What? See me?"

Melvin shrugged. "You said it."

Carter snapped, "Cool it!"

Archie moved closer to Melvin who bared long yellow teeth.

"I said, stop. Now," Carter's voice cut through the tension. He had his hand on his holster. "I mean it, Arch."

Archie sat down but not before giving Melvin a searing look of hatred..

"Wow," Keisha said, diverting the conversation. "You think… could it be someone shapeshifting?"

"Not likely." Carter looked at Keisha. "Have you ever heard of morphing into a water creature?"

Lily shook her head. "No."

"What do you make of this?" Melvin pulled out one of the round rocks from his backpack and placed it on the table.

Carter leaned over. "Keisha, maybe you should have a look?"

The door slammed, and John Raven, Lily's great-uncle, walked into the room. John Raven was all corded muscle despite his age, and with the hungry look of a predator. He was clean-shaven with a headful of long graying hair pulled back into a ponytail.

Carter held the rock, absorbed in studying it. John Raven moved closer to see. He glanced sharply at Keisha and said, "What's up with Tocho? He stalked right past me."

"I'm not sure," she said, and Melvin wondered why he felt tension emanating from her body.

Keisha reached out to hold the rock. Her brown fingers glided over the rough surface. "What do you think it is, John?" she asked.

Raven's brow furrowed in concentration. "Where did you say you found this?" He sniffed it, frowning.

"Jade's been picking them up from the lagoon." Melvin smiled. "She likes to decorate our home with them," he added sheepishly. "She likes pretty things."

"I think…" John Raven said. "I think this is an egg."

"What?" Melvin looked up.

There was a screech of metal, and the room tilted, sending John and Keisha tumbling against the corrugated wall. Keisha's head cracked against John's. They both went down as if they had been coldcocked.

"Earthquake?" Carter attempted to stand.

The desk slid, and Lily fell to her knees. Metal groaned as the trailer was torn from its pilings. Lily fell forward, wedged against the wall by a desk.

Melvin pulled himself to the window. "Holy crap!"

A huge face moved over the opening. The oversized hand reached in and pulled Melvin by the shirt. "No need you!" the voice roared. He touched Melvin's head with a surprisingly gentle hand. "Look at you. Red hair."

The giant stood thirty feet tall. He laughed, and Melvin was buffeted by the gusts of wind blowing in his face. The odor was familiar. It was the same stench he had smelled by the rocks. The creature tossed him away like discarded garbage.

Melvin landed with a painful thud. He heard Carter and the others tumbling in the trailer. Two enormous humanoids moved the structure as if it were a building block.

Melvin heard a feral growl and a mountain lion jumped from a cluster of bushes attaching itself to the back of one of the giants.

The creature bellowed, it's partner slapped the mountain lion from its back, slamming it against the ground where it lay motionless. It raised a big foot to crush the skull. The giant lost its balance and missed the cat's head.

"No!" Sean, Wyatt's younger brother, dashed from behind a stack of boxes. Melvin reached forward and yanked him to safety. Sean landed on the ground next to him.

"Stay!" Melvin ordered.

"I'm not one of your dogs!" Sean yelled, trying to escape. Melvin held onto the back of his shirt, pushing him down hard onto the earth. "They're huge. Look what they did to that cat. Wait until we can regroup and do something with a strategy."

Sean's eyes were bugging out of his skull. Melvin placed a reassuring hand on his shoulder. "D'ya think I'd let anything happen to any of you? Let me figure this out."

Gunfire exploded around them from Carter's police force. Melvin's jaw dropped. The bullets bounced off their flesh as if they wore armor. Carter's officers were scattered all over the perimeter, hiding behind other trailers, firing on the invaders. The giants batted away the bullets like pesky flies. Melvin looked for Tocho snarling when he realized was nowhere to be found. He had fled.

The monstrous man turned, his eyes landing on the younger boy. He reached over, flicked Melvin away, plucked up Sean, and dropped him in the trailer like a fisherman collecting bait.

Melvin lunged after them, a giant hand flicked his head, sending him five feet into the air. He landed, his skull connecting with a rock, and before he passed out, he heard the giant rumble, "I got all six. Let's go."

CHAPTER 15

UNSINKABLE

ROSEMARY STOOD IN the rear of the control center, her back against the wall. Her father's well-oiled machine seemed to be running smoothly. She admired the way his employees worked, they seemed happy, not intimidated at all by him. After finally meeting him face-to-face at the dinner last night, resentment had lodged itself on her shoulder and she had trouble meeting his invasive gaze. He was not what she expected. She paused to look around, and then sized her father up. The air of menace she felt the evening before was gone and in its place was this affable and engaging person. He appeared to be a born leader, her chest expanded a bit with pride. *An inherited skill?* She wondered briefly about his parents, her grandparents. Rosemary's brows furrowed, she hoped she wasn't allowing others like Shandy to influence her feelings about him. They had talked about Vincent at length last night, Shandy urged her to remain alert. He advised her to keep her distance.

She watched Vincent's every move, as if trying to prove to herself that perhaps she had judged him unfairly. She waffled from the need to escape to fascination with someone she was related to and all he had accomplished. The place was awesome in its scope. She was baffled and confused by the unfamiliar sensation of uncertainty.

Rows of computer screens lit up the faces of the technicians manning them. Her father lurched around the room, his gait awkward and uneven.

"Where did you get your staff in these difficult times? Most people are afraid to leave their homes, or what's left of them," she said.

"Money is a great motivator. I hold all the cards."

Dreg, his little lackey, tagged along behind him, picking up whatever her ungainly father dropped from his uncoordinated hands. Vincent sipped continually from a souvenir chalice that read *Monsterland for a Monsterthirst*. The clear plastic was filled with the thick purple fluid.

Every so often, Rosemary would look up to catch her father observing her. She met his gaze boldly, refusing to let him know he had the ability to unnerve her. Vincent seemed tickled by her independence and she noticed a glint of admiration in his eyes. It had a strange effect on her, and she caught herself sharing a smile with him.

Rosemary tapped her cheek with a finger while she tried to identify the curious feelings in her heart, an organ she long felt had hardened into a tiny object. Yet, she felt it slowing thawing. She was drawn like a moth to a flame to her father. He was so different, strange and exciting at the same time. While last night was overlaid with a sensation of threat or menace, today as she toured the facility, Vincent was charming, his attention devoted solely to her. He created a camaraderie and closeness as if she was the most important person in the world. They were alone, except for the fawning troll of a man, Dreg, who trailed their steps with slavish devotion.

A large screen took up the entire wall before them, different colored electronic dots moving across a vast map of the world.

"That's you right there." Vincent pointed to a red dot. "The ship I gave you."

Rosemary turned to see her father standing closely next to her. She sneered at Dreg, her mouth turned down and responded boldly. "Yes, and speaking of that, as your *daughter* don't you think I deserve something a bit more substantial?" She walked away, putting distance between them.

Vincent laughed. "I like your spirit, Rosemary! I have much better things in store for you. Give that ship to your lackeys and let them leave." He stumbled over and placed his arm around her. "They don't exactly fit in." He was leaning heavily against her.

"What does that mean?"

"Shandy's got an attitude problem. He'll never take orders, not even from you."

Rosemary face reddened. It was true she was the captain, but Shandy was her mentor, not the subordinate Vincent described. He'd stepped out of the leadership role willingly so that she could learn.

"And the giant is too stupid to be of use." Vincent's voice was dismissive.

"Jötnar is not stupid!"

"Really, my dear, it's not a reflection on you, but destiny has put you in the palm of my hands and the greatness they hold for you."

"Maybe I'm not interested in what you are offering" She shook off his arm from her shoulder and moved away from him. "Maybe I like my life the way it is."

The sound of all the blips and beeps, the absolute unnatural silence of the workers around her, and the canned air made her nervous. She didn't like where the conversation was going. Alarm bells started to ring in her head, but she silenced them. *Curiosity killed the cat,* she head Shandy's voice warning her. Rosemary firmed her lips. *I'm in control and I'm not a cat.*

"Oh, I'd recognize that expression anywhere." Vincent laughed and directed his attention to Dreg. "Well, did you find my phone yet?" he demanded, his voice raised.

Dreg glanced around the room. He leaned forward and whispered something.

"What? What? Speak up, man! I can't hear you when you mumble!"

Dreg cleared his throat. "You had it last," Dreg said in a squeaky whisper.

Rosemary looked away, her face turning hot. She knew she was smirking, so she faced the monitors.

"Me? I gave it to you." Vincent walked forward, his hands outstretched. He pushed Dreg on the chest, each word spoken with a shove. "*I. Gave. It. To. You!* You're always losing things. You can't keep track of your own head. Go find that cell phone! Leave me!" He threw his Monsterland container at Dreg. "If you can't remember where you've put my phone, do you think you can bring me another drink? This time fill it all the way to the top," he ordered.

"We're running low." Dreg held the container up.

Vincent sneered.

Dreg limped away, hugging the oversized cup to his chest, repeating the demand like a litany.

"Your phone is missing?" Rosemary tried to keep her voice normal. She was going to tell Shandy to chuck it in the ocean the next time she saw him.

Vincent gave a long-suffering sigh. "Help. It's such an issue. I wish the zombies could be trained. *Oh* well." He looked at her. "Where are those guard dogs of yours?"

Rosemary lifted one shoulder negligently. "Shandy and Jötnar? They're outfitting that poor excuse of a vessel you gave me."

Vincent wagged a finger. "You don't appreciate my gift? It's a good ship. Unsinkable. You think I would put my only daughter in an unseaworthy craft?" He paused and moved closer, his voice soft. "It would be better if you to put your wandering days away."

"I'll decided when I'm ready to do something like that."

"I admire your spunk, I wouldn't want to confuse it with stupidity."

Rosemary bristled, then took a deep breath ignoring where the conversation was going. "It's small. If you'd give me the Destroyer..."

Vincent pointed to the screen before them. "It's gone already. Sent it to New Patagonia. There are reports of an illegal zombie colony. They are headed there to clean it out and bring me the survivors."

Rosemary frowned. "No one cares about the zombies anymore." She opened her mouth to complain about their presence on this island when he smiled.

Vincent laughed. "I care. Walk with me." He took her arm, leaning heavily against her as they strolled toward the corridor. He patted her hand with affection. "You know, I am so very impressed with you and all you've accomplished."

Reluctantly she allowed him to lean into her. "You have the time to leave your work?" Rosemary asked, gesturing to the control room.

"I can spare the time for you," Vincent responded. He smiled sincerely, and Rosemary's breath caught with bewilderment. Here was the paradox again. Now he was charming, effervescent, all signs of hostility gone. Vincent was making her feel, she searched for the word...*cherished*. It was a novel sensation. For a minute the ice defrosted in her heart, Shandy's cautionary words becoming faint in her memory.

She shook herself, trying to produce the distrust she felt for him, but found herself letting her guard down. Shandy would disapprove, call her a gullible sad sack. For a moment she reveled in the sensation of being part of something larger than Shandy and herself.

Vincent hung on her every word. She had to remind herself again what Shandy warned, yet for the first time she doubted her old friend. *Why did he choose this moment to inform her that her mother had been a zombie, with the implication that somehow Vincent was involved?*

She had nothing. Vincent had everything. It was her nature to take. Wasn't that what Shandy had drilled into her most of her life? There was no reason not to *take* advantage of this situation.

Vincent kept her close to him. His ragged breathing vibrated against the skin of her arm where he held her. She matched her steps to his awkward ones and finding it funny that walking in tandem with him left her giddy.

Rosemary's brain played havoc with her emotions. Little vignettes of what her life might have been with a father played out in her mind. Father/daughter dances, princess birthdays, and her first valentine rushed through her troubled thoughts. Her logical half sneered to grow up and stop being desperate. She had trouble separating her emotions for the first time in her life. She didn't know where to place these foreign thoughts.

Dreg shuffled into the room, and the warm feelings Rosemary had evaporated when she spied the strange man's eyes on her. Dreg glared like a jealous lover, his dark orbs smoldering. She disengaged from Vincent, and her hands automatically looked for her dagger or pistol, both taken from her when they first arrived. She was still close enough to feel Vincent tremble with suppressed rage.

"What is it?" Vincent hissed.

She must have gasped because her father growled at the crooked little man, snatching the vessel Dreg held and downing it in a single long gulp.

"What else can I get you, Vincent?" Dreg groveled.

Vincent smiled, his rotten black teeth a broken trail in his mouth. Vincent patted Dreg's head like a favored pet.

Dreg fawned. She swore he looked like he was going to fall to his knees and roll onto his back like a dog. He was staring with slavish devotion. Rosemary recoiled, wondering if she looked at gullible.

Was this her future? Would she trade who she was to become some sniveling slave looking for crumbs of Vincents approval for the delusional thoughts of belonging to a family.

Who was she fooling? Vincent wasn't her family. She looked around at the rock-like walls, the canned echoes of their voices, the lack of sunlike and fresh air.. She didn't belong underground in this tomb.

Rosemary scrubbed the spot where he had touched her arm. As she backed away, her face burned. *What was wrong with her?* A little condescension from this accidental gene pool and she dissolved into a weak puddle of neediness. She stood taller, straightening her back. She had to get away from this place. It was changing her. Sometimes a blood connection had no more impact than a transfusion. She needed to be with the people who understood her, Shandy and Jötnar.

Rosemary shuddered with revulsion, her skin crawling. Even though Dreg was bowed in supplication, she saw his eyes darting up at her malevolently. She looked at Vincent. Who had Dreg been before he'd met her him? What part of his soul did he sell to be in his company? She studied both men. Resentment and suspicion flooded as all her warm feelings evaporated. *What exactly did her father expect from her?* Did he seriously think she would grovel for anything? She felt the comfort of her barriers returning.

Vincent stared at her in the gloomy hallway. He sighed, and she could see something spark behind his eyes. Her gut tightened with apprehension and pasted a phony smile on her face.

"Well, thanks for the tour."

"Don't leave." It was a command. His voice softened again. "I have so much more to show you."

"You can go now, Dreg." Vincent shooed him with his grayish oversized hands. Rosemary noticed the beds of his nails were turning black. He patted his chest pocket.

"Where is that thing?" he said absently. "Dreg, you must find my phone. Locate it and bring it back here."

"Is that normal?" Rosemary pointed to his fingertips. "I've taken too much of your time. Perhaps you should rest."

Vincent shrugged. "Rest! When I have so much to do? I must

drink the fuel to keep myself alive. If the body is failing, as I think it is, I will have to find another host soon enough. Are you still here?" he snapped at Dreg. "I gave you an order! I want to be alone with my daughter."

Rosemary swore she heard Dreg's teeth gnash. He growled, "Of course, Vincent. Why wouldn't you want to spend quality time with your child? I only wish I could spend some time with my Natie… you know, my son, the president."

Rosemary froze where she stood. *Impossible. Dreg related to Nate Owens.*

Vincent ignored him.

"Nate… His son is President Nate Owens?" Rosemary demanded.

"Yes. He *was* the president for a short time. Put his nose where it didn't belong. I told him to stay quiet, that he'd be protected. But did he listen? No! Put himself and my plans in harm's way and was taken out by the military in a nasty little coup d'état." Vincent's voice rose with indignation. "He had explicit orders, and now look what happened! Instead of being in the White House, I'm stuck on this godforsaken island in the middle of nowhere, hunting for marine life to finish what we started. If he'd followed instructions, I'd have a fleet of nuclear subs and wouldn't have to resort…" Vincent paused breathlessly, the fathomless holes for eyes resting on Rosemary. He grabbed her arm in an iron grip. "But then you wouldn't have gotten this chance to shine, my girl, and that's what you did by bringing me the giant octopus. I'm so proud of you."

She watched Dreg slither out of the room, his lips frozen in a sneer.

Vincent opened his mouth. Rosemary was assaulted by a foul odor. She tried to disengage, but Vincent held her fast and refused to let her go. She pried his fingers from her arm, feeling trapped. Her thoughts returned to that closet again, but this time instead of seeking the warm cocoon she was overwhelmed with horror, she felt a mounting need to escape.

Vincent turned to one of his subordinates and ordered, "I want to know when the *Carpathian* docks in New Zealand, and tell the captain of the *Stargazer* to prepare for departure."

The tech typed in the orders and paused when an electronic message came back.

"He's on the radio for you, sir. He'd like to talk to you," the tech said.

Vincent pulled away impatiently, stomping over to the console with his angry, awkward steps. Rosemary looked longingly at the door. She began to inch toward escape.

Vincent turned to her, shouting, "Stay where you are!" Rosemary froze in her tracks.

The screen above them opened up with the outraged commander of the *Stargazer* on the screen.

"I can't abide this, Konrad." The captain held up a sheaf of papers. "It's unconscionable."

"When I last looked, I was in charge of our navy," said Vincent.

"You can't expect me to follow these orders. They're insane."

Rosemary's attention was diverted to the growing tension emanating from Vincent. Her eyes were glued to the large screen. The man wore the uniform of a captain.

"Captain Pufahl, I can and you must," said Vincent. "This is war, and we must control the port cities."

"Unleashing zombies on the general population goes against everything we are supposed to be doing. I question if these are the orders of a mad man."

"You dare to mutiny?" Vincent said with deadly calm. "Me? You're the supreme commander to whom you swore an oath?"

The commander threw down the papers he was holding. "I swore an oath to protect—"

"Cut his sound!" Vincent hissed.

Rosemary's breath caught in her throat. *Unleashing the zombies! It was inhumane!*

Vincent motioned to one of his men on an upper deck. He held his hand out like an emperor of ancient Rome, turning his thumb down. The tech nodded, twisted to his control station, and depressed a button.

"Ours is not to question why; ours is—" Vincent said in a singsong voice.

The ship took a direct hit, the bridge exploding into chaos of smoke and noise. Another hit and the screen went gray with static, the last image of the panicked faces of the crew.

Vincent continued his song: "—to do or die."

"You killed them." Rosemary›s face was drained of color.

"Just so." Vincent walked toward her. "As leader of the world, I can't lose control of my troops."

Rosemary backed away from him. Any kind thought she might have still felt for him evaporated like smoke.

"You're a monster," she whispered. "Those were *your* people."

"There are things you don't understand, Rosemary. I answer to a higher—"

"You're mad!"

"No, not exactly. A little pissed." He shrugged. "They mutinied, forfeiting their lives. You know the rules of the sea."

Indeed, she knew the rules of both the land and the sea. She was a pirate, raised by Shandy, a rogue from the top of her head to the bottoms of her soles, but she was not a murderer.

She knew then that she couldn't have anything to do with this biological mistake. Her decision was made. She needed to get on board her ship and get as far from this fiend as she could.

Instinct told Rosemary that she had to resist the urge to run. He'd blow her to kingdom come if he had the chance. She'd find Shandy and Jötnar, figure out a way to get out of there, and take the damn octopus as well.

Vincent clamped his hand on her arm again. She struggled as they walked into the corridor, personnel rushing past them. He ignored her movements and continued to his tour of the facility as if she were compliant.

Dreg approached them again, holding a heavy silver tray with another jug of the strange fluid. His smile faded when Vincent brushed past him as he continued their stroll.

Rosemary turned around to see the hunchback's face twist with hatred.

"You're hurting me."

"Nonsense." He smiled down at her.

She tried to disengage from him. "Let me go— "

Vincent discussed the flora and fauna of the island. Rosemary kept her responses cool, just shy of uninterested.

They walked toward the end of the corridor, then turned and entered Vincent's lavish dining room again. The sea undulated around them in the panoramic windows. Schools of fish, like gentle clouds, shimmered in the murky water.

Rosemary extricated her arm from his grasp. The weight of the water was smothering her. She longed to be on the deck of a ship. *Her ship.*

"Sit, my child. We need to talk. We need to discuss my succession plan," Vincent said, interrupting her racing thoughts.

"What?" Rosemary's voice came out in a croak. She turned to stare at him. "I don't understand you."

"We plot, we plan.... Nobody lives forever, my girl. Do you understand me now?"

"Are you talking about me?"

"You... or your child?" Vincent turned away to face the seafloor. "For whom am I saving the world... myself?" He laughed again. "It was always for you, for the children of the world. The next generation."

"You don't give a crap about me, or anyone else!" She made a beeline for the doorway. She was getting out of there.

"Can you condemn a man for caring too much?" Vincent stood

unsteadily, staring out of the window, his eyes bleak. "You can't blame me. I do what I have to… what others promise, I accomplish. It may hurt, but that is the price of saving this planet. Now, as for you, I won't be cheated out of the experience of bringing up a child of my flesh and blood."

She paused at the portal. "Our reunion is over, Vincent. I think we both realize this isn't going to work."

"I'm not so sure of that, Rosemary. I want to bring up a child that you are going to bear for me. This is bigger than us. The world is run by fools. Left to their own devices, humankind is ruining the globe." He turned to face her, his eyes fierce now. "Rosemary, dear, that tough world where I left you to grow has made you stronger than others. You think on your feet." He walked toward her. His cold gray hand caressed her face, no longer clumsy but tender. "Hard choices have to be made, and I have watched you. I think you have the stomach for it. There is no doubt you are my child, Rosemary. Of this I am sure."

Rosemary shook her head. This was too much. She watched him, a chill running up her spine. She shrunk back from him, frightened. He was observing her, his eyes hard like marbles. She felt exposed, vulnerable. This was scarier than any dark closet she'd ever entered.

"I just want a ship, and I want to go. I'm not interested in power. I brought you your creature." She was surprised at how her voice came out like a whine. She cleared her throat, but he stopped her.

"Yes, you did. You alone did it, proving your superiority. I will use your gift to gain the attention of what's left of world leaders and teach them they cannot thwart my plans. Then, Rosemary, my dear, you shall procreate, and my genes will carry on…"

"Wait… *procreate?* What are you talking about? I don't want to have a child." Rosemary backed out of the room. Vincent meant to use her as he had used all the other people in his life. *How stupid she'd been.* What was she thinking? He never cared about her.

"You may not, but I do. Wait, Rosemary!" Vincent shouted to her retreating figure. "Don't you want to know whom I've chosen?"

Rosemary ran, Vincent Konrad's laughter filling her head as if he were mocking her.

Dreg sidled up to Vincent. "Yes," Vincent said. "Now, you go and bring her back for me. Take her to the laboratory." Vincent cautioned him. "Don't hurt her too much, Dreg."

Dreg galloped after her, using the tray in his hands to clobber her on the head, bringing a senseless Rosemary to her knees.

CHAPTER 16

A DERANGED OLD FOOL

S HELDON GRABBED HOWARD around the shoulders and hugged him. Howard's brother turned and smiled broadly at Wyatt. "I told Dad you'd find us."

"Well, we couldn't have done it without Commander Etan." Howard was never one to take all the credit.

Sheldon turned to look at the soldier, his mouth dropping. He pulled off his glasses to peer closely at the other man. The three commandos surrounded Etan as if they were protecting him.

Sheldon jumped to attention and shouted, "Sir!"

Etan pulled off his glasses, a broad smile on his face. He gave a quick salute back, yanking the scarf from his head, and replied, "At ease, Sergeant. Take me to your leader."

"'Take me to your leader.'" Howard laughed. "You crack me up, Etan."

Wyatt rolled his eyes, then asked, "You know this guy?"

Everyone went absolutely silent.

"You mean to say you *don't?*" Sheldon squeaked. "You can't seriously be that dense." He turned to Etan. "We heard you were dead."

Etan smiled and replied, "Fake news."

Wyatt looked at Etan and the meatheads surrounding him. The color drained from his face, and for a moment dots swam before his eyes. Etan's skin was burned everywhere except where he kept his sunglasses on. His scarf hid the unmistakable head of premature gray hair.

"Of course, Etan… Nate. It's an anagram," Howard exclaimed with dawning realization. "How did I miss that?" He scratched his scalp.

Sheldon pushed the gawking Wyatt out of the way and said, "Follow me, Mr. President."

"Mr. President?" Wyatt was aghast. "What?"

Howard and Wyatt rushed after the group. The girls were led to a building across from the zoo, a museum dedicated to some old Western star.

Sheldon didn't enter the zoo but rather walked along the road past the entrance. Etan/Nate, or whoever he claimed to be, peppered Sheldon with questions as they made their way deeper into the park. Wyatt trotted along, trying to keep up with the newly revealed president and Sheldon to hear what he was asking, but his attention was diverted to the ragtag troops, some in uniform, others not, populating the hillside.

Howard pointed to people camped out in makeshift shelters resembling something like a homeless camp. It comprised a variety of tents, as if someone had raided a sporting goods store. They littered the dips and crags that made up Griffith Park.

Campfires crackled, the wood smoke smell filling Wyatt's nostrils. He never remembered LA smelling so good. He realized it was quiet. No planes roared overhead. Music didn't blare. Horns didn't honk. If he hadn't known any better, he would have thought he was back in rural Copper Valley. The one smell he did recognize was the cloud of weed that hung over the place.

A general feeling of tension permeated the park. People stopped to stare at them as they walked through the pathways. A group surrounded two men who strummed guitars. Some girls were dancing, their flowing skirts twirling around them like a cloud.

Wyatt turned to stare at the valley below him. Smoke spiraled from several spots, indicating wildfires in the distance. No cars moved on the freeway. Here and there a straggler ran down the road as if he was afraid to be stopped.

They moved deeper into the park, the greenery closing over them like a canopy. Soldiers, some even with what Wyatt supposed were their families, clustered around giant black walnut or maple trees, their drying laundry resting on bushes. The clothes were ragged and torn looking. Children played tag, and others clung to their parents, their eyes frightened. Men and women were perched on the low-hanging limbs of the trees, binoculars over their eyes as they observed for activity in the distance.

Wyatt stopped for a second to look at the scope of the fighting force. *Will they be enough to overcome Konrad?* he wondered. He looked for arms but saw a limited number of weapons. It wasn't looking very good.

They climbed up a small hill that revealed a clearing with a cluster of tents. They entered a large tent toward the center of the camp. The interior was empty except for a desk and a group of mismatched chairs. A uniformed man sat behind the desk.

"Dad!" Howard shouted and ran to his father.

Colonel Drucker rose to embrace his son. "I knew you'd make it, Howard. You're well?"

He turned to Wyatt and held out an arm to him as if to include him. Wyatt moved toward them in a daze.

"Glad to see you, son."

Colonel Drucker snapped to attention and shouted, "Sir. Glad to see you survived."

Wyatt opened his mouth, something snarky on his tongue when Howard blurted, "I still don't understand how you were able to fool us. I can see clearly now that you are the president."

One of the guards smiled.

Owens said, "Hypnosis. You saw what you wanted you to see."

"I was not hypnotized!" Howard shouted, his voice outraged.

Yerbol, the commando, walked past Howard and snapped his fingers. Howard's eyes slid shut while he stood still.

Nate Owens, or Etan, as Wyatt knew him, softly said, "That's enough, Yerbol. Let him go."

Yerbol shrugged, snapped twice, and Howard repeated, "I was not hypnotized!"

Wyatt watched in horrified silence. "How? When?" He wasn't sure whom he hated most, Vincent Konrad or President Nate Owens.

"We accomplished it after we knocked you out," Owens told him. "You were hit first. One of my guys tapped Howard on the head as well. It was right before you came to."

"Are the girls involved?" Wyatt snapped.

Owens shook his head. "No. Somehow they never recognized me. They are an odd group. We think they belong to some cult in the desert."

Colonel Drucker added, "I saw them when you arrived. The girls are uncannily large. Identical. Busting out of their clothing. Strangest thing I've ever seen. Doesn›t make sense. Could they somehow be related to the theme park?"

The president shrugged. "I think they are the product of inbreeding. There was no doubt they had no idea about my identity. They haven't given us any trouble. Just the opposite, in fact. They've managed to help us out enormously."

"We heard that you were dead, Mr. President," Howard's father said.

"We had to put out false reports," the president said, looking at Howard's father's insignia. "Colonel."

Colonel Drucker saluted smartly. "Colonel Drucker, sir. Acting commander of the western front. Happy to have you here." He smiled warmly.

Wyatt opened his mouth, the shock wearing off. "He's in league with Vincent Konrad!" He pointed to Nate Owens. "He's part of this whole mess!"

The three guards stepped protectively around the president. Owens placed a hand on one of their shoulders and pushed his way through.

"I know that's what it looks like," he began. He walked slowly toward Wyatt, who backed away.

"Your father, Dreg, told us he placed you in Vincent's pocket," Wyatt said.

"My father is a deranged old fool."

"You're lying!" Wyatt was screaming. "You're part of Vincent's plan! Everything that's happened is your fault!"

Colonel Drucker moved to stand between them. "I'm sure you don't know the whole story, Wyatt."

"His father told us everything. He's working with them, Mr.… I mean Colonel Drucker. You can't trust him."

"If I were working with them, Wyatt, why am I here all alone and not with Konrad?"

Howard blurted, "I knew you weren't a soldier!"

Nate looked at him and smiled. "I'm not. I'm actually a pilot."

Howard's father nodded. "One way or another, we'll sort this out," he told the room at large. "I'm afraid that until we do, I'm going to stay in charge." He turned to his second-in-command. "Appel, hold their weapons until we can resolve this."

She moved toward Yerbol. Yerbol bristled. Owens motioned for him to relax and ordered, "Stand down. Give her your guns."

"I don't like this," Yerbol grumbled.

"They have a right to be distrustful. I would be," the president said, his voice reasonable. "I am confident things will fall into place."

"Well, I'm not," Wyatt said through gritted teeth.

"That's enough, Wyatt," the colonel ordered. "I'd like some kind of debriefing. If you'll walk this way, we'll have dinner in my personal tent, and we can talk. Sheldon, go prepare your mother so she doesn't drop our meal on the floor when she sees Howard and Wyatt."

Sheldon ducked out of the room. They walked out into the fading sunlight toward a tight cluster of tents.

Mrs. Drucker was waiting at the end of a long table, her eyes shining brightly. When they entered, she walked briskly to Howard and gave him a tight squeeze. She didn't let Wyatt pass without a hug as well. When she finished examining both boys, she looked up, gasping when she realized who their next guest would be for dinner. She opened her mouth to begin questioning and was interrupted by Howard's father.

"Let's get dinner on the table, Maggie, and then we'll get down to business," Colonel Drucker said.

Wyatt's mouth watered when he saw the mounds of mashed potatoes and chipped beef being brought into the room. He felt his eyes sting a bit, remembering the last meal he'd had with his mother. She made the best potatoes in the world. For an instant, he wished his stepfather and Sean could be here with them, and his insides clenched with longing to be in their company.

Wyatt stared resentfully at the president, thinking about how he could prove the man was up to no good. Still, Owens had saved his life a few times during their trip here. Wyatt bit his lip in confusion. He was just beginning to like Etan, and now his distrust meter was off the charts. He felt rootless, as if he were unbalanced on a stormy sea.

Wyatt sat down abruptly at the table as everyone settled around him. Colonel Drucker was deep in conversation with the president at the end of the room. Wyatt thought resentfully that Howard's father had surrendered the head seat of the table too easily.

Wyatt glanced around at all the people and noticed part of their group was missing.

"Wait, Colonel," Wyatt interrupted. "The girls who traveled with us on the bus… where are they now?"

The colonel rubbed the stubble on his chin. "Yes, the girls. Bizarre group."

"Because they're sextuplets?" Howard asked.

"No, Howard," the colonel laughed. "Because of their size. Damn unusual."

"They are a large group," Howard agreed.

"It's more than that. One of my men debriefed them. It's as if they've lived under a rock their whole lives. They know nothing of life."

"That's what I've been thinking!" Sheldon commented. "They've never played a video game or watched television."

"So?" Howard shrugged. "Not everyone likes television."

"It feels like a puzzle." The colonel sighed. His eyes were drawn to the opening of the tent.

Wyatt thought Howard's father looked very old all of a sudden. The lines seemed to fold in around his narrow face.

"I've got them all tucked in. They were exhausted, poor things. Fed them when you first arrived. They can put it away like champions. Half starved." Mrs. Drucker shivered, then smiled when she looked at her sons. "Never you mind. Sit down with the colonel and eat. Then it's off to bed with you two."

"Mom," Howard whined, "don't treat us like babies!"

She clucked a bit and rushed from the room, her eyes wet.

"Attacked by the clowns, you say?" Colonel Drucker asked once he was settled.

"Glendale?" He looked at Sheldon and murmured, "They've moved out of Burbank. They're spreading like a damn virus."

"They're worse than the zombies," Sheldon added.

"Yes. They were armed to the teeth, Dad," Howard said between mouthfuls of food.

"You know about them?" the president asked.

"They started out as a small band in Van Nuys. Mostly

homeless, they broke into the makeup departments in the studios when Hollywood closed down. At first we figured it was some kind of fetish, but it's been growing, apparently."

"Yeah, each neighborhood appears to have a special makeup style that defines the group they associate with," Sheldon offered.

"Like a street gang?" Howard asked.

Appel shrugged. "Could be. They are well organized. Their strategy is not stable. We've had a tough time anticipating what they are planning."

"West Point didn't prepare you for enemies like this," Sheldon said to her with a smile.

"Batshit crazy," Yerbol said dryly. "They're certainly not entertaining."

"Who said clowns are entertaining?" the president said. "I find them off-putting." He leaned forward, his elbows on the table as if to confide something. "Like the strange role my father played in Vincent's circus."

"He seemed willing enough," Wyatt responded. The table went quiet, but Colonel Drucker wasn't finished talking about the clown problem. Wyatt lost his appetite as his gorge rose.

"No one can identify them with all that crap on their faces. At first we thought that was their tactic, but something strange has been happening, and I think it is much more diabolical than that," Colonel Drucker said with a sigh.

"What do you mean, sir?" the president asked.

Everybody started asking questions at the same time. The colonel waited for the noise to die down.

"We thought they were using the makeup as a device to hide their identities. For a while, we believed they might be zombies under disguise, but their movements are too precise. They fight dirty too. They get you under their comic spell and then, *wham!*"

"We think they use clown makeup as some way to identify each other—" Sheldon offered.

"Or as a means to communicate," Appel said, finishing Sheldon's sentence.

"Ingenious," Howard said thoughtfully, looking at his brother drool in his food as he watched Lieutenant Appel.

"It's almost as though they have found a secretive mass identity and can hide behind the masks to behave as disorderly as they want," the president added.

"*Oh*, sort of like the social networking problems of the last decade?" Howard said.

"What do you mean?" Colonel Drucker asked.

"Don't you remember when online bullying was rampant until the zombie outbreak?" Howard asked. "Nameless and faceless, they were able to cyber-torture anyone who was different."

"Affirmative, people didn't have time to do stuff like that after the zombie plague. Aside from that, most people could claim at least one zombie in their family. You can't make fun of everybody," Yerbol said in his clipped commando way.

Wyatt sat numbly, his thoughts on his own father.

"Whether people hide behind the mask of social media or face paint, they are capable of doing the unthinkable. They feel powerful enough to step out of their comfort zone and not be afraid of consequences," Owens said grimly.

"I told you clowns were evil." Wyatt shuddered.

"Freud said—" Howard began

"Not now, Howard. I don't care why they do it. I need to know how to stop them." Colonel Drucker cut him off and changed the subject. "Anyway, I think it's something bigger. Sounds like they've recruited more people into their army."

"We didn't say they were an army," Nate Owens replied.

Colonel Drucker nodded. "They were a formidable group when we fought with them last month. If they've taken on more members and spread that far, it means they've morphed into a larger outfit."

"*Buncha* nuts," Yerbol said, dismissing them. "Sir," he added.

"I don't think so." The colonel shook his head. "We've tried negotiating with them. It seems they have a king and queen. Strange little guy. The woman is large with reddish hair, like those girls you brought in with you."

"We tangled with them. She was huge. I think she shot the little guy," Wyatt said in a rush.

"At least you got out of there alive," Sheldon said, his eyes suspiciously wet.

Yerbol chuckled. "They're just a bunch of crazies masquerading around."

The colonel banged the table with the palm of his hand, causing everyone to jump in their seats. "Don't underestimate them because they don't wear camouflage. Those *crazies* capture their victims and eat them."

Wyatt's mouth went dry. Both he and Howard looked at their plates.

"What?" Owens was aghast.

"Food ran out rather quickly in most of the big cities. You know this country depends on trucking. Within weeks, markets were set up for trading, but lawlessness closed them down. I didn't have enough troops to keep the peace. LA is just too spread out. So people left. The ones who stayed were starving. The clowns started off luring their victims in playfully. They were soon penned like animals and harvested for meat."

"Killer cannibal clowns!" Wyatt exclaimed. "I thought they wanted our bus."

"Nope." Sheldon shook his head. "They took the valley; they have plenty of cars. Just think of all the abandoned ride sharing vehicles. They wanted you for the meat. It's becoming scarce everywhere."

Forks clattered onto the table against the metal plates.

"No, no. We had plenty of rations." The colonel misinterpreted their reaction.

"They're using people as a food source?" Howard choked out.

"These things do happen in war, son. I'm afraid to tell you I've seen worse," the colonel answered.

"What could be worse than that?" Howard cried.

"They keep the food source alive, cutting off body parts until there is nothing left," Lieutenant Appel said, her voice a mere whisper. "They captured an entire scouting party. There were eight of them." She wiped away a tear that rolled down her cheek. "One of the men escaped. He returned. His arm had been amputated… and eaten. They ate them all." She lowered her head.

"That's insane!" Owens shouted.

"As insane as a theme park with monsters," Colonel Drucker said with deadly quiet. "I can't believe I ever voted for a government that enabled the unholy enterprise."

"Look, I was against the whole thing. It was a deal between President McAdams and Vincent Konrad. I thought the entire idea was abhorrent." Owens's voice was harsh.

"So says the man whose father was Konrad's right hand," Howard said.

Owens fisted his hand. "We all believed him at first. He was a great humanitarian. Don't you remember how bad it was for the zombies?"

Wyatt flushed to the roots of his hair. Everyone was quiet, caught up in their own complicity. "We were starting up impeachment proceedings. McAdams had deals with foreign governments. He was like a dictator doing everything by using executive actions. He lied to everybody. He was the one in Vincent's pocket."

"Why did he kill him then?" Wyatt asked.

President Owens shook his head. "I can't explain anything—" his voice trailed off.

Wyatt looked at Owens's tortured face. For the first time, he sympathized with Nate Owens. Wasn't his own father guilty of enabling the zombie containment camps with his job as Vincent Konrad's attorney? Nate Owens wasn't the only one who had trusted Vincent Konrad.

Guilt reared its ugly head. Wyatt looked around the table. Vincent

Konrad didn't spring up overnight. The entire population of the world had sat by and enabled him just by doing nothing, saying nothing, staying selectively blind to his plans. There were signs that all was not right, yet the politicians and the press had reported only what they wanted people to see. Very few people had been against Vincent's plan, because they were happy to hand over the problems to someone else. Wyatt couldn't think of one person who saw through Vincent except for his stepfather.

"I believed in Vincent Konrad as well," Wyatt said, his voice miserable. "Carter would call it 'twenty-twenty hindsight.'"

The room went silent again, each person reflecting on their role in the chaos. For some it was jumping on the bandwagon; for others, plain old apathy. *But make no mistake*, Wyatt thought, looking at each face. *Everyone is guilty for allowing it to happen.*

They simultaneously bowed their heads as if in prayer. Perhaps they were all asking for forgiveness. Wyatt knew he was, for not paying attention and seeing past the public relations and glossy facade.

Owen reached over and grabbed Wyatt's wrist. "Don't beat yourself up, kid. We're all guilty, and now we have to get ourselves out… together."

"There's more." Sheldon broke the mood. "When the food runs out, Dad says we'll have to start using up the inhabitants of the zoo."

"No!" Howard cried. "Not the giraffes!"

"Meat is meat, son. Even I have to worry about how I will feed our people. We think that's why they're massing. They want to capture the zoo."

"Where is the rest of the population of LA?" Nate Owens asked.

"We evacuated what we could up north. It was mayhem. Many people lit out from here on their own to God knows where. A lot of the outer communities were sucked dry by some purple foamy stuff."

"The Glob," Howard and Wyatt said at the same time.

"Explain." The colonel leaned forward.

"Alien jet fuel used by Dreg," Wyatt said, watching Nate Owens for a reaction. "He reanimated Vincent's dead body with it."

"Alien jet fuel, from Area 51?" Colonel Drucker confirmed.

"You know about that, Dad?" Howard asked.

"Everybody knows about that. I wonder if they took the aliens as well. Did you see any?" the colonel asked.

"Aliens?" Howard exploded. *"Gosh,* I would have given anything to see them. How many? How did they keep them alive?"

"Not now, Howard. That's the least of our problems." The colonel closed the conversation. He looked at Nate Owens. "What were you doing in the middle of the desert during this meltdown?"

Owens turned to Colonel Drucker. "I was on my way to stop my father. I was afraid of something like this happening. He became unhinged. I knew if I found my father, I'd find Vincent Konrad. Yerbol was going to take him out."

"You had the entire joint chiefs at your disposal," Colonel Drucker said.

"Most were killed at the opening of Monsterland. I wasn't sure where anybody's loyalties were. Washington was a disaster. I've been cut off from everyone. We need a plan. What else can you tell me?"

The colonel shook his head. "Not much more to tell. Zombies started raiding the towns on the coast. We think they may be holed up on one of the barrier islands. We got out as many civilians as we could. One thing about LA people—they follow directions well. It was quite a convoy on the freeway. The clowns started popping up not long after that. Took out whoever was left, and my guess is they are attacking anyone who passes by."

"Why haven't you eliminated them?" the president asked.

"You think we haven't tried? It's a big city out there, and further-more, if they got to you that far east, they've expanded their territory. We're blocked in on both sides."

"What about the people who were evacuated?" Yerbol asked.

"A buddy of mine, a retired captain, is organizing them in Bear Mountain. They are relatively safe, I think," said the colonel.

"You think?" Wyatt asked.

"I'm limited in what I can do, son. If I don't have the resources, no one is safe."

"Not if I can get this country back on its feet," the president interjected. "Time is of the essence."

"I'd like to hear what Wyatt has to say, sir," the colonel said.

Wyatt haltingly started. "Vincent Konrad planned the whole thing from the beginning. He was going to throw the entire world into turmoil."

"Well, he certainly succeeded," the colonel said grimly.

"You see, he had inside help. They told us that… Nate Owens supported him." Wyatt nodded toward the president.

"No, Wyatt, it was the other way around. Vincent Konrad controlled both President McAdams and me. He used his influence to get us elected. I thought he and McAdams were great friends. Personally, I… I didn't trust him. He hired my father. I'm not even sure how."

"He told Carter, my stepfather, that you were embarrassed by Dreg, and he'd done you a favor by keeping him out of the public eye so you could get elected."

Nate Owens stood abruptly. His face reddened. Wyatt wasn't sure if it was anger or shame. "No, no. I would never. I love… loved my father." He turned to face Wyatt. "Stop calling him that silly name. His name is Andrew. Andrew Owens. This is so warped; I don't know where to start."

Wyatt continued, "He took him in, allowing you to win the election and knowing you'd be president once McAdams was assassinated."

"He didn't allow me to win. He tampered with the election." Owens punched his fist into his palm.

"I thought only Russians did that," Wyatt retorted.

"Russians, Vincent Konrad, what's the difference? People are easily swayed by social media."

"It's like herding sheep," Howard said.

"You don't have much respect for the American people," Wyatt sneered at the president.

"I have the utmost respect for people who have the ability to interpret facts and not follow someone with the trendiest catchphrase," Owens replied.

"Why didn't you leave the ballot, then?" Wyatt asked softly.

"Because I love my country and want to help, Wyatt. I'm not here to be in a history book. I chose to make a difference in people's lives. Improve them. You can't do that sitting on your backside eating popcorn and watching television."

"I don't—" Wyatt's face got red.

"I'm not talking about you. I'm talking about the people who allow terrible things to happen and don›t do anything about it."

"Konrad was convincing," Colonel Drucker said.

"Yes, he was at first. He arrived on the scene during our darkest hour," Owens said.

"*Oh*, I don't know. I think we're in a pretty dark hour right now," Howard interrupted.

"Howard, I want to hear what President Owens has to say." The colonel's voice was firm.

"He seduced the public with his plan. No muss, no fuss. It was an easy way out of our dilemma. I will admit he made a lot of sense in the beginning."

Wyatt smiled shyly, happy to hear that from Owens.

"It's just that the public got lazy. These were not new problems." Owens held out a palm to stop him from interrupting. "Yes, yes, I know the werewolves were considered a myth, and the vamps were non-threatening and on the verge of extinction anyway, but when the plague hit, everybody wanted a quick solution, one that wouldn't inconvenience their lives." He paused for a minute. "I think we're better than that."

He had Wyatt there. It was exactly what Carter had told him. Wyatt bit his lower lip. He couldn't find a way to respond.

Owens continued, "I opposed him, and he knew it. Konrad wanted me eliminated and planned to kill me. There was a change of plans. My helicopter exploded in midair, killing the secretary of state instead of me. The army was fractured; the navy fell apart. I knew only one thing: I had to do the job myself. Yerbol, his detail, and I secretly left town to try to eliminate him. I was on my way to Monsterland when the battle took place. When I got there, there was nothing left but some kids living in the werewolf exhibit."

"Melvin," Howard and Wyatt said in unison with a smile.

Wyatt felt the hatred drain from him. It was too exhausting to stay angry.

"I haven't spoken to my dad in months. I did not support what he was doing. It was a mockery of his disability. I begged him to leave. Before all this happened, I contacted Vincent and told him to let my father out of his contract. He laughed and hung up the phone. I oppose everything he stands for. I didn't trust his plan. It's no way to treat people," Owens said bitterly. "A theme park filled with vampires, werewolves, and zombies—what were they thinking?" They were each lost in their own thoughts. Owens murmured, "How the hell did he manage to get everyone on this planet to drink his *Kool-Aid*?"

"You said you did in the beginning." Wyatt said without looking up.

Colonel Drucker's tired voice said, "I think we all are guilty of that. When you fail to react and become numb to wrong, there is a collective guilt for all humanity."

Lieutenant Appel cleared her throat, her hands folded, and said softly, "'The only thing necessary for the triumph of evil is for good men to do nothing.'"

"Edmund Burke," Howard added with a nod.

It was an intimate moment, each person reflecting their own role in the destruction of their world.

Wyatt's jaw dropped with the realization that of them all, Owens was the least guilty. He had tried to do something while Wyatt was busy going to the opening of Monsterland, supporting the idea of exploiting those less fortunate.

Blinders fell from his eyes, and he felt ashamed of himself. "What's going on outside of here?" Wyatt asked.

"Well," the colonel began, "Vincent tipped the world on its axis. Government's been pretty much disbanded. We can't get our troops organized. Many of them have gone rogue anyway. I've been working with the northern troops, but they are a small group and limited to protecting the population that's camped there. The cities are in turmoil. Once public services shut down, there was complete anarchy. Nowhere for people to go. Food not being delivered. No water. That purple goo jet fuel took down most of Arizona, Nevada, and Southern Cali. People were sucked dry, their bodies left to decay. Then an offshore colony of zombies escaped. They've terrorized half the state, infecting victims as they go, like it was Spring Break in Miami." He shook his head. "Damn shame."

"Well, at least all the vampires have been eliminated," Howard said.

The general shook his head. "Bunch made it out of Monsterland, Paris. They are cutting a swath through Europe."

"How do you know that?" Wyatt asked.

"We've got a wireless. Werewolves are roaming too. Mostly in South America, but we've had reports they are traveling north. You say Vincent Konrad is still alive? How could that be? I heard his head was ripped off."

"Yes sir. He's changed. His head was sewn on another guy's body," Wyatt said.

"It's gruesome, Dad," Howard interjected. "Do you think the monsters will organize themselves?"

Owens answered instead. "Vamps are feckless and care only about themselves. The werewolves never wanted much to do with humanity, but at this point, I'm pretty sure revenge is on their minds. They must be angry about what Konrad tried to do to them. The zombies are sick… poor sick people."

"We've been corralling them and imprisoning them in the Crypto Arena," the colonel said. "I have a platoon there."

"Do you have any idea where Vincent's gone?" Owens asked.

Colonel Drucker stood and walked over to the giant map hung on the wall. He pointed a finger to the southern coastline of California. "There's been some activity on one of the small islands off the coast, right around here. We're thinking the zombies are sneaking in from there."

Wyatt peered closely at the cluster of islands on the map. "Isn't that Great White Shark Park?"

The colonel looked at the map. "Yes. Yes, it is."

"The Shark Park was one of Vincent Konrad's enterprises," the president said.

"I'm going to need someone to survey the area, but if the clowns have taken the city, we won't be able to get there."

"Can we talk to them?" Owens asked.

"You know what they want," the colonel answered. "Much as I'd hate to do it, we could use what we have in the zoo."

"No, Dad!" Howard wailed.

Colonel Drucker's face was lined with worry. "Son, I hate the idea as much as you. But we are running out of food for the animals as well. Some of them are sickening already. It's a tough decision, but it saves lives. Do we even have a choice?"

Howard put his head on the table. "If we can get to the sea, we can fish and feed our people."

Wyatt nodded. "That's true. Sometimes, though, you have to make terrible choices. It's the lesser of two evils."

The colonel stared at their faces for a long while before he said, "Yes, sometimes you do." He ruffled his son's bushy hair.

"Were you worried about me finding you?" Howard looked up and asked his father.

It felt like a private moment, and Wyatt noticed Nate Owens was watching the father and son intently.

"Not for a minute. I was waiting for you to arrive," the colonel replied.

Howard smiled, his glasses lopsided on his pale face. Wyatt wondered if Carter would feel the same way about him, and he was surprised it actually mattered.

The flap burst open. A soldier entered breathlessly. "Colonel Drucker, you've got to come and see this."

"What is it?" the colonel demanded.

"Fires, sir. The entire northern side of the hill is lit up like a torch."

"I was afraid of that." The colonel shook his head.

"It's fire season," Wyatt added.

"I know that, but this is the work of the clowns, and there is nothing we can do about it. We are effectively cut off from any help from the northern forces."

"Do you mind if we follow you, Colonel?" the president said.

Colonel Drucker gave a curt nod, and they all walked briskly from the room.

Wyatt's eyes constantly moved back to Owens. He stared at his face. In the cold light of day, Nate Owens was clearly who he said he was. The real question was could Wyatt be sure of where this man's loyalty actually lay?

A hand landed heavily on Wyatt's shoulder. Colonel Drucker's sympathetic face was staring at him as if he knew Wyatt's churning thoughts. "Get some sleep, son. You can wrestle with it tomorrow."

Wyatt opened his mouth to argue, then snapped it shut. The colonel was right. He was tired. Dead tired.

CHAPTER 17

MELVIN OF MONSTERLAND

MELVIN WATCHED THE creatures plod through the sand, dragging the trailer across the ground. He searched the surrounding area for some sign of where they came from but saw only the vast high desert and the new footprints that pocked the ground like small craters. An identical-looking giant grabbed the other side of the structure and with a partner carried the trailer, swinging it merrily between them.

Forcing himself to morph, Melvin closed his eyes, and though his tendons screamed from elongation, he welcomed the switch to a predator's body. His tufted ears caught the thumping sound of his friend's bodies within the trailer. He winced with each bump. HIs sharp eyes caught the mountain lion he'd seen earlier at the camp creeping among the bushes and tumbleweed, dogging their trail. Melvin sniffed, his nostrils twitching. The mountain lion had a familiar scent, but he couldn't place it.

He fought the urge to howl, refusing to bring attention to himself, trotting after the giant's footprints. His ears picked up the rapid breathing of the occupants in the trailer. At least they were alive. He could hear Carter's calm voice telling everybody to link arms and hold onto the parts of the structure that were bolted onto the floor to keep them from being tossed around. He was able to separate the individual sounds of his friends and counted the rhythms of their breathing. The metallic odor of blood gave him a sense of urgency.

Scanning the grounds, he looked for the mountain lion again. It was gone, but he could still detect it's scent. He knew it was nearby, but out of sight. Melvin took off after the large men.

They walked for hours on the burning sand, stopping when they arrived at a huge cliff. The giants placed the trailer down with a crash that made Melvin breath catch from the cries inside. The creatures slid down, exhaling with relief.

Melvin hid in a cluster of bushes, panting. He was thirsty. He could only imagine how Carter and the rest of them were baking in the hot metal.

The ground vibrated as if it were an earthquake. Melvin crouched, his large paws raking the sand, his canine eyes opening wide. Four identical monsters with flaming red hair approached the sleeping giants. One, who appeared slightly shorter, broke into a run, causing rocks to tumble from the cliff above them.

The sleeping giant shook himself awake, stood, and bellowed, "Brontes! Stop! You'll crush us all!"

"Grillos, you found them, the girls? My girls?"

"Not the girls, brother. Tomorrow we'll trade these for your daughters in their City of the Sign." He slammed his hand on the top of the trailer, causing the metal to buckle.

"The Sign." Brontes nodded.

Melvin's ears rang from their loud voice. *They were headed to LA!* He wondered for a minute about the comments regarding a trade.

"We leave at nightfall. Rest so we may walk this wasteland minkins call home."

The six creatures arranged themselves around the dented police station, and soon the canyon filled with their snoring.

Melvin circled the encampment. He smelled the wolf before he saw it, it's strong scent overpowering the ever-present odor of the mountain lion. Melvin turned, his teeth bared. It paced a few feet from him, its eyes sharp. Its large shoulders undulated as it moved. The fur was startlingly black with a streak of white under its chin.

The wolf sniffed the air. *You are the changeling?*

Melvin eyed him warily. He didn't know him. He hadn't seen any wolves since the debacle of Monsterland. He communicated mostly with coyotes and hybrids.

I come in friendship, the wolf growled.

Melvin stared at him, wondering if he too was a werewolf. *What are you called?* he asked.

I am known as Max, Mad Max.

Melvin chuffed a laugh. *Lost your mind, eh?*

Max tilted his head. *I'd say I had reason enough.*

I thought Vincent Konrad caught all of you.

Max shook his head. *Si. I was there, but I got out. I saw the handwriting on the wall. I warned Billy he should get out too, but he wouldn't leave the others.*

You knew Billy? Melvin's eyes got misty. He wiped them with a paw.

I met him at Monsterland. He was a good man. We became friends.

Go on, Melvin said warily. He was not convinced.

They beat me, Vincent Konrad and his ilk. I almost died. If not for Billy I would have. But then those monsters threw me to the zombies. I escaped. I leapt over the fence to freedom. I came back for Billy, but he wouldn't leave. He was like my brother, he said in a sad whisper. *But you, Melvin of Monsterland, you have become a legend.*

Melvin blushed under his fur. The wolf lowered his head in

respect. Melvin moved closer, feeling kinship. This was a link to Billy and the birth of his new life. *Are there others?*

Si. I hooked up with them in Mexico. There are hundreds of us south of the border. They call us chupacabras. He snickered. *Listen, Melvin. You must return home. Your mate… there is trouble.*

I left friends behind to protect her.

They are dead, amigo.

Melvin tensed, his body going rigid. *What are you talking about? Did you pass through there? If you've done something—*

Hold on there, brother. We're all friends here. We wouldn't never hurt another one like us. There's been an incident. By the time we got there, it was over.

Melvin looked back at the trailer. *I must leave.*

Max hung his head. *I know. It is the least we can do for our brethren, Melvin of Monsterland. We will stay and follow these big humans when they begin their journey,* he told him.

Melvin shook off the shiver that raced through him. The clearing was filled with a ragtag pack of wolves. They shifted silently, but Melvin knew without counting there were at least fifteen of them.

Melvin considered the sleeping giants. *I don't think they are human.*

It doesn't matter. Anyone who walks on two legs is the enemy, a dark-furred wolf growled from the pack.

I walk on two legs sometimes, Melvin shot back. *Why would you help me?*

Go home, brother, Max interrupted. *Find out what happened to your mate and then follow our trail. We will help you.*

I say we destroy them now, one of the wolves whispered. His long tongue swiped his snout. *Especially the tender flesh in the box.*

No! Melvin shouted. *They are my friends. They are good humans.*

The dark-furred wolf barked, The only good human is a dead human.

Max sneered as he warned him, *Cállate, Donner. He said they are his friends. That means they are our friends too.*

What do we care about humans and their so-called humanity? Look where that got us! Donner came close to Mad Max's face.

Were we not all humans at one time? Max asked quietly.

Melvin watched them lower their heads with murmurs of agreement except for Donner, who remained defiant.

We stand together as one, brothers and sisters. The pack is life, and our life is the pack. We must protect any of our kind who are left.

They're not our kind, Donner snarled.

They're mine, Melvin barked back.

Then we will protect them, Max replied. *Back down, Donner.*

Donner narrowed his gaze. Melvin felt his feral stare.

We can take them now and rescue his friends, Donner said, his voice a crafty snarl.

No. Melvin shook his head. *We are not enough.* He hesitated for a minute. *My friends are in LA. We'll need their help.*

You mean Wyatt Baldwin and Howard Drucker? Mad Max said in awe.

The wolves became restless. Melvin could hear them whispering to each other.

You've heard of them… I mean us?

Los Tres Amigos, si. We have heard of their daring exploits. Mad Max bowed low. *It will be an honor to fight side by side.*

Melvin glanced at Donner and saw that he was kneeling as well.

Go. Time is critical, Max urged as he regained his footing.

Melvin walked in a tight circle. All the wolves nodded. He heard them murmur, *Go…. We will guard your friends.*

Melvin looked at the white trailer, his heart heavy with sadness. He could hear the rapid breathing of the people inside. He had to get home and see what happened. They had to be wrong, he sighed, his heart heavy. Speed was of the essence. He could make it to Monsterland in less than an hour and be on his way to LA by nightfall. He nodded to Max and the others, racing in the direction of Monsterland and Jade.

CHAPTER 18

ADVANCED TECHNOLOGY

THE WORLD WAS muted as if smeared by watercolors. Rosemary came awake slowly. Her vision was fuzzy. She tried to rub her eyes, but her hands were tied down. Opening her mouth, she cried out, her throat aching as if it were rubbed raw.

"You were not an easy patient." Rosemary heard a voice that made her shudder. She turned her head on the pillow to see her father sitting in an oversized chair beside her bed.

"What happened?"

"Do you want a drink?" He rose unsteadily to his feet to hand her a cup with a straw in it.

Rosemary knocked it away, her movements clumsy and as uncoordinated as her father. The cup fell with a clatter.

"My straws are not made of plastic," he said with mock dignity. "I assure you they are safe for the environment."

"I don't want anything from you." Her words sounded slurred. "What did you do to me?"

A white-coated man came into the room. "Don't upset her, Doctor," he said to Vincent.

"I assure you, I won't rile her up, Doctor," Vincent replied.

"Doctor." The white-coated man nodded.

"Doctor," Vincent acknowledged.

"Stop!" Rosemary screamed.

The two men exchanged looks. She saw the physician take a hypodermic needle from a tray and inject something into her IV. The room faded before she could call out for Shandy.

When next she awakened, Rosemary turned her head to see Vincent watching her keenly. She opened her mouth to ask how long she'd been out when Vincent held up a finger to stop her. "I can keep having them drug you to keep you safe, or you can use the Konrad survival techniques to listen before you react."

Rosemary mulled his words over and then nodded curtly.

"Good girl." Vincent patted her hand lying limply at her side. "You'll want to know how long you've been here."

Rosemary gritted her teeth. Of course she wanted to know and it irritated her that her father knew that.

Vincent went on. "It's been five days."

Rosemary struggled against the straps holding her down. "Five days! Where is Shandy and Jötnar!"

"Truth be told, I have no idea where they are. We tried to find them. They've vanished." Vincent picked at a fingernail. It peeled away from his skin and fell onto the floor. "Deserted you, it seems."

"They would never…If you've hurt them—"

"You wound me, child. I would never do anything like that to your playthings. After we detained you, they simply left. My guess is they've abandoned you. They are a pair of degenerates, after all. Perhaps they ventured onto the beach." He leaned closer as if to confide a secret. "Remember; I use zombies as watchdogs." He winced. "I hope it was quick for them."

Rosemary willed her eyes not to tear. She refused to show weakness in front of her father. "You're despicable."

"Have faith, Rosemary! They may have taken off in the shark-infested waters. I have a report that claims your boat has gone missing, and we haven't found any huge femurs around, so at the very least, your giant has escaped. You realize he is a giant, don't you?"

"Stop talking nonsense. There's no such thing as giants. Next thing you'll tell me that gremlins are real."

Vincent ignored her and continued. "Giants have been around for thousands of years. I first met them when I drilled for natural gas. Came up against a clan. They have some strange familial habits."

Rosemary eyed him up and down. "Really? You're talking about strange family habits?"

"I'm glad to see your sense of humor has returned. They birth litters, sometimes as many as six at a time. You see, because of their large size and the lack of space, they allow only one member of the litter to have children for the next generation."

"You know this because…?"

"I had to negotiate with them. They worked with me setting up each of my parks. Their size makes building efficient and quick. No need for big expensive equipment."

Rosemary lifted her head to look at him. "Why would these *giants* help you?"

"Because I left them alone." Vincent downed a mug of purple fluid. "They've lived underground in a network of caves for eons. Lovely creatures. They want nothing to do with humanity. They've had their fill, you know. Civilizations have abused their skills for years. Giants constructed the pyramids… and Stonehenge. Never got paid a nickel for it except for some bad press from one of their kings. You know the whole Goliath thing? I paid them full for the work they did at the theme parks. Let me tell you something." He leaned close, his voice a gravely whisper. Rosemary pulled away. "They like me. They really like me."

Rosemary groaned with frustration. "Is that your *Oscar* speech? Listen carefully," she said through gritted teeth. "I don't care about giants! I don't care about you! Where are my men?"

"*Aha!* Now you sound more like the old chip off the block. I told you, I don't know." He smiled. His large front tooth wobbled and fell onto the bed.

"*Eww*. You're falling apart." They sat in silence for a moment. She pulled at the restraints. "What have you done to me?"

Vincent sighed heavily.

"Tell me!" she yelled.

"We've harvested your eggs and have replanted them inside you. You are well and truly pregnant with my grandchild."

"Impossible. Five days is not enough time. You're lying."

"I assure you I am not. I have advanced technology—"

"From where?" Rosemary demanded.

Vincent was quiet for a minute as if he were weighing telling her.

"I don't want to be," Rosemary complained. Then with dawning horror at his smug expression, her eyes opened wide and she looked at him with revulsion. "I don't believe you. That takes months, hormone treatments. You can't know that I'm pregnant already."

"Science is my specialty. I have a team of doctors who can jump hurdles and overcome silly little things like hormone treatments and time. Rosemary, I am a genius."

She whispered, her face colorless, "Who… who is the father?"

Vincent laughed. "I am not *that* depraved, Rosemary. I want a healthy child. Strong, intelligent, invincible. Just so happens I had the perfect specimen."

Rosemary looked away, sickened. "You are an animal."

"No, I'm not. I am continuing our bloodline. It's all about the succession. I've failed you by not being in your life. You are filled with nonsense and ideals that Shandy's drilled into your brain. I will teach this child from the beginning of its life. Would you like to meet him, the father of your child?"

"No!" Rosemary shook her head.

"You'll like what I have to tell you. He comes from a gentle race. His DNA is very close to our own. I can't wait to show him or her the world!"

"Not this child," Rosemary screamed, her strength returning.

"It's my baby, and I will do what I want with it," Vincent said with deadly calm. "I've worked too hard to achieve all this."

"Make no mistake." She pulled at the restraints, ripping them from their moorings. "This is my baby. Not yours. This is Rosemary's baby."

Vincent caressed her cheek and said with a smile, "I knew you'd come around." He left the room, laughing all the way into the corridor.

CHAPTER 16

GROUND ZERO

MRS. DRUCKER CAME back and escorted Wyatt and Howard to a tent behind the mess where they'd eaten. Clean clothes had been laid out on the army cots. Wyatt sat down heavily, his legs wobbly. He was tired; his eyes burned.

"I think you won't have any trouble falling asleep. I won't anymore now that all my chicks are here together. I'm including you too, Wyatt. You're one of my boys now." Mrs. Drucker patted his head.

Wyatt's eyes stung. "Thanks, Mrs. Drucker." He looked up at her fussing with Howard. "How are the girls doing?"

"They're all sleeping already poor things. They were exhausted. Where did you say they came from?" she asked but continued talking without their answering. "Strange group. I'd swear they're younger than they appear despite their size. They act kind of childish."

Wyatt looked up. "What do you mean?"

"Their demeanor. The things they asked for. It's more in the vein of, *uh*, I don't know, like a middle school child. I don't know where I'll find garments big enough to clothe them." She shook her head. "Well, it doesn't matter. Time for talking is done. We'll discuss it in the morning."

She left the room, closing the flap from the outside. Wyatt stripped from his travel-stained clothes and changed into the clean ones. He would have loved a shower but was promised an assigned time tomorrow.

The scarf floated onto the bed. He picked up his shirt and emptied his pockets. He stared at the scarf, not quite sure why he was holding onto it. He wasn't interested in Danai in that way. It was just that he felt that if he let it go, somehow they'd disappear, and he'd never discover the sisters' secrets. He picked it up, the fragile material snagging on his callused hands. The scarf was like a link, binding them in some mysterious story. Wyatt shivered, though no breeze came into the tent.

Danai was connected; everyone was connected in some giant chain of humanity. They each needed the other to overcome the monster that was Vincent Konrad. He just wasn't sure how it was going to link together.

Two gray kestrel feathers fell out of his pocket. Wyatt picked up a feather and sniffed it. It smelled faintly of the scarf he had stuffed under his shirt. He held it to his nose, seeking Lily's scent, panic overwhelming him when he couldn't detect it. All he could smell was Danai's floral scent. It had overwhelmed Lily's, and for some reason that filled Wyatt with dread.

Howard leaned over pointing to the other feather. "That Lily's?" he asked.

Wyatt nodded.

"At least you have a feather of hers to keep. All Keisha had for me was one of her snakes, which I declined."

"She'll have feathers by now if John Raven succeeded in teaching her to morph into a bird."

"*Huh*," Howard said with a smile. "I'd rather sleep with that under my pillow than one of her snakes. G'night, Wy." He turned over on his cot, his eyes heavy facing Wyatt. "I'm glad we did this together."

Wyatt sank down. "Me too," he said.

The feather fell from his hand onto his chest. He looked down to see it, then placed it carefully under his pillow. The scarf remained tightly in his grasp. He raised his arms and stared at it as if it could give him an answer.

"Why do you have that?" Howard asked drowsily.

"I'm not sure. I'm not ready to give it back."

"Well, you should," Howard grumbled as he turned over. "It feels… I dunno, inappropriate."

"Maybe tomorrow," Wyatt murmured.

Every time he closed his eyes, the leering faces of the clowns filled his head. He tossed and turned. The dark corners of the tent seemed filled with a presence. He pulled the pillow over his face. The echoes of the clowns' laughter screamed inside his skull. He listened to Howard rustling around and knew he wasn't asleep.

"Howard?" Wyatt asked tentatively. "What scares you?"

He heard Howard sigh heavily. He looked across the room to see his friend sitting up, his eyes shining in the dark.

"Losing my family," Howard said after clearing his voice.

"Monsters don't get to you?"

Howard lay back down and put his hands behind his head. "We were never afraid of vampires, werewolves, or zombies, right?"

Wyatt nodded, then realized Howard couldn't see him. He cleared his throat and said, "No, never. Even when we fought them."

"And while I hate mummies, they didn't scare me much. Did they scare you?"

Wyatt was silent for a minute, his mind going back to the frightening battles. "I'm not sure. I don't think I had time to be afraid."

He glanced at the darkness of the corner and gulped. "I wasn't afraid then, but I'm feeling something weird… now."

"The clowns did it. They rocked you. It's a common enough fear. They look so, you know, like they shouldn't be frightening, and then—boom! They do something unexpected. Like when you have a zombie coming at you, all pus and moaning, you expect it to do something like that. But a clown is supposed to make you laugh." Howard sat up. "I'll tell you what scared the crap out of me—when Keisha turned all catatonic and had a nest of snakes in her head. That was freakin' scary."

Wyatt rested his head on the flat pillow. "Yeah. I think you're right. Clowns really get to me. I understand that now. Howard, you know what else gives me the creeps?" Wyatt whispered.

"What?"

"Politicians. It's the same as the clowns. You think they're all out there for the good of mankind, and then—"

"Yep, I know. They wear masks too."

It was quiet in the tent for a few minutes, the air filled with their own thoughts.

"I don't think Nate Owens is a bad guy," Howard said.

"I didn't think Vincent Konrad was a bad guy, and look what he did." Wyatt sounded close to tears.

"Ernest Hemingway said, 'The best way to find out if you can trust somebody is to trust them.'"

"That's what I'm afraid of," Wyatt grumbled.

"Franklin Delano Roosevelt was famous for the quote 'The only thing we have to fear is… fear itself.' Have some faith, Wyatt. Maybe that's what you need."

Wyatt didn't answer. He rolled over to face the wall of the tent instead of facing his fears.

Wyatt fell into a light doze that didn't last. He rose just before dawn, slipping on his shoes as quietly as he could. He ventured outside. It was hot. The sky was still dark; a smattering of stars filled the inky blackness. He could hear the lull of the zoo animals making their noises, a growl followed by the shrieks of the monkeys.

A campfire burned outside his tent. Several men had gathered there. Yerbol had his back against a tree. His eyes were alert as he watched Wyatt leave the tent. The flames popped and crackled, illuminating the big man's face. "We didn't lie to you and your friend on purpose," he said, sitting straighter.

"*Oh*." Wyatt raised an eyebrow. "So you lied to us by mistake?"

"That's not what I meant." Yerbol waved his hand, then turned away. "Forget it."

Wyatt stood indecisively for a minute. That was the most he'd heard out of Yerbol since he'd met him. He sat down on a log opposite him, his face open. "I'm listening."

Yerbol paused, then stretched out by the fire. "We were his detail. He's a good man."

Wyatt fought the urge to shrug. Yerbol continued, "I would follow him anywhere." He glanced around, then leaned forward. "He took care of his father. He's, you know—" He circled his temple with a forefinger in the universal symbol of crazy. "We think McAdams actually made the deal for Konrad to take the old guy. Andrew, you know 'Dreg', thinks it was Nate who did it." He shook his head. "The president's not like that. He's a great guy. The father was totally devoted to him, but somehow he got derailed in the company of Vincent Konrad."

Wyatt nodded. "I know a few people who were under his spell."

"Yeah, well, once Owens got wind of that he was going to be eliminated, he started nosing around. McAdams never saw it coming. He didn't realize he was on Konrad's hit list along with everybody else."

Wyatt watched the fire play with the shadows of the commando's face giving him silent permission to continue.

"We tapped Konrad's phone calls. That's how Owens escaped.

We were a few steps ahead of them and beat them to the punch, but barely."

"Why didn't you get word to McAdams?"

"Unexpectedly, Konrad cut off communications. They had no idea that was going to happen. We headed out here to take down Konrad and prevent the massacre, but didn't make it in time, so we returned to the White House." Yerbol shook his head. "Make no mistake, we were in the same position as you—didn't know who to trust. Everybody was ready to jump on Konrad's bandwagon—the army, the navy, the air force. Owens was quite alone except for the secretary of state. The actual coup was generated by the armed forces beginning sometime after Owens addressed the country as the new president. We got him out of Washington secretly before they could finish what they started. President Owens and the Speaker of the House separated with the plan ensuring one might survive, and the president did. Believe me, I lost a few good friends who went with the Speaker. Don't you see? President Owens didn't know where any-one's loyalties were."

"Why did you come to Copper Valley?"

"You mean Ground Zero? We were trying to find his father so we could get to Vincent Konrad. When his father didn't surface, the president was sure Konrad had survived."

Wyatt watched Yerbol's face when he spoke, wondering if he could believe him.

"I'm sorry we did what we did to you, kid, but we couldn't be confident of where your loyalties were," said Yerbol.

"I'm not sure I trust any of you," Wyatt blurted.

Yerbol smiled. "You remind me of my kid. She don't trust nobody." He pointed a twig to his temple. "Smart kids. A lot smarter than the adults around here."

Wyatt took a deep breath.

"You don't have to believe in us, Wyatt. I think we'll earn that back when you see that the president's actions meet his intent. He's one of the last good guys." He paused. "Like you."

Wyatt bit his lip with indecision. He knew what he felt in his heart. He had seen bad things since this had all begun. For a minute, he wished time could unwind and go back to when all he worried about was which monster would win in a fight or if could get Jade to go on a date with him.

But life was different now. Jade was with Melvin, changed from the girl he'd adored. Monsters were no longer entertainment. They were real, unpredictable, and deadly on purpose. That's what it was, he realized. That was what made them scary. It was their intent. The monsters of his youthful dreams weren't deadly unless provoked, similar to the lions or tigers in the zoo. They reacted instinctively to defend themselves. The new monsters that filled Wyatt with dread acted with deadly purpose. They desired to kill whether it was for sport or greed. Their lust for power drove them to behave the way they did.

He thought about Nate Owens. The man had protected them all from the time they'd met until they reached the safety of Colonel Drucker's forces. He had to admit that while he didn't like him, he did feel safer when he was with the group.

"Say whatever you want. I think you all suck," Wyatt said, but his voice had no power.

Yerbol winced and Wyatt felt almost as if he'd hurt him physically.

Wyatt considered Yerbol's comments. Part of him wanted to like this new talkative guy who reminded him somewhat of Carter. The other part enjoyed the rebelliousness and distrust that sustained him on their journey. Hate had fueled him, and in a strange way, he started to like the feeling, to look for things to accentuate it. He found that sneering or answering angrily got him more attention than being the boy his mother expected. Well, his mom was dead, and he could do what he wanted. If he didn't want to forgive anyone, choosing to seethe and be angry, there was no one there to tell him otherwise.

Yerbol watched him and said, "Mind if I share a story?"

Wyatt nodded.

"My grandfather was indigenous. I'm part Cherokee. I used to stay with him in the summer. He told me this legend when I was young. I have kept it tucked away in my brain, pulling it out from its dusty box in here." He tapped the top of his head. "A Cherokee boy was sitting with his grandfather. The grandfather tells him there are two wolves in your body that are always at war with each other. One wolf is kind, compassionate, thoughtful, and forgiving. The other is mean, greedy, angry, and always wants to fight. They are locked in a fierce battle. The young boy looks at his grandfather and gasps, 'Which one will win the fight?' The grandfather points to his heart and says, 'The one you feed.' Which one are you going to feed, Wyatt?" Yerbol asked.

Another guard stepped out of the shadows. "He's asking for you, sir."

Yerbol stood with a sigh. Wyatt could hear his knees crack. Yerbol handed him the stick. "Don't forget to feed the fire. We all need light in all this darkness."

Wyatt took the stick and stared at the fire until his eyes watered. He broke the stick in half and threw it into the flames. He watched it disintegrate, knowing his anger was dissipating as well. "Okay," he said. "Maybe we'll give President Owens a chance," he said to no one in particular. He tucked the other half of the twig into his shirt pocket, just in case he needed to feed another fire.

CHAPTER 17

BLOOD IN THE WATER

MELVIN RAN SO fast, his eyes teared from the scorching desert wind. He leaped over dry ravines, not stopping even for a drink at the gullies he passed on the way back home. His heart lay heavy in his chest; the blood raced in his veins. In his animal state, he had known an absence of anxiety, and now his worry about Jade returned like a tidal wave. The freedom from fear he had enjoyed as a lone wolf was gone, replaced by terror for his wife, tethering him to his old world again.

His paws clawed the earth. He slipped, scrabbling on the boulders of the hills in the desert, leaping over barriers that could slow him down.

He worried about what the other wolves had said. What would he find? What happened to the coyotes watching Jade? If they neglected her— he'd... he'd skin them alive. He reached the outskirts of

Monsterland, panting wildly, the skin under his fur dripping wet, his tongue lolling in his mouth.

The gates loomed before him, the sky darkening. He walked more slowly, his pulse loud in his ears, filling the dull silence of the theme park.

He entered the park and ran under the turnstiles, down the frozen escalators past the entrance booths. Tumbleweeds rolled past him on the cracked cobbles. Broken glass glittered on the streets. The place had been stripped bare by the army, leaving only rubble. A few stores held a jumble of merchandise left after the park had been razed. The only building left standing was the Old Copper Valley Inn.

Melvin paused to see white lights floating by a corner of the building. He stopped, listening to the low wail from the orbs. One glowed brighter. It materialized into the crusty old miner who had guarded the hotel and prevented Vincent from developing it.

A smaller, fainter orb wobbled next to him, then slowly made its way across the path. Melvin ducked away. The orb caressed his fur, enveloping him in warmth, then bounced back to the miner. The old ghost pointed his axe toward the lagoon with a sad shake of his head.

Melvin groaned with despair. Part of him wanted to turn around and not go any further, to forget about the last few days and pretend nothing had happened. His body was filled with dread. Doom hung over the park, and for the first time since his change, he hated his life. A tear rolled down his snout. He whimpered, wishing he could turn back time. Taking a steadying breath, he moved through the park, the dread growing with each racing footstep.

He slowed when he reached the main street of the amusement park. Walking carefully, he hugged the walls of the faux village, skirting around the ruined Werewolf River Run until he came to the lagoon surrounding the private island he shared with Jade.

He howled then, long and low. It was their signal, an inhuman sound that carried an intimacy just for them. He waited, his ears alert, the tiny tufts of fur on the points quivering with anticipation for the answering call. The coyotes didn't respond either.

A buzzard screeched. Saliva dripped from his tongue as he panted. His legs shook. He stepped into the lone boat moored to the pilings.

"Jade?" he called softly, his voice choking.

There was no answering call. Realization that something had happened to his wife filled him with horror that turned his insides to stone. Throwing caution to the wind, he barked Jade's name loudly. The boat made its way slowly across the murky water. He peered over the edge of the craft, looking for anything to ease his fears. The outline of two lumps lay like sacks on the beach.

He leaped out of the boat. His paws sank into the sandy beach. He walked cautiously to the first pile. A headless coyote lay torn and bloody on the sand. Melvin glanced over and saw the other animal was a broken wreckage.

Taking off, Melvin ran to their hut, knowing in his gut that it was empty. Billowing white curtains Jade had hung only last week waved in the wind like a flag of surrender. He burst in and found the room was bare. Everything, including Jade's prized decorations, was missing.

Melvin smelled her blood. His world spiraled.

A dark puddle seeped out from beside their pallet. He walked over, spying something soft and pale next to the covers. Using his snout, he nudged it out, his world going black. It was Jade's hand. Her body was nowhere in sight.

"Jade, Jade, Jade." He ran outside, dizzy with fear.

He circled the beach, coming to the end of the shoreline where the sand drifted into the water of the lagoon. There he saw two distinct grooves in the ground, the mark of a body being dragged into the secret depths. He howled again. Leaping forward, he took a deep breath and sank to the bottom of the water.

Squinting, he saw the lagoon bed was littered with plastic bottles of Whisp, the soda long gone. Ferns undulated along with small fish. A tail whipped past him, and he turned to see an alligator slither away.

He held his breath, panic making it hard to do so as he searched the bottom for signs of Jade. Those small, round, shell-like objects that he recognized from his home dotted the sandy bottom. They lay in pairs and trios, tenderly tucked into beds of seaweed and grasses.

He reached out and touched the back of a turtle that jerked away and swam as fast as its feet allowed. Melvin felt lightheaded as his oxygen gave out. He rose and inhaled a huge amount of air. His eyeballs felt close to bursting. He pushed on, his lungs full again.

He'd know if she were dead. He'd know. He screamed. She couldn't be gone. He searched the bottom, his paws frantically pushing things around. He was bitten by something, an eel. He didn't care. He smacked it hard, propelling it away with a bloody trail.

He surged upward, coughing and choking, sucking in the fresh air. He gulped another deep breath and dived down again.

The turtle swam past him, their eyes meeting. It rolled in a circle around him as if it were mocking him. As the turtle darted past Melvin, its flippers appeared to beckon him. Melvin's body pulsed with adrenaline, pushing his powerful hind legs to follow the turtle.

He saw it then, the monster, holding Jade's lifeless body. It was smaller than before, its arms little more than stubs. Her eyes were open and staring at nothing. No bubbles escaped her mouth. Her hair floated like a blonde curtain around her face. Her arms, one handless, flopped uselessly. Melvin's cry was suffocated by the water. The creature never heard it.

Melvin surged forward, his teeth bared and ready. The pounce he made barely registered with the sea creature. It dropped Jade's body and pushed off the seabed floor to wrap its powerful arm around Melvin's neck.

Rage made Melvin strong. He twisted, forcing the monster onto the floor, and he held it there. It bared its teeth in a feral grin. Melvin could see rows of tiny sharp teeth gleaming in its black mouth.

Melvin snapped his jaws, breaking off pieces of the creature that floated in the water around them. Melvin snarled and ripped, and though he needed air, he didn't stop. The monster went limp, and Melvin abandoned it to paddle quickly over to Jade. He nudged her with his snout, his eyes dulled by tears. Melvin moved underneath her, his front paws lifting her body to take her home. He reached the surface, wheezing and coughing, but was able to gasp a mouthful of air.

A powerful blow to his back caused Jade to fall from his grip. She drifted down to the lagoon floor to lie on the round objects as if she were on a bed. The creature was behind him, pummeling his spine. Melvin dove after her, landing on all fours. The sharp nails on his paws punctured several of the circular things. They disintegrated, his weight crushing them.

The sea creature shrieked, the sound traveling through the water like a warped siren. Looking down, Melvin realized the round things were filled with tiny replicas of the monster.

John Raven was right. *They were eggs!*

Only in Monsterland and through the evil genius of Vincent Konrad could some new species be found. Why here and why now? Melvin's mind raced.

Jade would have loved knowing they were eggs, he thought sadly. She would have never harmed them. He turned to the monster and screamed, *We didn't know!* It came out as a garbled mess.

His lungs burned, along with his eyes. He sprang to the surface, took another deep breath, and went back for Jade.

The creature lunged for him, but this time Melvin was ready. He hacked away with his teeth, breaking off chunks of the shell exterior.

In another time, he would have tried harder to communicate with this life-form. He couldn't. He hated it with every fiber of his being. It had taken the most precious part of his life from him, his Jade, his wife, his family.

He thought only about revenge. His naturally curious mind was closed and locked off from him as if it had been extinguished. Only thoughts of how to defeat the aggressor rattled in his brain. It was a creature of the sea. It needed water. *Get it out of the water,* Melvin told himself, almost as a mantra.

They engaged in battle. Hacking and clawing, they rolled. The creature wrapped its shortened arms around Melvin's neck, but it was no match for Melvin's grieving frenzy. Melvin used his sharp teeth to bite pieces of the creature. His long nails raked the shell, breaking it into bits.

Melvin pulled the monster up and out of the lagoon, dragging it onshore. He rested his huge paws on its chest, immune to the struggling. He squinted as he looked up at the bright sun, a hot disk in the sky. Melvin knew the heat of the sun would dry a seahorse or starfish; so would the sunlight dehydrate this monster from existence.

Exhausted and grief-stricken, Melvin stood over the sea creature, watching as the sun did its damage, drying the brittle surface. He heard the crackle and snap as the fibers dehydrated. It gasped, its eyes pleading to let it go.

Melvin snarled as he grabbed the creature by the neck and squeezed his jaws tight. The head snapped off. It gurgled, seawater gushing from its brittle lips.

Melvin didn't move until it collapsed underneath him, nothing more than dust.

Wearily, he reentered the water and smashed every egg he could find, crushing them into oblivion. Exhausted, he went back to retrieve Jade's body. It was nowhere to be found.

He combed the lagoon floor, back and force, back and forth until his legs burned from the effort. He crashed around from one side to the other, his heart heavy in his chest.

As the sun dipped behind the mountains and its light extinguished, Melvin swam one last time, shaking his head in disbelief. Jade somehow disappeared into the depths of the Monsterland lagoon never to be found again.

Only then did he retrieve Jade's hand and bury it. Only then did he allow himself to weep.

I'VE NEVER LET YOU DOWN, HAVE I?

FRUSTRATED AND ANGRY, Rosemary pulled on the tethers holding her to the bed. A nurse had disconnected her IV earlier and brought her a tray of food, which she refused to eat. Her inner arm pained her, but she saw nothing.

Fury made her rigid. Her breath came in short bursts, her nostrils rimmed with white. *Where the hell was Shandy?* How could her two trusted crew members have let this happen? They'd always managed to squeak through all kinds of tough situations. They abandoned her. Shandy and Jötnar should have done something by now. At the very least, they could have set the place on fire!

The nurse, a bland-faced male, looked at the full tray, his lips turned down. "If you don't eat some nourishment, they'll force-feed you." He smiled benignly, his face devoid of humanity. "Your father entrusted your health to me. I am to make you as comfortable as possible."

"Well, I'm damned uncomfortable," Rosemary grumbled.

The nurse patted her hand. His touch was cold and impersonal despite his forced smile. "I'll leave this with you a little while longer. Maybe you'll change your mind."

She noticed he had a name tag that read *Oscar*. Rosemary called his name as he turned to leave.

Taking a steadying breath, she tamped down her resentment by speaking slowly, as if he were a dimwit. "How do you expect me to eat when I'm tied to the bed, Oscar?"

She batted her eyelashes at him and thrust out pouty lips. The nurse barely noticed. He began fussing with the blanket at her feet. Rosemary gritted her teeth until her jaw cracked. With a shudder, she took a deep breath, then forced her face into a charming smile.

"*Ahem*, Oscar…" She cleared her throat. He turned to look at her, his face as blank as it was before. "I'm sure my father would feel better if I could move around. It will be good for the… you know… *baby*."

Oscar straightened. He looked at the door with indecision, standing stock still as if digesting her comments.

Rosemary clawed the air with her trapped hands, then gushed, "I'm so excited about the news. I can't wait to share it with my friends."

Oscar tilted his head. "Your father said you were quite angry."

"Angry? How could anyone be angry with the news of an infant? I've waited a lifetime to do this. True, I didn't expect it to be under these circumstances. Oh, Oscar… Do you happen to know who the father…? No, don't leave! It's okay. I don't need to know anything so trivial."

Oscar stopped his retreat to the door, giving Rosemary a chance to continue her performance. She gave a heartfelt sigh. "I've accepted my fate. I'm even looking forward to it. But I'm hungry now, and I want to sit up."

Oscar glanced at the doorway, then at the intercom on the wall. Rosemary rushed on, hoping to distract him from summoning Vincent.

"Once my father sees my change of attitude, he'll applaud your foresight. Oscar," she whined, "please?"

Oscar paced for a second, wrestling with the decision. He fished a pair of scissors from his hip pocket to cut the gauze imprisoning her. Rosemary stretched her fingers to get the blood pumping. Picking up the spork, the strange utensils that was neither spoon or fork, she eyed Oscar's frozen grin. He moved toward her in an odd rush, as if he were on wheels. Rosemary recoiled, dropping the utensil. The tray, balanced on her knees, wobbled. His face was strange looking, and it unnerved her. She found herself laughing nervously, Oscar seemed unaffected, his eyes disconnected from emotions. She wondered if Konrad had everyone in the place either drugged or hypnotized.

She considered the doorway. Oscar walked over and opened it. "See? It's not locked. You're not in a prison. As soon as you're able, your father said you're free to go. No one will hurt you. I'm here to help you."

The door wasn't locked. Better and better. Rosemary smiled.

Oscar moved around the room mechanically, his arms waving at a strange angle. "It's not a prison. Your father selected me to assure you that you are welcome and safe."

Rosemary shoved the chicken around on her plate, trying to think of small talk. She needed to find out more information. "Have you worked for my father long?" she asked, taking a sip of milk. It was thick and viscous, just like she remembered. Rosemary gagged. She hated dairy.

The nurse continued to clean the room, his movements precise.

"Where did you live before your job?" she asked in a disinterested voice.

"I've always worked for Dr. Konrad."

Rosemary studied the items on her tray as well as the tray itself. It was smooth, no sharp edges. A barely touched milk carton rested on top. No help there. The plate was *Styrofoam*. Clearly her father wasn't intent on saving the earth ecology-wise. Shame on him. She tossed the plastic spork on her barely eaten meal. It was useless.

Keeping up a stream of conversation, she inquired about the island, his coworkers. Oscar gave perfunctory answers that neither revealed much nor gave her information, the frozen smile never moving.

Rosemary used the time to scope out the room. It was a small cubicle—one door, no windows, a small grill on the wall near the ceiling. A breeze blew through the air-conditioning vent, chilling her. "It's freezing here. Do you think I can get some of my clothes?" she asked with a shiver.

"You are cold?" Oscar asked.

"Yes. Aren't you?"

Oscar didn't answer. He adjusted the thermostat. Rosemary rested her head on the stack of pillows behind her with a sigh. Annoyed, she let the anger drain out of her. Fighting the fleeting lethargy that stole over her, she forced her mind to find a solution.

She stared at the vent, calculating how high she had to jump, swallowing the gasp that almost escaped her lips. Dirty fingers stuck out from the grill covering the vent she observed on the wall. She'd know those filthy fingers anywhere. The hand disappeared, and she saw Shandy's bright eyes watching her from the other side. He raised a finger to his mouth to silence her.

Rosemary systematically began to remove all the items from the metal tray holding her meal onto a side table with cool deliberate movements. Her fingers gripped the edges until her knuckles turned white. Shandy laced his fingers through the grill to remove it. They needed a diversion.

Rosemary groaned loudly. "*Oh*, I don't feel well. I think this food made me sick."

Oscar approached her, his brows comically raised.

Metal screeched as Shandy pushed the vent out. Oscar did a one-eighty as Shandy dropped into the room.

Rosemary grabbed both sides of her metal tray, smashing it on the back of his head. The metal crumpled in half. Oscar didn't budge. It was like hitting a telephone pole.

Rosemary's eyes widened when she took in the large dent in Oscar's head.

There was a shrill whine like air squeezing from a balloon, the source appearing to be the crack in Oscar's scalp. He pivoted to face her. Smoke poured from Oscar's nose, his eyebrows moving up and down in a jerky movement. Holding out stiff hands, the nurse walked toward Shandy, who whipped a gun from his waistband.

Rosemary realized two things at once, her beloved crew had not deserted her and Oscar wasn't human.

"I don't want to fire, Rosemary!" Shandy's eyes were wild. "It will bring the whole place down on us," he called out, dodging Oscar's mechanical steps. "What is this thing?"

Oscar grabbed Shandy by the neck and lifted him off the floor in one smooth movement. "Help," Shandy squeaked. "Hit the bugger with something." Shandy gurgled, his face turning red, the vein on his temple bulging.

Rosemary slid off the bed. Dizziness assailed her. She forced herself to focus. Slamming Oscar on the shoulders was like hitting a mailbox. Her fists ached. She grabbed his shirt and yanked him backward. He listed to one side, then pulled away. One of his arms jerked out, coming inches from her face, the other holding Shandy in a death grip.

"Must not hurt Dr. Konrad's daughter," Oscar said, then repeated it four times.

Shandy was gasping, his bloodshot eyes rolling backward.

Rosemary jumped on Oscar's back, the rear of her hospital gown billowing, the breeze dimpled her skin with cold. She pounded the nurse with her fist without results. Shandy's nerveless fingers dropped his gun, his face slackening.

Sparks flew from the dent where Rosemary had clobbered Oscar. She leaned backward over the bed. Stretching her fingers for anything to aid her, she clutched at the milk container from her side table. Her hand grazed it. She could hear Shandy choking. Rosemary made a desperate grab for the milk container, holding it tightly when she finally got it in her grip. Bringing it closer, she concentrated on not dropping it, then poured the contents into the crack on Oscar's head.

Oscar released Shandy so fast, her old friend fell like an empty sack on the floor. Oscar waltzed in an awkward circle as if he were unbalanced. Weaving drunkenly, he looked like a sailor returning from shore leave, with Rosemary plastered to his back.

Rosemary heard the fizzle of short circuits. The room filled with the smell of burning rubber. The robot slammed face-first into the wall, leaving an imprint of his body in the sheetrock. Rosemary was jarred speechless from the impact. Weird noises came from his spasmodic mouth. Smoke and steam sprayed from his joints, setting off the alarm overhead. Water exploded from a sprinkler head, drenching them with fluid.

Oscar gave a final moan before going dead, the light in his eyes fading.

Rosemary slipped off the still form to land on shaky legs. She wobbled over to Shandy and helped him rise.

He weaved over to the bed, breathless. Rosemary watched him climb on reaching for the vent and demanded, "What are you doing?"

He gestured to the vent. "I brung your clothes! Let's get out of this dump!" he shouted over the roar of the sirens and water.

"I'll get it." She shoved the oversized chair to the hole and reached up, pulled down a bag of clothes, quickly slipping a jacket over the hospital gown. Struggling into the pants, she then shoved her feet into her boots.

Shandy cautiously pushed the door open to see the chaos in the hallway. "Nobody knows what's going on," he said. "I spoke to some of them while you was missing. As far as Konrad's concerned, we've been treated as guests. Won't have no trouble getting out of here."

"Nobody noticed I was missing for five days?" She was incredulous.

"He's a secretive bastard, he is. Anyway, they was all excited about you. Called you his *succession plan.* You're revered, like a saint or something."

"Right," she answered, her voice full of sarcasm.

"Listen, we hid out, and they never came lookin' for us. The whole thing is strange."

"I guess he figured you had nowhere to go. He told me either the sharks or zombies would get you."

Shandy shook his craggy head. "True, that. We've been plotting our escape the whole time. Me and your big bosun. He's pretty handy." He smiled at her. "You was right about him."

"Konrad told me you both left me." Her voice caught.

Shandy studied her tenderly from under his lowered brows. "You're my girl. I'd never leave without you. You know that, Rosie."

"He underestimated you."

"Seems like you did too?" Shandy looked hurt.

Rosemary leaned over and hugged him.

Rosemary shook her head. "Never. Much as I'd like to continue our *Hallmark* moment, we have to get out of here."

"Yeah." Shandy chuckled. "Konrad thinks he's smarter than he is. That's when you're most vulnerable."

"Never mind that. You said you have a plan?" she asked while she stuffed her hair under a hat.

Shandy nodded his head, his earring glinting. "Aye, and it's a good one."

"Right. I see how good it is," Rosemary responded, wanting to say something snarky. She was wet and cranky. "You were lucky the milk shut this guy down. Otherwise, you'd have to shoot him—"

"Trust me, Rosie. Trust me. I've never let you down, have I?"

Rosemary didn't answer right away. She leaned over to kiss his cheek. "Never."

Water rained down from the ceiling in the hallways. The alarms were deafening. Vincent's people hurried in the corridors. Emergency doors were slamming to contain any flames.

"There's no exit!" she shouted over the din.

"We're going to walk straight out of here. Act natural," Shandy said.

"That's your idea?"

"We're leaving through the back door."

"That's nuts. We can't do that."

"Haven't I been walking around here like the King of England these past few days?"

"He said you were missing," Rosemary's voice was forlorn.

"We've been hiding in plain sight. Jot escaped through the roof."

"Jötnar?"

"Aye, Jot. I kept your big fella under wraps, but I'm telling you, I've been in and out every day. As long as they think you're staying on this side of the mountain they don't bother with you. They think you can't escape from up there." He pointed to the ceiling, his eyes twinkling.

The corridor was filled with uniformed people running, some holding folders over their heads to avoid getting wet, others cradling tablets to protect them from the water. Rosemary straightened her back and walked purposefully in the hallway, Shandy following her.

"Behave like you belong here. Smile." Shandy whispered behind her.

Rosemary continued walking purposefully, nodding to the people she passed. They barely acknowledged her.

"This way." Shandy pointed to another corridor. It was empty. They splashed in puddles spreading across the stone floor. He moved to a doorway.

"This way," he said.

Sunlight assaulted her eyes when they opened the portal to the outside. She recognized it as the door they used after their dinner together when they first arrived. "That was easier than I thought. He has no security."

"He told you. He don't need it, girl. Place is protected by that monster you brung him in the water and zombies on the island."

"How are we getting out of here, fly?"

Shandy led Rosemary to a path she had walked with him days—or was it eons before. They were headed to the highest point of the island.

She could hear Shandy huffing from the effort, so she slowed down, allowing him to catch up with her. His face was beet red from the effort. She started to ask if he was okay, but Shandy waved her off. They continued their trek, going higher.

Below them she saw the zombies roaming aimlessly on the beach. They crested the last hill, her feet aching from the rocky path.

A rope had been strung up on one of the sturdiest trees. Shandy motioned for her to step onto a broken boulder that had been rolled under the rope. She climbed onto the rock.

"I told you it was a good place for a zip line," he said with a smile. His sailor hands ably knotted the rope around her bottom, creating a harness. "That giant of yours made us a nifty escape."

Rosemary could see that the rope connected with the ship her father had given her down below them, where it bobbed in the harbor.

The sound of men yelling made them pause. A group was climbing up the hill after them.

"Hurry, Shandy! Get on behind me. It can support the two of us." A feeling of dread overwhelmed the adrenaline rush of their escape. Her eyes opened wide with the dawning realization of Shandy's plan.

"Don't you worry. I'll be right behind you," he assured her.

Rosemary looked at the swelling crowd of troops climbing up the hillside. Her heart sank with the knowledge Shandy was lying.

"We can do this together," she urged.

Shandy shook his head. "No time. Jötnar is waiting on the boat for you." He pulled Vincent's phone from inside his jacket and tucked it into her shirt pocket. "Pit monster against monster. You could head north and stay out of this business or turn to the shore and make an alliance with someone. I think you'll be safer on land right now. From what we saw, he's stuck here. Most of his ships are strung out across the globe." He pinched her chin. "What, did you think I was twiddling my thumbs these last few days? You've a good reputation. I've always seen to that. Keep it that way. You're too good for him, Rosemary."

He touched her cheek with a rare show of emotion, something he hadn't done in her entire memory.

"Shandy…" she started. Her heart beat a rapid tattoo in her chest.

Shandy shook his head. "You filled my life with purpose, Rosie girl. I have no regrets. If I could have had a daughter, I'd have wanted her to be just like you."

"No, Shandy." She grasped his shirt with her hands.

"I'll be right behind you," he said again, but she knew it wasn't true.

The hillside was flooded with armed troops racing up the hill.

Shandy smiled sweetly. "Keep out of closets. You'll be safe from the monsters!"

He pulled her back, then shoved hard, sending her spiraling toward the choppy water. Rosemary screamed as the harness tightened around her groin. Behind her she saw her father's men cresting the hill. "Shandy!" she screamed.

Gunshots rang out, and she heard her father's tinny voice booming of a loudspeaker. "I said no guns. Bring them back alive!"

Shandy saluted her, their eyes holding each other for a long minute. He waved to Jötnar, who stood ready to receive her on the deck of her Coast Guard cutter.

Shandy reached up, grabbed the line, and pulled it off its moorings. She saw him struggling to keep it taut.

Rosemary dipped, her weight dragging it down. Beneath her, the gray shape of the octopus filled her vision. Its dark shadow moved sinuously under the waves. At the other end, Jötnar stood on the deck of the vessel, the muscles of his arms shaking from the effort of holding the other end of the rope that was attached to the mast. She picked up speed as she spiraled, racing to collide into Jötnar's sturdy body.

She heard Shandy shout, "Now!"

Jötnar reached forward, snatched her from the harness, and dropped the line into the churning ocean. He looked up and shouted, "Jump. I will get you!"

Horror engulfed Rosemary as Shandy was pulled from the cliff to free-fall into the path of jagged rocks.

Shandy reached for his ear and yanked off his earring. He flicked it toward them, a smile on his face. His aim was true. Rosemary barely registered the clink as the gold hoop landed on the deck near her boot.

Jötnar wasted no time. He gunned the engines. The craft rose from the water, taking off for the falling man.

Rosemary held onto the railing. "Faster, Jötnar! We're not going to make it!"

Shandy shook his head, looking as if he were enjoying his free fall. His eyes once again locked with Rosemary's. He pointed to the mainland.

Rosemary watched helplessly, then realized she had her father's phone. It controlled the octopus. She fumbled for the mobile but couldn't unlock it. Her fingers worked furiously, trying different combinations to open the cell.

The ocean parted, the water spraying her as the octopus's tentacles burst from the surface. They jumped fifty feet in the air, the massive arms closing around Shandy.

"No!" she screamed.

Jötnar cursed loudly.

The octopus squeezed Shandy and dragged him beneath the surface of the water.

"I can't stop. I'm sorry. He told me this might happen," Jötnar called out and turned the boat to the coastline.

Rosemary sank to the deck, dropping the phone, a strangled sob in her throat. "Shandy, Shandy…"

Something shiny rolled next to her foot. It was his earring. The gold hoop glinted in the bright sunlight. Rosemary picked it up and closed it in the palm of her hand.

He was gone—Shandy, the man who had saved her again and again.

Rosemary wiped the tears streaming down her face. She considered the earring. It was all she had left of him. She touched the pointed post and pressed it against the soft flesh of her earlobe, piercing it. It hurt, the sting minor compared to the ache in her heart. When she looked at her fingers, she saw the stain of blood on her fingertips. She wiped them across her shirt, then pressed her hands to her belly.

She looked back at the island. Zombies massed on the beach, preventing her father's guards from pursuing her. She reconsidered Shandy's plan. She glanced at the mainland.

"We have to get out of here, Jötnar. Can you pick up speed?"

She saw three boats appear from around the other end of the island.

"Watch me!" the giant yelled.

Rosemary held on as the boat took off again. She lost her hat, and her hair whipped around her face, stinging her skin.

The octopus changed direction toward the trio of boats, catching up to them instantly. Its parrot's beak opened wide, its head slicing through the water like a shark's fin. It reached the first boat. Its arms surrounded the craft, crunching the metal and crushing the men on board.

Rosemary winced from the sound. It smashed the other boat with its swinging tentacles. The third boat made an attempt to follow them but was tossed in the air like a plaything and then swallowed whole by the wide maw.

Vincent Konrad's forces were no match for her Coast Guard cutter or the octopus terrorizing the water. It seems Shandy had been right about everything. The boat was a great gift for its speed and ability to maneuver, and the monster she delivered had been the death of him after all.

CHAPTER 19

STOMPS

THE SMELL OF smoke awakened Wyatt from a deep sleep. He rolled over to see that Howard's bed was empty. Rubbing his eyes he groaned as he rose, unsure of where he was when the memory of yesterday rushed at him. He fell back on the flat pillow, too tired to move.

For the first time in days, he felt a sense of relief. He rested, being present in the moment, listening to the wind rustle the branches outside his tent. Just knowing he was with Howard Drucker's parents took him back to the time before his world had imploded, when all he worried about was who held the remote and how he could sneak out to do the things he never told his parents.

His sense of well-being was ruined by an overlay of sadness. It pulled at him; he teetered on the edge of a dark hole. He explored the abyss, knowing he was sad, as if his entire world had lost something he'd never realized was there. It gnawed at him, making his body heavy with sorrow.

Wyatt sighed. Things had changed. He considered his new reality. He'd been tested under fire and in action. Like a newsreel, battles flashed in his mind, his scalp tightening, his palms growing damp. Life would never be the same, and neither would he.

Wyatt lifted his fingers and studied them. He had killed to survive. While his hands looked the same, a different person lived under the layer of skin. Balling them into fists, he pressed them against his eyes trying to blot out the past few months.

His mind couldn't turn off the gruesome newsreel. Zombies groped, vampires slithered, werewolves prowled, and mummies marched. At the head of the grim army, Vincent Konrad loomed, his body swelled to giant dimensions. Gunfire, mixed with maniacal laughter, echoed in his brain.

Wyatt sat up abruptly, his heart racing. He had seen Carter struggle but never understood the depth of his pain. He placed a hand in the center of his chest. It hurt. His legs trembled as if he had lost all his strength. He doubted he could stand. Carter had never complained, yet his mother had alluded to nightly terrors that stalked his stepfather.

He had resented Carter's comments about his war-inspired video games. A shiver shook Wyatt. The video games—his mouth twisted with disgust—how juvenile and trivial. His face flushed with shame. Wyatt felt silly for all the time he'd wasted, the childlike adoration of the avatars that made him think he could mimic the experience of battle.

Fatigue swept through him. His skin felt like a shell holding up old bones. War had tested him and won. The old Wyatt was dead.

He thought about the Druckers and the feeling of security they provided. He wanted to give in to the illusion of being a teenager again even if it was for a few short hours. For all that he had been so desperate to grow up, to find independence, he missed Carter and his brother. He was tired of appearing strong to squash his insecurities. He wanted to let go of this mantle of adulthood and stop worrying about making life and death decisions.

Life had flipped in the blink of an eye. One year ago, his choices had been a lot less lethal, his outlook filled with promise. All he'd had to think about were test grades and Jade. He'd spent so much of his time planning his future, and for what? The buffet of choice had been closed, probably never to reopen again.

He stared bleakly at the dirt floor. He was not going to attend college. He doubted if he'd find a school even functioning anymore.

The sense of entitlement in which he'd wrapped himself for years was like a shroud smothering him. The patina of overconfidence in the divine assurance of his future lay like a broken wasteland of doubt. He never considered these kinds of consequences or the possibility that his choices could be eliminated. The assurance of his status in the world, his placement among promise had been replaced with a sense of doom.

He shook his head, a sad laugh of resignation escaping his lips. Even after the plague had struck and life had gotten harder, there had been no doubt that his parents would find a way to prevent his life from derailing.

He peered out the flap of the tent, remembering his surroundings. Hollywood, the land of promise, the land of dreams, his dreams. Here, the good guys always won.

He had raced to escape the smothering small town of his home to find himself reeling from the lack of anything to ground him in the city. He wondered at the differences he'd discovered and how he'd never noticed it before. LA held no appeal, no future. He missed Carter and Sean. He missed home.

Everything that was important to him had been reshuffled in a new deck of cards that left him unbalanced, as if his inner ear were off.

He never imagined there would be a time when he wouldn't be

able to talk to his mom. He'd never said goodbye. All those meals when he barely noticed her, listened to what she was saying, floated in his memory like seeds of a dandelion blown carelessly away. He wanted to gather them, safeguard them, but his mind rebounded in every direction. It was filled with all the new terrors waiting for him.

Wyatt dashed a tear from his eyes, his throat clogged.

He lay back down, depleted, watching the give-and-take of the canvas material above his head. It was as if the tent were breathing. The world had morphed into a living hell filled with savage beings that made the monsters he worshipped when he was a child appear tame.

Wyatt thought about home, not the location so much as the feeling of home that rested in his heart. He rolled over, knowing he would never take anything for granted again.

Howard burst into the tent, his face flushed. "You up? My dad wants to talk to us. Come on." He held a wrapped square in each hand. He offered one to Wyatt.

Wyatt placed a pillow over his head.

"Come on, Wy. I've been waiting all morning for you."

"I don't want to move," he mumbled.

Howard Drucker sat down on the edge of the bed. "This isn't like you." He pulled at the pillow to peer down at Wyatt.

Wyatt made a face. "I don't even know who I am anymore."

Howard pulled at his lip thoughtfully. "I understand exactly what you mean. I feel like I'm standing in quicksand, not on solid ground anymore."

"Yeah, like I can't get my balance." Wyatt sat up abruptly. "I'm… I'm afraid," he admitted with an embarrassed shrug.

Howard swallowed and replied, "You and the rest of the world."

"This is new for me. I've never been afraid of anything. I was so sure of everything in my life, even the zombies."

Howard shook his head. "It's not new for me. I feel like I've been scared of stuff my entire life."

"What?" Wyatt asked.

"Climate change, for one. I worried about world peace, terrorism, if we'd run out of food. The plague practically paralyzed me."

"That's just it. I never worried about those things before. I always believed—"

"That's the irony, Wyatt." Howard gazed at the opening of the tent. "Those things were not real inside your bubble. The biggest issue you had to deal with was your parents' divorce and your mom bringing Carter into the family."

"Seems pretty stupid from this end of the lens."

Both boys nodded in agreement.

"Yeah, lame," Wyatt said in a faraway voice. "I just remembered something my mom used to tell me all the time. When I complained about, you know, Carter, she said, 'You don't know what you have until it's gone.'" They sat in silence for a long minute. "You think she was talking about Carter?" Wyatt asked.

"It could have been him, or even your dad, her old life. Who knows?" Howard swallowed. "Either way, it's all gone now. Except for Carter—and your brother."

"And your folks," Wyatt added.

"And Melvin," Howard finished. "I miss him. Are you afraid it won't go back to the way it was?"

Wyatt sat up to put on his boots. "Nothing's going back to the old way. I think I want to go back to Copper Valley. What's that smell?"

Howard walked over to lift the tent flap. "Los Angeles. Remember the fires last night? They've turned into uncontained blazes. It's moving closer to us."

"Is it bad?"

"Well, it's not good. No fire departments to put out the blazes."

"Are we evacuating?"

"Not yet. Right now they are blowing the other way."

"We should leave. I've seen these fires spread. They're deadly," Wyatt said grimly.

"Where do you expect us to go? Clowns to the left of us, fires to right," Howard replied in a singsong voice.

"And here I am, stuck in the middle with you," Wyatt finished with a grin. They laughed at the absurdity of the conversation. "Seriously," Wyatt said.

"Seriously, they're making plans to pull out of here but hoping the fires burn themselves out and it won't be an issue. You know, hope for the best, plan for the worst."

"Yeah… the worst," Wyatt said darkly.

Howard pushed up his glasses and took a closer look at Wyatt. "You better?"

Wyatt shrugged.

"What else?"

"It's… you know… I never believed that this could happen to us."

Howard tilted his head. "Why? 'Cause you live in America?"

Wyatt didn't answer.

"You studied history, Wy. This is nothing new. What makes anyone think it can't happen to them? Stuff like this happened all the time. We were just protected from it in our happy little town. But believe me, people all over the world have had their lives upended through political crises, droughts, illness, holocausts, economic crises. It's nothing new. Ours was disrupted by monsters. It's all the same. There's no force field around the United States dictating shit isn't allowed to happen here."

Wyatt grunted a response. Howard was right. He'd been naive. He guessed most of the country was equally stupid.

"Not for nothing, it was a pretty dumb idea to corral all the monsters in a theme park for people to gawk at them," Howard finished.

"Yeah," Wyatt sighed. "What could possibly go wrong?"

"Right. We 're just a bunch of Icaruses."

"What?"

"*Oh* man, I miss Keisha. The dude who made wings of wax and flew too close to the sun," Howard explained.

Wyatt stared at Howard, then sighed. "Howard Drucker, I miss Keisha too. I don't know what you're talking about half the time, and I'm tired of trying to figure it out."

"Never mind. You better eat something." Howard handed Wyatt a sandwich made from uneven slices of bread. Wyatt had to hold it with two hands to eat it. "My mom made this. There's no time for a hot breakfast." Howard scarfed down the other sandwich.

"Why didn't you wake me earlier?"

"My mom wouldn't hear of it. She said you were dead on your feet and needed the rest."

Wyatt looked at this overstuffed sandwich, missing his mother again. He sighed heavily. "Have you seen Danai… I mean the girls?"

"Yup. My dad's debriefing them," Howard said. "Come on, I'll take you to them."

They exited the tent. Birdsong filled the air. Wyatt could hear the roar of the lions from the zoo. The elephants trumpeted their unhappiness.

"They're hungry." Howard frowned. "My dad said they are running out of food to feed them."

The sun's rays were dusted with smoke. The air was heavy with it. Wyatt looked toward the horizon. A funnel of gray swirled into the sky. The hills were smeared with fiery orange patches that looked like angry wounds on the dull surface of the mountain. Worry bubbled from Wyatt's chest again, and his mind filled with all the possible scenarios.

Howard put a hand on his arm. "Stop, Wy. You don't have to carry the weight of the world on your shoulders. Leave it to the adults now."

"*Uh-huh,* look where *that* got us," Wyatt grumbled back, but he admitted to himself he was happy to let Colonel Drucker and President Etan or Nate take it from here.

Wyatt could hear the sounds of the camp. They walked back to the command tent, their feet crunching on broken twigs, the air a smoky, dingy gray.

"Those girls are a puzzle," said Howard. "My dad's been questioning them all morning. I can tell you he's not getting anywhere with them."

"Howard?" Wyatt turned to his friend. "Do you think they could be clones?"

Howard shrugged. "Not sure. They could be. It's just…"

"Yeah?"

"It's just like they've lived under a rock their whole lives. They don't know anything. If they came from a lab, you'd think they'd pick up something about today's culture."

Wyatt nodded. "I know. There's a weird innocence about them. *Oh*, hey, I forgot about something Danai said. She talked about living under the mountains. It doesn't make sense."

"Under the mountains? Like, underground?" Howard asked.

"I don't know. She's very close-mouthed, like she's afraid of sharing information."

"My dad will figure it out."

The camp was stirring, people packing their belongings in case they had to move. The blaze was far enough away not to cause panic.

Apparently the colonel had given up questioning the girls. Wyatt and Howard found them huddled around a campfire, a light detail of soldiers watching them. Wyatt sat down next to Danai. Even though she was smaller than the others, her size dwarfed him. She seemed to have gotten larger overnight. Mrs. Drucker had given them super-sized army fatigues that would have swum on him.

"Did you tell them anything helpful?" Wyatt asked.

"Helpful to whom?" Danai responded tartly.

"They know you're lying," he told her.

Danai shrugged. "We're not lying, precisely."

"Precisely?" They both laughed at the absurdity of the

conversation. Howard had moved over to Becca or Candace; Wyatt still couldn't tell some of them apart. Howard's head was close to the girl as they talked.

Danai observed their whispered conversation. "Candace, remember, it's my secret to tell," she called out to her sister. She turned to Wyatt and confided, "It won't matter in a minute. Candace can't keep a thought to herself."

"I thought Erin was the one—"

"*Oh*, they're all irresponsible. See, nothing is expected from them. I am to be the clan breeder's wife." Wyatt's eyes widened. He opened his mouth to ask, but Danai went on. "There's limited space, you see."

"No, I don't see."

"Where we live, you know. Underground." She gestured to the mountain behind them. "We moved underground when it became impossible to share the earth with your kind. You made us into the enemy because of our size."

"What are you talking about?"

"Poor Goliath and King David. Grimms' fairy tales. The giants are always mean and nasty. We're really not."

"Wait, are you implying that you're all… giants, like… *real giants?*"

Danai didn't answer. Her face was enough to make him want to apologize for his tone. "I mean, there's nothing wrong with—"

"Do I have to say 'Fee, fi, fo, fum' to make you believe me?"

Words froze in Wyatt's throat. He fought the urge not to laugh. Danai's next comment brought him plummeting to earth again.

"Minkins… I mean humans made us out to be monsters. We're not. We're really nice."

"Peaceful." Adriane had scooted over. "Only one in each generation gets to mate. The shortest one." She looked at the smallest sister. "Danai's the chosen one. Danai's fiancé has disappeared. We were looking for him."

Danai huffed. "*Some* of us were looking for him. I don't care if I never see his ugly face." She stood and walked around. "*I was running away.*"

Adriane put a large hand on her sister's shoulder. "You know that's not true."

"I don't want to be his wife," Danai responded, shaking her head. "I don't want to go back. I like it here." She smiled tentatively at Wyatt.

"Where did you come from?" Howard asked. Their circle had tightened so they were practically sitting on top of each other.

"Did you tell him?" Danai asked Candace.

"Not yet, but he's so curious." She smiled at Howard. "And cute. You can answer his questions better."

Dania shook her head.

"Please, Danai," Howard pleaded, "if we understand what's going on, it can only help."

Danai threw up her hands. "Alright. Eons ago, we were harried underground. We shared the land with minkins, lived in communities around the world. We built monuments, worked together. Our strength gave you access to doing things your kind only dreamed about. The pyramids, Stonehenge, the Mayan cities were all built by giant hands, giant strength, and I think giant intelligence. We worked together, pooling our resources. Then, somehow, things started changing. It began with a drought; maybe a war might have been the catalyst. Your kind drove us from our homes, persecuted us for our size. People claimed we ate too much. Our proportions, once our greatest asset, became an inconvenience. Malicious things were said that couldn't be unsaid. Blame from fires like that one." She pointed to the blaze on the other hill. "A poisoned well, bad crops… anything negative and all eyes turned to us." Danai sat down again as if she were exhausted. "We abandoned the surface of this planet. We didn't want to live where we weren't welcome. We are a peaceful society."

"Wow," Howard said. "I never knew you existed."

"That's what they wanted. They wiped our presence from the

earth's history, except in fairy tales. You know, we did make the world a better place. It's been downhill since our species parted ways."

"If that's true, Danai, why do you want to stay here with us?" Wyatt asked.

Danai bit her top lip. "Our babies are born in groups of six, always six. We needed to make sure we didn't overpopulate, and the elders decided that only one child from each family would procreate. They chose the smallest, the runt of the litter, to be the one to create the new generation."

"Natural selection," Howard said with wonder.

Danai agreed. "Exactly. Each generation is smaller than the one before."

"It gives us breathing room," Becca chimed in.

"Maybe someday we can share the sunlight with you. It's really nice up here, and you don't have to deal with grubs," Erin said sweetly. "If we all look like you, maybe your people won't hate us anymore."

Wyatt felt sick. They were the nicest people he'd ever met. How cruel was the human race? he wondered.

"I am that child. I must be the one to bring forth the next generation," Danai stated.

"Even if you don't want to." Howard was aghast.

"Why don't you want to have babies?" Wyatt could barely breathe.

"It's my body, and I don't choose to do it." Danai firmed her mouth into a straight line.

"So tell your father that," Wyatt said.

"That's the point. He says it's the law, and I must follow the law."

"But it's your choice!" Wyatt responded. "Nobody should dictate what you should do with your own body."

Howard nodded. "Everyone should be able to decide what they want. It's not fair to have your parents or anyone else determine your fate. I mean as long as you're of age?"

"We are considered young," Frannie spoke out. "But we are over twenty."

Howard's jaw dropped. "Even though you're big, you look—please don't take this the wrong way—and act young."

Erin smiled at him. "You're so sweet. We mature at a different rate than you."

Frannie continued, "It doesn't matter. Our parents know best. That is what they teach us."

"You said we would just come up here for a lark and go back. I don't like it," Adriane complained. She pointed to the guards in front of Colonel Drucker's tent. "These minkins scare me."

"Everything scares you," Danai said. "Where are you going?" she asked Howard, who was moving toward his father's tent.

"I have an obligation to share what you've told us."

"They won't believe you, and I'll lie when he questions me." Danai stood close to seven feet tall and crossed her arms over her chest.

"Why?" Howard stopped in his tracks.

"Because I don't want to go home," Danai said loudly.

Wyatt took Danai's hand. "Nobody is going to make you do what you don't want to do."

Two troopers burst into the clearing and ran to the soldiers guarding the officers' tent. "Permission to see the colonel."

"What is it?" one of the guards demanded.

The private whispered his answer and was admitted immediately. Seconds later, Howard's father, President Owens, and his commandos ran out of the tent.

"Come on, let's see what's going on!" Howard yelled as he followed his father. Wyatt joined him.

When the girls rose, they were commanded to stay put by their guards. Wyatt shrugged and followed the group. "We'll be right back," he called after them.

"This way, Colonel," the aide shouted, leading Howard's father to a large outcropping of rocks on the top of a steep incline.

"What is it?" Colonel Drucker demanded, breathless from the effort of the climb.

"Over there," the soldier said, pointing to the opposite hill.

The group pivoted to look across a deep valley. Wyatt couldn't help the curse that escaped his lips. The area was so silent, but for the sound of stomps coming toward them.

Howard blurted. "Giants!"

CHAPTER 20

STEADFAST DETERMINATION

MELVIN'S PAWS BARELY touched the ground, so fast did he travel. For a while he saw nothing. His eyes were blinded by tears. The world was a muted smear where the lines softened, and the charcoal sky faded into the gray lumps that served as mountains.

Birds might have chirped. Hawks and bats flew overhead. The flutter of their flight meant nothing to him. He caught a glimpse of a mountain lion running nearby, but he couldn't stir up enough interest to acknowledge it.

Melvin had gone deep into himself. He could have been running in the Sahara for all he knew. His nose led him as it followed the scent of the large creatures and the pack that followed discreetly behind him.

His body appeared to have shut down. He felt no hunger. His

mind was blank. It hurt too much to think. If he blinked, his eyes saw only Jade, and his heart constricted with the loss.

Yawning canyons rimmed the rocks on which he ran, the darkness a reflection of the shattered remnants of his heart. Only the thought of his friends kept him focused. Wyatt and Howard, and Keisha, —they needed him now. Even his father-in-law was in desperate straits. Jade would have expected him to help.

The stars layered the heavens in a swirling pattern, the sharp pinpoints of light always delighting him. Now when he considered the sky above him, all he felt was lost in a pain-filled vacuum. A buttery moon followed him, its smile mocking his sadness. Yesterday, he might have howled at the bald face of that moon, Jade joining him, her soprano harmonizing with his alto. There would be no more music for him, no warm furry body curled next to him at night, no heartbeat that matched his own.

His eyes smarted; his throat choked. Melvin's soul acknowledged his loneliness.

He ran as if possessed. He supposed he was at this point. His life had irrevocably changed. He climbed a cliff, the rocks cutting into the soft pads of his paws. He felt no pain but the emptiness inside his soul. He reached the highest point and looked out at the winding road leading to Los Angeles, the desolate valley spread out before him painted blue by the moon's light.

He observed the plodding giants with the rectangular trailer swinging between them, the pack of wolves following a pace behind. One giant paused. It's great head swiveled to look at the outcropping of rocks where Melvin stood. The eyes of the creature glowed orange like the deep pits of hell, yet Melvin knew he was as invisible as a ghost, his coat blending into the rocky backdrop.

Melvin inhaled deeply. He raced down the cliff, eating up the distance. When he approached, the group of wolves melted away, losing themselves in the shadowy landscape.

Even though Melvin couldn't see the other animals, he sensed they were nearby. He put his nose to the ground, the fresh scents assailing his quivering nostrils. He detected not only the harsh smell of the giants but also the odor of his friends inside the trailer. The air reeked of fear from the prisoners, anger from the monsters.

Regret washed over him, making him shiver. Jade's father was inside that trailer, and he was going to have to explain what had happened to her once he rescued them.

He trotted with determination. He knew he was going to get them out of there, though he wasn't sure how he was going to do it. He needed Wyatt and Howard. With a shocked gasp, he realized he wasn't the lone wolf he believed himself to be. He longed for the comfort of his friends.

Blinking back tears, he thought back to his careless remarks, wishing he'd never said anything about his life being perfect. He'd jinxed it, ruined it once again.

Was it only yesterday that he had a home, a mate, and a calm existence? It was gone now, wrecked, and somehow he was responsible.

He had failed Jade, leaving her to be dragged off by that shell monster. Lulled by his own self-confidence, he'd assumed he had killed the creature. Instead, his cockiness had caused him to lose the most precious part of his life.

His mind was tired, his body working like a robot, one foot walking in tandem with the others, his grief enveloping him. All he saw was a gray cloud surrounded by dust and sorrow.

He plodded on, his head hanging low, chains of saliva dragging in the dust.

His ears betrayed him, the silence of the desert smothering him. His keen sense of hearing was deaf to the teeming life surrounding him. Still the animals persisted poking through the curtain of isolation.

Thick cries of sorrow filtered through his haze of grief. The calls from behind rocks and bushes fought to intrude behind the dense veil covering him. He lifted his head, realizing they were talking to him, calling his name. The mournful call of a dove shivered through him. It warbled an age-old song, singing a death of their own was a loss for them all.

The cries of his animal friends reached him. Though his feet were heavy, his breath became less labored. Bit by bit, he stood taller and looked around.

They asked if he needed help and tried to give him solace. Melvin tasted the salty wetness of his tears. They streamed freely now, as if his brethren had given him permission to release his feelings. His chest heaved silently as he pursued the giants with steadfast determination.

By the time the giants stopped in a valley hemmed in by tall rock walls, Melvin was able to swallow past the lump in his throat. The creatures took a break, sitting in an oval, the trailer in the middle.

Melvin circled the perimeter of the valley, searching for a vantage point. He caught sight of the mountain lion, but it slinked away before he could speak.

His ears perked up as he started to distinguish the sounds coming from the brush around him. He was surrounded by all types of life: rabbits, coyotes, birds, and insects. The pack of wolves that refused to leave whispered words of commiseration. The animal world cried out in shared anguish. His burden was not to be suffered alone.

We are here for you, they called. They repeated, *The death of one is a death for all of us.* The melody of their combined voices became a lifeline. The comfort of the message pierced the thick armor hiding his heart, melting his resistance.

Melvin thought back to when his mother had disappeared. Nobody spoke of it. He didn't remember anyone touching him with gentle understanding. Conversations ended when he entered the room, and beyond the obligatory casseroles people sent over for his grandfather and him to eat, not a single person shared his burden of grief.

There were the ubiquitous murmurs of "sorry" and what a

shame it all was, though they eventually petered out. Then came the impatience. His grandfather told him to move on with his life, get over it. Melvin was expected to put his messy feelings away and forget his mother had even existed.

Melvin growled back a sob. He had never let go of his mother, and he refused to allow Jade to be forgotten. He didn't deserve to live. He had failed to protect her.

The cries and growls of his companions breached the clouds of grief, refusing to allow him to sink. He was grateful, but his skin tingled under his fur. He didn't deserve their comfort. As if they sensed his thoughts, they whispered that they accepted him unconditionally, even venerated the horrible things he'd done. *I'm not good,* he whimpered back. *I'm nothing special. I couldn't even keep her safe.*

With gentle persuasion and kind sounds, they let him know it was the way of their land. Nothing was his fault. She was a part of the universe now, returned from where she came.

Their unconditional acceptance filled him with more sorrow than made him feel better. He sensed, sadly, that he didn't belong with them anymore. They were too good, too unselfish. It didn't feel quite right. He was right back where he'd started, neither fish nor fowl, man nor nerd. Part of him longed for the old days, to be back with his friends Wyatt and Howard.

Whatever he expected to happen wasn't going to, and he would have to forge a new path. He had wished for so much. He sighed. *What did they say about being careful what you wish for?*

Coyotes howled their support. Bats swooped down grazing the top of his head. Soft condolences filled his tufted ears. Melvin looked up, feeling dizzy. His fellow creatures were there for him, unlike the human counterparts.

He paused, his thoughts whirling. That was not exactly true. Howard Drucker and Wyatt had never let him down. While they didn't speak much, they gave him the peace of silence and understanding, suggesting a quiet video game that allowed Melvin to be himself.

They never offered empty words. *Howard Drucker, Wyatt, and Melvin. The coyotes, wolves, and denizens of the desert.* Where did he belong now?

The complexity of the question made him draw his brows together in consternation. He took a shuddering breath. He was caught between two realms, humanity and this new one. The added worry dragged him down as if he carried the world on his shoulders.

Despite his grueling pace, the animals following Melvin hadn't deserted him. Murmurs washed over him, showering him with compassionate words about Jade. Her sweetness, the things that made her special danced on the air. *We won't forget her*, the brotherhood of animals lamented, as if they could read his mind.

Looking sideways, he caught glimpses of his friends, bowing their heads with sympathy, their comforting eyes letting him know they embraced his pain. Tormented as he was, he found solace in this community. He took a deep breath, his chest expanding, the freshness of the air cleansing him.

Melvin settled behind a tall cactus. His head swiveled in the direction of the sound of four padded feet.

Mad Max stepped out of the velvety darkness, the moon lining his fur so it looked silver.

They said nothing for some time. Max finally cleared his throat and murmured, *It sucks.*

Melvin nodded. He moved closer, hovering, their breaths intermingling. *Yes. It does.*

They killed my mate four months ago in Mexico. She was shot.

Melvin nodded mutely.

Max lay down next to him. *Life will never be the same.*

Melvin whispered, *I don't know how I can—*

Max pressed his paw against Melvin's. *Don't say it. You will adjust. She'd expect you to. One day it will just be different.*

Melvin opened his mouth to argue, but Max shook his head. *I didn't say better, just different. You'll have a hole in your heart where she belonged. It will never heal, but the river of life flows. You will keep her alive in your thoughts.*

Melvin glanced at the sky, spotting the bright light of Sirius.

It's been our way for all time. One dies, but the other must go on, Max continued.

It should never have been her! Melvin said, resting his head on his front paws.

But it was, and she would not wish for you to waste your life or drown in sorrow.

Melvin took a deep breath while Max sat down next to him

Melvin didn't say anything. He nodded his head, choking back tears. Max was right.

I'll take it from here. I can do this, Melvin added softly. *You can go.*

We won't be far, Max said as he rose and then stopped. *Why do you care so much for human scum?* He gestured to the dented trailer where the rasp of labored breathing drifted in the night air.

Not all people are bad.

Mad Max laughed with a bitter sound. *Really? Your humanity is showing.*

Melvin locked his eyes with Max's. *You're not obligated to help. You can go.*

You're contemplating suicide? Unlike your human friends, we are obligated to one another. We will help you, my brother. Animals follow their nature, and it is our instinct to do the right thing… even if it is for humans. He paused and added thoughtfully, *I hope they are worth it.*

Melvin answered fiercely, *I know they are.*

Mad Max nodded and whispered, *Then we will do the right thing. We are honored to join Melvin of Monsterland,* he murmured as he melted into the night.

I'm a fraud! Melvin wanted to scream. He was not Melvin of Monsterland. He had failed the most important person in his life.

He missed the comradeship of his old friends. They saw him for who he was, and he realized he was tired of being strong. He wanted to be himself. Melvin of the Video Games, Melvin of Instaburger. *I'll have fries with that burger, Melvin."*

For a minute, he wished he'd never gone to Monsterland and gotten bitten.

It didn>t make his life better. In fact, it had made it worse.

He had tasted being part of Billy and his clan, had felt his heart swell with love for Jade. The agony of losing all that was worse than the pain of not fitting in. He'd take the years of abuse by his peers a million times over the black hole of depression he now felt. Life was not better. Not belonging, being different applied to both worlds. Besides, if he hadn't bitten Jade, she'd still be alive today. His thoughts tortured him. Would his friends even want him anymore? He felt his heart beat fast. They were dependable. He was secure in their feelings for him. He put his head between his paws, thinking briefly of morphing back into a person. He sighed, knowing it was not safe. His monster form kept him from the dangers of the desert.

Melvin didn't sleep, his brain racked with images. The echoes of the animals comforted him; the memories of Howard and Wyatt meshed together. The mountain lion prowled nearby.

By daybreak something had shifted. The tightly coiled fury, the overwhelming sadness had dissipated. His thoughts crystallized, and for one last minute, the band of grief tightened its hold again. He fought the feeling, panting, forcing it to contract into a compact ball until he felt it dissolve.

For a while he felt the absence of everything, as if he existed in a time warp. Slowly but surely, gravity came first, followed by the keen understanding that life would go on.

Jade would remain his and his alone, alive in his mind and heart, a treasured part of him that would never be separated. Their love was locked in timeless amber, preserved by his devotion. He knew Jade would live forever.

As for his identity crisis, Melvin realized he would forever straddle two worlds, dedicating himself to both.

Wyatt needed him. Howard needed him. He needed his new animal friends. He belonged nowhere yet belonged everywhere. Melvin inhaled the fresh scent of a new day. His grief was still a living thing but manageable. His animal side would endure; his human side would cope. He knew one thing for certain: he was not alone, not in either world.

The giants rumbled as they rose, stamping their feet and beating their chests. The earth shook from their movements as they resumed their journey. They walked carelessly, crushing Joshua trees with their oversized feet that smashed the landscape. Stomping over the terrain, their footprints left the ground as desolate as the moon.

Melvin rose to follow. His ears picked up the sound of Carter's encouraging words inside the trailer.

The monsters neither ate nor drank. Melvin could hear grunts that passed for conversation. A shorter one seemed more agitated than the rest. Another offered responses with a voice that reassured with gentle persuasion, reminding him of Carter Wright.

That's odd, he thought. The conversations mirrored each other. Their confident words applied to either group.

Twice Melvin ducked behind a tree, beady, suspicious eyes turning his way. He cursed all monsters, hating himself for having a fascination with them in his long-lost youth. What kind of a creature was he, lionizing and worshipping them?

They had consumed him. Shame washed over him.

His mother had left him to be a willing drone for the vamps. He had hated her for that, and yet he was little better. How did he not see them for what they were, instead creating warm and fuzzy creatures that charmed rather than told the truth? He glanced down at his furry legs. Did that make him a monster too?

Were the compassionate wolves that supported and consoled him monsters as well?

He thought about Jade, her winsome personality, her sweet smile. She could never be considered a monster!

Melvin turned his gaze to the oversized creatures walking before him. *They were monsters.* Their enormous hands carried his blameless friends, who lay injured on the inside of the trailer. They took what didn't belong to them.

The sun poked its head through the mountains as Melvin crested the last hill into Los Angeles. He stopped.

The giants swung the trailer between them the way one swings a small child. Melvin's canine ears picked up Carter's moans.

He heard the growls and whispers, the padded feet in the hidden brush. Melvin smiled at the small army of coyotes, wolves, foxes, and the lone mountain lion that tailed him as he moved toward his human friends. The future had brought him home to his friends. Behind him, he felt the assurance that his back was protected. Either direction he went would bring him comfort and support to continue his mission.

CHAPTER 21

ZOMBIE BOATS

ROSEMARY HELD HER breath as they took off, afraid her father would blow them to smithereens. She remembered when he had detonated a bomb that destroyed a ship with a mutinous crew only a few days ago.

She stood next to Jötnar, his rock-hard arms steering the ship toward the shore. Jötnar tilted his head, questioning. Rosemary searched the shoreline, shrugged, and said, "Shandy pointed to the land."

Jötnar grunted a response she determined was useless. She looked back to the sea where Shandy had gone down. He had picked a fine time to sacrifice himself, she thought, her eyes welling with tears.

She panicked for a minute. Her situation was dire. They had neither enough fuel nor supplies to take a chance on going onto the open seas, not to mention guns or ammunition.

She went through the crates stacked in a corner. "Is this all you could take?"

It was mostly equipment and tools. No food, water, or fuel.

Jötnar shook his head. "The minkins—I mean the humans— were watching us. It was impossible. The zombies hold the beach. We had to load it when they contained them."

Rosemary observed the big man closely. "Why are you referring to them as humans? We're all humans."

Jötnar nodded his large head.

"Who are minkins?" she asked absently but received no answer. Feeling exposed and vulnerable on the ocean, she knew they'd be overtaken by her father as soon as he could get his boats filled. "We have to get out of here fast."

Jötnar pointed to the west. "Open water?"

Rosemary shook her head. "No, it would be an easy target." She pointed to a barrier shielding a harbor. "Head in that direction."

"You want to go to land. There may be zombies."

"Even if they are, we'll outrun them. We'll be able to move around." Rosemary nodded decisively. "Yes, let's go there."

The boat moved hard to the right, Rosemary's fingers digging into the chair she held for support.

Jötnar slowed the craft as they approached a crowded inlet. Small boats bobbed around the water like buoys on restless water.

They traveled to a jetty just inside a scenic cove. They slowed, their eyes darting around. Rosemary evaluated the other craft in the water. Stopping as they neared an expensive yacht, she moved toward the lee side of the boat to observe. A chill shook her. It looked like a ghost ship.

"Zombie boats," Jötnar said, echoing her thoughts.

"Steady as she goes," she said softly. She raised her leg to leap onto the other ship.

Jötnar said firmly, "No, take the wheel. I'll go."

Rosemary opened her mouth to countermand him. The giant

looked pointedly to her waistline and leapt nimbly onto the deck of the yacht that he'd secured to their boat with a grappling iron.

Her hand went protectively to rest on her flat stomach. "Be careful," Rosemary called after him.

Jötnar nodded, his weight making the other boat dip when he landed with a heavy thud. Rosemary shivered as a breeze stole under her shirt. Smoke from fires that burned in the hills smudged the sky.

She was used to the quiet of the sea, the peaceful lapping of the waves, but the silence here was oppressive. It surrounded them like cotton batting. She glanced up at the gray sky, squinting to search for any signs of life. It was warm, yet there was no warmth. The sea ebbed and flowed, the creak of the boat loud in the deserted marina.

Far above the hills, she spotted a light in the sky. She watched it arc gracefully, then spin a tight circle. It was joined by another two lights that hovered above the ridge of the mountains for an instant, then disappeared as if they weren't there. Rosemary blinked, rubbed her eyes, and decided it was a reflection of sunlight.

She paced the deck. Time hung heavy as the lifeless clouds above them. The sun burned through the haze, stifling Rosemary. Sweat rings appeared under her arms. She searched the vessel for water and could find nothing to assuage her thirst. Her lips were dry, her tongue like sandpaper. She gauged the time, pursing her lips with impatience. Holding up the hanks of her hair from her neck, she fanned herself.

Her bosun was taking too long. She thought for a minute about going after Jötnar when she heard the steady thump of his boots. Jötnar lumbered back from the other boat, his arms laden with supplies and a lone oar.

"What are we going to do with that?" she asked, pointing to the single oar.

Jötnar held it high. "Useful."

Rosemary shrugged. "If you say so." She nodded with appreciation when she noticed a gun. She moved back to the wheel.

Jötnar grumbled, "No bullets."

Rosemary made a sour face. "Was there any water?"

He pulled a plastic bottle from deep inside his pile. "Take it easy with that. I could find only one." He tossed it to her.

Twisting the cap off, she took a satisfying gulp. She offered the bottle to Jötnar, who took a small sip.

"You'll need water. Take more," she told him.

Jötnar shrugged. "I'll do until we get on shore."

They both looked at the deserted coastline. "Well then, let's get going," said Rosemary.

Jötnar dumped the pile of supplies on the floor and resumed his place on the deck. He motioned to another boat anchored a short distance away. Rosemary nodded her head. "Aye. I guess we should check that one out before we dock."

They moved through the water. Jötnar hooked a line between the two boats. Rosemary resumed her spot at the wheel, her eye catching a movement behind the main cabin of the other ship, her breath catching. Her nostrils quivered; the stench was overpowering.

She waved frantically as Jötnar started to jump on board the abandoned craft, her shrill scream stopping him. "No! Jötnar!"

The big man turned to see four zombies making their way toward him on the deck of the other ship. They moved with determination, their grunts and squeaks breaking the silence.

Rosemary scrambled for the gun and aimed it. Her finger depressed the trigger. The gun clicked uselessly. She cursed loudly. Jötnar had said there were no bullets. Damn, not even one in the chamber. She cursed again.

Jötnar grabbed the oar he'd taken from the other ship and smacked the first zombie in the head as he swung his leg over the side of the boat. The zombie flew backwards and landed in the water with a splash, taking the oar in the fall. Its head separated from its body. Jötnar watched the oar float away regretfully.

The second zombie opened its mouth to bite Jötnar. Rosemary

spied a bucket filled with sand. She pulled it off its hook, her arms burning from the effort. Swinging it with all her might, she hit the zombie squarely in the chest, leaving a huge hole in his torso. The monster landed spread-eagled on the other ship struggling to rise.

Rosemary jumped onto the deck of the other craft. Spying an ax abandoned on the floor, she dove for it, then in a graceful arc cut the zombie in half. A third and fourth zombie wrestled with Jötnar, his bare arms exposed. She screamed his name. Jötnar swatted his attackers, avoiding their gnarly mouths and rotting teeth. Rosemary threw the axe. Jötnar caught it with one strong hand and pivoted gracefully to cut the two creatures in half in one fell swoop.

"Let's get out of here," Rosemary said breathlessly as Jötnar helped her across the side of the ship. He dumped the bodies into the sea.

Jötnar directed the ship toward a sandy piece of land. He cut the engines. They floated for a minute. "Are you sure?" he asked.

Rosemary looked at the bleak shoreline. The freeway overlooking the beach was usually filled with cars. The powdery sand was devoid of life.

She turned to look at Prendick Rock, now a smaller speck on the horizon. Four speedboats took off from the base.

"Trouble," Jötnar muttered.

"They must have managed to contain the zombies to follow us." She watched the boats spread apart, one coming directly toward the small cove where they'd taken cover.

Slipping her father's phone from her hip pocket, she tried to open it, but it was locked. She stared helplessly at the illuminated screen.

"Punch in your birthday," Jötnar said.

"Come on." She rolled her eyes.

Jötnar shrugged. "Try it."

Her fingers flew over the face of the screen, pressing in the date of her birth. It opened, revealing a screenful of apps. Rosemary laughed out loud.

"Told you." Jötnar smiled.

She searched through the apps until she found an icon in the image of a baby shark. *Really?* she said to herself. It revealed a toggle. She touched the joystick on the screen, moving it upward.

The air filled with the shrieks of a flock of seagulls. They took off from the water in a cacophony of noise. A heavy splash echoed in the harbor, and a tentacle broke the surface of the ocean. The enormous body slithered through the waves, moving into the open Pacific. Rosemary tentatively experimented with the simulated joystick, moving it to the left, and watched in fascination as the octopus changed course.

"Well, Jötnar, here goes nothing," she said, a devilish smile gracing her face.

As she pushed her finger forward, the octopus took off after one of the boats moving in their direction. Their pursuers were oblivious to their being followed.

Rosemary held her breath. She looked at the phone, not sure if she had to stimulate the octopus to attack. The animal was hot on the tail of the speeding boat. Its enormous head rose above the waterline like an erupting volcano. Rosemary and Jötnar watched in horror as it grabbed the boat in its mighty arms and snapped it in half. The guards' screams filled the air, and Rosemary could only imagine her father's realization that his handy-dandy tool of destruction was missing.

The cries of the doomed sailors reached her ears, but Rosemary rested her other hand on her belly, showing no pity. She realized she didn't have to manipulate the octopus. Its instinct was enough to annihilate Vincent's navy. It turned and made short work of the other boats.

The phone rang, making her jump in surprise. She chuckled. Her father was requesting Live Chat with her. Rosemary touched the phone, allowing her father's purple face to light up the screen.

"Hi honey. Time to come home." Vincent said and though the words were spoken lightly, Rosemary detected menace in his voice.

Rosemary looked at his face with a smirk. "I don't think so."

"I'm tracking my phone, silly girl. It's time to turn around. The party is over."

"Not on your life, you beast." Rosemary spat.

"You won't get away. I found you once, I'll find you again," he ground out through gritted teeth.

"Is that a threat?"

"No, Rosemary, dear. That's a promise. Don't make me blow up—"

Rosemary cut off his rant. "If you were going to blow up my ship, you would have done so already. Face it, you can't stop me. You're stuck on that island, surrounded by zombies, and now half of your forces are gone."

Vincent laughed. "You think that's the only trick up my sleeve." He held up another phone, this one with a steady pulse that beeped. "Do you know what that is? It's a homing device I had planted inside of you. You'll never find it. Besides, did you think that was my only phone? I misplace them all the time. It's these damn hands." He showed her fingers that could barely bend. "Never mind. Watch me take back control."

The sea bubbled where the octopus made a lazy circle and appeared to dive underwater, disappearing beneath the waves.

"Here you are, my pretty." He turned the phone camera around so that Rosemary could see the octopus back in the underwater aquarium.

Rosemary recoiled, wondering where the transmitter had been implanted on or in her. She had to find it and rip it out, even if it killed her. She looked back at the shoreline. She needed to get as far away from him as possible.

"Come back, Rosemary. All is forgiven. You are very smart, and it proves without a doubt that you are my daughter. I would have done the same thing. Come home, my dear. It's not safe up there."

Rosemary shook her head. Words clogged in her throat. She looked at the endless ocean, feeling adrift. She missed Shandy's advice. She longed for his company. She didn't want to think her actions reflected anything to do with Vincent Konrad. While she knew she could be labeled as bad, he was evil.

"I can come and get you anytime I want. Go, have your fun. Rosemary," he said in a conciliatory tone, "just remember, I can hand you the world on a platter."

"Who said I wanted it? You can keep your world."

"You are being hasty. Too emotional. What have you got left? The old man is gone. Your only companion is that freak of nature. Come home, and we'll forget this episode. Time is of the essence."

"I have all the time in the world."

"No, you don't. Yours is not a normal pregnancy. It's not like any other you've ever seen. You are going to need me. Come home, my dear."

Rosemary looked at her father's face, all feelings gone. "I have no home." She pressed the red button, ending the transmission, then threw the phone into the water.

A wide swath of ocean separated them. She looked back at the craggy hills and the smoke-filled sky. She needed to lose herself on land. Absently, she rubbed her wrist where it ached.

Rosemary observed the approaching shore and said to Jötnar, "Find a place to dock. I have to think."

CHAPTER 22

MAYBE IT'S FOR THE BEST

HEY WERE ON a ridge across the freeway, six identical auburn-haired giants who stood at least thirty feet tall. Enormous with rough-hewn faces, they each had hands as large as lawn mowers. They were lined up against a backdrop of flames, their bodies illuminated by the glow of the fires.

Colonel Drucker was watching them with a pair of binoculars. "My word. Now I've seen everything," he said, his voice filled with wonder.

A dented trailer lay on the ground at their feet. Wyatt strained his eyes, peering at the sign over the open door. "That's the police station from the reservation!" he cried. He looked back at the girls who had followed them. "They told you to stay back there."

"What are they going to do, lock us up?" Becca laughed. Wyatt glanced up at her. She appeared taller standing up than she had before.

"Who are they?" he asked, pointing to the giants.

Becca looked at the ground, her freckles standing out starkly on her pale face. "*Uh-oh.*"

Danai twisted her lips and said, "My father and uncles. See? There are six of them like me. Only that one was able to have children." She pointed to the shorter one from the left. "That's our dad."

The male whom Danai indicated was her father picked up the trailer as if it were a building block and shook it. One by one, several bodies fell out. Two lay motionless on the grass.

"Keisha!" Howard cried. In the distance, a mountain lion screamed.

Wyatt was speechless. Sprawled on the ground were six people. Carter, Sean, and Lily were included in the group. He made a move to race down the cliff, but Yerbol's hand held him back. Wyatt tried to shake him off, but it was like trying to move a stone.

Colonel Drucker looked back at Danai. "What do they want?"

Danai swallowed, her eyes filled with unshed tears. "Us. There are six humans. They'll want to trade those six for us."

Danai's father moved forward. He opened his mouth and bellowed, "Give me my daughters or they all die!"

Danai backed away. "But I don't want to go with them. I like it here. Even with the clowns, I like it up here."

Wyatt looked from her tearstained face to the figures of those he loved most in the world. He couldn't lose any more people.

Colonel Drucker glanced up to Nate Owens. "Any suggestions, Mr. President?"

Nate Owens considered the situation and with cool authority said, "We are going to treat this like any other crisis. Let's see if they'll negotiate. Get me a bullhorn. What's your father's name?"

"Brontes. But you have to talk to Grillos. He is the clan leader, the elder."

Owens moved to the front of the group, the speaker in his hand. "Grillos. We need to talk. Perhaps you'll join us in our camp?"

One of the large men laughed. "You think giants are stupid? If we go into your camp, you'll trick us. We will start killing these humans by dawn every hour on the hour until you produce our children."

"He will do it," Erin said softly. "If you want, I will go and trade myself for the young boy."

"I'm not going back. They cannot force me to marry Jötnar." Danai's voice was shrill.

"Who's Jötnar?" Howard asked, but everyone ignored him.

"We don't even know where Jötnar is," Frannie replied. "I want to go back anyway. With all your fires and crazy zombies, it's not so much fun."

"No! I don't want to be forced into a marriage!" Danai cried. "I don't want children!"

"You don't have to go back. No one should be forced into doing something they don't like." The words tumbled out of Wyatt's mouth. He didn't know where they came from.

Owens turned around. "Wyatt's right. But we still have to figure out how to get our people back."

"You don't understand our ways. If we don't return, my uncle will start killing those people," Danai said.

Owens looked at each of the girls' stark faces. "Is this true?"

All six nodded. Erin glanced over at the giants across the freeway. "He's very mad."

"We have no way of knowing if they're going to return those folks," Lieutenant Appel said. "I think we should plan some sort of attack."

"No, they'll murder everyone." Wyatt considered John Raven's still form and wondered why Lily and Keisha hadn't transformed into birds to escape.

Howard must have read his mind because he murmured, "Keisha's not moving. I don't like it. Something's wrong."

"I have an idea," Wyatt said to the president.

"Well, I'm all ears and open to just about anything," he replied.

"Just tell him you'll give him your reply in the morning. Yes, tomorrow morning," Wyatt said, his face set.

"It's crazy," Colonel Drucker said, shaking his head after a meeting at the command tent.

"It will work," Wyatt responded with confidence he didn't feel. He wished Melvin were there to help out.

"You're plotting a strategy based on a book, Wyatt, a story written over two hundred years ago. I'm still not convinced. One of them is bound to stay awake," Colonel Drucker said.

Wyatt chose not to share he was basing his theory on an animated cartoon he'd watched every Christmas as a child. He had never read the book but decided it was prudent not to tell them that. Besides, he had read the *CliffsNotes* in middle school.

"Yes," Howard replied. "That's where the sedative from the zoo comes in."

"We can just give back the girls," Lieutenant Appel offered.

Both Howard and Wyatt responded simultaneously, "No!"

Howard shook his head. "Some of the girls don't want to go home. They should have a choice."

"Those fires are getting closer. We have to do something. Time is running out," Colonel Drucker said.

"You can start moving people out. We can do this with a small detail," Nate Owens stated. "It'll be with Yerbol and his men, Wyatt, Howard, and me."

"Sorry, sir," Yerbol interrupted, looking at Wyatt and Howard. "You've put yourself at risk enough. I'll do it with my team."

"You're going to need us," Wyatt replied, his face set. "It won't work unless we go along. We know all the prisoners."

"I don't know…" Colonel Drucker started.

Howard met his father's eyes. "Keisha's there, Dad. I have to go. She's barely moving. If she's startled and transforms into Medusa, she might turn our forces into stone. It's too risky."

"We'll be finished before anyone realizes anything," Yerbol stated.

"You don't know Keisha," Howard replied.

"He's right. Once it starts, all hell might break loose," Owens added.

Colonel Drucker nodded in agreement. "See if you can learn anything from those girls," he told both Wyatt and Howard. Howard opened his mouth to protest. "That's an order, son."

"Come on!" Wyatt yelled as he left the tent.

Wyatt returned to where the girls sat in a large circle. He moved to Danai. "We've come up with a plan. Let's go over there." He pointed to a spot where a huge sycamore shaded a group of boulders. They walked away from the camp to a small incline with half-buried rocks. Wyatt sat down on the largest one, now face-to-face with Danai.

"I'm afraid." Danai moved closer to him, her eyes large in her face.

"No one's going to get hurt." Wyatt patted her hand. She had changed since he'd met her. She was even larger than before. It was as if her pituitary gland had taken over and wouldn't stop.

Danai traced the veins on his hand. Her finger looked like a tree branch. "It's our puberty… all the good food Mrs. Drucker's been feeding us."

Wyatt smiled at her. "Why did you run away?"

Danai looked off into the distance. "It's stifling there. It's a closed society." Her eyes moved around the camp. "You have so much diversity here—tall, short, all different kinds of people." She shrugged. "It's nice."

Wyatt nodded in agreement.

"Our generation is getting tired of following the old ways," said Danai.

"That's in every society, but I don't know if I'd run away," Wyatt said, then caught himself knowing he'd done the same thing. He wondered why it was so imperative for him to leave Carter and Sean. He missed them fiercely. "Anyway, they should let one of your sisters marry the guy."

"It's not so easy, Wyatt. The other girls were all sterilized when they were young to prevent unwanted consequences. Besides, I told you before, I'm the shortest. Each generation is being bred smaller so we can fit in our limited space."

Wyatt reared back with revulsion. "That's horrible. What right do they have to do that?"

"Only the smallest child from each set of sextuplets is chosen to have children. The others serve as aunts and uncles. Didn't you see the size of my father and uncles? There is not enough room where we live to have a population explosion. We'd run out of food, even air to breathe. We're trapped underground, and our resources are limited."

"Why didn't you return to the surface of the planet?"

"Really, Wyatt? Look at them. They'd be hounded to death," Howard said as he joined them. "Just consider what humanity did to the Neanderthals, or even Goliath."

"I miss Mama." Candace pouted. She sat on the ground close to Wyatt, leaning on his leg. Her weight was comforting. She patted his knee. "I'm not hurting you, am I?"

Wyatt shook his head. The others slowly joined their conversation, surrounding them like tall fir trees.

"Well, I don't. I'm never going back," Danai said.

"Then our clan will die out," Erin said sadly.

Danai shrugged. "Maybe it's for the best. I don't want to crawl underground anymore. I like the sunshine." Her eyes met Wyatt's. "I like the people here."

"They'll break your heart, just like they did to us in the past. They don't like people who are different from them. Look what they've done to the vampires, werewolves, and zombies. They were people too."

"*Hey*, I didn't do anything!" Wyatt was indignant.

"You told us that you went to the park on opening day. That makes you the same as Vincent Konrad," Adriane said bitterly.

"How do you know about Vincent and the parks?" Howard demanded.

"Who do you think built Monsterland? Did you ever wonder how it was accomplished so quickly? He used and abused our tribes. He made a deal and then didn't do his part." Adriane sniffed.

Erin continued. "You see, our people are getting tired of living beneath you. It's affecting the intellectual development of some of the offspring." She cast a meaningful glance at Becca and Candace. "They decided it was time to see if we could coexist. Vincent Konrad offered us a place on the surface of the earth to help him build his parks, and he would create a new homeland for us, make the world recognize us as a part of it."

"Only it never happened," Danai said. "We built his parks in under a year. Practically moved mountains. When we finished, he sealed all the entrances, locking us in."

"Yeah." Erin laughed. "We did the heavy lifting. Get it? The heavy lifting?"

"How did you get out?" Wyatt was horrified.

"The trapped gasses under the Earth's surface would have killed you without proper ventilation," Howard added.

"Grillos and many of the other tribal leaders never trusted him. Our uncle communicated with the foreign clans, and they had a network of tunnels prepared for escape. If your army hadn't destroyed the park, we would have leveled it," Danai said.

"*Shush*. Don't say that," Erin advised. "You'll scare them, and they won't want us near their homes."

Wyatt shook his head. "*Nah*. I could never be afraid of you. You're all sweet and gentle."

"Gentle giants, how cliché," Danai said. She shook her head. "Doesn't matter. I'm staying here. I don't want to live under a rock anymore, and I'll marry who I want."

Wyatt nodded. "I understand." He turned to the rest of the

group. "If some of you want to return with them after we release your family, there'll be no problem. What happened to your groom?"

"He probably saw Danai and took off." Frannie laughed.

Wyatt smiled. "No, he didn't. You're all equally beautiful."

"Who knows why he left? We never saw him. He came from a Nordic clan that lives under Oksskolten."

"*Ah*, Norway." Howard nodded. "A perfect spot."

"But Danai, the ancient customs and traditions," Becca pleaded. "We must respect the old ways."

Wyatt looked around. They were all so different, as varied as a village. He smiled, thinking there had been a time he couldn't tell them apart. Erin was funny, and Adriane had a sharp tongue. Danai was all compassion, and Becca, Candace, and Frannie still had that childlike innocence.

"I saw how respectful of the rules you were, Becca. You ran away with me." Danai laughed. She touched her sister's hair tenderly, putting an errant reddish lock behind her ear.

Becca stood up indignantly. "I followed you to make sure you didn't get into trouble."

"See, that's the thing," said Danai. "I don't need to be watched. I have an independent mind. I can think for myself, and I don't need to be told whom to marry."

"I don't know why you want to stay here," Adrianne said. "Look what Vincent Konrad did to this world, and they let him."

"We were just as vulnerable," Danai answered. "Vincent Konrad made a commitment to our people. We worked for him, and he promised to find us a place to colonize above ground."

"Only he didn't. He's a cheat."

"You're not the only ones he cheated. He used you. He used the entire world." Wyatt stood. He had gotten the information he needed. A plan had been formulated in his mind. He glanced at the tall ridge where the giants huddled in a circle around the trailer.

Yerbol's bulky form emerged from the tent. "Stop your flirting and come to the tent. We have to discuss the mission," he said.

"Let's go, Howard. We have work to do!

CHAPTER 23

IT MEANS PROTECTOR

MELVIN SAT ON his haunches quietly observing the giants settle in for the night. He sniffed the air, knowing his friends still lived. There was no stench of decaying flesh.

The giants had dumped out the captives briefly, then put them back into the trailer as if they were finished playing with toys and were cleaning up. The trailer was behind them. A couple of the large men rested their backs against the corrugated walls. To the northeast, the fires crackled, burning the dry brush.

Melvin glanced at the early morning sky. He swallowed the impatience that bubbled up from his throat. He tilted his head, thinking about the sounds of the pack behind him.

He was surrounded by fifty or so additional wolves, hybrid coyotes, and even a few foxes. With every mile, his pack had swelled, the new members swearing loyalty to him. Several members of the pack never failed to mention his attempt to defeat Vincent Konrad. The story of when he ripped off Vincent's head had grown to epic proportions until he wanted to scream for them to stop. He was hailed as a savior for canine-kind, a true friend to four-legged creatures, big and small.

Melvin looked back at the clusters of animals grouped in the shady spots under the trees. He stood, his four feet bracing the ground, feeling tall. Blood pumped through his veins, filling him with strength and power.

He considered the army camp on the next ridge but decided not to go there. His gut told him Howard and Wyatt were nearby. His nose reconfirmed it. Melvin detected their distinct odor the way a policeman reads a fingerprint.

I know you're here, he said, looking at the base camp.

There was the rustle of leaves and the mountain lion stepped out from the brush.

Melvin squinted. *Do I know you?*

The mountain lion snarled, *We've met.*

Melvin studied him. The air around them shimmered, and Melvin stared hard at him. His gaze narrowed to the mountain lion's eyes and he said, *Tocho.*

Tocho in his mountain lion form, broke eye contact. *I assume you plan to attack. I will be with you when you charge.* He turned to leave.

We could work together, Melvin said, but the lion melted into the shadows.

Melvin sat and resumed studying the giants.

The creatures appeared to be family beings, clannish, thrown away by society for their appearance. In some small way, Melvin identified with them.

A few of his new canine friends shifted on the grass. *Anything?* a gray wolf named Renaldo whispered.

Not yet. Melvin shook his head. "They'll make a move today. I wish I knew what they were thinking."

What are you thinking? Renaldo asked.

I'm not sure yet, Melvin whispered. *But it seems Tocho will follow our lead.*

The mountain lion? Mad Max strolled over. *I don't trust him.*

Why, because he's human.

No, because he's angry. His judgement will be clouded. What would your friends want to do? Mad Max growled.

There are other people in charge now. They'll have to follow what they are told.

Why? Renaldo barked.

Melvin managed a credible shrug. *They are young. They don't give orders.*

Ha! Renaldo laughed. *That's not what I've heard. Your friends are resourceful and don't follow orders. The three of you together are unbeatable. My bet is on what they will tell their superiors to do.*

Mad Max nodded in agreement. *We want to join forces. With you as our leader and the humans Wyatt and Howard, we'll be unstoppable!* Max was excited.

It's not so easy. You're giving the three of us more credit than we deserve. Melvin hid a wry grin, remembering how he and his buddies had been treated back in Copper Valley, as if they'd had the zombie plague.

Max went on, unaware of Melvin's thoughts. *The tale of Melvin and his human companions is the stuff of legend. I'm sure you are going to do something spectacular and bring us all glory!*

Perhaps. I know we'll be here to cut off the giants from escaping, Melvin said, calculating the terrain as if it were a battleground.

See, I told you you'd think of something. The older wolf nodded, circled for a bit, and lay down in the shadows.

Mad Max came close to Melvin who eyed him sideways. *Why do they call you Mad Max?*

Why do you think?

Melvin smirked. *It's a cool name. Not much you can do with a name like Melvin.*

I don't know, amigo. I think you've changed the perception of it already.

Really? Melvin was nonplussed.

Don't you know the meaning of your own name?

Melvin shook his head. *I never thought about it. I always thought it was a mean trick my mom played on me when she had me..*

Si. I've heard a new generation of cubs being born. Their mothers are calling them Melvin. It means protector. It has always meant protector. It suits you. It is your destiny.

Mad Max bumped Melvin affectionately and advised him to get some rest. Melvin's eyes burned from lack of sleep, but he didn't lie down. He watched the giants stirring.

He thought about his name. *Melvin* meant protector. Big deal. His mother could have easily named him Charley, like his uncle, or George, after his grandfather. A name couldn't determine your personality or qualities. Names meant nothing.

Melvin drifted, his eyes growing heavy. As sleep claimed him, he realized that only his actions would define him and steer him in the direction of his future.

CHAPTER 24

GROWING TIME

THEY LANDED IN an inlet. Jötnar was able to pull the boat onto the beach and camouflaged it with debris of broken lumber. Rosemary worked alongside him, dragging planks of wood and discarded canvas to help.

Rosemary glanced at Jötnar as he worked. He was intent on his job, barely acknowledging her. She stopped to watch the sun traveling west. It was growing dark. The air chilled. Birds screeched overhead, diving for the water.

Rosemary walked down the deserted wharf to look at the vast ocean. It spread out before her, meeting the horizon, the whitecapped waves like the surface of an endless tabletop. She loved the ocean.

Holding her hand out in front of her, she measured its size against the backdrop of water. The sky above weighed down on her, making her feel no bigger than a tiny speck, a mere particle of nothingness. She whispered a prayer for Shandy, missing him greatly. It was as if a piece of her were gone.

Glancing back at Jötnar hard at work, she observed his bald head glistening in the setting sun. Time slowed, and the air around her became thick like molten sugar.

Memories of her mother flickered in her mind like an old-time movie. Rosemary saw her in sepia tones as she tried to recall her expressions. Her mother was always in motion. She had never spoken about the hardships of life or the loneliness of her existence.

Rosemary pressed her hands on her flat stomach, wondering how her life was going to change. Her ankles wobbled, her knees weakening with the pressure on her shoulders. She reached out to grab something for support, but there was nothing there. Her hands clutched the air, and she gripped her fingers into fists, her knuckles turning white with the effort. Fighting the wave of panic overwhelming her, Rosemary rocked on her feet.

For the first time in her life, she felt small and alone. At least when she was born, the world wasn't a smoking wreck of itself. Life promised a future to everyone.

Her brows furrowed, the tension in her head tightening. Squinting, she searched the distance as if she could divine her future there. Pressing her palms into her temples, she realized she knew nothing. She wasn't even sure who the father of her child could be.

"Help me," she whispered to the water. The sea was her haven. She felt safe there. The rhythm was as predictable as the stars that shone at night or the moon's pull of the tides.

Indecision gnawed at her. Her brain had ceased to function. As much as she tried, all she came up with was a dull blankness. Refusing the urge to sink to her knees in the churning surf, she planted her hands on her thighs, breathing deeply of the sea air.

Rosemary stared at the waves lapping the shoreline for a long time, her feet sinking into the soft sand. Lassitude overcame her. The clean smell of the ocean, the heat on her face. The pull of the water sucked at her shins. She sank down, her heels digging in, rooting her to the ground. Soon her feet disappeared, and she was covered to her ankles with sand. The waves rushed in, pushing her, and though her body swayed, she refused to be moved. Power pulsed through her soul, firming her calves rock hard as she fought the pull of the water. She invited the pounding of the ocean, each wave making her resistance a triumph.

She straightened. Shading her eyes, Rosemary searched the vast ocean with the realization that the answers were not to be found there. She twisted toward the beach, watching Jötnar work to hide the boat. Her mind cleared. She knew she would get no help from the sea.

"Leave it," she ordered, her voice swallowed by the crash of the surf.

Jötnar looked up, a question in his eyes. "Wot?" he asked, his eyes widening. He looked at her for a long minute, then went back to work, ignoring her.

"I said stop!" she shouted, pulling her feet free from the well where they'd been buried. She struggled as she walked in the sand to his side. "We're moving inland. There's nothing for us out there."

Jötnar scowled, his body frozen, but his hands gripped the planks of wood as if he hadn't processed her order.

"You can pout all you want. We've no supplies. We have to get away from my father. He's stuck on that island, but he could deploy another ship. He'll be less comfortable on the mainland."

"You don't know that. Water is safer," Jötnar replied.

Rosemary nodded. "Not this time. Konrad planted a transmitter somewhere on me. Until we find it, it's safer here. We'll head east."

Jötnar shrugged his shoulders, his eyes downcast. "We won't be safe until you find it."

"It's only a matter of time before he gets here or comes after us with that helicopter," she agreed.

Rosemary tugged the plank from Jötnar's hand and let it drop onto the ground.

Jötnar was sulking. The thought of it made her skin crawl. She might have been the captain, but it helped having Shandy behind her. Now she had no one and didn't like the tight ball of worry planted in the middle of her gut.

Jötnar's brows lowered; his jawline hardened. Rosemary tried not to shiver. She studied his face for a clue, catching her breath when she recognized fear in the big man's face. "What is it about the land that scares you?"

Jötnar stalked off and put together a pile of supplies to travel with, his movements jerky. Rosemary observed him unhappily. No crew, no Shandy, only this brooding giant. Taking a deep breath, she watched him, thinking of how to convince him it was the right move.

Rosemary studied Jötnar's powerful shoulders as he worked. Aside from the fact that he rarely spoke, she admitted she hardly gave him more than a passing thought. He was always in the shadows, a big, hulking specimen that gave off nothing more than menacing impatience. He followed orders well enough, but that was when she had Shandy.

It had never bothered her before with Shandy by her side. She never doubted her authority. What did she really know about Jötnar other than his great strength and the fury when he defended what he was ordered to protect? She walked back to him.

"You never told me why you went to sea," Rosemary said as she helped him fill a canvas bag.

Jötnar grumbled a response.

"What? I don't understand you," she said.

Jötnar shook his head like a shaggy bear while he rolled a length of rope around his arm. "Not important."

They faced off opposite each other for a moment. Rosemary was the first to look away, then cursed herself for showing weakness. He ignored her, standing abruptly to drag over another crate. Rosemary simmered, wondering if their relationship had changed as their circumstances developed.

A cool breeze stole over her, making her shiver. Without thinking, she hugged her arms to her chest.

Jötnar returned, threw down the ropes he'd been carrying, and shucked off his shirt to place it around her shoulders. It was slightly damp from the spray of the water but warm enough from his body heat. It smelled of Jötnar, a clean but earthy odor.

"No." She tried to take it off.

Jötnar stopped her. "You need it."

"I'm not some wilting flower," she snapped. "I am still the captain." They were silent for a long minute, each reflecting their circumstances. "Shandy was with me for life. He would have followed me anywhere." She regretted the words as soon as they left her mouth. She sounded like a petulant child.

"Maybe it was the other way around," Jötnar said.

"I'm not some weak woman. I know what I need to do."

Jötnar sighed as he sank down on a wooden box. She realized he was as exhausted as she was. She had no idea what was going on inside his head. "What do you want?" she asked.

He shook his head. "You are the captain," he said simply.

Her spine relaxed. The tension holding her uncoiled. "Yes. I am the captain, and you are my first mate now."

Jötnar nodded and with a rare smile replied, "I am your *only* mate." He rose to finish packing their supplies.

They would be traveling inland into unknown territory. Rosemary relaxed. She might not have Shandy, but Jötnar might turn out to be the next best thing.

Brushing her hands together to wipe off the dirt, she noticed a discoloration on the inside of her wrist. She ran her forefinger of the spot and felt a small lump. Squeezing the skin together, she gasped when the hard piece of material pressed against her flesh.

Jötnar looked up, his brows furrowed. "Wot's wrong?"

"The transmitter. I think it's here."

Jötnar lumbered over and moved her hand. His gentle fingers

probed her arm. "I think you're right." He glanced up to her eyes. "I need a fire to sterilize the knife."

"Do it now. We have to remove it so he can't find us."

Jötnar opened his mouth to argue, but her stoney face stopped him. Cradling her arm like a fragile bird, he made a quick slit, and squeezed out a small transmitter.

Gritting her teeth, Rosemary smothered her gasp and smiled at him. Her eyes watered. Jötnar ripped the tail end of his shirt with his teeth and fashioned a bandage. He picked up the small plastic device and crushed it between his fingers.

"It'll do." Rosemary nodded and staked off, lest he see the tears that threatened to fall.

"We should get moving." She looked towards the setting sun. "We'll scavenge supplies as we go. Maybe find a car." Her wrist throbbed, but she refused to show how much it pained her.

Jötnar shook his head. "I won't fit in the small vehicles they have here." He pointed to abandoned electric cars that looked like toys.

Rosemary gave him a once-over. It was true. He appeared to be growing by the minute.

They had to get moving. "True. We can walk all the way—"

"Walk where, Captain? Where are we going?" He glanced darkly at the passing scenery. "Over there." He pointed. "That's their airport."

Rosemary shrugged. "LAX. So planes have been grounded. Nothing's flying. If you couldn't fit in a car, I doubt you'd fit in the cockpit of a plane." Jötnar nodded in agreement. "Still, I think we should look for a place to settle ourselves," she continued. "Dig in. Find supplies to trade."

"Trade with who?" Jötnar asked.

"Whom," she corrected. "There's got to be somebody here." Rosemary held out her hands, her words echoing as she spoke.

Jötnar turned to stare at the sea, his lips a firm line of disapproval.

"Aye. I miss the sea too." She eyed his big body. "The ship and you. It's not practical anymore. Do you have some sort of disorder?"

Jötnar laughed, a big booming noise that sounded unnatural. "Something wrong? Ask my Pa. Something is very wrong."

Rosemary opened her mouth to respond, but Jötnar's lowered head froze the words in her mouth. She placed a hand on his arm.

"It's okay, buddy. There's something a little wrong with all of us."

They walked for miles. The stores along the way had been picked clean. Neighborhood after neighborhood, they found deserted buildings, abandoned and useless cars.

The sun had set, and without lights, it was pitch black. Jötnar's ability to see in the dark gave them a tremendous advantage. Rosemary discovered he had an acute sense of hearing as well.

She opened her mouth to comment when he clamped his hand over her lips and scooped her up like a doll. He slid between a row of stores into a dark alleyway, avoiding smashing into any of the oversized trash containers lining the path.

"*Shhhh,*" he cautioned.

Rosemary could feel the thud of his powerful heart. Then she heard the backfire of an engine. She poked her head up, and Jötnar placed his hand over her skull, pushing her down. His big body loomed over her.

"Wait here," he ordered. He took off after the vehicle.

Rosemary rose to follow, then sank down again. It was so dark, she couldn't see her hand in front of her face.

There was the roar of a motorcycle taking off, followed by the screech of tires and then the sound of a scuffle. Fist thudded flesh, an exhalation of air, and a deep moan.

Minutes later, Jötnar returned, dragging the bike behind him.

It was a chopper with a long front wheel and a lowrider seat. She could see Jötnar's eyes gleaming in the darkness.

"You wouldn't believe the strange creature riding this," he told her. He raised his other hand to reveal an unconscious… *clown* dangling from his grip. "What is *this*?" he asked, shaking the man in the baggy polka-dot suit.

Rosemary peered up, her face going slack with surprise. "Bring him over there." She pointed to an area where the light from the moon silvered the street. She continued, her voice choking with laughter. "It's a clown."

Jötnar brought the man closer to his face. "Do they bite like zombies?"

"Haven't you ever seen a clown? Didn't you ever go to the circus?"

Jötnar shrugged. "Scary. I don't like it." He tossed the lifeless form over his shoulder, and it sprawled onto the pavement. He climbed onto the bike and motioned for her to join him.

Rosemary moved into the cradle of his arms. The bike squeaked, bending lower, but appeared to support their weight.

Jötnar turned on the engine, and they took off into the night.

They traveled the 405, passing town after town. The surrounding hills had patches of fire burning brightly. Here and there, she could see entire areas lit up with flames, the houses of Los Angeles serving as kindling. The blaze roared like a living thing. It was a monster and Rosemary sighed for the destruction of it all. Despite the crackle of the fire, the city was eerily silent. She worried her bottom lip thinking of the victims, the people displaced, and resting her hand on her stomach, she thought about the children.

The white letters on the street signs sped by like ghostly signposts. Rosemary might have dozed. She realized she was groggy. She shook her head; her hair was blowing around her face. The smell of burning trees filled her nostrils.

"Stop! I need a break!" she shouted over the roar of the motor.

Jötnar pulled the bike onto the dark shoulder, where Rosemary was able to pull herself up a hill behind some trees to take care of nature.

They had to find some food, she thought as her stomach grumbled. She hadn't eaten since last night, and that had barely been a meal.

"Let's head up there and see if we can rustle up some grub." She pointed to the overpass before them.

"I don't like grubs. They're dangerous." Jötnar made a face and mounted the bike.

"I said grub. It's another name for…oh forget it." Rosemary slid into her spot. Her body jerked against him when they took off.

Culver City looked like the set of an apocalypse movie, Rosemary thought. Moonlight lit the streets, but the approaching dawn painted everything a dull pewter. Papers flew in the roads. Doors banged. The protective gates attached to several of the buildings rattled as if the inhabitants were trying to get out, only there were no signs of life.

They stopped at a drugstore that had been picked clean. Rosemary found a squashed energy bar that Jötnar refused to taste. He insisted that she eat the whole thing. He found a tube of half-used antibiotic cream and bandages forgotten in a first-aid kit in the bathroom.

Water gushed from the side of a building. Jötnar tasted it first, declaring it palatable. Rosemary couldn't stop drinking once she started. The tepid water felt wonderful on her face and down her throat. Her body absorbed it as if it was parched.

They drank their fill, then searched for containers so they could fill up and take it with them. Since plastic had been outlawed, there was nothing they could find to hold water.

A Chinese takeout yielded soup containers and some foul chicken that Jötnar happily consumed, maggots and all. The smell made Rosemary gag, but the big guy had no problem with it.

She found a package of dried fish pieces called *Drunkards Fish Chunks* wedged behind the door. The smell wasn't strong, and she could tell by the expiration date that it had a few months before it would go bad. She chewed on the salty fish, bones, skin, and all, eating slowly. Jötnar popped a few pieces into his mouth, groaning with delight. It was no worse than some of the salted fish they had caught and dried on the ship. It certainly beat the moldy chicken.

Her belly nominally satisfied, Rosemary suggested they bed down for a few hours in the shelter of one of the buildings. It was growing lighter, and she had mixed feelings about riding in full daylight.

Jötnar left to see if he could find bedding. Rosemary wandered out of the restaurant and walked toward an abandoned theater. She pulled at the boards covering the door. The rotted wood gave easily away. Jötnar approached from behind and peeled away the wood as if it were *Band-Aids*.

Rosemary fell back, her legs giving way. A wave of fatigue washed over her, making her head feel disconnected from her body. Jötnar caught her up by the armpits, lifting her on his back when she stumbled. She could barely wrap her arms around his broad back. The ground looked quite distant from her perch.

"Jötnar," she asked weakly, "are you… growing?"

Jötnar grimaced. "It's begun."

Rosemary leaned on his shoulders. "What?"

"My growing time. My birthday passed last week."

Rosemary paused to think of how to ask. "Just how old are you?"

He was bursting from his clothes. "Old enough," he grumbled. "Old enough to decide for myself how to live my life and marry whom I choose."

"Marry whom you… Jötnar, what are you talking about?"

"Long story."

"It seems we've got the time," Rosemary said with a chuckle. "I'd like to know."

Jötnar hefted her higher. "I don't know where to start, Captain."

"Well, start at the beginning, and that's an order."

Jötnar continued to pull at the boards over the door of the

building and spoke while he worked. "I was born on a mushroom farm under the fjords in Norway."

"I thought you were Scandinavian," Rosemary replied, then settled herself comfortably for the rest of his story. Her eyes felt heavy, and she realized she was beyond exhausted.

"I am the youngest of six, the smallest, the runt of the litter, and for that I am forced to marry a bride chosen for me." Finished gathering supplies, he sat down to change her bandage. His touch was feather-like. Rosemary let her lids fall.

"How gothic!" she breathed.

"That's my point. I'm not ready to marry. Besides, maybe I've got other plans."

"You do? Who is she?" Rosemary's eyes snapped open and leaned closer to ask.

Jötnar's broad shoulders bunched. His face reddened. "I said maybe, didn't I?"

"Okay, never mind." Rosemary laughed. "Who is this paragon your parents chose for you?"

"That's the point. I never met her. I was supposed to attend the betrothal ceremony in a few weeks, but I left."

"*Hmpf*," Rosemary said, getting comfortable. "I would have run away too. What a pair we are, *hmmm*, Jötnar?"

"Pair of fools, walking around this godless place."

Rosemary closed her eyes, feeling safe. "You sound just like Shandy," she said.

"I miss him too."

Rosemary dozed for a short bit. When she woke, Jötnar had placed her on the floor of the lobby of the old theater.

She was lying in a pile of smelly carpets that felt wonderful despite their repellent odor. She was wrapped in a velvet curtain that gave off clouds of dust when she moved. Rosemary sneezed, then shivered.

A pile of carpets blocked her view. They moved, and with a start, she realized Jötnar was underneath them.

Jötnar took off his covering and tucked her into it.

"No, no, you need it." She tried to give it back.

Jötnar waved her off. "Where I was born, this is like summer."

"I wish we could make a fire."

"We'd burn this place down. Besides, weird creatures live here," he said grimly.

"Yes, that's what I've heard. This is LA. Weird creatures have always lived here, even before the apocalypse."

"Go back to sleep. I will watch."

Rosemary leaned against him, feeling safe.

She awakened to find a feast of candy before her like a treasure. *Kickers Kandy Bars*, a half-eaten *Wee Wanda Cake*, and bright red licorice made for a satisfying meal.

"How far into this place do you want to go?" Jötnar asked as he walked into the room. His head was wet from what she assumed was a washing.

Rosemary wasn't even sure what she was looking for. She bit her lip. "We need a place, a base of sorts where we'll be safe from Konrad's reach. A place where we can defend ourselves."

She touched her stomach. She had time, but with the country in its current state, they would have to find a home where she could finish the pregnancy safely. Only after the baby came would she be able to figure out their next move. She wasn't quite sure what Vincent was talking about the timing of this pregnancy. She was a human and expected it to be the normal nine months.

It was daylight outside. Rosemary could see the full effect of the devastation. She realized with a sinking feeling it was going to take a while to find a place to settle.

For a minute, she wondered why she wanted to travel inland. It was a wasteland. They were better off at sea, but there she ran the risk of facing her father.

Here and there they met up with a mindless zombie that Jötnar dispatched with a huge tree limb he'd placed across the front of the bike. They got back on the 405 and continued their trip. Twice they got off to look for gas. She knew their time with the bike was coming to an end.

Deep in thought, Rosemary glanced up to see Jötnar equally quiet. His eyes were distant, but every so often she saw them move to study the mountains surrounding them, his brows lowered with worry.

The smell of the fires grew stronger. The air turned gray and sooty.

Rosemary wiggled, her legs going numb. Jötnar pulled off the highway next to an abandoned landscaper's truck. They lost several hours while he salvaged the small trailer, hooking it onto the motorcycle.

She was against taking the trailer, but Jötnar refused to listen. She argued that they had a limited supply of gas, and the trailer was probably going to be useless soon, but Jötnar would not be dissuaded.

While he worked, she managed to find a supply of Whisp soda. The stuff was horrible, but Jötnar adored the sugary taste. They also stocked up on a case of vegan crackers, the only product left behind in a garage of the house they pillaged.

"Feels like old times," Rosemary said wistfully, stuffing shirts into a knapsack. "What do you need the hose for?" she asked when he packed it into the trailer.

Jötnar replied, "Useful."

They took off, deciding to travel the side streets for a while.

Jötnar drove slower, stopping by an SUV on the side of the road. Taking the hose, he ripped open the gas tank and put one end of the hose into his mouth. He sucked deeply. Seconds later, he gasped and ripped the hose from his mouth, liquid gushing from the end. He placed a hand over the hole, then brought it to the bike, where he filled the tank.

Rosemary nibbled on a vegan cracker, smiling. They now had a full tank.

They took off, and Rosemary was jolted from her thoughts when Jötnar stopped abruptly. She slid off the bike, lost her balance, and landed in a boneless heap.

"What's wrong with you?"

Jötnar stood, the bike between his legs as if he'd been poleaxed. He pulled her up and moved over to a trash receptacle to peer at something in the street beyond them. Crouching under a sign that read *West Hollywood*, they hid in an alley off a main street.

"What's the matter?" Rosemary whispered.

"*Shhhh…*" Jötnar pointed to a group of wildly painted creatures running in the streets like a demented circus. "More of those *clowns*."

Rosemary made a face. "*Ugh.*"

Jötnar looked at her blankly. "Why are they dressed like that?"

"I don't know, but it's stupid. Some people like them. They're cute in a way."

Jötnar leaned closer. "Look."

He pointed to a sewer drain where a white-gloved hand beckoned them closer. "You think *that* is *cute*?" he asked, his eyebrows comically raised.

Rosemary got on one knee to peer closer.

The clown grinned, it's macabre face alight with twisted humor. "Hiya Rosemary."

Rosemary snorted, tickled by the clown in the sewer. "How did you know my name?"

Jötnar kneeled down next to here, completely unamused.

"What a nice boat." In the darkness under the sewer the clown held up a paper flyer with an image of Vincent Konrad and a photo of Rosemary. "Look at the size of that reward." He giggled loudly.

"Where'd you get that?" Rosemary demanded.

"The clown's all over LA know your name," it responded with a chilling smile. "Your father Dr. Konrad been dropping these flyers everywhere. He says you stole his boat."

"What's your name?" Rosemary said with an inquisitive look.

"Why, I'm, Dollar Foolish, the lazy-ass clown," the creepy clown said. "Yes, Dollar Foolish, meet Rosemary and," he paused. "Rosemary, meet Dollar Foolish."

"What the hell are you doing in a sewer? Wait don't answer that. It's probably cleaner and safer in the sewers than it is on the streets of Los Angeles."

"There is a storm coming Rosemary and I am hiding. *Yuk, yuk!* A storm is coming from very high above that will blow this whole circus away. Can you smell the circus, Rosemary? There are peanuts. Cotton Candy. Hot dogs. *Yuk, yuk.* And…"

"Popcorn?" Rosemary asked, playing into the clown's idiocy.

"Popcorn!" Dollar Foolish repeated. "Is that your favorite?"

"Only with lots of hot melted butter, of course."

"Mine too! *Yuk yuk!* Because they *pop.* And *pop, pop, pop, pop!*"

Jötnar raised an eyebrow. "This is dumb."

Rosemary side-eyed Jötnar and agreed. "I think we're going to get going now Dollar Foolish."

"Without your boat?"

Rosemary leaned in. "Ship. You mean a ship."

"Take it Rosemary," the clown grinned evilly holding out the flyer..

Rosemary bent over and reached into the sewer.

"Oh, please," Jötnar's voice broke the silence. "You're gonna put your hand down there?" He rolled his eyes. "LA clowns suck." Jötnar reached into the sewer grate and grabbed the clown by its scrawny neck, its eyes bulging from the white-painted face, and yanked him from the depths. Jötnar shook the strange creature and spat, "Not funny or nice!" With a powerful wind up, he chucked the clown into the heavens.

Rosemary stood and watched the creature fly upward, finally hitting a billboard of *Vincent Konrad's Monsterland*. After a loud *splat* that sprayed blood all over the theme park advertisement, Dollar Foolish slid down slowly and fell to the pavement motionless.

"Now that's funny!" Jötnar laughed.

Jötnar and Rosemary were interrupted by the commotion of a huge bonfire that roared in the street. It was ten feet high and had two forked poles on either side of it.

A woman as tall as the hanging traffic light and wearing a red wig came out from behind one of the buildings. Everything stopped. All the clowns running rampant in the streets fell to their knees.

Jötnar sat ramrod straight.

"What is it?" Rosemary demanded.

"Aunt Henny," Jötnar whispered. "I thought she was dead."

"You know her?"

"Yes. She disappeared from home when I was a young boy." He stood up. "I'll go talk to her."

Rosemary grabbed his forearm. It was as big as a log. "Do you think that's wise?"

"You didn't mind talking to the clown idiot." Jötnar was thoughtful. "I don't see a way around them." He paused, his eyes drawn to two clowns marching into the street, a large railroad tie resting on their shoulders. Hanging like some captured deer, a man swung from the pole, tied to it by his hands and feet. His head dangled; his eyes were rolled back in his head. They were heading to the fire.

Rosemary covered her mouth. "*Oh* no."

"This is not good," Jötnar said.

"You can say that again," Rosemary responded.

Jötnar broke the silence. "We cannot go around them. We must go through them. Or can we turn back?"

Rosemary thought about their meager supplies. "If we are to make a successful escape anywhere in this wasteland, we have to move forward."

"I'll talk to Henny."

"Henny? What are you talking about?"

"The redheaded woman. My aunt."

"You're not even sure that's your aunt."

Jötnar cocked his head. "It looks like her."

"No! You can't go." Rosemary tried to stop him.

"I am not afraid," he told her.

"But I am."

Without looking back, Jötnar strode out into the street.

CHAPTER 25

LILLIPUTIANS

THEY CREPT UNDER the cover of darkness, Yerbol in the lead. Wyatt and Howard's faces were painted camo green. The boys laughed when they saw each other, but Wyatt had to admit it felt cool to be part of the presidential elite commandos.

Lieutenant Appel brought up the rear. Each of them carried rolled coils of thick cable that Wyatt swore weighed a ton. Rolling his shoulders, he thought they would break from the heaviness. Wyatt clamped his mouth, refusing to be the first to complain, especially when all the other soldiers carried a coil on each arm. It was brutal.

They traveled stealthily through the brush, using prearranged hand signals to communicate. Yerbol admonished Howard and Wyatt when they became too zealous with their hand signals. Wyatt's ears still rang from the harsh-voiced tongue-lashing. Even though Yerbol whispered, it sounded as if he could be heard all the way to

Ohio. Wyatt didn't mind it, though. He felt part of a team, and Yerbol reminded him he couldn't act like a kid anymore.

Wyatt was afraid his breathing would give him away, he was panting so loudly. Still, he kept up with the commandos. Once he heard Howard curse softly, but his friend was silenced by a glare from Lieutenant Appel. She carried two spears dipped in heavy sedatives. There was a black trash bag, bulky with drenched bath towels in it tied to Sheldon.

They slipped down the incline, their feet muffled by rags. They moved quietly over the highway and climbed the other side of the hill. Grabbing onto roots and tree limbs, they fought their way through the thorny bushes until they were halted by Yerbol's final hand signal.

The commander's sweaty face was gleaming from the huge bonfire behind a row of cypress. He parted the branches, and they all stared at the lumpy shapes surrounding the trailer.

Yerbol motioned for Lieutenant Appel to move forward. She peered through the trees, nodding once. Handing one spear to Yerbol, she moved closer to the giant's encampment. Sheldon awaited her signal, bagged sedatives attached to his back.

Wyatt looked through the foliage to see the back of a large giant leaning against a tree, his eyes half-lidded, his wide chest moving up and down, the air escaping his lips like a mini cyclone.

With the grace of an athlete, Appel leaped over a hedge and moved quickly past the terrain, her feet barely touching the ground. She stumbled once, and the giant's great head swiveled toward them.

Wyatt's breath caught in his throat. Appel froze, her body fading into the scenery. Howard opened his mouth, but a warning glance from Yerbol cut him off.

The giant belched loudly. The others stirred. One giant sleeping close to the roaring fire flapped his arm and admonished, "Be quiet!"

His feet rooted to the spot, Wyatt stood so still he could hear his own heartbeat. Nobody moved. The soldiers barely breathed.

Wyatt saw Lieutenant Appel's teeth flash with a menacing smile. She moved deliberately toward the back of the sleeping giant, Sheldon following closely behind, a gas mask covering his face. He held a dripping towel in outstretched hands.

Sheldon nimbly climbed the tree, his feet slipping silently over the branches, then swooped down, landed on the giant, and stuffed the rag in his mouth before any sound could come out.

The guard giant struggled, tearing at the towel, his cries muffled by the material and the sedative soaking it. His movements became lethargic, his grunts lower in volume. Lieutenant Appel jabbed the spear into the giant's exposed shoulder. The creature heaved his great body once, then slid down into the dirt, his eyes closed and his breath even. He gave a loud snuffle and rolled onto his side in a deep sleep.

Sheldon stood on the giant's stomach, a look of relief on his perspiring face. He jumped down, taking one of the coils of rope from a commando.

Yerbol motioned for them to move forward. They rushed the camp, silently creeping from the bushes, five teams of two each. The troops snuck up to the encampment, each one in position near one of the giant's feet.

Yerbol held up his hands. *Three, two, one.* They pounced on the large bodies, yanking feet and wrists together, hog-tying them the way cattle are caught on ranches. The combined roar of the giants awakening was deafening. The cries reverberated against the hills surrounding them.

Like the Lilliputians of *Gulliver's Travels*, the soldiers wound the cables around the giants' feet and hands, pinning them to the ground. The strength of the prone men was astonishing. Wriggling like huge snakes, they pulled the ropes confining their hands. Soon, massive fists were flying. The giants grunted with each painful blow.

Wyatt struggled with the heavy coils that were too bulky for him to wield. He dodged a hand, but the commando working with him was not so lucky, and the swinging palm knocked him senseless.

Wyatt was alone. He wrapped the rope around the thick ankles, making a tangled mess. The creature worked his clumsy fingers to unravel the cable as if it were twine. Teeth as large as tombstones snapped, and Wyatt dodged fingers as thick as telephone poles.

He glanced wildly and saw Yerbol high in the air, trapped by a fist squeezing the life out of him. Lieutenant Appel was under the sole of a foot, the cable clutched uselessly in her hands.

Sheldon screamed as he ran with a spear to jump on the giant holding Appel captive, but large hands plucked him off, snapped the spear in half, and tossed him in the bushes like trash.

Howard was racing toward Wyatt, his face stark in the moonlight, a giant in hot pursuit behind him.

The red-haired creature he was trying to imprison swatted Wyatt like a gnat. His vision filled with colorful stars that circled his head. Wyatt was lifted off the ground. The air *whooshed* from his lungs when the distinctive howl of a wolf brought him rushing back to reality.

CHAPTER 26

WHO ARE YOU?

MELVIN ROSE WHEN he heard the group approach the clearing. Scents came to him. His nostrils quivered as he sniffed the air. He smelled the fear in the trailer, not to mention blood and sweat.

Wyatt was near. He grinned, his canine teeth exposed in a happy smile. Howard was right behind them. They stank like nothing he'd ever smelled before. They must not have had much in the way of showers at the army encampment. Melvin's nose twitched from their offensive odors. He counted the scents of others, older, meat eaters. The heavy camouflage paint on their face choked him.

Mad Max moved close to him. *I count ten of them.*

Melvin shook his head. *Nope. There are twelve. They've brought two for each giant.*

What do you think that means? Max asked.

Melvin shrugged. *I don't know. I smell something else. I'm not sure.*

I smell dinner. Alfonso laughed, licking his side whiskers.

Melvin pounced and grabbed the hair on the scruff of his neck mercilessly. The older wolf crouched, whining. Melvin bit down harder. *Make a sound and I'll rip your throat out.*

Okay, okay… Alfonso grunted.

Not a hair on their heads. Not a nip or scratch, Melvin said through gritted teeth. He shook the older wolf, then turned to face the group, dropping Alfonso with a thud.

Got it, got it, a coyote called out. *We won't hurt the humans, but what about the giants? One of them could last the group of us for at least a week.*

I said no one, unless they threaten my friends. Melvin's voice was low but harsh. *What has become of us?* He turned in a tight circle. *When Billy bit me, he told me werewolves stayed to themselves, were peaceful, and tried not to hurt others.*

Mad Max looked down. There were a few murmurs. The group sat on their haunches, listening to Melvin.

Billy told me he killed to eat but not humans. He stayed away from humans.

That's just it, mi amigo, Max said. *They started it. We didn't care for them. They stringy anyway. With all the sugar they eat, they're too sweet for my taste, but honestly, Mel, they started this war.*

Melvin glanced back to where he knew his friends had climbed the hill. *In a few minutes, I am going to help my friends. You can come along or not; it's your choice. I don't hate humans; I never did. It's our job to educate them. They do what they do out of ignorance. It's up to us to break their perceptions.*

There were murmurs of approval. Two wolves stood to leave, their mouths caught in vicious snarls. *You can't reason with hate,* one of them called out.

Melvin nodded. *True. But you can reason with compassion.*

You're not going to change them. Max held his gaze.

Then maybe I'll die trying. Who is with me?

A group got up to leave. The majority didn't move. Each coyote, every single wolf that remained seated, lifted their paw. *I'm with you,* a few murmured.

Melvin's got it right, another said. There were barks and howls of agreement.

An old wolf rose. He cleared his throat. *I've been this way longer than some of you have been alive. I like humans. They amuse me, make great pets. They react only when they are threatened. Well, most of them are that way. Melvin's right. Vincent Konrad is the real enemy, not mankind. A wise one once said, 'The only thing necessary for the triumph of evil is for good men to do nothing.' If we don't unite this planet, then evil will prevail. Nobody will win. I say let's go help those people!*

They all rose, their eyes shining, their tails wagging. Melvin's chest filled with pride. They say a dog is man's best friend. Now he was going to put that theory to the test.

Tocho moved next to him and growled, *If you don't do something soon, there'll be nothing left to save.*

Screams erupted behind them. Melvin leaped over a row of bushes to see the giants' camp in chaos. The commandos were on the defensive, many imprisoned in a giant's huge grip. One of the monsters was sprawled against a tree, snoring, a rag over his mouth. The other five were standing around the campfire, fighting with the commandos.

Melvin assessed the battle at once. He understood what they were trying to do. Scattered on the grass were coils of heavy-duty coils of wire. *Who's with me?* he called to his pack.

Me! Me! Me! they howled back.

Melvin quickly barked out orders. Within seconds, the army of animals bounded into the camp.

Commandos shot their guns at the giants, their bullets useless on the thick skin, their weapons easily plucked from their hands. The soldiers were no match for the enraged men. They were picked up, then tossed into the trees, where they draped the branches like tinsel.

The clearing was filled with the sound of barking canines. A collection of wolves and coyotes flooded the area and surrounded the giants, creating confusion. They ran between the tree-trunk-sized legs, contributing to the chaos.

Tocho attached himself to the back of the giant holding Wyatt, his roars echoed off the mountains.

Enraged giants waved their arms at the canine onslaught using the soldiers as weapons to thrash the oncoming wolves and coyotes.

Groups of animals picked up each end of the ropes. Grabbing them in their powerful jaws, they raced in circles, winding the ropes around the giants' ankles.

Higher! Higher! Melvin shouted as he directed the teams.

Melvin nipped at the giant holding Wyatt without breaking skin. The man swatted him with Wyatt, their heads connecting with a loud *thunk*. Wyatt's eyes rolled to the back of his head. He hung listlessly from the oversized hand.

Howard shrieked as his giant waved him around like a flag.

Melvin regained his balance and saw a gray kestrel escape out a window of the trailer to peck at the forehead of the giant imprisoning Howard. The small hawk managed to poke the monster in the eye. Screaming with pain, he dropped Howard onto the ground. On the other side of the fire, Melvin watched in horror as the giant stumbled around, his big feet about to crush his friend.

I got him! Tocho leaped off Wyatt's giant and weaved between the creature's legs. He caught the collar of Howard's shirt and dragged him to safety.

One by one, the cables did their intended job. With the thick wires tangled around their legs, the giants were caught in the fibrous web. Melvin directed the canines to pull tight, and each large man fell like a tree chopped at the root. The coyotes raced in and grabbed humans before they could be crushed by the falling giants.

The kestrel landed on Wyatt's chest, chirping wildly at him. The bird shivered briefly, then transformed into a disheveled Lily in a shimmering spangle of lights.

Melvin loped over to Howard to see him getting groggily to his feet.

"Melvin!" Howard wrapped his arms around Melvin's furry neck. Melvin buried his face into Howard's chest, holding back sobs of relief. "You wouldn't believe it, a mountain lion dragged me to safety!"

Some of the commandos descended from the trees and scrambled for their guns.

"Werewolves!" Appel screamed. She'd just awoken and had missed their rescue.

Pulling her sidearm, she rolled and aimed for Melvin's heart.

Wyatt rose unsteadily to his feet, saw the direction of her gun, and screamed, "No!" He raced between them, jerking as the bullet hit him.

Melvin's cry could be heard across the valley. Both he and Lily ran to Wyatt's side. Yerbol knocked the gun from Appel's hand, his face filled with disgust. "They were helping us, you idiot."

Sheldon patted her shoulder. "You didn't mean it. You were acting on instinct." He pointed to Melvin. "I think that's my brother's best friend."

"Your brother mixes with werewolves?" Appel sneered. She yanked up her gun and stalked away. Sheldon watched her leave mutely.

Melvin nuzzled Wyatt's chest, trying to make him move. Wyatt's face was covered with blood. Lily wailed as she held Wyatt's cheeks.

Yerbol pushed Lily and Melvin out of the way. He pulled Wyatt up and wiped his forehead with the flat of his hand. Wyatt's eyes fluttered. "Stop," said Yerbol. "He's okay. It's a graze."

Melvin whimpered, his nose pushing against his friend's temple.

Yerbol picked Wyatt up and adjusted him onto his shoulder. "Think you can help us move these monsters to the base?"

Melvin nodded his head. He looked up at Yerbol, his eyes pleading.

Yerbol said, his voice gruff, "I have no problem with you. You saved my crew. You don't have to worry."

Melvin moved off to organize the group.

"Let's get those people out of the trailer," Yerbol ordered.

Howard had already scaled the side of the building to climb in despite being wobbly on his feet. Lily joined him. It was dark and smelled foul of human waste.

Carter rose unsteadily on the tilted floor when Howard fell in through the window. They embraced. Carter held Howard away from him with both arms. "That was some fight," Carter said. "Where's Wyatt?" He took in Lily's tearstained face, his own going pale.

"He's okay," Howard assured him. "He was grazed by a bullet and knocked out, but he'll be fine."

The mountain lion stood protectively over Keisha.

Howard dropped to his knees next to her crumpled form. He reached over to touch her and pulled back when the mountain lion snarled at him. The cat's teeth were bared, it's warning clear. John Raven was spread out nearby, his face devoid of color.

"Keisha!" Howard cried ignoring the mountain lion. He raised her head and was relieved to see her eyelids move.

"*Oh* good." Carter leaned over him. "She's finally waking up. She's been out of it for a while now." He looked at the mountain lion and nodded. "Tocho."

Howard looked up to see a dark-haired man sneering at him. "You're Howard Drucker," he demanded.

"He is and you better stop," Lily told her cousin.

"He's lucky I didn't know before I saved him."

Sean and Melvin's father-in-law helped lift John Raven out of the trailer.

Howard cupped Keisha's head. "Lily, get me water."

Lily was back in an instant. Howard dribbled the water between Keisha's parched lips.

"Are you alright?" he asked, wiping her face with the end of his shirt.

Keisha pushed his hands away. Her eyes were still closed, her skin hot to the touch.

"She's burning up," he told Lily. "Why didn't you guys fly out of here?"

Lily gestured toward Keisha. "She and John were hurt from the start. We were all banged together. I was groggy for some of the time and couldn't focus." She wrapped her arms around her midsection. "Then they told us if we did anything to hamper them, they'd eat us all or any survivors if we escaped."

"Too much of that going on," Howard said grimly.

"What are you talking about?" Lily asked.

"There's a clown convention where people are the main course."

"That's horrible."

Keisha moaned, her eyes squinting as if it hurt to open them.

"You're going to be okay," Howard assured Keisha.

"Of course I am." Keisha's hand reached for the spot next to her. "Tocho? I thought I heard Tocho."

"Easy." Howard tried to push her back onto the floor. "Come on, I'll help you."

Keisha looked at him, her brown eyes focused and round, her lips a tight line. She pried his hand from her arm.

"Don't touch me. Who are you?"

CHAPTER 27

THE BIG MAN SAID TO GET YOU

JÖTNAR TURNED AROUND, and for a minute Rosemary thought he'd changed his mind. He told her to stay put, making her pulse beat from her ankles to her temples. Rosemary opened her mouth to talk him out of it, but he wouldn't be dissuaded.

She watched his large body melt into the shadows as he walked closer to the main street. Soon he was swallowed up completely. She slid onto the pavement, weary and afraid.

Loud music blared from speakers, the incessant beating of the drums primitive. The constant noise filled her aching body with dread. Twice motorcycles roared past her. Each one had two passengers, all dressed in garish clothes, their faces painted with demonic expressions.

The night air smothered her. Not a star could be seen in the sky, yet there were lights of some sort. She watched a trio of three sets of blue beacons zip around overhead in precisely orchestrated movements. They looked like the ones she'd seen earlier.

Rosemary wondered if they were helicopters sent by her father to find her, yet she instinctively knew they moved in a way she'd never seen any craft operate. They swooped from one end of the valley, in the distance to the other, then zoomed to the spot where she hid, hovering overhead. They moved with astonishing speed. She pressed herself into the darkness, allowing a commercial trash bin to provide cover.

The crafts appeared to freeze miles above her, a blinding light from each aircraft searching the alleyway. Rosemary strained her ears, hearing nothing but her own rushed breathing. The ship or whatever it was, made no sound.

The night was interrupted by multiple shotgun blasts. Rosemary covered her eyes with her hands. Her mouth was dry; she whispered, "Jötnar."

The gunfire went on for what seemed an eternity. Rosemary waffled with indecision, something new for her, and she didn't like it one bit. Usually decisive, she wanted to run but felt glued to the ground, half of her expecting Jötnar to come racing to her side, the other knowing she might have to face it alone.

She sensed a shadow looming over her. Peeking through her fingers, she saw oversized shoes on the ground next to her. Her breath frozen in her chest, she looked up and was hit squarely in the face with water from a squirting flower exploding from the clown's lapel.

"Gotcha!" he giggled with maniacal glee that sent chills down her spine. Fisting her hand, she whacked him in the head.

He bent in half, screaming with laughter, then extended a dirty, white-gloved hand. Rosemary stepped backward ready to defend herself in an all-out brawl, when his polite words stopped her in her tracks.

"The big man said to get you."

Rosemary relaxed and stammered, "I don't believe you. What have you done to Jötnar."

She looked behind him to see four others, all watching her with painted smiles on their faces. Her eyes darted around the confines of the alley for a way to escape, when her captor said, "I wouldn't if I were you. There are more of us down the street. If you don't come peacefully, we'll have to tickle you there." He poked her in the mid-section. "You're better off with us." He pointed to the dark, night sky. "The blue lights have been searching for you."

Recoiling from his touch, she assessed her options. She scanned the horizon. *So, it wasn't her imagination.* Deciding she didn't have a decent choice, she agreed to go with them.

She kept a watchful gaze on the skyline. The aircraft were gone.

Walking dejectedly, her head hung low next to the creature, who held her arm in a tight grip, she considered ways to escape. They rounded the corner. Rosemary felt a blazing heat.. A giant bonfire lit up the street. Dozens of clowns danced around the flames. The heat scorched her face. She held up a hand to deflect the waves radiating from the fire.

She realized they had stopped walking. She heard shouts of laughter, singing, and the racket from a DJ hunched over a station, his red dreadlocks bobbing to the rhythm of the music.

Rosemary recognized a voice. Her head swiveled to find an over-sized green velvet chair that looked like it had been poached from a movie set. A huge woman, her face covered in runny makeup, sat upright in it with a scepter in one hand. She wore a crown that looked like it had been made for King Arthur.

The woman inclined her head regally, motioning Rosemary to take the smaller chair next to her. It was the only empty seat. On her other side, the chair was occupied by Jötnar. He greeted her warmly. Rosemary's feet refused to move.

Jötnar leapt up to escort her to the chair, she punched him in the arm. "What were you thinking sending those clowns to me?"

He pointed his thumb to the huge woman. "She wouldn't let me leave. I told you I recognized her. This is my Aunt Henny. She ran away from home years ago. She just told me she left to join the circus, whatever that is."

CHAPTER 28

CHOICES UP HERE

"SHE DOESN'T REMEMBER anything?" Wyatt asked quietly. His head ached where the bullet grazed him. Mrs. Drucker had fussed over him and the painkillers helped a lot. Everyone had admired the groove just under his hairline and he beamed when Lily said it made him look dashing.

Sean was asleep on Howard's cot. They were huddled on Wyatt's side of the tent.

Howard Drucker shook his head, rubbing his eyes. "Nothing." He paused and added bitterly. "No, not everything. She remembers that guy Tocho."

"She forgot how to shapeshift?" Melvin asked. He was in human form and sprawled across Wyatt's bed, gnawing on a rib bone. "This is delicious. What kind of meat is it?"

Wyatt gave him a look of warning.

"What? I'm only—"

"Don't ask. It's horrible. Life keeps getting worse and worse," Howard said, his voice a ragged whisper.

"Don't I know it," Melvin agreed, his face downcast.

Wyatt looked at his friends. They were all casualties, wounded in ways the world could not see. Melvin cried when he recounted what had happened to Jade. Wyatt shed more than a few tears as well. Lily was quiet, and Keisha had a distant look in her eyes that baffled him.

They had been debriefed, followed by a warm meal. Mrs. Drucker had taken the girls to another tent. John Raven and Jade's father were being tended to in the triage center.

The giants had been corralled in the elephant pen while Carter met with the president and Colonel Drucker. Wyatt didn't want to ask what had happened to the animals. The zoo was strangely quiet.

"What do you think they're going to do with the giants?" Melvin asked.

"Owens said he's going to negotiate," Howard responded.

"You can't reason with them. I followed them for miles. They're not bad, so to speak; they just want what they want." Melvin appeared to be the resident giant expert.

"They want their own back. That doesn't make them evil," Howard replied.

Wyatt shredded the ends of his army blanket. "It doesn›t feel fair. Nobody should have to do things they don't want to do."

"You're speaking about those giant girls?" Melvin asked. "*We* had to do what our parents demanded."

"Yeah, but they weren't making us get sterilized or arranging marriages like some medieval kingdom."

"Marriage isn't so bad," Melvin said, his voice sad. "I liked it."

They all stared at each other, the silence heavy in the room. "Sorry about Jade, but that was both of your choices… you know, to be together."

Melvin bit his lip and nodded. "I would do it all over again if I could."

"Yes, but it was still both of your decisions. Nobody forced you to do it," Wyatt repeated.

"Mel," Howard said, "Jade told me you made her really happy."

Melvin swallowed, his Adam›s apple bobbed convulsively. He fought the urge to howl out his pain to the world.

Sean stirred, then sat up. He knuckled his eyes.

"You slept like the dead." Wyatt rose to move over to his bunk. He placed a hand on his shoulder. "Boy, am I glad to see you."

"You have no idea how happy I was to see you." Sean laughed. "What did I miss?"

They all stood. "Nothing much. Just catching up." Wyatt looked at his watch. "It's seventeen-thirty."

"Listen to you," Sean said. "All military-like."

Wyatt shrugged, his face reddening. "It's not a game, Sean."

"No it's not." Sean shook his head. "I miss just being like… you know… young."

The four stood in a circle, lost in thought. The air was heavy with lost dreams and regret.

"Remember when all you guys worried about was which was the strongest monster?" Sean asked.

"Yes. That feels like it was a million years ago," Howard said.

"Boy, we were stupid," Melvin muttered.

Sean asked, "What do you mean?"

Wyatt looked up, his voice grave. "We should have been worrying about who was the strongest human instead."

The wind whistled into the tent, making them all shiver. Wyatt cleared his throat and said, "We were told to be at Colonel Drucker's tent. Let's go."

They shuffled out together. The camp was eerily quiet. Low-pitched moans floated from the zoo.

"Are those the animals?" Sean asked.

Wyatt shook his head. "No, it's them."

"The giants?" Melvin asked. He sniffed the air. "I can smell them."

Howard said, "They're awake and in the elephant pen. They sound hungry."

"Are the elephants safe?" Sean caught up to them.

"They're not there anymore," Wyatt said hastily. He pinched Sean's elbow.

"*Ow*," Sean started, but a look from Wyatt cut him off.

"Just leave it," he whispered to his brother.

Howard was walking steadily ahead, his shoulders bowed.

There was a crowd outside the command tent. The girls had grown too large to be inside. Wyatt now came up to Danai's armpit. "What's going on?"

Carter came over. He had a bruise on his cheekbone and dark circles under his eyes. He was thinner than Wyatt remembered. Carter placed a warm hand on Wyatt's shoulder. "We're going in to talk to them."

"You're not making the girls go back," Wyatt said.

Danai answered before Carter could respond. "They actually took a vote with us. Two of my sisters want to return. The president is going to talk to my uncle and see if that will satisfy him."

"They don't seem like the type who take *no* for an answer," Melvin said.

John Raven exited the tent. He seemed frail. From the other direction, Keisha and Lily walked together. Wyatt watched Howard's face pale when Keisha failed to acknowledge him. She walked straight over to some guy who had been in the battle yesterday, named Tocho and stood behind him as if he were a barrier from the world. Tocho acted like he was guarding her.

Lily joined the boys, her eyes on Danai and Wyatt.

"You don't have to go," Wyatt told Danai.

"Maybe she misses home," Lily said, her voice low. Her eyes narrowed as she observed Danai.

Danai shifted from foot to foot, pushing her hands deep into pockets on a pair of pants that barely fit. "Vincent Konrad destroyed whatever home we once had. There's no reason to go back," Danai said. She hunched her shoulders defensively.

Carter glanced at her. "Are your leaders angry at him?"

"Wouldn't you be?" she asked. "He made promises, then double-crossed us. They'll never trust another human again."

"My people know what that feels like. Why do you want to stay here?" Lily's question bordered on rude, She glared at Danai.

Wyatt scratched his side and realized Danai's scarf was tucked under his shirt. His face flushed. He wasn't sure why he still carried it. He glanced from girl to girl, a light going off in his head.

Lily's brows were furrowed in a straight line as she spoke, the words careful and precise. *Lily was jealous!* If looks could kill, both girls appeared to be in trouble.

Wyatt thought it prudent not to return the scarf right now. He opened his mouth to say something when a thought occurred to him. "That's it!" Wyatt yelled. "Candace—or maybe it was Erin—told me they hate Vincent Konrad. That's the bargaining chip. We'll join forces to take him down!"

"They could just easily turn on us as on Vincent Konrad," Howard replied. "Danai just said they see humans as an enemy."

"It will be hard to form an alliance," Melvin murmured.

Carter's laugh held no humor. "What choice do we have?"

"Nate Owens will have to do it," Howard chimed in. "I think he's the real deal."

Carter shrugged. "His story adds up. Vincent Konrad played the biggest con in history. Only time will tell exactly where Nate Owens stands. Right now, Colonel Drucker trusts him, so I guess I'll have to as well."

Wyatt nodded. "I felt the same way."

"Past tense?" Carter asked.

"I think so. I think he means what he says. He's brave and loyal, things that Konrad is not."

"I trust your judgment." Carter motioned for Wyatt to follow him.

Wyatt bounced toward the path to the zoo, feeling lighter than air. Carter trusted his judgment, and that filled him with pride.

"Where are they now?" Wyatt asked.

Carter began walking toward the zoo entrance. "They've been at the elephant pens for over an hour. He's trying to talk to them but is getting nowhere."

Nate Owens was standing on an overturned box, a bullhorn in his hand. He looked disheveled. His hair was mussed, as if he'd run his hand through it in frustration. The giants rocked back and forth, humming loudly like a swarm of bees.

The president placed the bullhorn to his mouth to speak but was drowned out by the noise coming from the other side of the fence. The giants raised the volume of their voices so he couldn't be heard.

Wyatt watched the exchange. The giants were corralled together, their hands and feet tied. On the other side of the barrier, the military stood, guns trained on the prisoners.

"They're getting nowhere with them!" Lieutenant Appel muttered to no one in particular. "I don't know how long those restraints will hold them."

"They'll hold," Colonel Drucker said.

"You hog-tied them. No wonder they aren't listening. May I?" Wyatt asked, pushing his way toward the president.

Carter called, "Wyatt!" in an attempt to restrain him.

Howard put his hand on his wrist and said, "You said you trusted his judgment."

Carter lowered his arm. Wyatt held out his hand for the bullhorn. Owens exchanged a look with the colonel, who shrugged. "They're not hearing anything we say."

Wyatt held out his hand to the president. "Let me." He motioned to the bullhorn. Nate Owens handed it over.

Wyatt moved closer to the elephant pen. Taking a deep breath, he began, "Vincent Konrad killed my mother." The giants ignored him, humming tunelessly. "Vincent Konrad killed my mother!" he shouted over the din. He said it a third time, raising his voice so that the whole sentence became a mishmash of noise with no definable beginning or end.

Frustrated, Wyatt climbed to the top of the fence and jumped over before the commandos could stop him. He heard Carter shout, "No!" He ignored his stepfather, coming up directly in front of the one Danai had identified as the clan leader. Colonel Drucker had painted a big yellow dot on his shoulder so they could tell him apart from the others.

Carter's hands gripped the fence. Wyatt walked up to Grillos and, using the bullhorn, shouted the sentence again. Howard and Melvin raced to the barrier, watching the scene unfold.

A lone kestrel perched on the chain link, her eyes never leaving the giant's large body.

Wyatt shouted the sentence again, his cheeks red, the veins bulging on his neck and temple. The large man paused his humming to look at him. Wyatt touched his face, surprised to realize his own cheeks were wet with tears. "I know what Vincent Konrad did to you, and I know where he is hiding."

Grillos shrugged, his gaze locked with Wyatt's. He was silent for a long while and the humming died down. "Why should I care?" the giant asked.

"Vincent Konrad did the same thing to us as he did to you. You see my friend?" He pointed to Melvin, whose predatory eyes watched the giant. "He's a werewolf."

Grillos gave a startled gasp.

"And guess what? We don't care." Wyatt pointed to the troops on the other side of the fence. "None of us cares that he is different. We don't care if your kind is different either." Wyatt ran to the barrier separating him from the rest of the group. "Isn't that right, Mr. President? Nobody cares about those things anymore. Vincent

Konrad was the one who exploited differences. We have to share the planet with each other. No species is more deserving than any other."

"I don't believe you." Grillos dismissed him and started humming.

"No!" Wyatt ran from giant to giant and tried to break through their chanting, but they closed their eyes and ignored him.

He stopped in the center, breathing heavily. Looking down he saw a group of ants circling an anthill. He remembered something he'd read in his political science class last year. It was so dumb when he heard the story and he recalled making snide comments about it all afternoon with Melvin. "Listen to me," he cried. They didn't. The humming grew louder.

"Look, if you have a jar and put fifty red ants and fifty black ants inside, nothing will happen. But if you take that jar and shake it up, all the ants will start killing each other. Red thinks that black is the enemy and black thinks red is the enemy." Wyatt walked around. He noticed two things the giants had stopped humming and everyone was listening to him. "But you know who the real enemy is?" he asked, looking at each giant. "It's the person who shook the jar. The same is true here. Giant versus human, Vampire versus Werewolf, young ways versus old ways. Don't you see, before we fight each other, don't you think we should ask, who rocked our jar?"

He spun to face the giants, who appeared to be listening intently. "The girls don't have to go home. They are home and so are you. We don't want to shake up our home. Isn't that true, President Owens?"

Nate Owens approached the fence and directed Yerbol to lift the latch. Yerbol opened his mouth to refuse. Owens firmed his jaw and ordered, "Now."

The gate clanged. Owens joined Wyatt barely a handspan from the six giants.

"Can we put aside our differences and live together as we did in the old days? Yes, your nieces told us of the combined accomplishments when our species worked as one." Owens held out his hand. "I give you my word you are welcome here. Your nieces can come and go as they desire. You are not our enemy and together we will use science and our collective brains to stretch our resources so that there is enough for everybody. We have a world to rebuild and I believe we need each other to get it accomplished. We choose not to banish you from our society. We respect your civilization." Owens paused. The zoo was so quiet he didn't even need the bullhorn. He put it down. "I think we need each other. I believe if we are to all survive evil, it will be only as a unified force."

Grillos didn't move. Danai squeezed through the gate. "They are good people, Uncle."

The ground shook as the shortest giant jumped to his feet, teetering unsteadily. He looked about to fall. Wyatt moved next to him and wrapped his arms around the leg to prevent him from toppling over. Brontes looked down at his daughter. "Danai! You'll come home?"

Danai gasped as he began to list to the side. President Owens joined Wyatt in locking Brontes back into a standing position. "Remove the restraints!" he ordered Yerbol. Yerbol repeated the orders to his troops. Minutes later, two soldiers entered the pen with oversized wire cutters.

Danai shook her head. "I love you, Pa, but I'm not going back." She looked at Wyatt. "I like it here."

"But the clan will die out!" Brontes cried.

"Just because I'm not marrying Jötnar doesn›t mean the clan will die out. There are lots of choices up here. Anyway, Jötnar is nowhere to be found."

The air filled with the babble of the six giants speaking all at once. Released from their shackles, they huddled together, resembling a lumpy hill. Wyatt and the president backed away.

"That was a bold move, Wyatt."

Wyatt shrugged. "I think all we have left is bold moves, Et—I mean Mr. President."

"I could use you—"

The president was interrupted by the clan leader. Grillos stuck his head out and addressed Owens. "We think we can live with this idea. We will need a settlement in the mountains."

"There is no question about that. It will be arranged. The mountains will become your territory." Owens smiled.

Owens raised his hand again in friendship. This time, Grillos reached out to gently shake it with his pointer finger.

Wyatt spoke without the bullhorn. "We need your help first. We have to get through the killer clowns to reach Prendick Rock and stop Konrad."

Grillos chuckled. "That's easy. We'll plow right through them. Direct us to these clowns. We have to get there." He pointed east. "We will take you to The Sign."

"What sign?," Wyatt interrupted.

"The Sign, the big Sign. We have a tunnel behind the double *L*'s that will lead us to Konrad's base."

"Do you mean the Hollywood sign?"

The bowed their heads with respect. "Yes, The Sign. It's sacred to both yours and our culture."

"You don't even know where his base is," Wyatt responded.

"It won't matter. The whole area is filled with honeycombs that will lead us to wherever he is holed up. We can take you anywhere in the world."

"He's on Prendick Rock," Wyatt shouted.

"That's easy. Prendick Rock. If we don't have a tunnel, we will make one for you," Grillos said with a nod.

"Wow!" Howard exclaimed in wonder. "Did you hear that, Keisha?" he said as he walked toward Wyatt. He paused to notice Keisha hadn't moved from her spot. Her eyes were wary. "Come on, Keish. Don't you want to learn more?" Howard asked.

Keisha backed behind Tocho, who called out, "Ask them if they are the source of the earthquakes that plagued the area for centuries."

Howard turned to the giants, his brown eyes filled with sadness.

Grillos nodded his head. "Yes, it was us." He smiled a toothy grin.

"Go on, Uncle. Tell them you used to do it for the sport of watching them scramble!" Candace yelled.

A rumble of laughter went through the crowd of giants, the girls joining in.

"Well, it is fun to watch. Want to see?" Grillos raised his foot.

Wyatt shouted, "No! That›s a great story, but no, not right now."

"This way, gentlemen." Owens gestured toward the exit.

Danai's uncle lifted Wyatt onto his shoulder and pumped his fist in the air, bellowing, "We are taught that the children are our future. It's nice to know it's the same way for the folks of the sunlight."

Wyatt hung onto the giant's homespun shirt, his knuckles white. The kestrel fluttered up to land on Wyatt's shoulder. Wyatt relaxed and touched the soft wings. "I missed you, Lily." He pulled a gray feather from his pocket. "See, I always keep you next to me."

The kestrel chattered loudly, her response sounding like a song.

"Yes," Wyatt responded, "you're right. Together we'll be unstoppable."

CHAPTER 29

COUSINS

THE STRONG RAYS of the sun awakened Rosemary. She was curled up on an oversized pillow in a storefront. She must have collapsed on the softest thing she could find even though it was directly below a display window.

She rose up on an elbow. Someone had made the storefront homey by placing a well-loved couch in the center of the space. Rosemary sat up and considered her surroundings, deciding it was more like a haphazard collection of cushions than furniture. She was in the front of a large, airy store that at one time held sectionals and other types of pieces.

Glancing at the walls, Rosemary saw painted patches where artwork had once hung. A tall mirror the size of a king-sized bed took up an entire section of wall space. Sheets of canvas that must have been pillaged from a lumberyard hung across the area, dividing it into rooms. Everywhere she looked, everything from the furniture to the serving pieces on the floor was oversized. Trash pails served as drinking vessels, and garbage can covers were the plates. Rakes and machetes acted as silverware.

Rosemary gingerly rose to examine the remnants of a meal glued to the surface of the metal lid. The congealed mess made her stomach turn.

A commercial fridge hooked up to a generator hummed loudly. She opened the door to find six oranges. They looked mouth-wateringly delicious. She snatched two, peeled them as rapidly as she could, and enjoyed the fresh taste of the fruit.

She walked to the exit to find Jötnar sitting with his aunt on the pavement. At least three dozen scrambled eggs were on the inverted hood of a car.

"Sit, child. There's enough for you." Henny winked.

"Where'd you get those?" Rosemary asked.

"We've got hens and goats. We raided the houses in Bel Air that kept the goats for fire control, and the hens came from East LA."

Rosemary settled on the ground and scooped up a handful of eggs. They were rich and delicious.

"I almost forgot how good they are," she said between bites. "So, Jötnar, what happens now?"

Jötnar busied himself with eating. Rosemary looked at him, one eyebrow raised.

"It's nice here," he said finally after a long moment of silence.

Rosemary opened her mouth to say something, then snapped it shut.

"Anything you say to me, you can say in front of my aunt." Jötnar looked at the big woman with awe.

Rosemary got to her feet, brushing off the back of her pants. "I only just met her. Besides, you said I was the captain." Rosemary grimaced. She sounded like a child whose playtime had been interrupted.

Jötnar picked at a tooth with what looked like a knitting needle. "I don't see a ship."

Rosemary sputtered, "This is mutiny."

"I'll give you two some privacy." Henny rose unsteadily to her feet. She used a broken street sign as a cane. Ducking her head, she disappeared inside the storefront.

"What is going on?" Rosemary demanded.

"I like it. Henny is in charge. She's their queen. We'll be safe here."

"This is not exactly what I had in mind."

"I didn't expect this either, Rosemary." Jötnar paused when Rosemary gave him a dirty look. He nodded respectfully. "Captain, I don't see us going back anymore. We're moving further and further away from the sea."

Rosemary mulled over what he was saying.

Jötnar continued, "There's food—"

"That's a problem! Besides the eggs, you know what else is on the menu!" Rosemary stalked to the end of the sidewalk to stare at the extinguished campfire and the grim remains of last night's feast. She looked back at Jötnar with disgust. "I can't do this."

Jötnar shook his head. "I didn't eat—"

"I can't talk about it. It's barbaric. We have to get out of here."

She sat abruptly and drummed her fingers on her bent knee. "You and your aunt, where do you really come from? You're… *different* and you know it."

Jötnar's face colored up. "I am a giant," he said bleakly.

Rosemary's mouth dropped. She looked him up and down from his enormous shoulders to his oversized feet. She rose and paced in front of him. "It's highly unlikely," she said to herself. "There's no such thing. We would have heard about you if…. There's no such thing as real giants, is there?"

Jötnar hung his head. "I don't want to be a giant, but here I am." He stood, looking even taller than before.

"You're just tall," Rosemary said in a rush. "Like your aunt."

"You know it's not a size thing." Jötnar laughed humorlessly. "In my world, I'm small. So is Henny. For a while I almost fit in your world. Henny's been doing it for years. She stoops and hides her height."

"What are you talking about?" Rosemary asked.

"My people. Where I come from. Yes, we are different. We are giants."

"How can that be? It must be a gene pool thing or something, like those people with lots of facial hair in Mexico… a family thing."

Jötnar shook his head, his face sad. "We survive in small clans underground. Henny actually was born right here in Southern California. She moved to live with my people up north for a while. She originally was to marry someone from our clan, but she ran away. She's not really my aunt. It's a respect thing." He shrugged.

"People back out of marriages all the time," Rosemary replied impatiently.

Henny wandered back and settled down comfortably on a cushion. She took a deep breath and started, "I hear you talking, you don't mind if I explain? It's a little more complicated than that. I was the smallest of my family, and as such, it was determined that I would birth the next generation. I didn't want to settle down. I wanted to see the world, and I did. Just like Jötnar over here. He doesn't want to marry either. He ran away too."

"I know about that. Arranged marriages should be outlawed," Rosemary said.

Henny shrugged. "If he stayed, he'd have to do what they tell him, and that would be unnatural for you, right, boy?"

Jötnar's lips quivered. He pressed them firmly together.

There was the sound of a toy horn honking. A clown rode past them on a unicycle.

"What's up, Bob?" Henny asked in her deep voice.

"We got trouble, Boss. Take a look down Sunset."

The ground below them trembled as if a train were running underneath their feet. The three of them walked out into the middle of the road to see six giants marching down the road. They walked like an invading army, shoulder to shoulder, with a mass of humans following them.

Henny growled deep in her throat.

"Who are those guys?" Jötnar asked.

"Cousins," Henny replied, her voice tight. "I haven't seen them in over fifty years.

"*Oh* crap." Jötnar sat down heavily.

"What is it, Jötnar?" Rosemary yelled, her hands balled into fists.

"If those are her cousins, then one of them is my intended father-in-law."

Rosemary turned to see a wall of flesh walking their way, pushing resisting clowns away like pesky insects. Their big feet broke the blacktop, creating massive craters. They swatted at the clowns, flinging them onto abandoned cars. Sporadic shots of gunfire interrupted the quiet peace of the morning. Rosemary's jaw dropped. If Jötnar was big, these men were enormous. Her hands went protectively to her belly. Not only were they large, they appeared to be invincible. The gunfire was ineffectual. She watched the giants snatch the guns and crush them until they turned into pancakes.

Several clowns formed a line, shooting. There was the screech of tires, and two SUVs raced down the street, followed by a firetruck, to form a barricade.

One of the invading giants grabbed a stoplight and used it as a missile. He threw it at a group of defenders, sending them crashing into a wall. Two of the huge men brushed away the vehicles as if they were toys.

Henny wearily moved to the middle of the street. Jötnar followed her. They looked pathetically smaller than the giants approaching them. The six giants stopped abruptly on the other side of the intersection. One picked up the bottom of his foot with annoyance and peeled a clown from the bottom. He flung it away like a bothersome pebble.

"Henny." One of the giants stepped forward and nodded to her. "I should have known."

Henny flung her red hair defiantly. "I managed to elude you long enough."

"That you did. Broke your Pa's heart."

"I had to live my life. I hated it in Oslo, Grillos."

"Cold." Grillos nodded.

"Yes. They weren›t what we expected."

Grillos looked at Jötnar, his brows drawing together. "Jötnar? Is that Jötnar? Where have you been hiding?" he demanded. "You're long overdue. My niece has been waiting for you."

"He can't marry one of the girls, cousin."

"It is our law!"

"Yes, and I broke the law. Nothing happened," Henny retorted.

Brontes spoke up. "The Oslo clan died out."

"No great loss to the world."

Nobody responded to that.

"Still, Danai needs the match!" Brontes shouted.

"Brontes, he can't marry your daughter."

"It doesn't matter. He's here now, and we will seal the match!"

"Brontes! He doesn›t like *girls*."

Brontes walked forward, his hand outstretched. He appeared to be speaking directly to Jötnar. "It's always like that in the beginning. They grow on you. After a while, you'll get used to her."

"You don't understand," Jötnar mumbled, his head low.

A tall redheaded girl peeked from behind the other giants. She looked from Jötnar to her father, fear on her face.

"I understand that you have to marry my daughter!" Brontes ground out.

"He doesn't like girls, Brontes. He prefers men!" Henny shouted so loudly it silenced everyone in the group.

"It's true. I don't want to… I mean, I can't—"

Brontes's face changed from red to purple. His eyes narrowed to slits.

Rosemary saw the impending response in the balled fists of the older giant. Instinct took over, and without thinking, she grabbed a trash can cover as a shield and ran out to stand in front of Jötnar, looking pitifully small. "It's alright, Jötnar. You're perfect the way you are, and they are going to have to accept it." Straightening her shoulders, she looked the opposition in the eyes and growled, "You'll have to go through me to get to him!"

Brontes roared with laughter. He took a step forward, and Grillos laid a restraining hand on his arm. "There's no time for that now, Brontes." He looked back at the crowd behind them.

"Let's go!" President Owens›s voice bellowed through a bullhorn.

Henny stepped forward and slammed her signpost into the asphalt. She hit the ground so hard, it stuck in the blacktop, vibrating like a violin string. "This is our territory, and you can't just waltz in here and do what you want."

Grillos pushed her out of the way. "This is not about you, Henny. We're taking them to the Sign."

"The Sign is a secret, a sacred place," Henny said in a shocked whisper. "I've never even told any of my subjects about it."

Grillos looked at the crowd, cowering behind Henny. They were dressed in bizarre costumes, their faces painted with oversized smiles or red noses. Grillos laughed out loud. "You left the safety of our society for them?" He pointed to Bob, who inched his tricycle forward, then honked the horn. Grillos and his brothers stamped their feet, shaking with laughter.

Reaching out, he picked up Rosemary with his thumb and forefinger and plucked her off the ground. "If I wanted to, I could crush you like an insect." He held her up to his face. Rosemary went completely still. "You intrigue me. You would go against impossible odds to protect this big baboon?"

Rosemary sputtered for a minute, then replied fiercely, "He is a member of my crew!"

Henny stood tall, her imposing height dwarfed by her relatives. "You'll not make fun of others because they are not as strong as you. Loyalty isn't measured by size. She has a pure heart, not like the others of her species."

"Don't speak to me of loyalty, Henny." He turned his attention to Rosemary, who was vibrating with rage.

Grillos laughed hard, his great belly shaking. He wiped his eyes, his chuckles subsiding. Still holding Rosemary, he bowed low. He turned to his cousin, his face solemn. "But of course, Your Majesty. I respectfully ask you to allow us to cross your, *er*, territory so we may reach the Sign."

"Go ahead, but I won't come with you." She pointed to the humans behind them. "They will use you and destroy you."

He held Rosemary up in the air. "You said this one didn't use Jötnar. She risked her life to defend him. I believe we will consider humans on a one-on-one basis for now." Grillos shrugged. He looked back at his nieces. "Like it or not, we are taking them to Prendick Rock, and then we will destroy Vincent Konrad."

"Vincent Konrad? He's on Prendick Rock? I thought he was dead. I'll rip that bastard's head off."

Melvin stepped forward. "Sorry, ma'am. I did that already, and it didn't work."

Henny's lips turned into a snarl as she loomed over Melvin. She reached for him menacingly. A pack of wolves crouched and growled, moving between Henny and Melvin. She snapped, "I've heard about you. You're the wolf boy. You can't expect to send a werewolf when a giant is the only one strong enough—"

"I was never against you, cousin." Grillos pointed to the campfire with the charred remains of the gruesome meal. "This is what you left us to become?" He twisted to Jötnar. "Is this what you want?"

Henny seemed to shrink before his eyes, tears welling in her own. They streamed down her face, smearing her makeup. "I'm sorry," she cried. "I don't know why we did that." Her hands went from aggressive to pleading. "We were hungry. Starving. We didn't have a choice."

Howard was on one knee, poking a stick into the smoking coals of the fire. He rose then and walked over to Jötnar and Henny. "Did you eat the meat last night?"

Jötnar said, "No."

Rosemary turned pale and yelled, "Never!"

"Well, whoever did is in trouble. That corpse was a zombie. You've all got the plague. I wouldn't give you more than twenty-four hours, even less in some cases."

Henny backed away, her eyes wide with horror. "No!"

Panic caused the clowns to start shrieking. Some ran. Others fainted on the street. A hush overcame the army.

"Say it isn't so!" Henny cried. She turned on Bob. "You stupid, stupid man. How could you have let this happen?"

Bob shrugged. "I thought he was an actor," he whimpered.

"What?" She smacked him over the head with her large hands. "I told you not to take the green ones."

"It looked like make-up," Bob whined.

"Henny, it's too late for that now. What will you do?" Grillos called, interrupting the tirade.

Henny looked forlorn. "What can I do? The deed is done. You must go. Go quickly. Go before we change."

"I'll stay and take care of them," Brontes offered.

Henny yelled, "No! Get Konrad. He's the architect of this. He released the zombies here."

Grillos took one last look at his cousin. "We never stopped loving you."

Before their eyes, her face turned green, and an open sore bloomed on her cheek. "Get away from here, and when you have the means, get the humans to bomb this place."

Brontes held out his hand. Henny shook her head violently. "Go now! Forget you ever saw me!" She spun in a wild circle, yelling at the top of her lungs. "Get inside and let them pass!" She stopped, wobbling as if dizzy. "Not so funny now." She laughed. The clowns looked at her for direction. "Let them pass."

One by one, the clowns slithered into the storefronts until all that was left were Jötnar, Rosemary, the giants, and the human and werewolf army. Papers blew across the deserted streets. The sun dazzled the glass of the windows. The sour smell that accompanied zombies filled the area.

"We'd better get out of here," Wyatt said. "Zombies are bad enough. Zombie clowns are probably worse."

"They'll be dropping like flies in no time," Howard said.

Brontes turned around. "We're not afraid of zombies. They're very slow."

"They still bite," Melvin said, watching the streets warily. He had mustered his group of werewolves and coyotes. They surrounded him as if he were a shepherd.

"We'll protect you from the monsters." Grillos patted Melvin's head.

Mad Max bristled as he growled, *But who will protect you from us?*

Melvin shot the wolf with a look of warning.

"Are you coming with us?" Grillos turned to Jötnar.

"I won't marry her." Jötnar planted his bare feet firmly on the road.

Grillos held up Rosemary so they were eye to eye. "I like you."

"You have a route to the island?" she asked, ignoring his remark. He nodded once. "Good. Get moving, you big lummox."

Grillos placed Rosemary on his shoulder, then waved his arm at the troops. "Move out!"

They fell in rank and began their trek toward the sign.

"So, you don't like girls?" Rosemary yelled down to Jötnar from her perch on Grillos' shoulder.

"I like you," Jötnar responded with a grin. "But not in the way you're thinking."

"I get it. It's okay. It's really okay."

CHAPTER 30

AN UNCERTAIN FUTURE

THEY MARCHED THROUGH the streets, trekking through empty neighborhoods. Wyatt looked back where he knew the clowns hid behind windows of houses in their territory.

"What do you think will happen?" he asked Howard.

"You're the zombie expert," Howard replied. "It won't be long before they cannibalize each other. There's no one else left for them to eat." He looked at the werewolves trotting nearby and said wistfully, "I wish at least some of the vampires had survived here. I heard a few escaped in France." He hefted the gun he'd been given from one shoulder to the other as if it were uncomfortable.

Wyatt was armed as well. He had an antique Uzi that seemed lighter.

They raced through the throngs of soldiers, where Carter walked with John Raven. Wyatt moved forward. Carter placed a hand on his shoulder, and they began a spirited discussion.

Howard hung back, his eyes boring into Tocho's back as if his gaze alone could melt him. Tocho turned around and gave him a penetrating look. Howard glanced to the other side and realized Melvin had loped off to be with his furry friends. He was alone. He focused on the broad shoulders of Lily's cousin, resentment simmering on his face.

Lily's great uncle, John Raven slowed his steps until they walked side by side. "Keisha is a special girl. Very smart."

Howard saw that John Raven was watching him intently, his dark eyes wide and unblinking as a bird. Bristling just a bit, Howard gave a surly shrug.

"She has a great heart," John Raven continued.

"What do you know of her heart?" Howard spat, instantly regretting it. He was not used to being rude. It wasn't John Raven's fault Keisha moved on.

"I know her heart belongs to you and no other." John Raven nodded sagely.

"But... but... she—"

"A schoolgirl crush, nothing more." John sidestepped a hole in the road.

Howard picked up speed to catch up with the older man and stumbled against him. John Raven righted him with one powerful hand. "But Tocho—"

He shrugged. "He's wild about her." Howard opened his mouth to speak, but John Raven held up a hand stopping him. "I know what you think, Howard. She never left you. She never stopped talking about you. Keisha needed someone for a while. She lost her parents. You left."

Howard opened his mouth to retort, and John Raven said, "Let me finish, I didn't mean that you deserted her. You didn't. These are hard times, and there are going to be consequences. She is learning heady stuff. It confuses them sometimes."

"Are you insinuating she was having an identity crisis?"

John Raven raised an eyebrow. "Aren't you?" He looked back at Colonel Drucker and nodded his head. "Having your parents accessible makes things easier. She needed a friend."

Howard flushed, his cheeks going red. He looked at Melvin, Wyatt, Lily, and finally Keisha. She trailed behind them, her head down, her shoulders slumped. Tocho was speaking to her. She was not the same girl he had left on the reservation. She had changed, as if her spirit had been broken. Keisha had always been so sure of herself. Her resilience and strength served as the backbone of their relationship. Her cocksure confidence had led them through calamity, and now she needed him to be understanding.

He was the luckier one. His family was intact. Howard hung his head, ashamed that he hadn't realized it sooner.

John Raven chuckled. "It's alright, Howard. It's all part of growing up. Seeing the pain around you. It's real, *eh*? It's never been real before."

Keisha's self-assurance was what drove their connection. Her coolness under fire had been instrumental in cementing their relationship, especially when he had been a supreme dork.

Howard's insides quaked with fear. Insecurity curled its way from his tailbone to his stomach. He looked from Keisha to Tocho, his face red with shame. Taking a deep breath, he realized he'd been unfair to Lily's uncle. "No sir. I'm sorry. I was rude to you. I guess I blame everybody for our—"

"Distance? Give her time, Howard. She has to figure out what she wants."

Howard looked at them bleakly.

"Don't be so down, Howard. I have a feeling things will get better," John Raven said softly.

"I don't see how it can. She doesn't even remember me." He looked up at the older man. "Besides, Tocho is your nephew. Don't you want it to work out for him?"

John Raven laughed. "Tocho thinks he's in love with her. He's an alley cat. He will move on soon enough."

"He'll break her heart!" Howard was outraged.

"Perhaps, perhaps not. I'm sure it will all work out."

"Will Keisha remember?" Howard knew he wasn't asking about her time as Medusa.

"To morph?"

Howard spoke his voice low. "Everything."

John Raven looked thoughtful before answering. "You mean you? She never forgot. It's all there, waiting for the curtain to open." He stopped and placed his hand on Howard's shoulder. "What was the biggest issue in your relationship?"

Howard thought for a minute while they resumed walking. "She was always annoyed because I didn't seem interested. It… Keisha always made the… you know, first move," Howard added quickly. "It wasn't like I was missing signals, really. I was always thinking about science because I thought she liked that."

"Well, Howard, I think it's time to put science aside and let Keisha know she comes first."

Howard stared at the floor, wondering how he was going to do that. When he looked up, John Raven was gone.

Howard glanced around, realizing he was encircled by his friends.

They walked together, just like the old times. Melvin was unarmed and was followed by his canine army. , Wyatt, Howard, Sean, and Lily. Keisha caught up to them, her face blank. Howard looked for Tocho and saw him walking with his uncle.

He turned and saw Keisha tripping. He reached out and caught her in his arms. The group continued on, pushing into them.

The world narrowed to the two of them. They stood still, oblivious to the marching army. Howard held onto her arms, their eyes meeting.

"Get outta the way, kid!" someone yelled.

Howard pulled Keisha to the side of the road where they could talk.

Keisha was staring at his tanned hand supporting her arm. He knew he looked different. The months of hard life and deprivation had hardened him. He had to convince himself he wasn't that gawky teen anymore, and for a minute, his stomach flipped. Keisha loved that boy, the indecisive, preoccupied person who missed all her cues. In spite of his fumbling nature, he knew she was attracted to him.

He looked at the wreckage of Los Angeles. Nothing was the same, not even Keisha, and yet he loved her so much, it filled every fiber of his being. He might have looked like he was no longer a child and on the verge of adulthood, but inside he felt like that same stupid boy who couldn't find the right words, especially when he stood next to Tocho.

He watched the uncertainty in her eyes, hating the fact she remembered nothing.

Sweat beaded Howard's brow, his nerves jangled as if he were caught in a five-alarm fire. What if she never remembered him, or even worse, what if she decided she didn't like him, or wanted to be with the other guy?

Regret washed over him, leaving shaky knees in its wake. His eyes scanned the desolate streets, the bleak landscape. He had taken so much for granted in his life. He thought back to the time before Monsterland, his careless acceptance that everything would fall into place. How smug, how stupid to think the vagaries of living would leave him untouched. He had been incredibly naive to believe that nothing could happen, that tragedy and sorrow were for others. He looked at the back of his friends' heads as they walked away, knowing they were all scarred and would never be the same again.

Howard knew only one thing for certain. He needed Keisha as much as he needed air to live. They belonged together. Howard touched the region of his chest where his heart beat dully. It ached, and he wondered at the thought of a broken heart. His breath came out in a rush, understanding the pain Melvin must be living with or Wyatt's overwhelming losses. They couldn't bring their loved ones back to life.

Firming his lips, Howard knew he couldn't trust time to fix his relationship with Keisha. Flushing, he remembered their conversation at Monsterland, when he disappointed Keisha by not responding to her declaration of love. Realization came with the force of a tidal wave. He had to make sure Keisha knew what she meant to him. He didn't want to wait another minute.

Howard pulled her into an alleyway between a cluster of buildings. The world faded. Howard felt the silence lie over them like a thick blanket. They stood in the shadows of the buildings, letting their eyes grow accustomed to the dim interior.

Keisha stared at him, her brown eyes huge. Fumbling with his gun, Howard rested it against the brick wall. Taking a deep breath, he took her hand between his and held it tenderly. She snatched it away. They stared at each other.

Howard tried to read her eyes. She seemed uncertain, her gaze darting to the line of people passing them.

Finally, Keisha cleared her throat. "Lily told me that we are… we were—"

Howard placed a finger over her mouth. "Nothing's changed. You need some time, is all. It will come back."

"You don't know that." Keisha pulled her hand from his. "Things are different. I'm different." She turned from him, and he could see her shoulders shaking.

"Keisha." He moved in front of her, wrapping his arms around her. As tall as she was, for the first time, Howard felt taller, bigger, as if he could take care of her. "Then we'll create new memories." Pressing her against a building, he rested his forehead against hers. "I love you, Keisha. I always have."

Keisha lowered her head. "Howard, I… I—" She glanced through the opening of the alley at the troops moving past them.

Tears leaked from the corners of Keisha's eyes. "I wish I could remember you, Howard. I can't."

Howard swallowed and said, "Yesterday is gone. Tomorrow has not yet come...."

Keisha continued with her soft voice, a spark passing between them. "We have only today. Let us—"

"Begin." Howard finished the quote. "You remembered." Howard smiled.

Keisha gave a watery laugh. "It's just a quote."

Howard drew her close. He whispered into her ear, "I'll take it. It gives me hope."

Keisha's temple was resting against his. "I don't know."

Howard caressed her cheek. "Take as much time as you like. I will wait forever."

Keisha moistened her lips and for a minute, Howard wanted to kiss her, but he didn't. It wasn't the right time. He had to be sure, and all he saw was indecision in her eyes. "Promise me, you'll think about it."

Keisha nodded. "I will."

She pulled away to walk with Lily, leaving Howard alone in the alley. He meant what he said, he'd wait forever for her.

Howard ran out and caught up to Wyatt and Melvin.

"All's right with the world?" Wyatt asked with a smile.

Howard gave a lopsided grin. "Still working on it, but I'm hopeful."

The group picked up their pace and climbed the mountainside, their mood as well as their steps lightened. Together they crested the hills until they reached the Sign.

Four of the giants sifted through the bushes until they found what appeared to be broken tree limbs. They were huge torches fashioned from wood and straw. Within minutes, a fire was produced by one of the soldiers, who then lit up the end of the wood.

Four of the giants pulled away the double *L*'s of the Hollywood sign, opening a portal to a new world. Wyatt and his friends waited as the army began its march through the doorway created by the giants. The group of teens rested on a boulder, Tocho sat on the top.

The setting sun painted the sky orange and gold. Night turned into a ceiling of stars. Wyatt lay back on the rock to look at the bright light of Saturn. Without city lights, it blazed in the sky like a beacon.

Howard was sitting at the base of the rock. He called out to Keisha. "Make a wish."

"That's rather fanciful," Keisha responded.

"'Look up at the stars and not down at your feet. Try to make sense of what you see, and wonder about what makes the universe exist,'" Howard said, quoting Stephen Hawking.

He could hear Tocho snarling at him. He ignored it.

Keisha thought for a bit and responded, "Keep your eyes on the stars and your feet on the ground.'"

"Here comes Shakespeare," Wyatt said out loud..

Howard did not disappoint. "'Doubt thou the stars are fire,/ Doubt that the sun doth move,/Doubt truth to be a liar,/But never doubt I love.'"

Wyatt exchanged a look with Melvin, who rolled his eyes and said, "We should leave."

Wyatt shook his head. "No worries. He's going to start naming the stars in a second."

"Alnitak, Alnilam, and Mintaka, the Three Kings," Howard stated.

Wyatt raised his eyebrows and mouthed, *Told you.*

"Sisters." Keisha's voice sounded firm. "They're called the Three Sisters, Howard Drucker." Keisha sat up abruptly and gasped. "I used to call you that," she said.

"Yes!" Howard's face filled with joy.

Tocho stood. "We better move inside with the others."

Keisha was staring at his face, then she looked up at Tocho. "I... I."

"Move out!" Tocho ordered.

Everyone rose and pushed toward the opening.

"I love you, Keish," Howard said. It was low, and he cursed his timing. She was already near the entrance.

"I think it's sweet." Lily smiled at Wyatt. "Howard and Keisha." Her face filled with longing. He reached out for her. They walked hand-in-hand toward the entrance of the sign. "You never talk to me that way," she said wistfully.

"And I'm never gonna," Wyatt responded, then added, "Not my style."

Lily laughed. "Oh, you have a style?"

He plucked a feather from behind Lily's headband and kissed it. He placed it in his pocket, next to his heart. Lily smiled winsomely, and Wyatt patted his pocket, feeling the scarf underneath this shirt.

He didn›t know why he held onto the scarf, but it was time to let it go. He pulled it out of his shirt, and as they reached the top of the hill, he tossed it onto the breeze. It hung in the air for a minute, then floated down the cliff.

He glanced back at Danai, who walked with her five sisters. She raised a hand to wave her fingers, grinning widely. It was as if he let her go. Their eyes met and they watched the fabric dance on the breeze and float to freedom. Wyatt raised his fist in the air and she returned the gesture. He caught Lily regarding him, her expression wary.

"Is there anything I should be worried about?" she asked.

Wyatt looked at her, his eyebrows raised. "What?" He saw her look at Danai. "You mean Danai? *Nah*. She's a great girl, interesting. You'll like her." Wyatt smiled back, very sure of himself. "No doubt."

They walked into the dark tunnel together.

Howard caught up to Keisha and tapped her shoulder. She turned and he grabbed her hand. "I missed you.".

"I... missed you too," Keisha replied, staring back at him. She looked him full in the face. "Why does this *feel* different?".

"I was a moron. I never… what I mean to say is I never had the guts to say what I what was in here." He touched his chest.

Keisha shook her head. "No, I think you did."

Tocho brushed past, banging into both of them. It didn't even rock them. Howard heard Tocho curse as he walked away. Stopping for a second, he glared at Howard. Holding Keisha's forearm, he turned her so they were face-to-face and she couldn't notice Tocho's hateful stare.

"I think I never gave you a chance to take the first steps," she said as if this revelation just occurred to her.

"It's a lot like dancing. We have to learn how to move together," Howard said.

"I'll need time, Howard." She looked back for Tocho.

"He moved on," Howard said.

Keisha nodded. "Maybe. Maybe not. I have to talk to him too. It's only right."

Howard kissed her knuckles. "I agree." His eyes met hers. "I'm not concerned," he said with an impish grin that turned into a satisfied smile when he heard her quick intake of a breath.

"Enough!" Sheldon yelled as the group came up next to them. "Fall in. They're about to close up the portal. We have work to do."

Side by side, Keisha and Howard walked into the entrance and an uncertain future.

"What do you think is going to happen?" Keisha asked.

Howard shook his head. "I'm not sure, but as long as we're together, it'll be okay."

The door slammed shut behind them.

CHAPTER 31

TOY IN A BATHTUB

"**Y**OU'RE TALL FOR a minkin," Grillos said without looking at Rosemary, who sat perched on his shoulder.

"Are you talking to me?" Rosemary nodded. "You mean a human? Taller than most. My father is very tall." She looked away. They were trekking through a vast network of tunnels, the rock walls striated in patterns of sandstone and red.

"Pretty," Grillos commented.

Rosemary looked down to find his gaze resting on her hair. She smoothed the wild tendrils down, feeling feminine and petite for the first time in her life. Blushing, she averted her gaze.

"Is it really a problem with Jötnar?" she asked.

Grillos explained their complex society and the reproduction demands.

"Surely it won't be an issue if you move to inhabit the surface of the planet." The road was uneven, with dips and valleys. Rosemary clutched at Grillos' shirt to hold on. "You can put me down, you know."

Grillos didn't answer for a bit. She saw his watchful eyes glancing at the president.

"We haven't had much success with your kind. While we are very trusting people, we really don't know whether humankind will live up to their promises."

"Yet you are helping us." A wave of fatigue washed over Rosemary. She paled, feeling light-headed.

"You are tired." Grillos's voice was soft, as if he understood that admitting she was exhausted threatened her sense of leadership. "You are safe. Lean against me."

Rosemary rested her head against his deltoid muscle. It wasn't soft so much as comfortable. Grillos's scent enveloped her. It brought her back to the sea, surrounded by her crew. Her eyes drooped. "Jötnar carried me once," she said dreamily.

"*Hmph*," Grillos huffed. "He is a boy."

She moved herself to speak close to his ear. "And you are a man?"

Rosemary felt the ridges of his muscles flex, as if they would embrace her.

"Is it possible for our races to mix?" she asked, placing her hand on the side of his neck. She caressed his skin, marveling at the softness. A pulse beat lightly against her fingertips.

"We are not so different, I think," Grillos said. "It's all about adjustments."

Rosemary chuckled. "I presume you have some experience in these things."

Grillos's laughter filled the corridor, ricocheting off the walls.

"Are you married?"

"No, Brontes was the smallest, so he married to have the girls. I never had a need to settle down."

"Still, you could find someone to be with," Rosemary said. "Don't you have something like… GDate in the App Store?"

Grillos' booming laughter filled the tunnel.

"What's so funny?" President Owens asked when he caught up with them.

Grillos looked down on the tiny army surrounding them. "I think you've found your first ambassador to represent humans with our people." He turned his head so his eyes met Rosemary's face. "Do you think you would like that? Living with us?"

Rosemary glanced down at the president. "I don't know. What do you think, sir?"

President Owens smiled. "Since the government is experiencing a shortage of employees, I'll take any volunteers. Are you willing to take on the task? I believe the young giant introduced you as his captain...." He waited for her to supply a name.

"Just call me Rosemary." Rosemary turned to look at the five other giants. "I am looking for a new home. Yes, I think it might do."

"It's settled, then... after we finish our business with Vincent Konrad," President Owens said.

Rosemary's eyes narrowed, her thoughts on her father. "Yes, after we finish with him." She tugged Grillos's earlobe. "And you—you think I can fill those shoes? I'm new to this."

Grillos shrugged. "If you are indeed Jötnar's captain, then I trust you are experienced in making decisions."

"I am used to being in command," she responded.

Grillos's shoulders shook with laughter. "We'll see about that."

"What do you mean?"

"Well," Grillos explained, "in our culture, men are dominant."

"If you plan to live on the surface, you are going to discover things will have to change."

"Why?"

"In our world, women are valued as equally as men. All sexes are respected."

"I see how you respected the monsters and the sick people," Grillos responded.

"That was one man, not the whole world," Rosemary shot back. "Don't judge humanity by one demented person."

Grillos took a while to answer, as if he were considering his words carefully. "Yet your world let him, even encouraged him to do it. They closed their eyes to his depravity."

Rosemary found no answer. She fumed at Grillos' words, angry at her father. Her face flushed with shame. The giant was right. "Maybe I'm not right for this job," she said almost to herself.

Grillos's voice rumbled beneath her head, which was resting on his shoulder. "Perhaps taking baby steps with giants will lead to giant steps for your kind." Rosemary didn't answer. Grillos continued, "This should prove to be an interesting experiment. It is settled. You will live among us and help with our resettlement." Grillos dipped as he approached a junction, and the ceiling space narrowed.

Rosemary shrieked, sliding from his shoulder. The giant caught her with his other hand and perched her back on his collarbone. "I think we have a lot to learn together. It's strange, but I sense I can trust you. I've never felt that way before with a minkin. Do they just call you Rosemary? What is your clan name?"

Rosemary's face went wooden. She said blankly, "I have no clan."

Grillos' heavy eyebrows rose to his hairline. "No clan. We must see about that."

Wyatt and his group grew silent as they walked through the cathedral-like caverns. Wyatt could hear Howard's and Keisha's whispered comments as they marveled over the polished rocks. Tocho fumed nearby, stalking them like a wild cat.

Wyatt's gaze wandered, and he was struck by the giants' superior knowledge and workmanship that had enabled them to create a vast network of underground tunnels. The caverns were tall and well formed. The top of the giants' heads grazed the ceiling.

"…There's no leakage." He heard Howard's voice. Indeed, there was no dust or evidence of water dripping. The floor was just as solid, and an idea struck Wyatt.

He patted Lily's hand. "I have some unfinished business."

Wyatt paused at a corner, hanging back until Danai caught up with him.

"The tunnels are incredible," he told her with awe. "I can't believe what they've managed to accomplish. I want to ask you something."

Danai nodded.

"The earthquakes—"

Danai giggled. "Yes, it was us… except for the Northridge quake," she added hastily. "That one was natural."

"*Wow.*" Wyatt tried to wrap his brain around what he just learned. "Wait until I tell Howard. It is going to blow his mind." He moved to catch up with the others when Danai's hand came down gently on his shoulder.

"Wyatt?" Danai asked, keeping her voice down. "I saw you let go of my scarf. I just want to say… Thank you."

Wyatt flushed. "I'm sorry. I should have given it back to you."

Danai giggled and shook her head. "We both know it's too small for me now."

Wyatt watched her face, wondering if she was talking about the scarf. She was so tall, he had to crane his neck to talk to her.

"I knew you had it. I didn't understand why." She blushed a bit.

"Finding something like that in the midst of all the craziness, you know, I felt like I couldn't let it go. If I did…" he stammered, his face red.

"I understand," Danai interrupted. "That's exactly what I'm searching for. Back home, we have very few comforts."

"That's it! The scarf brought me *comfort*. It reminded me that there is still beauty in this world, and I wanted to hold onto that."

Danai nodded gravely. "I thought it was something like that. I never believed it was anything deeper."

Wyatt cleared his throat. "*Um*… you're lovely, Danai—"

"Don't be nervous, Wyatt. I was trying to think of a way to let *you* down gently." She looked at Lily, who was walking a few yards in front of them. "I can see now… well… no matter. It's all okay."

"I always thought of you as a friend. We call that the *Friend Zone* up here."

"Yes. I like that." She waved her arms around. "When you let the scarf go free, it was liberating." Her eyes were brighter than he'd ever seen them. "I don't feel tethered to the underside of the earth anymore. I can't wait to go above ground and explore. There's a whole planet to discover, even if it's a little bruised. Besides, there must be thousands of eligible guys around. I want to take my time." She looked down at Wyatt. "You made it all possible with my family, and for that I will never forget you."

"I won't forget you either, Danai," he replied.

"Be careful!" she called as he jogged away.

As they neared their destination, the tunnels became more cramped, the walls rough-hewn, less finished. They walked for at least an hour in the narrow part. For the first time, water trickled down from the ceiling, puddling at their feet. It was muddy, a beaten track as if many large feet had flattened the path. The air was thick with a growing humidity.

Howard touched the water and tasted it. "It's seawater." He looked up, his Adam's apple bobbing in his neck. "I think we're under the ocean."

They were damp, sweat coating their bodies, their shirts sticking to their skin. Wyatt looked at Melvin and realized he'd morphed into a werewolf. He was panting, his blue tongue hanging out. Wyatt noticed Melvin had a backpack on his back that he supposedly carried his clothing.

"You okay?" Wyatt asked. "You want me to hold that?"

Melvin growled a response, and strangely enough, Wyatt understood that he was fine. He smiled at the absurdity of it.

The front of the group slowed until they were bunched together in an immovable knot. The air became stifling. Wyatt used his tee to wipe his face.

Wyatt pushed forward, holding Lily's hand, the two of them squeezing between the large shoulders of the officers surrounding Colonel Drucker and the president.

Grillos was speaking, Rosemary standing next to him, dwarfed by his size. The giant was pointing to a tunnel that veered eastward.

"This one tunnel goes all the way to Hawaii, then on to our brothers in Asia. There is a large community thriving in the Himalayas."

"And the other?" Colonel Drucker gestured to the dark interior of the one before them, the flashlight someone had attached to his helmet illuminating the darkness.

"We used to vacation there years ago. It's what you minkins call Prendick Rock."

Wyatt heard the order for the army to stand down as it echoed past him. He looked up to see Carter next to him.

"What now?" he asked his stepfather.

"Not sure. They'll figure it out."

"Yeah, but what would you do?"

Carter considered the narrow opening. "We have the element of surprise. The problem is that we make our entrance on the beach where all the zombies are roaming. By the time we manage to get through them, we'll lose our ambush—"

"Not unless we let the werewolves get them first," Wyatt interrupted.

Carter exhaled. "That's a great idea. The werewolves can outrun and outfight the zombies. They are not affected by their bite. Where's Melvin?" He looked around.

"Mel!" Wyatt called.

Melvin emerged from the shadows in his human form.

"The giants will open an entrance on the beach that's filled with zombies."

"Want us to take 'em out?" Melvin asked.

Rosemary's voice rang out like a bell. "There is a way into the subterranean building from the top of the mountain. It's how Shandy and I escaped. I can lead you to the opening."

"Where will that put us?" Colonel Drucker asked.

"Right in the heart of Vincent Konrad's control center."

"*Hmmm…*" The colonel was thoughtful. "But the zombies on the beach—"

"Sir!" Carter called out. "Wyatt has come up with an idea to take out the zombies."

Carter disappeared into the fold. Wyatt stood on the tips of his toes, Lily's hand encased in his sweaty one, but he couldn't hear anything else. He watched Melvin fade into the darkness, he guessed to communicate with his band.

"That was pretty smart," Lily told him.

"I'd give anything to hear what they are saying."

Wyatt felt his hand go slack and heard the flutter of wings, the soft feathers brushing his cheeks. He smiled as a dainty kestrel maneuvered her way to hover slightly above the giants' heads, where she perched on a broken piece of shale, her bright eyes flickering in the torchlight.

She was back minutes later, morphing into a girl once more. "They've got a plan. There's a spot for us in the corner." Taking Wyatt's hand, they squeezed between the bodies, silently pushing themselves into a small spot to the right of Rosemary.

Rosemary dictated while Lieutenant Appel drew a map on the rock wall using a broken piece of rock. Wyatt craned his neck, watching the illustration take shape. The crude drawing of the island was small, the beach surrounding a giant man-made hill, Vincent Konrad's control center miles below the ocean.

Wyatt shivered. Vincent was so close. Wyatt's body hummed with anticipation. He touched the gun slung over his shoulder, reassuring himself he'd be ready this time when he met his nemesis.

Wyatt glanced at the president, wondering what he would do when he encountered his father, Dreg. Wyatt's gaze moved to Yerbol, a chill racing down his spine. The commando's face was like granite, stone cold, his lips firmed into a stern line. Yerbol's eyes moved to meet Wyatt's. They stared at each other for a long minute. Wyatt looked at the president, and Yerbol broke eye contact.

"We should release the werewolves in oh-four hundred hours," Colonel Drucker said.

Everybody looked at their wristwatches to confirm the time. Carter moved over, motioning for Wyatt to follow him.

"They're going to storm the control center. I want you to stay here with Sean, Howard, Lily, and Keisha," Carter said in a low voice.

Wyatt shook his head. "Not going to happen."

Carter opened his mouth to reply, saw the five sets of eyes watching him, and snapped it shut.

"This is war, Carter. You can't protect us. Besides, I have a score to settle…"

"Wyatt, you can't take a chance that Vincent Konrad will escape again."

"It wasn't my fault!" Wyatt exploded. He started to storm off when Carter grabbed his arm.

"No one said it was your fault." Carter looked at the crowd surrounding them. "Can I have a word with you alone?"

Wyatt shook his head. "Where? The tunnel is packed. Anyway, anything you say to me, you can say to my friends."

Carter took a steadying breath. "It's going to get chaotic. I just wanted to keep you safe."

"There's no such thing as safe anymore, Carter," Howard said.

"You have to let us grow up," Wyatt added. "It can't be any crazier than it was at Monsterland."

Carter looked up and then back at their faces, his eyes distant. "You're right."

They bedded down anywhere they found a few feet of space. It was quiet. The air was filled with electricity, the hushed voices of soldiers like a steady hum in the tunnel.

Lily rested in the crook of Wyatt's shoulder, his cheek against the silk of her hair.

Wyatt saw that Keisha was asleep, her head on Howard's thigh, her breathing even. Howard's hand rested on her shoulder protectively. Tocho was crouched, brooding in the corner.

Melvin had gone off to be with his pack. Soon Wyatt saw them trotting through the tunnel. Everybody cleared away as they moved forward, a surge of fur, teeth, and raw power. At the head of the group was an auburn wolf. The wolf paused as it passed Wyatt and his friends.

Wyatt stood, then reached out to embrace the wolf's neck. "Be careful, Mel."

Wyatt heard an affectionate growl.

Colonel Drucker's voice rang out. "Are you ready, then?"

Melvin nodded, his teeth bared in a ferocious grin.

"Open the door!" Colonel Drucker commanded.

There was the grind of metal against metal and the groan of an unused door being pushed open.

"Are you ready to give the command, Mr. President?"

Nate Owens moved next to Colonel Drucker. "Attack!"

The pack of wolves charged out the portal, baying and howling as they escaped the tunnel.

President Owens turned to face the troops. "This is it. Some of you will make it; others won't. This is our Apocalypse. We have to take back this country from that monster. Good luck and Godspeed."

Rosemary nodded and, on the back of Grillos, waved them forward. "Follow me!"

Wyatt heard Howard murmur, "Boudica."

"What?"

Keisha sat up, rubbing sleep from her eyes. "An ancient Iceni queen who led her people against the Romans."

"*Hmph*. What about her?" Wyatt asked.

Lily came to stand next to him, her face troubled. "Brave and fearless."

"That's good for us. What happened to her?"

Keisha looked back at him, swallowing. "She ended up poisoning herself after her defeat."

The teens watched the troops pour out of the tunnel after Rosemary.

Sunlight assaulted their eyes when they emerged from the dim interior of the tunnel. Wyatt followed the commandos as they scrambled up the sandy hill. Gorse and branches tore at him, ripping his shirt, leaving long scratches down his arm. The gash on his head pained him a bit, the pills Mrs. Drucker had given him were wearing off. He looked up to see Lily flying high above him. She pointed her wings downward, and Wyatt peered over the edge of the cliff to see zombies clamoring on the beach, werewolves swarming around them like a tide. Body parts were flying; the pale sand was stained with blood.

Sirens went off, the element of surprise ruined.

Bullets whizzed past him. One tore at the shoulder of his shirt. Wyatt threw himself on his belly, making himself a smaller target. He saw Keisha and Howard crawling on their stomachs next to him. Behind him, Sean crouched behind a cluster of bushes.

Vincent's troops poured from an opening on the top of the hill. Wyatt could see Rosemary and her giant fighting with the enemy as if they were one person. The giant swatted away the oncoming soldiers as if they were pesky flies. Rosemary shot at them with a single-bore rifle.

Howard Drucker landed next to Wyatt. Sean was now on the other side.

Wyatt looked around wildly. "Where's Keisha?"

Howard pointed upward. "Her memory is flooding back. She finally remembered what John Raven taught her."

Wyatt looked at the crest of the hill to see two kestrels flying in tandem, pecking on the enemy soldiers.

"Well, that's progress," Wyatt replied. Nearby a mountain lion prowled, its eyes on Howard Drucker.

They heard the order to fire, and all three of them aimed their guns and commenced shooting.

Carter was in the lead group, next to the president and his commandos. Lieutenant Appel with Sheldon by her side had command of the lee side of the cliff. They were picking off whatever zombies were not ripped apart by the wolves.

Wyatt's body was pressed against a dune, his gun slamming his shoulder with every shot he released. He could see Howard spraying the enemy as they surged forward.

He saw one of the giants go down like a felled tree. The enemy soldiers climbed over him like a hill.

There was a screech like an avalanche, and all six girls, Danai in the lead, decimated the incoming soldiers. Fury made them wild, like the Amazon women Wyatt had read about in a comic book years ago. Their combined strength and anger made them invincible. Red hair billowing behind them, their faces set, they looked nothing like the sweet girls he'd traveled with this past week.

Danai had a cut over her eye, Candace a wound on her arm, but they moved with the might of a tidal wave breaking the line of the opposing force.

The air stank of cordite, making Wyatt's eyes water. Dust surrounded them, inhibiting visibility. The fresh sea breeze warred with the side effects of the battle. Bullets whizzed around them, mere puffs of deadly air. Wyatt heard Sean exhale in a rush and glanced at him, his voice squeezed out, "You okay?"

Sean moved sideways, revealing a dead soldier next to them.

"Stay down!" Wyatt yelled.

A movement made Wyatt turn to look in the other direction. Squinting through the fog of battle, he noticed a strange formation of lights hovering in the sky. He shaded his eyes with his hand but couldn't quite make out the aircraft. Tapping Howard, he shouted for him to look back at the mainland. Howard looked at him blankly, so Wyatt pointed to the east.

"What?" Howard yelled back.

"What's that?"

Howard peered at the horizon. "I don't know. The air force, maybe? The color of the lights are unfamiliar. I'm not sure if they are with us or against..." His voice trailed off as he watched the lights blink once and make an impossible turn, moving upward to disappear into the atmosphere.

Howard narrowed his eyes in concentration. "Wyatt, I don't know of any aircraft that can do-"

Wyatt interrupted, his voice urgent, "Never mind that, Look Howard! Look over there!" Wyatt was pointing in the opposite direction toward the sea. "They're here."

Lining the horizon four massive battleships appeared as if from thin air. Japanese flags fluttered proudly from their masts. White suited sailors filled the decks, arming the various guns along the sides of the ship, aimed at the island.

"They're going to attack Vincent!"

Wyatt stared at the massive warships, his eyes smarting. "They came!" he said in awe. "They're here to help us!! The other countries came to our aid." He looked for Lily and Keisha, he wanted to share the news. The heaviness he felt all day in his chest lightened, and for the first time, hope lodged there. He watched the commanders execute a wide turn maneuvering the warships to surround the island. All around him, he heard cheers amid the chaos. Gray clouds of smoke expelled as the first volley of missiles were released. Wyatt and Howard instinctively ducked as the explosions shook the earth. Huge chunks of the mountain fell away.

One of the ships tilted a bit.

"*Uh*, Wyatt," Howard said. "Those multi-purpose operational motherships aren't really meant to tilt like that."

Wyatt watched as two of the ships swayed as if the sea had turned stormy. Water washed over the decks taking screaming sailors with it.

Before another shot could be fired, giant tentacles whipped out of the sea like grappling irons and dragged the tilting ship under like it was a toy in a bathtub. They watched as the metal buckled under the pressure and the battleships broke in half.

Wyatt›s face melted into a mask of horror.

"Holy sh…" Wyatt's words were cut off by another set of tentacles ripping apart the second ship like it was paper-mâché.

"What is that thing?" Sean asked.

"I thought it was mythical. It›s *Octopus Giganteus.*" Howard's jaw hung open.

"English, Howard!" Sean yelled.

"A really, really, really, *really* big octopus." Howard blew air through his lips. "What's next, Bigfoot?"

"Bigfoot doesn't exist," Wyatt said matter-of-factly.

The other two ships turned to face the unexpected underwater enemy. Machine guns sprayed from the deck. Behind the vessels, the oblong-shaped head of the octopus emerged from the water.

A silence filled the air.

The remaining ships were pulled underwater, out of sight, the octopus slowly sinking with its capture.

The boys stood there stunned.

Wyatt noticed Nate Owens follow Rosemary and Grillos into an opening at the top of the hill.

Wyatt urged, "We gotta go guys. We're on our own." He, Howard, and Sean took off after them. The mountain lion creeped after them.

CHAPTER 32

MELVIN

MELVIN RAN DOWN the incline at the front of the pack. His group had swelled to hundreds. Howls filled the air, sending the zombies into a frenzy at the base of the cliff.

Melvin burst from the rocks, launching himself into a group struggling to get at them. He went down into a blood-soaked splatter, arms and legs flying everywhere. Soon his coat was matted with zombie guts, the ground slippery with muck. Alfonso was feasting on brains, his fur slick with it.

No time to eat! Melvin yelled. *Take down as many as you can!*

Alfonso growled back, but a shove from Mad Max propelled them both into another crowd of zombies that toppled like bowling pins.

Melvin raced along the beach shouting orders when a stray bullet hit Alfonso squarely in the jaw. He wobbled and went down, and four zombies tore him into pieces to chomp on his remains.

Melvin took off in the direction of the shot, weaving as bullets kicked up clots of sand.

Behind a group of barrels, two soldiers picked off wolves, shooting with deadly accuracy. Melvin hid behind a palm, looking for a way to get to them.

I'll go from behind, Donner said breathlessly, coming up behind Melvin.

It will never work. They'll see you coming. Melvin looked up. A crane towered over them. *If we could get up there...*

It's suicide. Donner shook his head.

You got a better idea?

It would be easier in human form, Donner suggested.

Especially if they think I'm a zombie.

It's dangerous. If one of them bites you in human form, you'll get infected, Donner warned.

A spray of bullets rained into a crowd of five werewolves. They could hear the survivors whimpering as the zombies finished them off.

Well, if I don't do it, we're all going to be nothing more than dog food.

Donner nodded. *It will be better if there are two of us. I'll go with you.* By the time he finished the sentence, he'd morphed into an older man. He pulled a pair of pants off a zombie, shook them out, and put them on. *Come on, man. We have no time to lose.*

You don't have to sacrifice yourself. I'm willing to do this.

Who's going to save us all if you don't make it? Donner smiled like a wolf, and Melvin found himself wishing they would both make it out so he could get to know him better. Melvin followed him, dressing in soiled surfer shorts he'd taken from a body near the tree.

They both hunched over, and widening their eyes, they lurched forward, dodging bullets, zombies, and werewolves.

A growl stopped Melvin in his tracks. Without moving his mouth, he ground out, "It's me—Melvin."

Caught in bloodlust, the wolf bared its teeth. Grabbing Melvin's arm, the powerful jaws clamped down. Melvin shook him off, but it wouldn't let go of his wrist. His skin tearing and his bones grinding against bone, he raised a fist to punch the wolf when a zombie leaped onto his back.

Drool mixed with pus ran from the zombie's open mouth, the fetid stench making Melvin gag. The heat of the fevered skin next to his made his hackles rise, but in his human form, he had less strength. Melvin felt himself going down, the hot breath of the monster on his back vying with the growls of the werewolf imprisoning his arm.

He landed on his stomach, the wind knocked out of him. The zombie's broken fingers pulled at his hair, the smell of Melvin's bitten hand making the zombie wild for blood.

Taking a deep breath, Melvin jumped upward, and his head collided with the zombie. One eyeball flew from the socket to land on the wolf's head. It looked up at Melvin with surprise.

"Get him, not me, you idiot," screamed Melvin.

The wolf's mouth went slack, and the canine turned on the zombie, forcing it to release its hold on Melvin.

Melvin leaped for the crane and scaled it to the top to find Donner hanging from a rung, his eyes vacant.

"You okay?" Melvin asked breathlessly.

Donner held up his arm. His hand was missing from his wrist. "They got me. We haven't got much time. You?"

"I'm good."

"I'm glad, Mel. You're a good guy."

Gunfire exploded around them. Melvin winced.

"You've got to promise me something," Donner said, his voice weary.

"What?"

"You've got to get them to change their perception of us. We're not bad."

Melvin went to place a hand on Donner's shoulder. He ducked

away. "Too dangerous. I feel the change coming on already. I'm going in. Don't follow me unless I don't succeed. You have work to do out there." He gestured to the mainland.

Donner saluted Melvin with his injured hand and, baring his teeth, let go. Bullets splattered around Donner's falling body. His body jerked twice, but he managed to land behind enemy lines. He smashed both heads of the gunners together. He rose, wobbling, to his feet. He swayed and fell face down in a puddle of blood.

Melvin watched the carnage from his spot. The wolves were winning. Zombies were piling up like cordwood. Mad Max barked loudly. Melvin nodded. Max would take it from here.

Melvin saw an opening to the building and, using the rope from the crane, swung himself into the doorway.

CHAPTER 33

WE MEET AGAIN

ROSEMARY JUMPED OFF Grillos' shoulder and ordered, "Follow me!"

They stormed through the corridors, looking for Vincent. Passing his dining room, Rosemary motioned for the president and a detail to wait in there.

"What are you doing?" Yerbol yelled.

"I'm going in." She pointed to a darkened corridor. "He must be in his control room. It's a quarter of a mile deeper."

Yerbol looked at the president, who nodded. "Bring him back to me."

"We may not be able to take Vincent alive."

Yerbol shook his head. "He means his father, Dreg, eh, Andrew Owens.."

Rosemary and the troops hugged the walls, bullets whizzing past them as they entered each new corridor. Grillos walked ahead, smashing into the resistance, pummeling the opposition, and clearing the way for the others. His remaining brothers split into different hallways, the imperviousness to the bullets making it possible for them to storm the enemy, allowing the troops to fill the corridors. The air was filled with the screams of the dying soldiers.

Grillos grabbed Rosemary when a spray of bullets pocked the walls behind them. These bullets shredded the metal as if it were butter.

"Wot's that?" Grillos pointed.

"Heavy artillery. They've got armor-piercing guns."

They slid onto the floor, Grillos filling the entire corridor. Rosemary motioned for Lieutenant Appel to move to the passageway on the left.

"The hallway intersects at the next corner. We'll surround them."

Appel nodded and took off, a group of soldiers following her.

Yerbol came up from behind. "What's the holdup?" he demanded.

A rapid hail of gunfire answered him. Yerbol landed on his stomach. The area above their heads was torn apart as if by a grenade.

Rosemary said, "Appel will circle around and get them from the other side."

Yerbol agreed. "I'll set up a sharpshooter on this side."

Grillos got to his feet, crouching so his head grazed the tall ceiling. "Bullets don't affect us. I will go in."

Yerbol looked behind him. "This is different ammunition. It's not what the others were using on the outside."

"A minor nuisance. Walk behind me."

Grillos moved forward, Rosemary, Yerbol, and his commandos in his wake. The hallways lit up as gunfire exploded around them. One of the commandos was blown backward, his vest disintegrated.

Rosemary looked up. Grillos was hunching more than ever, blood dripping down his legs. He plowed on, his hands dragging on the floor.

The sound of gunfire was so loud, the only thing Rosemary

heard was ringing in her ears. A cheer went up from the other side of the corridor, followed by a silence so profound, Rosemary thought for a minute she had gone deaf.

Appel stood in front of a pile of bodies, her face triumphant. "Which way now?" she asked. A loud whine, followed by a flash of light, split the air. As the words left her mouth, Appel collapsed on top of the enemy bodies, her eyes wide with shock.

Grillos jerked and fell forward, taking out an entire wall, his hand clutching his face. Yerbol twirled, his gun flying out of his hands, and Rosemary was lifted off her feet from behind. A purple-skinned hand squeezed her arms until she dropped her gun.

Beneath Rosemary, her troops lay sprawled across the floor. A hated voice sneered, "We meet again." Dreg limped out, holding a sleek cannon made from a material she'd never seen before.

Rosemary watched the smile fade from Dreg's face when the entire room shook as if hit by a cyclone. Everything went black.

CHAPTER 34

A MOLECULAR HAZE

WYATT AND THE others ducked through clusters of soldiers locked in battle, following the president into the entry of Vincent's dining room.

Bursts of gunfire echoed in the corridors. Wyatt heard the scuffle of booted feet, followed by a gunfight. They crept along the hallway, eyes alert.

Wyatt heard the howl of wolves. "Melvin!"

Melvin rushed into the room, his body matted with blood. He was in human form and wearing filthy surfer shorts.

The building shook as if impacted by a torpedo. Wyatt slammed into the floor, Sean fell on top of him. The lights blinked and went out.

There was the whisper of wings, and Wyatt felt Lily land unsteadily on his shoulder. He looked behind him to see Keisha next to Howard, a feather in her hair.

A minute later, Lily hopped onto the floor and came to herself. She moaned, "It was that thing that took down the ships."

"Yes, you okay?" Wyatt asked, squinting into the darkness.

"We flew right into the wall when that tremor hit."

There was another crash, this time shaking the floor. The walls groaned, metal grinding against metal, and dust rained down on them.

Wyatt rose, then grabbed Lily under the arms.

"We have to get out of here," Lily said.

"No. I'm not leaving until I finish Vincent," Wyatt replied.

Water spurted from the walls, running down to puddle at their feet. Howard got up, then slipped when he tried to walk. "It's close."

Keisha shook her head groggily. "It destroyed the Japanese navy. We can't beat something like that."

"You go," Wyatt yelled over the sound of rushing water. He helped Keisha rise and pushed them toward the door.

Howard pulled his arm. "I›m not leaving without you, Wyatt!"

There was a feral roar, and the mountain lion leapt onto Howard's back. He screamed as the animal sunk its teeth into his bicep.

"No!" Keisha yelled, grabbing the lion by the back and trying to peel it off Howard's body.

Melvin pummeled the lion with his bare fists, and Wyatt took a bead with his gun.

The shot was impossible, Howard was moving, Keisha and Melvin were locked in the struggle and he couldn't see where one body ended and another began. Howard moved back toward the wall slamming against it with all the force he could muster, giving Wyatt an idea.

Running forward, he turned his gun around holding it by the muzzle and tried to get close to the grappling bodies. Howard's grunts and moans filled him with urgency. Holding the Uzi over his shoulder he scuffled with them, their feet tangling together. This caused Howard to topple Wyatt underneath him. The gun skittered across the room. Melvin and Keisha went down behind them in a tumble.

Sean ran and grabbed the gun neatly clipping the mountain lion on the back of its head. The animal went out like a light, transforming into Tocho.

"*Ow, ow, ow,*" Howard complained, pushing Tocho's dead weight off his back. "How bad is it?"

Keisha lifted his shirt. "Not bad. He punctured the skin. He was mad. Tocho wouldn't really hurt you."

Howard's pithy response was cut off when the building shook again. This time a wall collapsed. "Grab him!" Wyatt yelled and they pulled Tocho with them. The teens scrambled deeper into the room, Melvin and Wyatt slamming the door behind them.

"*Woah,*" Howard said, looking at the panoramic view of the sea behind them, his wound forgotten.

Light from above filtered into the murky depths of the ocean. It felt as if they were in a fishbowl. Schools of fish eddied and swam around them. Stingrays did an aquatic ballet. Keisha moved forward, hypnotized by the undulating movement of the seaweed. The president was against the window, cupping his hands over his eyes as if he were looking at something.

The beast moved back, then rammed the glass, shaking the entire structure. The teens fell to the floor in a massive huddle. Tiles fell from the ceiling, hitting the president, who went down like a sack of flour.

A shadow moved past them, and Howard whispered in awe, "There it is, the *Octopus Giganteus.*" He moved the glass, appearing like a mere speck next to the giant octopus. "It's beautiful. Keish, look at its stripes."

Keisha choked out a response. "Yes, it's gorgeous. Now let's go!"

"Impossible," a new voice grated from the darkened side of the room.

Wyatt whipped his head around, his eyes going wide with dread. He knew that voice. He'd have known it anywhere.

"Come out, you fiend! Come out and show yourself!" Wyatt screamed.

"Wyatt Baldwin, no relation to Roy, the famous footballer," a hated voice came from the corner.

A large figure disengaged from the shadows, lurching toward him. Wyatt raised his weapon dropping the barrel when he saw Rosemary in front of Vincent, a gun to her head.

"Hold your fire," Wyatt ordered.

The uneven gait of Dreg broke the silence. He shuffled out, holding a strange weapon on them.

Rosemary's eyes moved to the window. "*El Fantasma Gris*," she whispered. She winced when Vincent squeezed her arms, shaking her violently.

Howard repeated, "El Fantasma Gris?"

"The Gray Ghost, a gift from my daughter," Vincent said silkily. He turned awkwardly to stare malevolently at the group. "You ruin everything. You make everything harder. All my well-laid plans are constantly being tested by your juvenile antics. My perfect defense, at least she won't disappoint me." He gazed at the monstrous octopus floating past the window. "My wonderful friend and ally, here to protect me, and you as well." he turned to the group. "You're all so stupid! Can't you see that I'm protecting you?"

"You're nuts!" Wyatt said.

Vincent lashed out, his fist impacting Wyatt's face. Wyatt smashed against the glass, sliding down, his lip bloodied. His eyes fluttered. Lily dropped to her knees cradling his face.

Vincent threw back his head and laughed.

"You're insane," Wyatt muttered.

"All geniuses are a little crazy." Vincent smiled.

"Who said you were a genius?" Keisha asked contemptuously.

"Always the bravest one in the lot. I liked you better with snakes in your hair. I could have used you."

"I'd rather die," Keisha spat.

"Okay." Vincent raised his gun.

Rosemary pushed back, hitting him in the chest with her shoulder, causing the shot to go wild. Howard raced to Keisha's side, colliding with her and landing in a tangle of limbs.

"Damn it, Rosemary. You spoil everything. You're more trouble than you're worth."

Feet scuffled outside the door. Wyatt heard fists pounding against the thick walls.

"They'll never get to you. It's time for all this to end." Vincent's voice cut through the room.

"Wyatt! Sean!"

Wyatt heard Carter screaming their names on the other side of the door. Another jolt shook the building. Outside, the octopus wiggled its tentacles, thrashing. It circled down and then surged upward.

"What are you doing to her?" Rosemary cried.

"Shut up. I'm not doing anything yet," Vincent replied. He dropped Rosemary and commanded Dreg, "Watch her."

Dreg pointed his gun toward her heart. Vincent struggled with his clumsy hand and pulled out his cell phone.

"Let her go!" Rosemary screamed.

"When you give a gift to someone," Vincent spat. "It's not polite to ask for it back. Besides, she's my monster."

"She's not a monster! You're the monster!" Rosemary tried to rise. Dreg shoved her down with the barrel of the gun.

The lights darkened despite the illumination of the emergency strobes.

"Look," Howard said, breaking the stillness of the room.

Outside, the fish scattered, leaving the seafloor empty but for the octopus.

Vincent pressed the buttons on his cell and watched as the

creature responded to his commands. Its large body fought the impulses directed by Vincent. While it struggled, a larger shadow, four times the size, moved toward the window. Vincent lowered the cell, his eyes going wide as an octopus the size of an ocean liner filled the glass.

"Holy mackerel," Sean said.

"That›s the mother of all octopuses," Howard›s voice trembled with awe.

The new octopus flashed her tentacles and smacked the glass, the suckers as large as truck tires. The violence of the impact created a network of spiderweb cracks to spread across the surface.

"It's going to kill us all!" Rosemary yelled. She rose, grabbing the cell from Vincent's nerveless hand, and pressed the release button. She threw the phone at the glass wall, where it shattered into pieces.

Dreg let off a round, peppering the air, one shot catching Rosemary in the shoulder. She went down as the smaller octopus, released from its electronic tether, slithered away. The bigger creature gave another whack with its arms, sending them crashing to the floor as water spurted from dozens of small holes. The octopus turned, following her baby into the abyss, leaving the stunned survivors to stare at the empty sea.

Water trickled steadily, but the windows held.

Vincent rose and smacked Rosemary in the face, sending her reeling. He turned to Wyatt and sneered, "I'll start with you, boy. You've been nothing but a thorn in my side for too long."

Wyatt rolled over, pulling his uzi from where it had fallen underneath him and shouting, "Well, I'm taking you with me!" He fired shots, watching as they hit Vincent's body.

Vincent jerked, his limbs going spastic, when the room filled with a purple glow and a high-pitched whine. Dreg yelped, letting go of his gun, his face a mask of fear.

Wyatt dropped his weapon and covered his ears as the sound grew louder. The teens watched stupefied as Vincent and Dreg rose several feet off the ground. Vincent looked lifeless. His body hung limply.

Nate Owens moaned from the shadows against a wall. Clutching his head, he sat up, a dazed look on his face.

The door burst open. Carter Wright and Colonel Drucker pushed their way in, guns drawn.

Dreg screamed, "Nate! Nate, is that you?" before disappearing in a molecular haze, vanishing into thin air.

Carter ran over to his sons. "Are you okay?"

"What happened?" Wyatt turned to Howard.

"Which part are you asking about?" Howard whispered.

"Where did they go?" Wyatt asked.

Tocho having regained consciousness, stared, his face blank at the space where Vincent and Dreg had been. "Ab-" he stuttered.

Melvin stared out at the seabed, his face stark in the gloom. "We're in big trouble," he said, his voice wooden.

Howard walked over to him. "The fish are back. That means the octopus and its mom are gone. It probably went back to where it came from. There's not enough food for it here."

"I'm not talking about the octopus," Melvin replied.

"I'm not sure what happened to Vincent, but Wyatt shot him dead. He was deader than a doornail."

"You killed him?" Carter asked.

Wyatt nodded. "I didn't miss."

Tocho pointed to the spot and licked his dry lips. "Ab...ab..."

Lily moved over to him. "What is it?" When he didn't answer her, she moved to help Keisha with the wounded.

Keisha pointed to a puddle of alien jet fuel on the floor. "Yes. That's what's left of his alien jet fuel blood."

"It still doesn't explain what happened to him or my father," Nate Owens said.

"We have a bigger problem," Melvin said from his spot by the cracked glass.

"He's right. We'd better get out of here before the whole building caves in," Lily called from her spot where she was bandaging Rosemary.

Melvin spun. "You're not listening to me! You see those things out there?" He pointed to the seafloor.

"That orange coral?" Howard asked.

"That's not coral. They're eggs, and when they hatch, a sea creature will emerge—the sea creature that killed Jade. Killing one of those fishmen was nearly impossible. There's hundreds on the seafloor."

The room grew silent. One by one they walked toward the cracked glass. The only sound was the trickle of water as it slid down the surface.

"How will we win against an army of deadly sea creatures?" Melvin asked, his shoulders slumped.

"We can, and we will prevail," Nate Owens said. "The only way we know how—to work together. We will unite what's left of this planet and take our home back."

Wyatt looked at the ceiling, wishing he could see the sky above him. The weight of the world was crushing him. Something bothered him, and left him with unanswered questions. He turned to Howard. "You still didn't explain what happened to Vincent Konrad and Dreg."

Howard shrugged, his face looking young and worried. "That's because I'm not sure. I'm not sure of anything."

Tocho stood. "Abducted," he blurted.

"What? What are you talking about?" Howard exploded.

"Don't yell at him," Lily said calmly. "Go on, Tocho, tell them."

"It's the aliens. They've been abducted. I recognize it from when they did it to me."

"Really?" Howard was intrigued, his anger forgotten. "We have to talk." He walked toward Tocho. "I have so many questions."

Rosemary shivered. She understood now. *What had he said? The*

DNA was similar to ours? Touching her belly where her unborn child lay safe from the shattered world, she knew where her father had gotten the DNA to create a new life. "The lights."

"You saw them?" Wyatt asked in a rush. "They were blue—"

"And moved like nothing from this planet," Howard finished.

They all looked up toward the ceiling.

"Impossible," Colonel Drucker said, shaking his head. "We don't know this for sure."

"Is it, Dad? Is anything impossible in this new world?" Howard asked.

Nate Owens walked toward them. He towered over the group. "I'm sure of one thing and one thing only: Vincent Konrad said that youth was the future, and he was right. You are the future of this planet."

The noise in the room hushed except for the dripping water.

"You." Owens looked at their tired faces, stained with worry and fear. "You hold the key to tomorrow. Your combined brains and courage will lead us from the darkness to our destiny."

"But how?" Keisha asked. "We're only kids."

"Not anymore," Wyatt answered before the president could say anything. "We're not kids anymore." He peered at the seabed and knew they'd find a way to protect their home. They'd think of something.

Howard moved next to him. "What do you call alien eggs?" Howard said.

No one answered.

"Eggstra-terrestials."

Melvin smiled. For the first time in a week. He walked to stand in the spot he always held. Wyatt glanced to his right and then to his left. They were together again, the way it was supposed to be.

"Don't tease them, Howard Drucker," said Melvin. "They can't take a *yolk.*"

Wyatt couldn't help the groan that escaped.

Lily pushed her way between him and Howard. He felt her arm brush his. Taking her hand within his own, he squeezed her fingers gently. A smile tugged at her lips. He saw Keisha take her place at Howard's side, joining their group.

"Come join us, brother," Wyatt called Tocho.

Tocho hesitated for a minute.

"Yes, you belong with us," Keisha said, holding her hand out to him. "Right?"

Howard nodded and Tocho rose to join them. They lined up, strength coursing through their bodies like an electrical current. Wyatt felt invincible. These were his people, this tribe. He thought about a line from Shakespeare he'd read in what felt like a hundred years ago, in high school English. He understood it now. He looked at each of their faces, including Tocho. They may be different, they might even be a bit weird, but together they would take on the world. Monsterworld.

"We few, we happy few, we band of brothers—for whoever sheds his blood with me today shall be my brother. However humble his birth, this day shall grant him nobility."

Wyatt, Melvin, and Howard Drucker smiled.

ABOVE

VINCENT KONRAD CAME to awareness slowly, the unfamiliar beeps and whistles rousing him. Gingerly, he turned his head, satisfied with the mobility until he realized he couldn't feel anything below his neck.

Vincent shivered, knowing eyes were watching him. He was not alone. Pushing upward, he saw Dreg seated and staring at him intently.

"What's wrong with me?" Vincent demanded, his voice as cranky as an invalid.

"Nothing, Vincent. They saved us—I mean you. They worked for days after they transported us."

Vincent blinked. He didn't remember this room. "Where are we? I'm thirsty. Dreg, get me a drink."

Dreg shook his head. "They said no liquids for you."

"Never mind. Help me up." Vincent struggled to rise, but his body refused to listen to his commands. "What's going on?"

"We've been here for months. You've been out of it." Dreg looked at him with pity. "They almost couldn't save you. Why didn't you tell me about Nate?" Dreg's eyes filled with tears.

Vincent frowned. "I didn't know. Dreg, we are surrounded by incompetents."

The door opened, and a slight green figure floated into the room. It had long, spindly arms and a large head with almond-shaped eyes atop a sticklike neck.

It wore an iridescent gown that sparkled with all the colors of the rainbow.

Vincent recognized the creature and smiled, his blackened teeth filling his grin.

"*Ah*, Spekator. It was you. You saved us. I don't remember much from the time that vile boy shot at me."

Spekator inclined its head, the voice coming out in a nasal whine, much like a machine. "It killed your host body. We had no choice but to find you another." Spekator raised twig-like arms, did something with bony fingers, and a machine whined. Vincent felt himself jerked forward as if on an escalator. The room spun, and he tried to focus to stop the dizziness.

"What nonsense is this?" he roared. "What have you done to me?!"

"Now, Vincent, don't get upset," said Dreg. "These nice creatures tried their best, and given all they had was a *Roomba,* I think they did a—"

"They've attached me to a vacuum cleaner?"

"Well..." Dreg shuffled his feet. "It was either a *Roomba* or pressure cooker, and I thought with your temper—"

"You thought.... You thought...." Vincent charged at Dreg, the *Roomba's* treads eating up the distance in the little room.

Spekator squealed with pleasure and clapped his thin hands. "I love humanity and their silly inventions!" he cried with delight.

Vincent opened his mouth to bite Dreg when gravity launched them into the air; they began spinning in a circular motion.

"It won't be for long, Vincent," Dreg pleaded. "Just until we find you another body."

Vincent gnashed his broken teeth. "I'll give them your body when I catch you."

"Patience, Vincent. We're about to land. Spekator will find you all the bodies you need. Besides, they tell me the birth is imminent. Don't you want to meet your new granddaughter?"

ABOUT THE AUTHOR

Michael Okon is the award-winning, best-selling author of *Witches Protection Program*, *Pokergeist*, *Stillwell*, and *The Battle for Darracia* series, all of which were written under his *nom de plume* Michael Phillip Cash. Michael writes full time and lives on the North Shore of Long Island with his wife and children.

Connect with Michael

Web: michaelokon.com

Instagram: @IAmMichaelOkon

X: @IAmMichaelOkon

OTHER BOOKS BY MICHAEL:

Michael Okon

Monsterland (Book 1)
Monsterland Reanimated (Book 2)
Monsterland Below (Book 3)
Monsterland Above (Books4)
Witches Protection Program
Dragged Down Deep

Michael Phillip Cash

Pokergeist
Stillwell: A Haunting on Long Island
The Flip
The After House
The Hanging Tree: A Novella
Brood X: A Firsthand Account of the Great Cicada Invasion
The Battle for Darracia Schism (Book 1)
The Battle for Darracia Collision (Book 2)
The Battle for Darracia Risen (Book 3)

Michael Samuels

Just Ask the Universe
The Universe-ity
Keep Calm and Ask On

ACKNOWLEDGMENTS

Monsterland and its predecessors are complete works of fiction. While it takes place in the US, and you may recognize some locations in Los Angeles, Prendick Rock is a subtle nod to the protagonist in H.G. Wells' *The Island of Dr. Moreau.*

Monsterland Below was a joy to write. Watching Wyatt and his friends grow and mature as they face the challenges somehow built a deeper connection. I really like these kids.

The journey as an author has been both exciting and amazing. I would like to thank my beta readers. Your comments helped shape the direction of *Monsterland.*

Special thanks to all the readers who write reviews. Those reviews are key in the development of each new part of the series. I hear you, and more importantly, so do Wyatt, Melvin, Howard Drucker, Keisha and Lily

and Jade.............

I am lucky to be surrounded by a wonderful team.

Jon Levin

thank you for believing in monsters.

I couldn't do this without the total support of my family. Thank you to Sharon, Alexander, Cayla, Eric, Jennifer, Hallie, and Zachary. You set my imagination on fire in so many ways.

Mom

my work would be nothing without your voice. You make all my dreams come true.

Dad

I can't see you, but I know you're moving the chess pieces around. Thank you for helping me out from over there.

And finally thank you to my readers. Three monster books in and number four is waiting in the wings all because of you.

Look to the skies for *Monsterland Above*.

Michael Okon
Long Island, New York

www.ingramcontent.com/pod-product-compliance
Lightning Source LLC
Chambersburg PA
CBHW051433190726
48289CB00001B/167